SEE THROUGH YOU

EXPLORE MEN OF THE HAMPTONS
BOOK FOUR

LULA WHITE

CONTENTS

ONGOING SERIES ADVISEMENT

This novel has a prequel novella!

Thanks for checking out *See Through You*. This book can be read as a stand-alone romance with an HEA, but your reading experience would be greatly enhanced if you read the prequel stories first:

Christmas Down Under - available for free
Overheated for Summer - available for sale

This series is a spin-off of the *Sag Harbor Black Romances*, all of which span nine books. While the *Sag Harbor* series could be read out of order, and this book provides a complete love story, it is highly suggested that you read *Explore Men of the Hamptons* in order.

Here's the order in which to get acquainted with this world. The events do not occur based on order of the books:

Brown Sugar This Christmas
Hot Chocolate This Winter

Flinging All Spring
Overheated for Summer
One Tasty Night FREE Novella
Explore You
Rouse Family Christmas
Christmas Down Under (FREE Download- website only)
Taste You
Drink You
See Through You
Find You

It all started with 3 childhood friends
Books 1-4

Maddy

Chrissy

Adella

The Old Hamptons Money

ELLIS/PAGE BLOODLINE

Maddy marries Jerrell
William
Marguerite

TOWNSEND COUSINS

Chrissy marries Sheldon
Cher marries Kevin
Neeraja marries Roland

ENGLISH FAMILY

Solomon marries Chaitra
Lonnie
Constance
Rachel
Martin
Adella marries Desmond
Ilyana

MIDDLETON SONS

Lion marries Kamila
Brendan
Kevin marries Cher

These Black families have thrived in New York since 1700s & 1800s.

The English family arrived in the 1970s & 80s during the real estate boom.

Explore Adventures is created by Keenan, Solomon, & Kevin

New Hamptons Money, Books 5-12

ROUSE FAMILY

Roland marries Neeraja
Sheldon married Chrissy
(ex-wife is Eugenia)

Etta
Kamila marries Lion
Jerrell marries Maddy

These Black families arrived in New York after 2000.

MCLAIN FAMILY

Chaitra marries Solomon
Desmond married Adella
Keenan loves Eugenia

CONTENT WARNING, DISCLAIMER & COPYRIGHT

*** TRIGGER WARNING: This book contains a physically intense sex scene that could be triggering for readers unfamiliar with these characters' pasts and the deeper issues they're acting out. Analyzing nuance beyond the scene is required, or this may not be the appropriate book for you.**

*** Additional trigger warnings: neurodiversity, mental health challenges, depression, discussions of death, suicide & homicide. Strong language and medium-heat sex depictions.**

This is a work of fiction. Sag Harbor is a real place and the author has included some of its actual neighborhoods, streets and history. However, all of the characters and plot are fictionalized as products of the author's creation, as well as most of the small businesses. Names of real businesses may be included from time to time, for benign purposes, and to lend authenticity. Any resemblance to actual persons, living or deceased, is entirely coincidental.

SEE THROUGH YOU PLAYLIST

Hey Loves, I have a music playlist for most of the books in the series. These are the songs I think are most fitting for this couple. In my more intimate posts on Patreon, I share the songs I listened to on repeat and which songs defined some scenes. Eugenia and Keenan are funny and fun, hot and urban. Their music is street and uptempo, with some serious soul and youthful fun.

On Spotify it's free to set up an account, open up the web player and listen for free. Here's See Through You You on Spotify.

THE RACE OF MY LIFE

EUGENIA & KEENAN

EUGENIA

"You're ready for that big math test today you and Dad have been working on?" I ask my son while squeezing in our morning fifteen-minute phone call.

"Yeah," he answers.

The haphazard tone tells me I don't have his full attention.

I wish I could write that off as typical nine-year-old behavior.

"You mean *'yes'*?" I press.

"Yes," my son manages between mouth-smacks of his eggs and French toast.

An inhale of frustration enters my lungs and I check myself, so I don't exhale a stern tongue-lashing that is not really connected to parenting. "Can I get a 'ma'am' in there somewhere?"

"Yes, ma'am. So when are you coming here, Mom?"

I pause from sliding on my running leggings. Finally, light from the overcast gray sky splashes onto me. "Oh, so you're missing your old mama, huh?"

"Well, next weekend—not this weekend coming up, but the one after that—Blake, Rome, Isaac, and I want to go to Six Flags Great Escape. Dad said I needed to check with you and make sure it wasn't during your visit," he replies in his proper English my ex-husband, Sheldon, has been hammering into him.

Tuh. Of course, Sheldon set this up to make me the bad guy. "Fella, next weekend is one of our visits, remember? And if the judge says it's okay, it'll be our first full weekend of just you and me. We're going for movies and go-karts and that pizza place you like."

Silence. That is, if we don't count the background noise of the whimpering, two-month-old baby that Sheldon has with his new bride, and my son's new little sister. And if we also leave out the arguing between Sheldon's two new stepchildren, who my son calls his brother and sister.

"Okay, yeah. All right," Hadar finally replies, not bothering to hide his disappointment.

Instead of jumping on him for the attitude, I switch subjects so an upsetting conversation with me isn't the last memory he carries through his day. And so there is no need for Chrissy, Sheldon's wife, to console him once we get off. "You know, Rashad and Marshall have been begging to get on a plane to New York to see you. Maybe I'll bring the family this summer when the judge lets us, so we can all go to Six Flags with you. We can visit the Statue of Liberty, see where the Knicks play, go to some concerts in the park."

"Okay, tell them I said 'hi.'"

Hi? Whatever happened to "get at me"?

"Well, all right then, it sounds like you're getting ready to—"

"Hey, Mama?" he interrupts.

My head bobs up as I tie my tennis shoes. "Yes, ba—"

"May I have the butterscotch pudding instead of this chocolate?" he calls out louder. Apparently, I'm not there to handle his pudding.

"We only have chocolate left, but Gustavo is having groceries delivered, and you'll get it in your bag tomorrow. That good?" Chriselle replies from another part of their new mansion, where the echo of her voice ricochets across its massive walls and into the tight, tiny rooms of my jam-packed mind.

I'm unable to focus on my shoelaces any longer. The weight of what I just heard sends me back on the couch.

"Yes, ma'am."

On the massive sea of emotions, under siege of a storm, my heart is a tiny sailboat I'm paddling to stay afloat. "Hadar, did Sheldon tell you to call Chrissy 'Mama'?"

A tiny whine is his first answer, before he mutters, "No, ma'am."

"Kids, your ride is here," Chrissy yells from a distance.

I imagine her ushering an end to our phone call with a silent stare, seven minutes into what should have been a fifteen-minute conversation.

"Well, who told you to?"

My kid sighs. "Dang, Ma, it's not a big deal. Don't be mad."

"I asked you a question, young man."

"Nobody, okay? I've got to go. I love you, Mama."

Who is he talking to? Me? Or *her?*

Before I can tell him I love him back, the phone disconnects.

Sheldon is likely already headed to his office, so Chrissy is probably the one who dialed the phone and passed it to Hadar while she stood aside silently and low-key monitored.

No more than thirty seconds have passed before I fire off my first text to Shel.

Me to Shel: *Who tells our son to call Chrissy "Mama"?*

After a twenty-minute wait, my answer comes.

Sheldon: *Nobody, G. He started on his own. Chrissy's kids call me "Dad." When they're with my family, they call my folks "Grands" and my sibs "uncle and aunt." There are no step- titles around here. He probably noticed and fell in with everybody else. No disrespect to you.*

Yeah, and I'll bet that couldn't have made Shel happier. After I massage this tightness in my chest, I resume.

Me: *My talk with him was seven minutes today instead of fifteen.*

Sheldon: *Kid is nine, getting his head right for a math test. He probably ran out of stuff to say.*

No, that's not what it is. My son never runs out of things to talk with me about. And there is no question Sheldon is enjoying this immensely—the shoe being on the other foot, or more specifically, payback.

Me: *Our phone visits are unmonitored now. There was a lot of noise this morning, and Chrissy and her kids were around.*

Sheldon: *We're doing the best we can with a full house. I'll make sure tonight your vid conference with him is just you and him.*

Translation: Busy little singer, Chriselle, can't trouble herself, in her fast-wheeling life of celebrities, interviews, and singing performances, to comply with the judge's orders for my son and me, and instead, sandwiches my calls in with his breakfast. Which was prepared by a chef for Hadar to heat up in the mornings. So my son's not getting his meals personally made with the love and care I put into them. His life is high-tech and "designed" in less than a year.

All my objections curtly addressed and dismissed, I have

no other straws of involvement or control in my child's development to grasp at.

I'm certain Shel's probably gotten out of his Escalade and is rushing into his office while multitasking. He's good at that—not just blowing me off, but driving the knife into me, so our conversations end in a way that reminds me of what I did. In a way that reminds me I am utterly alone now. *Just you and him.*

Instead of taking off to jog, I let my body sink into the couch cushions. What else do I have if I don't have my own son? What's left? Hadar is the one perfect thing I put in this world. Without him, why am I even still...

I get up. But why, I don't know.

Once I'm outside my River North condo, my tennis shoes pound the sidewalk. One leg at a time, I take off. Through the tears building up, I manage to see my way toward the Loop in Downtown Chicago. As long as I run, these lungs have no choice but to breathe.

KEENAN

"You sure?" Stepping out of the SUV rental, I glance at the piece of paper again.

520 W. Superior Street.

"I'm sure. This is the building," the private investigator replies.

I reach back inside the car and grab the bouquet of two dozen pink roses. My initial impressions of Eugenia tell me she's not a "roses" kind of woman. And I seriously don't believe her personality vibes with this shade of cotton-candy, dollhouse pink. But since I don't know yet what her "thing" is, the only way I can express the big question mark she drew through the center of me is with some simple, cliché-ass roses.

I stare at my watch. "Seven o'clock?"

It's 7:02.

"Seven o'clock," the investigator replies, taking a smoke.

Why in the hell did I go with pink roses? I probably should have gotten a more sophisticated color like purple or royal blue. Why did I spend a hundred and fifty dollars on these for somebody I barely know?

As I stare at my sneakers for whether they're white enough, the answer pops into my head: Eugenia is a mysterious storm I can't turn away from .

"There she is," the PI notes.

Dark-gray jogging tights come pushing through those double doors. At the sight of her, lightning throttles up my dick. In those leggings are the lithe legs that delivered one of the best Christmas gifts I've ever received. The black sports bra framing her breasts, even the loose-fitting tank falling over her chest and abs remind me of the soft, firm gifts she bears underneath, and more important, the energy. She heads toward the Chicago Harbor, and her poofball ponytail starts swishing.

Negro, do what you came to do. My feet don't move; throat dries up. What if she reacts the way she did last weekend at her son's birthday party?

But Sheldon Rouse and his family, and all those Hamptons folks, aren't here.

"You doing this or not?" the PI presses me.

I inhale and get ready to say it with my chest.

"Eugenia!" My pounding heart prays she turns around.

She speeds up her stride.

"Eugenia!" I shove the flowers at the PI. "Take these and follow us."

I hit the sidewalk after her—a graceful, statuesque work of art who conjures up images in my head of a black Statue of Liberty. Through a yellow light, she bounds, but the crosswalk timer warns it'll soon change.

Since she's put a good amount of distance between us, I get caught at the red light. Some force inside me cringes at the thought of spending any more time lagging. Hell, it's been five months already. That force propels my legs through the light.

"Excuse me! Sorry about that." I place my arm on an appalled lady to hold her steady, and then race through the light after cars pass.

Down Superior Street, Eugenia doesn't just jog light. Those legs must pump the gas of ferocity. She turns onto North Noble Street. My determination beads up in droplets of sweat. I play basketball with my boys, swim, lift, surf, rock climb, and ski, and she is *still* doing a damn good job of outpacing me.

I could have followed her from inside the SUV while the PI drove me, but what man of passion watches a woman run while he rides in the car? Lazy as hell. And my adrenaline rush right now will not allow me to just sit in the car, idle and inactive, after I've waited for months.

So in these $450 Air Jordans, I keep pumping after her. Of the two blocks that separated us, I've now cut the distance down to a block. Her concentrated intensity communicates to the world it should move out of her way.

For what must be several blocks, I put in a good jog in these inappropriate shoes that are now hurting my feet. But as she reaches a park, I'm closing in. Throwing in a few more puffs, an extra burst of motivation, I speed it up. With more muscle, I fling myself into this half a block of separation now, toward a butterfly maybe no one else managed to catch or understand, or could even hold on to for long, before letting it go.

"Eugenia!" I manage, huffing and puffing like hell now. With everything in me, Stunt Man from B'More muscles ahead, my curiosity giving me the fuel to push through my fatigue.

Finally, on a clear stretch of the path, almost a mile from where we started, my arteries pulsating in overdrive, lungs about to burst, I'm at Eugenia's side. My arm brushes her, and we keep running against each other. She peers over her shoulder and practically jumps from her skin. Shock fills her eyes, knocking her off kilter, and she swerves off the running path, tripping into the grass.

"Eugenia!" I reach for her so she doesn't fall, but her feet stumble.

In her state of apparent disbelief, she jerks back. I lunge forward, and we land in a pile on the grass. I'm on top of her, covering her svelte, catlike, slinky body I held for a few precious hours.

"Hello, gorgeous."

Her chest drags in big breaths and her chocolate-brown eyes still might be processing if I'm real. "Kee..." she murmurs between breaths.

The jolt of her chest precedes her eyes frosting to ice. Writhing underneath me, she scurries backward.

"Keenan." Her voice axes through my fantasies of how this reunion would play out.

"Hey, good morning. I called for you back at your building, but—"

"You were at my place?"

"Well, yeah. I wanted to pick you up and surprise you, take you to breakfast."

I've wanted to take you to breakfast since Christmas morning. Hell, I've wanted to eat you for breakfast since Christmas morning.

Those athletic legs vault her off the grass and away from me. "How do you know where I live? How did you get my address? What are you doing here?" Wide-eyed between each blink, still catching her breath, she silently accuses me. "I thought I asked you to stay away."

Now it's me who blinks, stunned as hell, still trying to reclaim my own damn breaths that won't come, so my lungs tighten up. The lack of oxygen chokes off my coherent words and, shit, scrambles my brain waves.

"No, at the party, you asked me to leave. And I-I did. So I thought you and I could talk here in Chicago, your city, just us. Away from all those people in New York."

I say it as I pick up her earbuds from the grass after I knocked them from her ears.

"Well, you thought wrong. You shouldn't have come."

The words are boulders crashing down on me. I've never chased a woman, as in physically and actually chased her. Now I stand here wondering if this was the dumbest move I've ever made.

"Eugenia, damn, you act like I'm some masked murderer or something."

She shakes her head and worry lines crease her forehead, where a neon stoplight may as well be sitting. "No, no, that's now how I mean to come off." She waves her hands. Her labored breathing might no longer be from the workout. "But I can't. I-I *can't*, Keenan."

"Don't say what you can't do."

"Keenan, do you want these?" The PI comes toward us holding the roses.

As subtly as I can, with tiny quivers of my head and hands, I attempt to tell him "no dice," to stop. He misses my cues and shoves them at me.

Stammering now—which this nigga never does— I hold

them out to her. "I got these for you. I didn't know what your favorite—"

Eugenia's gaze bounces around, as if the boogeyman is around the corner and she might get in trouble if she's seen with me. Is she searching for a dude? Did my PI screw up and miss that she might have a man?

"I can't take those," she tells me.

A little annoyed at this point, after I almost chased her nearly a mile, I throw up a hand. "Why not? They're flowers. Literally, just flowers. There's nothing in them. No toxic gas. No poison. No practical joke. Look." I stick my nose in them and take an exasperated, large sniff. "See?"

Seeming to recollect herself, she starts off, back in the direction of her building. "Stay away from me, Keenan. Please, don't do this again."

My sore feet and me, we start running after her again, but I'm keeping up this time, I don't care how bad it hurts. Fuck it, I grab her. "Why are you so scared? Can you stop a minute and give me just—"

"Did somebody send you here?" What must be the fear of God shakes in Eugenia's eyes.

The morning breeze cools my hand that she leaves empty when she snatches her arm out of it.

"Eugenia, what are you talking about? We had a damn good time together at Christmas—"

"*Stop* talking! We did *not!*"

"*What?*" Have I entered an alternate universe?

The panic attack on her face smothers all my eagerness that flew me here to Chicago from New York. I mean, she doesn't just land my plane. She's King Kong completely slinging my jetliner from side to side and then tearing off the wings and *smashing* my shit against a building.

"I asked you if anybody sent you here to *trap* me!" she loud-whispers.

"*No.* Look," I say, trying to reclaim my grip on *my* version of reality. "Our time together was dope as hell."

Eugenia's eyes blow up to the size of Italian meatballs. "Shut up!"

There's nobody around now, just her and me. So why is she acting like she's being watched by the KGB? "Do you have a man or something? Is somebody watching you? Threatening you?"

Apparently, she's sifting through whether or not I'm her enemy. "I *can't* be out here with you, and I don't know what you're talking about."

Whatever is behind those terrified eyes, I wish I could get inside her and remove it myself. Because the deathly way she's glaring at a nigga right now is a one eighty-seven.

Her frantic eyes remind me of seeing boys on the street held at gunpoint, as if she's a hostage saying all this against her will.

Confused about what's happening, crushed under the heel of the beautiful Black Mystique who has haunted my fantasies, I still hand her the roses. "At least take these. Don't let them go to waste."

Eugenia's gaze darts around us again, like her prison warden will appear at any moment. Snatching the roses, she struts to the nearest trash can.

In slow motion, I cringe as she dumps them inside.

"I appreciate the gesture, but I can't accept these."

Did she just toss a piece of me into that damn trash can?

But all of her volcanic womanhood that has dominated my head for months remains.

This is definitely not the mysterious dark star whose stellar mass drew me to her from a corner booth in Taste on Christmas Eve. Not the energetic force I dropped off in my helicopter on Christmas Day. Not the woman who stopped on the heliport and spun toward me—excited, maybe in awe, definitely curious, who forgot herself for a little while—and was still floating on cloud nine after our otherworldly night.

Instead, I face a shriveled, shrunken bottle of pent-up gas.

"A-all right. Fine, if that's what you want." I can't believe I just said that shit.

"It's what I want," Eugenia breathes. But in that breath is a whiff of hesitation. "Now will you *please*… go."

Something is off. She's too nervous and antsy.

I'm almost certain the traffic light in her eye is turning yellow, telling me to slow down, but not to stop.

2

WITH A BANG

EUGENIA

I pace around my living room before work, and clutch my phone like it's a strand of imaginary pearls. "So," I start, pausing for a breath, "how does that sound?"

"But, Genie, why are you having such a major reaction to an exchange so small?" Lillian asks. "I mean, all you did with this guy at Christmas was just have some dinner, talk a little and then you and him went your separate ways. Right?"

The light-hearted encouragement of my therapist is a boulder of weight falling on my next decision—whether to lie or tell the truth.

Shit! Maybe I shouldn't have called her. I should have just let it ride and prayed no one saw.

No. I know I must be right: Sheldon's got eyes on me. He is hoping I screw up, the same way he waited me out last summer. Keenan showing up this morning, out of nowhere— one week before my visitation hearing—is a test. It *has* to be.

Calling my therapist and getting ahead of the narrative is the right thing to do.

"Yes. Absolutely," I lie. "I just wanted to call and share

with you how proud I am of myself and report my moment of personal strength and discipline. There is no way I would have done this a year or two ago." Is the dry, dusty laugh I manage believable enough? "This is a nice guy and all, but I'm proud of myself for saying no."

More truthfully, I hope my social worker or her investigator didn't happen to see and plan to use it against me in their custody assessment. More than that, I hope Sheldon's private investigator was nowhere around.

"I'd say the way you handled it was perfect. Of course, you're a grown woman, free to do what you want. But right now, your son is your only focus. You're proving that you're finished with meaningless relationships that cause you to question your value. Being strong for Hadar is your priority. To the extent that new friends or potential dates come along, if they really care about you or have an interest in you, they can wait until you've taken care of yourself first."

"Exactly," I agree.

I blink back tears and wait for her to validate me. "I don't need any confusion or distraction in my life." The muscle cords surrounding my heart chamber contract and twist as I fight to keep my voice level. But I need to tell these next lies so she'll write positively about me in her report. "I've been so happy and settled these last few months. I'm filling my emotional cup with meaningful activities instead of empty sex or stupid lies men tell. And it feels good."

Hot emotion rages behind my eyelids and threatens to spill out my truth—I've been lonely, sex-starved, depleted of energy or motivation, and I hate number-painting and attending sleep-inducing group therapy meetings with boring, middle-aged, lifeless women.

Hold on. Just hold it together, G. You're almost home free.

Once I get Hadar back, he and I will be free. No more of Sheldon's family supervising us in public places. No more of

Sheldon's mother watching and listening to every word while we talk. My son and I can be alone, and he can tell me what he really thinks about Chrissy and her snooty family, and if Roland Rouse or Charles Rouse are picking on him about his eyeglasses, and about the private school Sheldon's sending him to now. Hadar can tell me the truth that he hides around Sheldon's sister, Etta, when I ask him if he's happy and his lowered eyes bury the answer in his shoes.

Though Sheldon is clearly using money, fancy events, and high-priced everything to make Hadar love being away from me, I know my son must also be feeling a way about numbering as one of *many* kids in Sheldon's new life.

"Girl, that's it!" Lillian beams and breaks apart my daydream. "You've come so far! I'm so glad for you, making better decisions. I'll check in with you in a few days for our meeting. Sunday, right?"

"Yes," I answer, the lead in my throat almost dragging down my falsetto. "Mhmm, it can't come fast enough."

No sooner do we hang up than I double over.

Those flowers were so precious, the most perfect thing anybody has done for me in a long time, not since Sheldon.

Keenan's face as I'd trashed them…

Stumbling toward the shower, barely getting the shower cap over my hair, I turn the knobs and let the water consume me.

I scrape to wash off my lasciviousness, irresponsibility, impulsivity…

But regardless of how hard I mentally scrub, the memories of Keenan's dick scrubbing my cervix still steam up the walls of my head.

His wildness. My need. His limitlessness. My hunger.

Hard, long, and commanding, not even a Brillo pad could remove his imprint on me.

My fingers make their way between my thighs, touch my

clit and swollen lips. My eyes press shut, and I'm back on the yacht with him again, in his arms, his whispers flooding my head, as we're suspended under the ocean, hidden from the world.

It was a different kind of hookup. The sex wasn't just him taking from me, but him giving and... appreciating? Worshipping?

Then he flew me to my son, just as he'd promised he would.

Curious, perceptive, and imposing, Keenan's allure is nothing like Sheldon's. Keenan's intellect wields a sharp edge.

Bitch, shut up. Don't be stupid again.

"Edge" means dangerous.

There can't be any flowers, cards, dinners, nothing.

I finish pleasuring myself to douse this tiny flame in me before work. This is simple. I haven't been with anybody since that night, so my womanhood is just frustrated. I've got this under control.

NELSON: *You coming to the Memorial Day barbecue if you don't get the weekend with Hadar?*

While sitting at a stoplight, I snicker at my younger brother's text.

Me: *No matter what the judge allows, I'm going to New York.*

Even if Hadar doesn't appreciate me being there and prefers to do cooler stuff with his cooler new family.

Nelson: *You could at least come through this weekend for some dominoes and grilling.*

As always, I ignore my brother's request and creep

onward on the backed-up I-90 East into downtown. My Snickerdoodle latte provides a sliver of heaven while Sade's mellow voice serenades me. Her smooth, chill vocals against the slight urban up-tempo never get old, and that's all the excitement I need this morning.

Hey, Mama?

Each time my mind recalls it, I allow Sade to escort me back to a calm mental haven, where I'm posted up in a large, wild garden. In that place of sanctitude, every plant, flower, and shrub springing up around me is one I planted.

Then, my son's voice jolts me back to the painful concrete jungle of reality I now travel.

There is no way to transport myself away from what I heard this morning, no matter how many deep breaths I take or visionary exercises I perform. In a last-ditch effort to be strong, I swipe at the tears burgeoning, which does nothing for the violent tears splitting my lung's air sacs. My vision blurred to the point I can hardly see, I drive into the building's garage where I work and turn the corner too fast, ramming my tire over the curb. The back fender of my Lexus truck scrapes the high concrete block in a loud, high-pitched notice to the world that I'm distracted.

"You okay?" somebody yells as I slide down my window and use my employee access card to lift the security gate.

"Yes, I just made the turn a little too soon. Thanks!" My fake cheer isn't quite on point, but it'll have to suffice.

I enter the Department of Social Services building, and glue on my happy mask to wave at other social workers and investigators and summon up my strength for another day of survival.

With my son's voice lingering in my thoughts, my daily mental checklist already scrolls through my mind—reports that are due to several judges, signatures I still need from supervisors, meetings I should hold with the team under my supervision, home visits I need to make, therapists to interview, all by the end of the day.

The rickety but trusty elevator delivers me to the seventh floor, and I barely enter the office door when eyes peer at me over cubicles.

I'm used to it, but their side-eyes are especially punishing today.

Oh, yes, that's right. The latest article in the *Wall Street Chronicle*. Sheldon's name is in it. Now the echoes of co-workers are louder than whispers: how I could have been so stupid to leave him.

Carrying my coffee and that of my work wife, Lus, I pretend to know nothing and to not give a shit as I walk down the aisle of shame, past the stares.

So focused am I on tuning out haters, I don't pay attention to my desk.

"Girl, it's about time you got here so you can open this damn card and tell me what's on it," Lus greets me.

Good grief. There is no room for me to sit in my cubicle. "Where did all this come from?"

My desk, chair, spare shelf space, leg area under the desk, and windowsill against which I sit, are all filled with roses of every color. Lus has also placed some of them at her desk.

She comes and takes the latte I bought her, now lukewarm. "That's not all of them. We had to put the rest in the conference room." She hands me the small car and leans closer to my ear. "Girl, don't say anything, but I actually caught Sherae and Leddy holding it up to the light and trying to read it."

Against my will, overthrowing my mindfulness techniques, and butting into my perfectly predictable, sane morning, a silver lining streams through me.

It's been a long time since...

The small, shiny card shakes from the nervous fumbling

of my hands. Thank God he was smart enough to seal it. Turning away from Lus, cupping it so she can't see, I read:

I still want to go to sleep in your pussy on an open mountain range. You never answered. I'm not accepting "no."

With a hand over my mouth, I suppress any outward hints of the giddiness bubbling in my nerves. His eager, impatient penmanship scribbles across my chest with the ink of excitement—excitement I don't need. Vibrant and romantic and hopeful, this kind of foolishness is not on my list of priorities.

"So what happened and I didn't get the tea?" Lus mutters.

I've already shoved the card back in its envelope and down in my purse. Back in my professional mask, I say loud enough for the others to hear, "How many of our mother clients will come here today, working hard to get their kids back, without anyone cheering them on? I'll call the front office to give out these flowers to people who need them more."

"That is really sweet, Genie," Leddy, another co-worker blurts. "So do we get to know who the special man is?"

"There is no special man," I clap back immediately to dispel the suspicions. "Just a kind friend showing his thanks."

"'Kind friend' must have some real friendly dick," Sherae notes to an eruption of giggles.

"Let's just mind our business and focus on work." I'm the supervisor for this office of Children and Family Services social workers, and work is what I need to stabilize my heart rate.

But I know I'll hear from my own social worker, Tabatha, by the end of the day. So rather than working, in my head, I begin getting my story straight about who sent all this and why.

Lus: *I wouldn't have given my flowers away to these ungrateful folks.*

Me: *You and I are not the same. And some of them do appreciate it.*

Lus: *So do I get the real story this weekend on a hike? That whole 'friend' bit sucks.*

Me: *It's true, though. Wow, would you look at the time? Client meeting. ;-)*

Lus is great. I don't distrust her at all, and these last three years she's been a solid work wife. She and I have traded notes over dates and boyfriends in the past. But as it concerns this particular situation, I'm not taking the risk of sharing about Keenan. Not when custody of my son hangs on by a thread and the wrong person even accidentally learning about Keenan could destroy me.

"Hi, Victoria, come on in," I greet a mother who's had her children out of her care for a year. Just a little longer than me. "You have your updated progress letters?"

"Yes, ma'am, I sure do," she says proudly, reaching into her purse for several envelopes containing Alcoholics Anonymous sign-in sheets, a letter from her sponsor about her level of commitment, her parenting instructor, drug rehabilitation coordinator, and from her individual counselor.

Sparks of satisfaction brighten Victoria's face, and she asks, "So, Miss Rouse, what do you think? Will you be recommending that my babies come home to me?"

Here comes the hard part. "Well, Victoria, I received your alcohol test results, and your last test was diluted."

A diluted urine test usually means they drank a lot of water to flush their system, which makes it hard to detect intoxicating substances. Parents in open social service court cases normally flush with water to hide that they've been drinking.

The big smile drops from her features. "Miss Rouse, I've done everything you and the judge asked me to."

"I understand that, but the lawyer who represents DCFS will be concerned when they read your diluted test unless you have a good explanation for it. And this isn't your first questionable test. You had one last month also that you missed. You haven't been seeing Tremaine, have you?"

She shifts in her seat, and her eyes dart around in search of a response. "He came to my job and I told him he needed to leave."

"Then why haven't you requested a restraining order?"

"Because I'm not seeing him. I can't control his actions. He hasn't threatened me or done anything to me. And what does his case have to do with mine?" Panicked breaths rush out of her chest.

"He's not doing his programs, Vic, and you are. You've been working really hard. But if the judge believes you are still seeing the children's father who is not enrolled in any classes and he's not addressing his own drug issues, the judge will wonder if you will expose the kids to him also."

"This isn't right. I'm not seeing him."

I look at the previous interview that was conducted by another social worker earlier in this case, with the children's father. Tremaine said he's off from work on Tuesdays and Fridays. When I review Victoria's diluted and missed tests, they occur on Saturday and on Wednesday. As if she's partying with Tremaine the day before, and when her letter is called the next morning, she spends the entire day drinking water to flush out alcohol before she goes to test.

My mouth opens so I can point this out to her.

"Eugenia."

The decibel levels cause a seismic shift in me and turn my head.

"Did that come from the intercom?" I ask.

"Eugenia Jackson." That insistent tone...

Victoria and I look up and around.

My brain cells flatline.

"No," I mutter, spinning in my seat. Nobody ever calls me by my maiden name. I haven't used it on any of my paperwork in almost nine years, so not a soul in this building would call me that.

"I think it came from outside," Vic replies.

"Eugenia Jackson, I'm asking you to come outside and give me an answer. Now."

Lus busts through the door. "Girl, is any part of your name Jackson? There is a fine-ass specimen out there, and *I'm* about to go be Ms. Jackson if that's not you."

"Excuse me," I say to Vic and follow Lus to a hallway window facing the street.

The lungs holding my oxygen are about to burst. In the middle of the street sits a large boat on wheels, *filled* with flowers. Keenan stands atop it holding a megaphone.

Her gaze still glued to him, Lus marvels, "Oh, he looks like he's got hella energy. So, uh, tell me that lie one more time about a friend."

I putter down the seven flights of stairs. With the goal of not tripping, I remember this is not good. Not exciting. Not thrilling. His audaciousness threatens to pop my safe, carefully constructed, perfectly predictable bubble of wise decision-making.

At the base of the stairs, I collect my composure so I can walk through the lobby gracefully, as if there's not a big-ass yacht on the street in front of my job.

Past the hordes of government workers who have already come down to pry, the front desk workers and bystanders, I fake a few shreds of calm as these wobbly legs carry me to a very firm and stalwart hot-blooded male.

Beautiful and chocolatey as a tall bottle of South African coffee liqueur, he stares down at me from some fifteen to twenty feet over my head. Keenan's jaw is set. My back to everyone else, I attempt to take control of this situation by playing it off as light-hearted fun between two friends.

"Nice boat," I say with a forced smile to cover my urge to drag his ass from up there. "Why didn't I think to take one of these to work this morning?"

"I don't know, but you're more than welcome to ride it home with me," he offers, slick and devious, with a little agitation of his own.

"But see, there's this whole 'job' situation I've got." I sweep my arm around. "You know? This government building here, where I must report until I win the lottery."

"Today might be your lucky day. Maybe you just won it. I'm not going anywhere until Eugenia Jackson leaves with me in this boat."

"Keenan, if you don't get down here right now," I say, my voice snapping a leather belt, "I'm calling the police."

He jumps down from all that height, scaring me and earning a collective gasp from all the admiring spectators behind us, as he lands in a deep squat.

"Oh my goodness! Are you o—"

The taut trunks of his thighs tighten under his shorts, and thick calves flex while his sneakers remain steady against the sidewalk. He stands with a pristine, relaxed grin. "If I'm not okay, will you leave with me and take me to the hospital, Eugenia Jackson?"

"You do know that is not my name." I'm struggling to keep my voice light. I worked hard to earn the name Rouse. To have that lasting connection to Sheldon's prestige, his success, and his… respectability.

When people learn I'm connected to Sheldon Rouse, they treat me like more than where I came from. As if they realize at some point in my life, I did something worthy enough to deserve attachment to someone of his import, and therefore, I must be important, too.

Keenan leans toward me, his flaring nostrils inches from my forehead, his Vaselined lips unsmiling, his clipped goatee as pointed as his presentation today. "I will not call you by his name. I will call you by the name your mama and daddy gave you. *That's* the woman I want."

"Tuh." I cover my mouth and try to decide on laughing or scoffing in my disbelief. "I'm not a piece of candy for sale on a shelf that you can decide you want."

Hands on his hips, genuine irritation in his pinched eyebrows, he must truly believe he is entitled to something. "For sale or not, tell me you don't want me to lick you and eat you like you're my candy."

The inevitable laugh bubbles up now, and I hammer it back down. All of this would be cute if… if… I can't remember all my reasons and objections I had just an hour ago. So blown away am I by the shock wave of Keenan, my brain can't think past all this to construct its logic fast enough.

"Keenan, all of this is very sweet and thoughtful." The boat is gorgeous, not as big as the one we rode on Christmas, more like an afternoon cruiser. Dammit! Brain, *work!*

Athletic, determined energy blasts from his eyes and engulfs me. "Then will you come out with me when you wrap up your 'job situation' today?" he asks, using air quotes.

I barely heard any of the words while mesmerized with the movement of his smooth, bonbon lips. His possessive swagger towers over me as if I belong to him already, the same way he approached my table with an air of authority on Christmas Eve. And thinking of that night transports me back to episodes of eroticism that squirt cream into my panties where I stand.

"No, Keenan. I told you already this morning. I *can't.*"

This young cat—who might be younger than my

youngest brother—hovers close, not easing up. "What do you have to do besides eat with me?"

Dumb and speechless, I actually stand here and search for a lie, or something that I should be doing tonight besides *This Is Us* or a good thriller novel. "That's not the point."

"Then what is the point of you turning down a perfectly good invitation?" he challenges.

Footsteps of authority approach behind me, specifically heels. In these final seconds, I give Keenan a pleading expression so he catches the hint that he needs to pipe down.

"Hey, Eugenia." The voice of one of my bosses, a DCFS administrator for this branch. "Are you all right out here?"

With all the fake professionalism I can muster, I answer, "Oh, of course. This is my friend, Keenan, who was gracious enough to organize the entertainment for my son's party a couple of weekends ago. As you can see, he is quite the entertainer, very good at what he does."

"Yes, he is," Miss Darcy says. She stretches out her hand toward him, her gaze taking a tour over Keenan's physique in a way that might irritate me a smidge. "Nice to meet you, Mr. Keenan. We certainly don't witness displays this 'off-the-chain' as they say, around here often. You'll have to forgive us if you have the attention of every warm body in the building."

This is when I cast a peek over my shoulder. On every level of the building, in nearly every window, my co-workers make no pretense of sipping this proverbial hot tea.

When Ms. Darcy lets her hand linger on Keenan's a tad too long, he must be hip to her game. Withdrawing it, he moves it to my hair.

"I appreciate that, Ms. Darcy," Keenan responds, taking that same hand to sweep one of my frizzy tendrils at the side of my face, "but Eugenia is the rockstar here. A fantastic mom, and from what I've heard about her, an amazing social worker. I just wanted to come and literally give her her flowers today. The great city of Chicago must feel fortunate to have her fighting for you all's families."

His gaze attaches to mine, and the seemingly harmless touch of his fingers along my ear—a move so small and inconsequential—is akin to lighting a chain of dynamite up to my brain. My thoughts race to guess what will emerge from his mouth next.

"You know, Miss Darcy," Keenan says, with his playful eyes on me, "if you and your office staff would ever like to join my friend, Eugenia, and me for a ride on the lake, we would all have a bomb time."

This little…

"That's certainly not an offer we get every day. We'd love to. We just might take you up on that, Mr. Keenan," Ms. Darcy replies.

"I'm happy to hear it." His eyes still parked squarely on me, he whips out his business card and passes it to her. "And if you're ever in New York, drinks on me."

This time I can't control my snicker.

I manage to capture the words on his business card as she takes it.

Keenan McClain
CEO & Founder
Explore Adventures
The Hamptons, New York

I can't help catching the whiff of admiration on Ms. Darcy's face when she sees the town and no address. Of course, the moment she's back inside, she will look him up. While Ms. Darcy still inspects it, I flash him a warning glare.

The smart-ass young slickster flashes me one of his own and tops it off with a mischievous smile. "So, Eugenia, my friend, where did you say we're meeting up to grab dinner again?"

Urgh!

Instead of giving us our privacy, a nosy Ms. Darcy turns to me and cheeses in anticipation of my answer. "You know, I can make some recommendations for you two."

I'm not supposed to want Keenan, but the throes of my vagina care not one iota about my child custody situation.

As far as my social worker, Tabatha, finding out, I'm certain she will hear of all this and hit me up with questions about who Keenan is. He's done the damage now. I will have to hustle up a solid explanation of why a man in which I have no interest whatsoever, who I barely know, rode a huge boat for me into the middle of Chicago.

To clear all this up and pass it off as fun and innocent, I will have to beef up the lie I fed the therapist this morning. The only way to handle this smoothly is by playing it off as a legitimate friendship. Any drastic moves—shooing him away, calling police or panicking—and such drama will draw unwanted suspicion, digging a deeper hole for me.

As if this pain in the ass senses I'm cornered, he stands with his chest out and a brag in his eye.

"There's a place called Delta," I say, even while my glare admonishes him. "It has pretty good selections. I have a couple of home visits to make, and then I can meet you there, probably about six."

Ms. Darcy thinks on my suggestion, as if I made it for her. "Oh, I've eaten there plenty of times. That spot does have wonderful food, but why don't you let Mr. McLain here take you some place fancy, like—"

"I'm not dressed properly since I'm working. Getting all dressed up in the appropriate attire requires too much time after work. Besides, I'm sure Keenan, as a Founder and CEO," I say, emphasizing his titles to ensure he hears the mockery in my tone, "has a ton of other commitments he must go attend. I don't want to take up too much of his time."

"My time is all yours," the African coffee liqueur replies through lips wet with lust. "Excellent. Six it is, beautiful."

My red blood cells must suspend in midair at the feel of his fingers sliding into mine. Lifting my hand to his lips, his eyes disabusing me of the lies I tell, he kisses my flesh. I'm too old for his cockiness and bombastic gestures. So why is my chest a boxing ring, in which my heart is an oversized wrestler throwing itself from one side to the other?

Miss Darcy goes to dismiss security and police, finally leaving us alone.

I'm thankful for a moment to inform him of what he needs to hear, what my situation *demands* I say. "Sandwiches and coffee, and then you *leave*, Keenan."

All his young swagger stares down at me, no smile, no playfulness to be seen anywhere on him. "Depends on what your answer is, Eugenia." He releases my hand that I only now realize he is still holding.

The brain of this forty-year-old mother of a ten-year-old son not in her custody reminds her to look away from this cocky, flagrant, explosion of a man—exactly the kind who has no place anywhere around me, the kind who's always been my undoing.

On the march back to the office so I can finish the interview with my client, I stew over the inevitable questions I'll field from *my* assigned social worker, similar to what I just asked Victoria.

How serious am I about getting back Hadar? Who is that brazen individual out there, who showed up at my job in a boat? What's his story? How safe is he for a young, impressionable child? Does he have mental health issues? Does he need to get checked for any?

The lie I told my therapist this morning wasn't a total lie.

My fling with Keenan was truly a one-time spontaneous act, a casual stress reliever that meant nothing and went nowhere.

There is no shortage of curiosity among my co-workers who jockey for answers.

"Hey, Genie, does he have brothers?"

"Does he have any friends, frat brothers, financial advisors?"

"Does he have a daddy?"

"Shit, does he have a mechanic?"

Hearty laughter fills the elevator, where I'm sandwiched between co-workers and investigators. "Does his mama or daddy have any candidates in their family tree?"

Miss Darcy levels me with a skeptical peek from the corner of her scrutinizing eye. "If only we could all have our children's birthday parties hosted by somebody so... charismatic."

"He does like to come in with a bang," I mutter. And that's not figuratively speaking either, as I recall him pinning me against the glass, under the ocean, in an underwater elevator.

Lus meets me back upstairs. "I hope you answered whatever question that man wants. If you don't answer, somebody in here will."

Back in the interview room with Victoria, she smacks her teeth with leftover anger. "Must be nice to be a social worker with a government job who works in a place like this. You college women get all the good ones."

I reach my hand out to her across the table. She snatches it back.

"Vic, you can have a good one, too. Regardless of whether you went to college or not. Just hold yourself to a higher standard and don't accept less."

"Easy to say when you have your pick of men," she mumbles back.

"That hasn't always been the case for me. I understand why it appears that way to you, but we've all gone through hard times. Men will treat you as you teach them to."

"So basically," she fumes, pausing to cock her head, "you're not recommending that my kids come home to me at the hearing in a couple of weeks."

"I'm going to ask the judge for a progress hearing in another two months, to give you a chance to deliver more clean tests and no signs of Tremaine in your life. This way you don't have to wait the entire six months before your next review."

With a violent shove of her purse, tears tumble out of her.

Nobody on this planet understands her predicament more than me—wanting two objects so badly that contradict one another so much. She'll either have to choose her son or her man.

I've been there, and it's a choice I'll never make again.

THE LIES YOU TELL

EUGENIA

"I'm glad you came to meet me," a more subdued Mr. McLain greets me at the door of The Delta. His athleticism broadcasts from his muscles easily throwing open the door for me, a reminder of how physical he is.

"Did I have a choice?" I ask. Nervous, looking over my shoulder, I follow him into the café.

"Sure you did. You could've said no, and I would've kept bothering you."

"Why? You don't have enough other women to chase on your playboy boats in New York?"

As we approach the small line to order, Keenan stands behind me. Close. Until I can feel the outline of his chest on my backbone and the outline of his manhood… at the edge of my back. "Do you have to plug yourself into my crack?"

Pressing closer, closing daylight between us, he drops his mouth to my ear. "Why not? Does it make you nervous?"

Keenan's lip brushes the tip of my ear and whispers to my nipples.

"It's inappropriate. That's why," I answer and step

forward to cut the flow of electricity from my socket to his plug.

"But you're grown. I'm grown."

"No, Keenan," I fuss under my breath. "I'm not just any grown, single person. I have a son." And I'm a woman who's screwed up enough times that I can't afford to do it now.

"Yes, I remember flying you to him on Christmas Day. But I am also aware he stays in New York with his dad most of the time, so why are you all tight?"

It's complicated. And I refuse to dive into my business. Although, if he knows my maiden name, where I work, where I live, my custody arrangements with Sheldon, he clearly must know about that other thing that happened last summer.

"I still have responsibilities that don't give me the time or headspace for… irresponsible entanglements."

"Who said I wanted the activities to be irresponsible? We can make it as responsible as you want. If you tell me to put on ten Magnums, I will. Shit, you damn sure will need 'em."

I balk.

"May I help you two?" the cashier asks.

"Yes, I'd like those smoked catfish hush puppies and the 'Easy Does It' beef and cush, and that 'Get Yo' Self Some Soul' drink sounds real nice. Let me get that. And the lady will have…" Keenan pauses and turns to me.

"The Delta sweet tea is fine."

"That's all?" he asks.

"That's all." I pull my eyes from him and take off to find seating.

Once we're seated, he links his hands lazily across the table and zooms his attention on me. "You're just as gorgeous as I remember. But more so today because I'm seeing you in daylight."

"You look younger in the light. And act younger," I point out.

"Damn, you don't have to crush a nigga."

"Apparently, I do. You were out there doing the most today, and you don't know what my situation is. How do you know I don't have a boyfriend?" I toss out a random possibility so he doesn't get hip to the reality.

"I'm sure if you did, that would've been the first thing out of your mouth." He smacks his lips for emphasis as he adds, "And I probably would not have given a shit, since he hasn't put a ring on your finger." Eliminating space between us, he bears his weight down on the table. "I've also got a gut feeling you don't have a boyfriend for the same reason I don't have a girl."

"Which leads us back to why are you here. All the way in Chicago, so far from New York or Baltimore. You're a young man who should be living his life with women his age, who have no responsibilities, can travel all over, be wild and crazy and fun with you."

The waitress sets down his plate, and he stuffs his mouth with the first bite of Mississippi beef cush. All sloppy, he chomps and smacks in a way that competes with cows. His tongue wipes excess sauce from his open mouth, the way my brothers' do. Though he's a young man of means, he definitely is not the prim and proper Sheldon.

He pauses to note, "And none of those chicks are Eugenia. You're the only woman that's been on my mind so tough. I try to push you out of my head. Lord knows I have."

"Try harder. You can't just bust into Chicago and start making demands from someone you don't even know."

Again, he slows from devouring his food to stare at me. Wiping his mouth, his eyes pin me down in an uncomfortable way that bunches up my panties.

"That's the thing, Eugenia. I feel like I do know you. I learned a lot about you that night."

"Impossible. It was just one night."

"No." He clears his throat, sips his alcoholic beverage, and spreads his fingers on the table to argue his case. "The time period may have only been twelve or thirteen hours, but in the place where both our heads traveled at the same time, with the same intensity, that was too much particle collision to relegate to time constraints here on Earth."

Just as I start to laugh at how crazy that sounds, my gaze crashes with his across the table. Under his lips, he rolls his tongue over his teeth, and no humor disturbs the seriousness of his face.

"Keenan, I'm sure that in your mind—"

"Not in my mind." He wipes his mouth. "Don't insult me."

I run my hand over my shoulder-length hair that needs a fresh trip to the salon and evaluate how to put this nicely.

"Tell me that night didn't light up every bulb on that tree in your pussy," he demands.

"Shh!"

"No, I will not shh. Just say it." Frozen, now ignoring his food, he awaits my answer.

I cannot admit to what we did. For all I know, Sheldon truly may have sent him here. They do business together.

"Keenan, I enjoyed hanging out with you on Christmas Eve while I waited to see my son, but it was only a friendly boat ride. What right does that give you to do this?"

The disappointment in his eyes immediately hardens into bestial determination. "Let me tell you something. The way you bucked and fucked on me that night, you may as well have taken a red-hot brand with your name on it and burned 'Eugenia' on my dick."

I throw my head from side to side to see if anybody is watching us. "Have some decorum."

He pushes his chest farther over the table, closer to me. Elbows hiked out as if he's about to snatch me up, his stare intensifies. "Decorum? Let me tell you what decorum is. Decorum is me not pouring this sauce all over your titties and licking until my tongue hurts. Decorum is me not gobbling your pussy the way I just scarfed down that cush. Decorum is me refraining from throwing coleslaw on your thighs and munching it off your little stretch marks you've got. With all these damn fantasies I've wrestled the last five months, and now you're here in front of me, I think I'm showing a *hell* of a lot of decorum right now."

I'm appalled, and stupefied. "What makes you think you can come here and talk to me like that! I don't date guys who say things like that to me!"

I yank up my purse with all the energy of somebody who's had enough of this damn glorified thug.

Keenan's hand shoots to grab my arm and hold me at the table. Rough, firm, his grip is a demand. "I'm not trying to disrespect you." He lowers his voice, stills his eyes. "But I can't lie to you. I meant every word I said. I can't be some fake nigga and shoot you some empty compliments that really don't mean shit just to impress you. Something tells me you've already had enough of that."

His eyes tear into my willpower the way his teeth ripped into his meat.

"I'm just telling you the thoughts that have lived in my head all the nights I wished for you, tried to satisfy myself with other females, to forget you, and I couldn't. And while you sit there picking and choosing your words carefully and pretending you didn't go HAM on me, a nigga just wants to lay you down and take off that mask you're wearing and see for myself if you really are sincere about those lies you're telling."

Keenan's take-no-prisoners approach to romancing a woman might have been cute twenty years ago.

"You need to go find a woman closer to your age who you can say all that to. I wish you all the best. Please don't bother me again."

This time when I jerk my hand from his reach, I'm quick to shoot off from my seat.

"Eugenia." At least he has enough decency to try and keep his voice controlled, though we're drawing attention anyway.

With him trailing me, I bust onto the sidewalk and race toward my SUV. His insistence chases me. The memories of him inside me, tossing me up, splitting open my cervix under the ocean, opening up closets in me I work to keep locked, all follow me in hot pursuit.

"Eugenia, let me show you I'm not playing with you. Seven years is nothing, so don't use my age against me."

"Easy for you to say when you have no kids and no commitments."

"No, you're wrong." He clamps my door against its frame as soon as I unlock it, leans against my back, pelvis-to-pelvis, his loaded breaths hot on my ear. "It was hard as hell for me to be this raw with you. I know the caliber of man you've been married to, a Wall Street banker, and I'm not that. I don't know how to be, and I won't even pretend I'm him. All I do know is you're raw, too, and your rawness puts me in a vice grip." With each inhale, his chest sweeps my back. "You belong in the wilds of nature where you can let go of all that untamed energy you hide. Before you tell me to kick rocks, think about how long you want to walk around with your body dry as a desert I can satisfy."

I'm a forty-year old woman, and while his passion is transfixing, sobering reality calls me. "I've heard all you had to say. Now will you please let me get in my car?" It took the strength of Sampson for me to push those words out.

He hauls his arm off the door. I dare not look at him. I'm too old to be weak. Too bruised and battle-scarred to lose again.

I'm proud of myself. Yes. I kept my focus, held my ground, and didn't give in.

All I need is my son.

4

IN SEARCH OF A BALM

EUGENIA

I made the right decision, I tell myself, ignoring this weight rolling around in my chest.

Multiple texts pop up from my family members with questions of news media they saw today.

Mom: *Somebody sent you a bunch of flowers today at work? What's this about a boat?*

Right after she texted, she calls. I hit 'ignore.' The day has already taxed my mental deposit account.

Then comes my older brother.

Eugene: *You finally found somebody who will treat you better than Sheldon?*

Then, of course, the inevitable family text thread, started up by my first cousin on my dad's side. It's always my dad's side.

Koi: *Damn, Eugenia, why do you always get the dudes with money?*

Valuable: *Don't screw this one up this time.*

Aunt Amy: *She didn't screw up nothing. Sheldon wasn't ever at home, probably had a whole other life over in Hong Kong, with an Asian wife and Asian kids. She was right to* *leave his ass and get them checks, instead of sitting there by herself all the time.*

Koi: *Shid, he can have all the wives he wants, long as I'm the American wife living in his American mansion and pushing out his American kids. He was bringing home that American cash, so I woulda kept giving him this American ass! Now she by herself.*

Zenaria: *Genie still lives good, in a high-rise, North Side, so what are you talking about?*

Valuable: *Not as good as Sheldon's new wife, in that big-ass castle they showed on* **Lifestyles of the Black and Famous.** *I woulda NEVA left him!!!*

My fingers whip across the screen, typing a savage response that'll shut her purple, horsetail-hair-wearing ass down. Feisty Eugenia erupts, pre-therapy. Fuck counting to some ten.

Me: *Bitch, really? You wanna talk about where somebody lives and the kind of man they've got? I would rather be by myself and paid than with six kids and a fuckboy who can't even make rent! Go somewhere and find you some fresh tracks. I heard his other baby mama tore out your last set.*

My finger hovers over the 'send' icon.

I have every right to defend myself. They shouldn't be talking shit, and Valuable clearly forgot who won the last time she and I threw down.

All this hot kettle of boiling grits that's been bubbling in me for months, I get ready to throw on her ass in this text. And after months of being the silent, "mature" woman who can't talk back or defend herself, who's had to play humble, this savagery will hit the *spot*!

The vase on the hallway table knocks over when I slam down my phone.

This is what they want.

The first thing they will do once my text lights up their

screens is screenshot it and email my social worker, Tabatha. They have probably already called Tab and alerted her that a man is in town looking for me.

Koi: *Bitch, you were the loudest one talking about what you would not take off Sheldon, telling her she needed to go.*

Valuable: *And who is dumb enough to listen to my stupid ass? I'm over here on the Southside, no fancy degrees, and my piece of a man ain neva gon be no banker. Shel wasn't my husband. I was just running my mouth. She should have stayed her ass right there in New York. Dumb!*

Aunt Amy: *Y'all, shut up, before she tries to kill herself again.*

Zenaria: *Genie, don't let them get in your head. They jus playin'. You straight?*

Valuable: *This dude in the boat must not know she crazy.*

Aunt Amy: *Eugenia, did you tell him the state of New York took your son and you shouldn't be seeing another man who could get your emotions up and send you to the mental ward?*

Koi: *Yeah, Eugenia, we're your family. We're just telling you what's good for you. You need to get rid of this new dude so he doesn't waste his time or yours and you can get Hadar back here.*

Their words—what's good for me—the backhanded slaps dressed up as family caring, are dust choking up my airways.

My mother messages me separately.

Mom: *I hope you're not reading those. Don't pay them no never mind. Just stay to yourself. You've come far, and you'll be getting Hadar back soon.*

Back on the family thread...

Koi: *What's Dark Chocolate's name, for real? Since Genie can't have him. He fine as hell. Where he work at?*

Valuable: *He don't want your tired, hood-rat ass. Those college professional men like their stuck-up females with a stank attitude.*

Koi: *Bitch, no you didn't. If I'm a hood rat, what is you?*

Valuable: *Hood Queen, heffa, and don't you ever forget it.*

Koi: *Haaa! I can't stand you!*

Koi: *But for real, though, Genie, what's that dude's name? Since you're tied up at the moment. I'm asking for a friend. Dude might like some hood cat, nice and deep, where he can drive his boat.*

Aunt Amy: *Genie, you coming to the barbecue Saturday? You coming down from your thrown to come play some bones?*

Instead of correcting her that the proper spelling is "throne," I leave the group thread. And then silence my phone.

Kicking off my shoes in the hallway of my condo, I stare at the pileup of my shoes and Hadar's. I never put them away after the judge gave Sheldon custody, because Sheldon bought him new shoes and an all-new wardrobe for his new school, new friends, and new siblings.

On the coffee table in front of the television sits two of Hadar's Avenger toys, exactly where he left them the last time he was here. Each time the cleaning lady comes and dusts, she knows to put them back exactly as they've laid for almost a year. The others still sit in an open toy chest, next to the wrapped-up cords of his video game console, all collecting dust. The day I offered to send it to him, he told me Sheldon had already bought him the latest model Play-Station and replaced mine.

An hour after rejecting Keenan's dinner, I'm hungry. I want nothing in my refrigerator and don't feel like cooking. But there is Raisin Bran atop the fridge and some almond milk left inside. Requires very little time or energy to prepare.

I tap my phone for the notifications. Swipe past my family conversations to see other texts from casual associates.

Mona from cooking class: *Hey, girl, where are you? Missing you at cooking class tonight.*

Lus: *What's popping, homie, you straight?*

Joy from group therapy: *Saw the news today! How exciting! Hope that man piece is in line with your goals of discipline and focus for your son.*

Translation: Don't get sidetracked and blow your custody.

I appreciate the positive sentiments from these women, but honestly, it's just too much sugary energy tonight.

Where I sit on a barstool at my island, my hands form a graveyard where I bury my face.

What's wrong with me?

I had it all.

Through the rush of tears I wrestle, I realize the lights are still out. The fingers of dying sunlight tease the edges of furniture in my lifeless home.

I sink down on my haunches until I face the cabinet doors to the storage area under the island.

In search of solace, praying for numbness, I open the doors. As a social worker myself, I know which areas we go for when we conduct searches for contraband and items our clients shouldn't have—the underwear drawers, glass and plate cabinets, fridge, bedroom nightstands, mattresses, and trash.

I pull out my large cooking pots and cutting blocks to reach for the Instant Pot in the very back. My lonely thirst shudders at the sight of temporary refuge.

The bottle of Cabernet Sauvignon has been sitting there since I got back from visiting Hadar over the holidays.

I grab a glass, open the bottle that's already been uncorked, and watch my liquid therapy pour out to me.

Keenan had one thing right. My desert wasteland stretches from my womb up to the cracks along the dustbowl of my heart and into my parched throat that starves for this wine. I raise it to my lips, smell sweet release. The first glorious swallow comforts my taste buds and soothes the dust cloud over my brain.

I'm yanked from my serenity when the buzzer at the front door screams at me.

My knee-jerk instinct is to ignore it and savor the only drink I've had this year. But I jump back into my social worker brain, into my devoted mom suit, into my reformed street-girl script, and start rushing.

A quick flick of my wrist dumps the wine from the glass, and I splash on the faucet to eliminate every scarlet drop of evidence. Shoving the topper back on the bottle, I pack it away inside the Instant Pot and cram it all back under the island, replacing all the big cooking pots.

In a couple of sniffs, I make sure there's no whiff of weakness on me, no hint I gave in.

It could be Tabatha, my social worker. She may have heard about Keenan's public display today and is stopping by as I do with my clients—a surprise, unannounced home visit.

I press the button. "Yes?"

"This is Reggie with a delivery from The Delta."

I thumb my fingers and think. "I didn't order anything from Delta. You have the wrong location."

"Number Four? That's what I dialed. Fried chicken sandwich and Kool-Aid pickles? I'll just leave this here at the front desk then, if you want to give it away, since it's already paid for. You have a nice evening," the delivery man says in my intercom.

While I sit here and contemplate whether to go downstairs for it, if this is, in fact, a setup, a knock raps against the door.

The peephole reveals it's Lus. She holds up The Delta bag.

She and my mother are the only two people on my permanent guest list who have spare keys.

"Did you buy this?" I ask her.

"No. The desk clerk asked me to bring it up, though." She peeks inside before entering. "Oh, so you've got clothes on. Anybody in here butt-naked?" She sniffs. "I don't smell ass and screwing."

Her reference to Keenan possibly being here is cute.

"Girl, nah. Come on in."

The food smells too good to toss out. I throw the bag open and pull out the deliciously scented takeout box. On top of it lies a note:

After a long day of shooting me down, you must be too tired to cook. Even if you won't eat with me, at least eat.

Before I think, the remnants of his cocky sensuality overtake my judgment and draw my hand to my nose. I smell the note. The faint aroma of his sharp, forested athletic prowess floats off it and into my subconscious.

"I wasn't sure if I should come check on you or who I would find in here." Lus interrupts my errant imagination. "You good, girl?"

She starts over in the direction of the paper towels.

"I'm straight. I had to turn down a man who rode to the job in a yacht, but no, other than that, we're good."

"You sure about that?"

I'm confused as she snatches a paper towel off the rack and walks back over to the island. To my horror, she dips down and wipes up a small ruby drop from the white marbled tile floor.

Since there is no other food or liquid in sight to justify that, I snap my mouth shut.

"Don't worry, girl," she says. "I remember those days. When a social worker would come to our house and check up on my mom. A so-called friend had stopped by and gifted a bottle of wine, and when the social worker found it, she took us away, a week after our mama had gotten us back. Those days of having an open case terrified the hell out of us. I'll never forget." She nods toward my food. "Go on and bust it open so we can get into it."

Our shared hard-knock lives are why Lus and I bonded after I moved back from New York.

We take out two plates and halve the food that Keenan delivered.

"Sometimes, it feels like, no matter how much work I put in, I'll never catch a break."

"I hate to be that person who sounds like a fortune cookie, but God usually takes us through these wack tests in preparation for something better," Lus says. "Take that for what you will."

"Yes, that does sound lame. A long time ago, I actually believed that, or I tried to, but I don't anymore. I think God takes us through strife just to ready us up for more strife." I've seen too much despair to believe anything else.

"That sounds negative and defeatist as hell."

"I've been negated and defeated a lot, so you'll have to excuse my side of the fortune-cookie wisdom."

"Looks like I got here at the right time, before you did something crazy."

I nod and keep munching on the good food from The Delta. "You're right. I'll give Tab twenty-four hours before she does a surprise drop-by."

"Then why were you taking that kind of risk?" Lus references the drop of wine she just wiped up.

"Because for a hot minute, I felt like I'd lost already." Again, echoes of my son's voice still call Chrissy "Mama" between these same ears Keenan's lips brushed two hours ago. "I'm running and running on a treadmill and going nowhere. Until all I see is a wall of defeat. I lost. I'm doing all that hard work, just to lose."

"But you're not losing. You're so close to unmonitored visits, and you know the social worker is going to come and check up on you after all that attention on you today."

"And I'm still doomed. Sheldon is good at that—running circles around me with his fancy friends and fancy technology and fancy family."

"Girl, stop. So, this guy, why is he under the impression that he can just show up at your job and bomb you with all those flowers?"

I've told Lus about losing Hadar. She is the one coworker I trust with information that I don't even entrust to most of my family members.

But I still give her a side-eye, in a silent stoplight that my blizzard of a Christmas Eve night with Keenan is not up for discussion. Lus is no fool, and I'm sure she sniffs out what must've gone down between Keenan and me at some point.

But the earthquake that night between him and me, and the geyser he unleashed in me, that won't leave my lips. I don't care if she knows I sat here and almost had a drink.

"All right then, girl, I feel you, loud and clear," Lus says. "But I don't have to remind you to jump your ass off that treadmill and hike a real mountain or something. Don't mess up winning your boy back for some dick. Stay strong."

Now she digs into her purse and pulls out a plastic bag that she sets on the counter. Once I see the label, my gut almost gives up the ghost from laughing. "Gina's Good Time Toys?" I read.

Inside is a vibrator.

"It's not a yacht, but you'll have to make do." She finishes up her part of the sandwich and Kool-Aid pickles. "He's fine as hell and looks like he's packing big sausage energy, I won't lie. Girl, you should've seen your eyes when he showed up. Oh, you tried to hide it, but your first mind can't lie."

For a few more minutes, we have a good roll over Keenan today, but I know my secret I haven't shared with her won't go anywhere. "Appreciate you stopping by."

"I figured you could use help keeping up your strength. This weekend, let's do yoga or a hike."

"All right, I'm game."

When she's gone, I have a hard time detaching myself from the door. Once again, I'm alone in my empty condo. No good loving in that bedroom, and no babbling child so excited about his day he can hardly explain it to me.

Work reports and tea make my evening company on the sofa. Around eleven-thirty, I finally pack it all up and go to the place I hate most in the world—the dark torture chamber of my bed. At times, I manage six hours of sleep on a good night. But as we roll closer to the custody hearing next week and my anxiety gallops the terrain of my head, sleep is more a punishment than a refuge. After a few minutes of a book, some stretches, and breath work, I finally turn out the light.

"Genie!" The ferocious bark from the front yard rips my eight-year-old mind from my play with the neighbor. "Get your ass out here and sweep off this porch right now!"

"Daddy, I already swept it!" I plead while trudging out to point at how clean it is.

"Who you talkin' back ta, li'l girl?" His large hands grab my neck and shove my face toward the wooden porch until my nose almost touches the dirt tracks my brothers left behind after playing in the yard. "You call that clean?"

The blood flushes from my humiliated face in front of my next-door neighbor who watches. "I didn't do this. Nelson and Odie did it after I swept."

The fumes of cheap whiskey seeped in his sweaty skin whip me before he pulls off his belt. "Imma teach you about talkin' back."

"She said she swept it already!" Niecy screams at him, and leaps next to me. "Stop it."

"Niecy, no!" I plead.

The fury of his unmet bills, overdue property taxes, and denied job promotion comes slamming down in that belt, on both Niecy and me. I reach out and grab for it at the risk of making it worse and him going for the stitching cord.

"Daddy, I'll sweep it. Stop! *Stop!* Eugene! Eugene! Eugeee… Euuuu…" Tongue stuck to the roof of my mouth, kicking and grabbing the covers, I moan a tortured, unintelligible cry in my tumble down the tunnel of sleep. "Mmmmm!"

At 3:38 a.m., the treadmill of my screwups rotating round and round in my head, I yield to yet another urge I shouldn't. Opening the nightside table, I reach for the small photo album inside. These photos shouldn't be a balm over my anxiety-riddled mind, but the hope and brightness blooming on every page provides a melancholy calm that brings me closest to peace. Sheldon's and my wedding day, the happiest day of my life, reminds me that real joy was almost possible. I grin at us on our honeymoon in Paris, and the night I showed him the pregnancy test. A few months later, the evening Hadar was born, the tenderness pouring out of Sheldon's eyes at me…

With my marriage to Shel, I thought I had finally left hell for good.

5

HER ONLY PRIORITY

EUGENIA & KEENAN

EUGENIA

The front door buzzer blares me from sleep. Peeling my face from the plastic album page on which I fell asleep, I shoot a glance at the alarm clock.

6:16 a.m.

In a slam, I shut the album, and shove it back in the nightstand drawer.

"Good morning, Eugenia, this is Tabatha."

Of course. I thank the universe for Lus coming over when she did and stopping me from giving in to my worst instincts.

No sooner than I throw open the door does Tabatha make her way through it. "I would've thought you'd be up by now."

"I needed a while to center myself and meditate," I lie.

Without asking for my invitation, she starts hunting in my kitchen. "I heard you had a visitor yesterday at work.

Who is the special guy? And have you ever told me about him?"

I regurgitate what I rehearsed yesterday so it's consistent with what I told my therapist. "He organizes special events and adventure activities in New York. They put on Hadar's birthday party a couple weeks ago."

"Oh! That group of guys called Explore Adventures!" she gushes. "When I interviewed him, Hadar could not stop talking about those guys. He loved his party."

I smile as Hadar's immense excitement flashes through my mind, of him running from one joy ride to the other. "Yes, he did." In fact, I've never seen him so happy. That worries me. "Anyway, the man who is the company founder clearly got a little attached. I told him I'm unavailable these days."

"That was quite a show he put on for you yesterday. Practically every social worker in the city is talking about it," she says while going through the cabinets. She opens up the door to the trash can, tilts it open, takes a peek in search of alcohol, marijuana, a needle, bottles of painkillers, anything that might indicate I cannot process my emotional hurdles without an intoxicating substance.

She moves over to the island, where all the cooking pots are stored, and throws open the wooden doors.

"Yes, Keenan is quite confident. I've looked him up, and his co-workers, flying around in helicopters, jumping from planes, skiing on the water, that sort of thing. He seems like a showy person." I hope the light conversation covers the egg beater of my heart churning at lightning speed. She peers under the island for signs of weakness.

"Yes, I've heard about that group myself. I think they're hosting a Sasha Static concert in a couple months, right?" Tabatha asks.

The mention of the big, extravagant event feels like rocks

being shoved down my throat. "That's the word. Hadar can't stop raving."

"I tried to hunt for tickets. The cheapest I found was four thousand, and it's been sold out for months. But Hadar says he and his brother and cousins have VIP backstage passes, where they'll get to meet her, and oceanfront seats on an Explore boat. You plan on being in New York with Hadar for that? That should be fun."

I pray she doesn't notice the spice in my face at the mention of Sheldon's and Chrissy's combined money and connections.

"He and I have not talked about it." It's yet another one of those activities where he'll take my son and not include me. Payback for all the years I did it to him, I'm certain.

"I'm not sure. As always, it depends on what Hadar wants."

"You should speak with Mr. Rouse about it. If the judge gives back your custody of Hadar, you and Mr. Rouse will have to work together. Everything that went down between you and him in the past will have to be resolved for Hadar's sake. He's such an interesting kid. Very smart. Mr. Rouse has been doing a lot with him this past year."

Like I need to be reminded.

She proceeds toward the back rooms as I follow, going to the bedroom and heading first to the closet, then the bathroom, bends over, lays one knee on the floor, and checks under the bed. Slides out one dresser drawer and then the other, goes through the underwear. Standard procedures for social workers to do home checks when they suspect parents have a reason to hide activity, as an unsuspecting person would've hidden Keenan last night. Countless times, I've discovered boyfriends cowering in showers, children's fathers crouching in closets, drugs hidden in bra padding, and guns in shoe boxes, when I showed up by surprise.

"So what are your plans for today? Your cooking class said you weren't there last night. How are you keeping yourself busy?" she asks with a faux friendliness that only thinly masks her interrogation.

"My co-worker, Lus, came over, we ate, and then I worked on some reports. Not much on Netflix."

"What do you have going on for this weekend?"

She wants to know if I'll be here stewing in depression.

"Lus and I will likely hang outside for a bit, go for mani-pedis. There's a family barbecue also this weekend, and I need to check in on my parents."

"Just be careful over that way. There were six shootings on West Washington just on Sunday. And as for this man who showered you with all that wonderful attention and had all the girls falling out," she says with a joking expression, "you know what he needs to do if he wants to be in your life. He'll also be in Hadar's life."

"No," I say, shaking my head. "You don't have to remind me. My son is my only priority."

"Good. So you'll be in New York next week for the hearing, and I'll see you via the video conference."

"Yes. Any clues on what you're recommending?" Now I sit in the same seat as Victoria.

"Eugenia, you've put in a lot of hard work this past year and come so far. But I'm not sure. What happened last summer was really serious. It won't be up to me. My bosses will make the final call as far as the recommendation to submit to the judge."

The helium filters out of my chest in a loud whizzing sound. "Oh, come on, Tab, I know your bosses are going to rely mostly on what you report. And then also, you're one of the bosses. I know the hierarchy." She and I are essentially on the same level as far as our government and agency job status—senior supervising social workers. She was assigned to me specifically because it would've been awkward and intimidating for someone who is my junior to oversee my case.

"I'll submit my input that I think you have done well. But our superiors will make the final call, Eugenia. And then the judge will hear from the therapist, from Hadar and from Sheldon, and will make her own decision."

She gives me the kind of response that's not really saying anything, meaning the news is bad and she can't say it to my face. Just as I couldn't tell Victoria yesterday.

The dagger of inescapable truth twists in my esophagus. I know what I would recommend if I were the case-carrying social worker in this scenario, who had the information they have against me—information Sheldon's investigative team provided.

If the decision were up to me, I would have grave concerns about turning over unmonitored access to an impressionable ten-year-old boy a year after a suicide attempt, my second suicide attempt. That they know of.

I'm over the reassuring smile she tries to offer that tells me nothing. Closing the door after her, I collapse against it.

Why am I still fighting? What do I have to offer Hadar now, after he's spent the past year in his father's clutches? How can I possibly connect with him after he's been meeting with Disney and NASA employees?

Each breath I manage only yields to one that is more shallow in the cage of my trachea.

Should I sign Hadar over to his father? I did all the heavy lifting while Sheldon traveled, hopped on jets and planes around the world, and hobnobbed with high-powered banking executives and political friends. I dealt with a yelling, screaming toddler, slow-walked my own social worker goals, potty trained him, and was essentially a single parent.

But he gets to sweep in now with his high life and be the hero. How will I ever win?

KEENAN

"So, boss man, what'll it be?" an exasperated Laney asks me over the phone and awaits my answer. "Should I book another flight, or will you finally ride this one?"

I should stop now.

My head rests on the glass of my hotel room, separating the city of Chicago from me, separating me from her.

I peek at the scribbled notes on the desk—where she attended high school, college, her activities, few friends, and even some family, provided to me by my investigator and a couple of friends from Chicago. Through some detective work and process of elimination, we figured out a few names of her clients.

Should I hunt for a lost woman who doesn't want to be found?

Maybe what's screwing my head around is, at Christmas, I thought we had a connection.

Sex with Eugenia is a line of cocaine.

I wasn't prepared for the way her ass bucked on me, and when I woke up four sweet hours later, I might have pulled my thumb from my mouth.

The moment I woke up and said, "Good morning," her restless body was already telling me she needed to go. Her first priority—her *only* priority—was dipping the hell off that boat. She wanted nothing more from me.

Now that's just damn unusual for a young black brother in my position. Most women my age—early thirties, single, no kids yet, professional and counting paper—try to stay in my damn bed as long as possible. At first fuck, the next step for them is marriage.

But not her.

Eugenia compartmentalized expertly that morning: *We're fucking and that's it; don't expect anything else.* That detached attitude is normally… my role.

Shit was a real head-scratcher. She dismissed me like the last situation on Earth she needed was some nappy-headed kid thinking he could play with her head. Her air of indifference—having more important priorities to worry about than me, or seducing me, or hustling up a place on my roster—only stoked the flames under my wood.

After our explosive Christmas Eve night, shit, I wouldn't have minded talking to her on the phone. But she was so antsy and nervous to be on time for her kid, it didn't seem appropriate for me to ask. And I am not an "appropriate" type of Negro.

Now here I am, months later, and my curiosity's got a man riding a boat down the street. No amount of sex I've had —no matter how phenomenal—comes close to the underwater depths Eugenia and I reached on Christmas Eve. That bond exceeded physicality, to spiritual heights.

I should leave her alone and get my hop on the plane to Baltimore, and then on to New York.

I *should.* But does Keenan ever do what he's supposed to do?

"No. See if you can find me a flight out for tonight."

Laney scoffs over the phone, because this is the third time she's had to rebook.

"Keenan, if you're really not leaving until tomorrow, then just say that."

"Fine. Tomorrow morning." That is when I really and truly will give up. But I feel that Eugenia has not experienced the absolute best and purest of Keenan DeWan McLain.

I pick up my phone and call my boy, Ian, who works in the government in downtown Chicago. He also throws the best kickbacks in town.

"All right, so hook me up with your cop friend."

"Bet that. I've got her schedule and list of clients for today. Go to the Gold Coast where some of us have a little hideout. Apartment eight hundred and nine."

I let out a small breath. She will likely be really pissed about me involving her job, especially after yesterday.

"Appreciate you, son."

"Kee, man, you sure this is the move? I know some of her family. They're kind of rough. And doesn't she have some kind of... issues? Didn't I read about something happening with her last summer? Was she married to that one guy who is, like, way up in the New York banking world?"

Though Ian is my guy for real, my public displays have already irritated Eugenia and had the reverse effect of what I intended. I won't take the risk of confirming she and I have linked up. I won't stir any more gossip among these city government workers than I might have already caused. Yesterday, I got a little excited. But I called myself sweeping her off her feet.

"She's somebody I care about, a great lady with a cool kid, and she's dope. Nothing serious."

"Uh-huh," Ian says in a tone that conveys he doesn't believe shit coming out of my mouth. "Just have my Sasha Static tickets ready, dude."

"Bet."

I head to North Lake Shore Drive, where Ian instructed. It's my understanding Ian's cop friend will direct her to this location. I can't bust up in her house, since I don't know her situation, or if she really does have a man.

My mind spins with ways to surprise her. She refused to drink on Christmas Eve night, so maybe not liquor. She wouldn't eat with me yesterday, so no food. Flowers are apparently out. But I do recall the drink she kept ordering the evening I approached her in a booth by herself at Taste.

The brand of pure chocolate paste that Solomon imports straight from the Ivory Coast, I'm not sure I can locate that here in Chicago. And since Solly and I are on the outs, I won't call him and ask if he knows any place around here that's comparable to the dishes he curates at Taste, which Eugenia seemed to love that day.

"Laney, I need your help."

She doesn't say it, but the impatience is evident in her tone. "What's up, boss?"

"This is the last favor I'll ask, and I promise you, I will be on that plane in the morning. I need you to ask Solly about places around here that compare to Taste's chocolate. You can probably already guess, he shouldn't know the request is coming from me."

Solomon hates my guts, and the feeling is mutual. Hiding his secret angel investors from me that included my own damn sister is the lowest a business partner can go.

Still, though I can't stand how tight Solomon is with his supplies, that dude knows what he's doing when it comes to his menu. Taste's quality cuisine add another level of distinction to the Explore brand and have no peer.

"All right. I'll get on it."

I don't know if this will work. She may call police on me. And I still can't figure out for the life of me why she's so damn jumpy. Looking over her shoulder, running from me like she'll get in trouble with a Boogeyman, she just might have a dude. Why else would she be so shook? Is she depriving herself of joy as some form of punishment—not drinking, not having fun, rejecting any dates? The weird shit reminds me of that religious priest in *Da Vinci Code* who walks around whipping himself.

But the underwater depths she and I dove to that night still have me in a headlock. Despite my doubts and questions, I'm going in.

6

JUST A TALK

EUGENIA

"This is Eugenia." Balancing the phone between my shoulder and cheek, I cram a sandwich into my mouth between home visits.

"Hello, are you the social worker, Eugenia Rouse?" somebody who sounds official asks on the other end.

"Yes, I am. And this would be?"

"I'm officer Larry Aiken, and I have one of your clients here with me who's gotten herself into a little situation. Looks here like she has violated her parole. She says she has been performing well with her drug tests and in her drug treatment program but she does not have the proof to show me here. She asked me to call you, instead of me arresting her and taking her to jail for court in the morning. Now, I'm willing to cut her a break if she really is doing classes and clean tests. Maybe she just got herself caught in the wrong place at the wrong time. But if she cannot produce proof, I'll have to take her in and she can tell the judge all about it."

This happens all the time—when my clients need help getting a job, applying for food stamps, seeking an apartment, or get into trouble with police. Rather than calling their attorneys, they ask the officer to call their social worker.

I swallow my food. "What's her name?"

"Victoria Tyson."

God, no, Victoria. She was probably hanging out with the wrong people. We just talked about this yesterday. I give her a quick phone call so I can hear her version of the events. Her phone has been cut off. There's no telling what may have happened, or if her baby's father keeps it in his name as a means to control her.

I start to call her mother and then think better of it. Parents with open child neglect cases normally don't want close relatives and parents to know the trouble they're in. Sadly enough, I know this firsthand.

"All right, sir, what's the address?" I wrap up my home visits for the afternoon and make this final stop.

This area of stunning, pricey Gold Coast is not what I was preparing for. I wonder how Tremaine and Vic got access to a place like this. Who do they know in such a nice place? What does he have her doing in such a swanky building that could land her in trouble with police?

On my way inside the high-rise condos, I scan for cop cars that always flood a crime scene, a big drug or gang bust. But it's just a posh setting complete with waterfall, reflection pool, high-end furnishings.

I flash my government badge to the front desk security officer.

"Yes, Mrs. Rouse, come on in. They're expecting you."

Now I'm baffled. When I'm signing in, I take a quick peek at the list but I don't see Victoria's name on it. This must be really bad if somebody snuck her in here. I've seen it all in my eighteen years doing this.

On the eighth floor, apartment 809, the scene is completely calm at the door. No hordes of cops or investigators or arrestees sitting around in handcuffs. I wrap my hand against the door, but this feels a little off. Inside my purse, my other hand rests on a switchblade knife.

The door opens, and yet again, the sight asphyxiates my brain cells. My feet don't turn fast enough to flee before he reaches for me.

"Come here, Eugenia, I just want to talk to you."

"But a cop called me… How did you…?"

Yanking my arm, he tugs me inside and closes the door behind us. Mechanical forces inside me move too fast, too organic for me to control, in which inner heat beneath my bones already transfers with his. The heat convection between our bodies, circulating under our surfaces, shifts my emotional plates and gears, realigning me without my permission.

His head bonds to mine. Already stroking my cheek are his nose and mouth. The sporty outdoorsman scent rising off his flesh already enters my brain, and those gorgeous lips already lock my breaths in his.

"I don't understand why you won't eat, or drink, or take flowers. But I do think I understand one thing," his voice drips into my ear.

All that cockiness that compels him to show up and infiltrate my life irritates me and hardens my nipples.

In a week, I've got Hadar's hearing, and I'm too close.

"I don't care what you understand. I told you to stay away from me." Fighting whatever wildly reacting forces take over me, I dash for the door handle. I'm floored. He jerks my hands over my head and pins them against the door.

He can't know his forceful energy wakes up my force.

"But that's just it. I can't."

"You're crazy." I don't care how good or otherworldly this feels, I can't be a fool again.

"Yeah, I am, a little bit." The cocky glint in his eye laughs at my willpower. "And you're crazy, too. It's why I like you."

He digs a hand into a bowl on the wooden hall stand, into some kind of mud. His fingers brown and messy, he reaches for my face.

"Don't you dare!" I dip down and lurch to escape.

But Keenan must have a compass to traverse my ocean, navigating my torrents and rough tides easily. He snatches me back to him.

"Let go of me!"

Shocking him, I grab the lightweight bowl and smack it against his head. While he holds one of my wrists, I use the other to smear him with as much mud as I can. Across the marble floor, he skids.

"Tell me you weren't thinking about my dick inside you last night."

At the very mention of Christmas Eve, I almost fall into a stupor. "There's nothing to think about!"

"That's a lie!"

My adrenaline up, I go for a plant on the floor, scoot it between us to trip him. He's ready for my fight. He steps through the plant, steps right through my brick wall of self-protection.

"Come here, Eugenia. I know damn well…"

He lunges for me, and I dodge toward the bar area, where I reach for another bowl to hurl. His hand cuffs my wrist, stops me. Into another bowl, he sticks his other hand and pulls out more mud.

"What the hell is this?"

"Come find out." He flicks off my protests like mental gnats and grabs my face, smears it with chocolate that smells like it's been whipped with caramel or toffee and sweetness. His fingers dirty up my flesh in muddy sweetness. The thrill of this little scuffle animates his eyes. "Why haven't you called police, Eugenia? There's the phone." He motions at the phone on the wall.

I grip his dick. "I don't need police! I can handle you myself."

"Really? Well come handle me then." He hikes my arm over my head.

I struggle to bring it down again, grunting. "Mmph!"

With another muddy hand on my neck, he closes in, his mouth open to break into mine.

He winces when I head butt him.

Fuck.

I wince, too.

Back when I was a kid fighting my brothers it didn't hurt.

"So you *are* crazy." Keenan's arm wraps around me, his pressure securing my body, disturbing my breathing, unnerving my strength. Out and in, our chests rise and fall, ribs fighting ribs, soul against soul, dueling one another's heat. Over my chest, he places his messy hand, as if it's a defibrillator delivering an electrical charge into my heart chamber. "I needed to find out for myself."

I pick up a wooden spoon with my free hand and, while he's distracted, smack him with it.

"Shit!" Undeterred, he rips open my blouse, exposes my chest and satin bra.

"You ruined it!" I yell.

"I'll ruin more than that."

I stick my nails in his fancy T-shirt and slash through it. What lies underneath transfixes me. I must've been so exhausted on Christmas Eve I didn't really pay attention. So nervous about reaching Hadar on time, eaten alive with guilt for sleeping with a stranger, I failed to properly savor Keenan. That firm chest sucks in air, sucks in me.

But he needs to understand I'm not one of his young playmates.

His fingers at my throat, he draws me toward him, spreads his hand over the slopes of my breasts. Smears whipped chocolate over the mounds of my flesh, thumbs my nipples. He lowers his face, slides out his tongue. I hit him in the head and on his back.

He lifts me and throws me over his shoulder. While I kick and writhe, he manages to unbutton my slacks.

"Put me down!"

Instead of complying, he yanks my pants and thong over my ass. We wrestle even as he sets me down.

Despite me shoving him, Keenan clasps my head and finally joins his mouth to mine.

I want to fight, to be strong and not falter. All my common sense pleads with me—he's too young, this will go *no*where, and he just thrives on the chase, the allure of an older woman.

His tongue pushes into me, tasting me, thrusting his way past the gates of my lips and over my tongue, invading my mouth until the tip of my vagina surrenders. Between us flows a symmetry, life-giving water that creeps along the crevices of my scorched desert land, in a way I both need and question.

"You act like you're in prison. You don't drink," he whispers and bites down on my lip, plucking its meat before letting go. "Or party." His tongue licks. "Or club." His tongue dips in and out of me. "But you fuck like you're riding a damn bull, a wild woman." His sweet-scented hand houses the side of my face. "Black Mystique." The heat transfer continues against my will, the shifting of emotional plates unearthing my exterior. "Unleash her on me again, the one you won't let anybody else see. Let her out."

I stick my nails in his skin. Instead of flinching, Keenan grimaces through the pain.

He shoves his fingers in my thong. Through my wet folds

that squish with cream, his fingers stroke me and play in my unshaven hair. The immediate ecstasy opens me up and involuntarily snaps me to arch my back for more.

How long has it been since I've been touched? Christmas Eve.

In the caves of my mind, inside my mountains of need and unfulfilled desire, the abandoned cries of my consciousness fade. In a last weak attempt to grasp for the light, I swat at his arm.

"Tell me to stop. Say it."

But the involuntary reaction of my body to his touch slowly bucks. My legs widen. My jaw falls at his finger twisting in my malnourished vagina.

I unbuckle his belt while our tongues flutter around another. In impatient jerks, I wrangle with his zipper. He helps me maneuver it over his erection.

I sink my teeth into his lip.

"Eow!"

"You shouldn't have come here," I mutter through my clinched teeth, still gripping him.

I don't remember touching Keenan's dick last December. He did everything. Which is probably why I don't remember him being this size. But now, dangerously thick and heavy, it thumps against my thighs.

"Then leave." He pulls off my slip-on shoe. "Call police, Eugenia." Flips off the other shoe. "Tell me I'm hurting you." He wrestles down my pants far enough until they no longer obstruct his manhood from penetrating me. "And you don't want this."

He slides me forward so my ass hangs from the edge of the island, and he dives down.

Inside my legs, he smears whipped caramel and chocolate through my unshaven hairs and pink folds. Shoving his face between my knees and rips his tongue over my dessert tray.

Sensations I haven't felt since he ate me at Christmas now blow the biggest scream from me. He tears my pants all the way from my ankles. My legs flail in the air and his mouth flails over the moist hills and valleys of my fleshy womanhood.

My carnality overtakes the safe, cautious mother. She succumbs to her need, thrusting and jerking, tilting her ass up more and tipping her knees out farther.

The sweet sounds of my juices on his tongue, mixing with chocolate. His taste buds crawling over every inch of my flesh, he sucks my pussy with desperate hunger I both resent and crave.

He doesn't miss an inch of my cracks and crevices, lifting my entire ass to lick. My nerves dance for sweet redemption. My messy titties bob over his head with every stroke, my ripped work blouse flapping open.

Like he summons my coming orgasm, it heats my womb, busts through my cervix, sizzles like hot grease thrown on my uterus. With me jerking and bucking, the boiling ecstasy is too much for me to keep still. Keenan persists, circling his tongue around the center of my pussy and my soul with his whole head.

Riding his face, losing control, I give up the fake restraint and let him rip off my mental slip he saw hanging.

An unrecognizable wail erupts from a woman who touches her inner beast.

I hop through the skies like in *Crouching Tiger, Hidden Dragon*. On the magic carpet in *Aladdin*, way up in the sky, my womanly canal soars. My womb is set free, still trembling and contracting.

While I'm in a drunken fantasy, he rises and sucks my mouth. My essence emanates from Keenan. His dick at my threshold, so many objections still echo from that distant cave in my head—I'm an easy fuck, he's playing me, I'll be another notch on his belt.

"When was the last time you were with somebody?" he asks.

"None of your business."

"I'm serious, Eugenia. It's been a long time—I'm talking years—since I've been in anybody bareback. I'm clean."

I'm impressed. He's responsible. No mischief or tomfoolery creeps anywhere on his expression.

Still, I'm stingy with a short answer that yields so much. I finally give it up. "You."

I don't appreciate the tender way he caresses my face at hearing that confession.

"Birth control?"

The sorest spot of my soul mumbles. "I can't have children." I immediately regret saying that. Or sounding so desolate. Despite his being responsible, he's so young and insolent. Now I tote my insecurities and stumble through the dark forest of confusion. "Never mind."

I move to go.

His hands clasping my head, he presses compassion onto my cheek in a simple kiss more massive than lust.

Keenan pushes his raw dick into me, and our lungs grasp for the same stunned, heavenly air.

I strap my legs around his muscular ass and his bare shaft sparks the sulfur tinder box of my pussy. In the deadwoods of my womanly canal, the sublime sensations jump to life. We meld together, mouths, fingers, pelvises, in heat. His pants still taut around his ass, I slide my hands in and cling to his cheeks. He rolls and swivels them, and his dick strikes the match, setting a wildfire in me.

"I haven't thought about anybody but you since Christmas." The taste of me on his tongue dominates my own tastebuds. His manhood penetrates me deeper. "Have you thought about me?"

Every night, sometimes all night. "No."

"That's funny." He shoves his dirty fingers through my lips. "You're fucking a nigga back like he owns at least half your head."

On his flesh is a fiesta of caramel, chocolate, and maybe even raspberry. Now I realize each of those bowls held a different flavor of whipped paste, so undeniably delicious I instinctively suck it off Keenan's fingers like it's candy, before I think to stop myself.

"Mm…"

"Shit, Eugenia." His breaths are quick and erratic, excited for every stroke.

I whine when he removes his fingers from my mouth, rubs my spit over my nipples.

My marble-hard tips on his tongue, he stares directly through me.

"You got some pretty, real woman titties."

I hate how I need this.

I hate the flames of his touch on my shoulders, him cradling my back, worshipping at the hills of my breasts, igniting forest fires in my womb. Where his wood burns and explodes, his log filling me up, pressing toward my diaphragm. I hate how my dry peaks and valleys, so caked up and scorched, open up in my legs and await the refreshing rain.

"You're in my head. No matter what a nigga do, I can't get you out. Other women only make it worse."

"Don't say that."

He lifts me from the island, my legs still wrapped around him, and he pushes me against the wall. "I didn't come all this way not to say it. I want you, Eugenia."

With more leverage, he shoves his dick harder into me, gripping and yanking my hips.

"Urgh!" Somebody inside me growls at the discomfort of him entering spaces that are rarely touched. "That's too much, Kee…"

I claw his ass harder, hanging on, hating how I love the pain of his pounding.

"I want to be too much."

Keenan buries his face in the crook of my neck.

My inner walls contract, creaming on his shaft.

"Aaah…" My toes ball up, legs hugging his ass.

"Yes, baby," he mutters, jackhammering my womanhood that crumbles under the pressure.

Against the wall, we buck and ride. With him still in me, we climb to the erotic pinnacles together, grunting and groping like we'll never get this again. My titties grind on his bare chest, my lungs hardly inhaling on my ascension to the clouds. Keenan beats on my pussy like he already owns it. On his shaft, my soul gallops like it wants to be owned.

My first vaginal orgasm in months…

The scream is not enough release. Through our shudders and spasms, we crest a raging wave.

On our descent back to Earth, and Keenan grips my head to his.

"You never answered my question."

"I'm not going to Europe with you." Already, even while the aftershocks still quake across my legs, I squirm to escape him.

But he holds me still, his eyes exiting the haze of our lovemaking. "Don't just automatically tell a nigga no."

"I'm automatically telling you no."

"Eugenia, why are you playing with this crazy vibe we've got? We need to explore this. What we just did wasn't fucking."

Both of us still gulp air to catch our breath.

His ripped, Hamptons-kissed arms are unyielding at the sides of my head. He's still inside me, still magnetizing my legs that clasp at his waist.

"That's exactly what it was."

He snickers and drops his head, clearly put off that I don't readily agree to what he's decided. "It's deeper than that or you wouldn't have done it. You wouldn't have given yourself to me. And I may not know you, but I've got a hunch you let me rub all this food on you, that you moan for mercy when my dick is digging through your bullshit, that you let me do it raw because you're tripping out on our vibe, too. It's been on your mind. You've probably replayed it a thousand times —all the ways I light up what you try to hide, the ways you sure as hell light me up, how good we felt sleeping next to each other by the fire. No matter how you fight it, Eugenia, our chemistry is burning up some shit."

It doesn't matter. Regardless of how beautiful all that sounds, I'm a screwed-up single mom on the verge of losing the one good thing I still have left in this world. "Put me down, Keenan."

With caked chocolate on his finger, he trails it down my cheek. "I'll set you on the floor, but I don't think I can put this down."

"No. This is where you stop, Keenan. Kick these fantasies out of your head. You seem like a very interesting young man," I note, sure to point out our age difference.

"Don't do that patronizing shit." His irritation flickers along his dick and twitches inside me, the dominant energy wetting me up again. We both feel it.

That can't happen. I can't open myself up to whatever that was.

"Go chase somebody your age. Plenty of women out there are just praying for a man like you."

No sooner than the words come out of my mouth does a phone buzz somewhere across the room. My wrist displays the time: 6:27 p.m.

"Oh Jesus! Put me down!" I tap on Keenan's shoulder frantically.

He sets me down, and I take off running. Toward the phone. I smack my hand to my forehead. Four missed video calls from Sheldon's phone.

"Shit!" My fingers skate across my screen to hit 'call back.' Then I see myself in a mirror, with my face smeared, hair a dirty rat's nest, chest caked in chocolate, my blouse destroyed with buttons missing. I look like I just stepped out of a women's mudwrestling match. I terminate the video call and make a regular call.

I turn toward a half-dressed Keenan and put my index finger over my lips. He nods his understanding.

"G, I thought you wanted to talk to him earlier, before he gets sleepy, and you don't pick up?" Sheldon starts in on me.

"My bad. I had a client visit that went over the time," I lie while searching for my thong.

Keenan holds it out, and I glare at him, snatching it off his finger.

"Genie," Sheldon continues, "you said you'd be finished around four and home between five and six and ready to talk. H had a big day in his science class he's excited to show you. He says you and him worked on this in Chicago. We'll call you right back on video."

Finally, a project between my baby and me that Sheldon and Chrissy can't hijack—his bug investigation.

"Uh, *no!*" I yelp, conjuring up another quick lie for why they can't see me this way. "I'm not home just yet and still driving," I lie with a heavy tongue. Untangling my slacks, I continue, "I got an emergency call from police about a parent, not on the schedule." That part isn't a lie, even if I was misled.

"Fine, we'll call you back in an hour, G. But this earlier time was your idea. I don't want to hear you complained to the social worker that I'm not trying to work with you." In the background, Chrissy's kids scream and laugh. Straight into my ear, a baby's happy, delighted squeal lights up the phone, like she's being tickled. Sheldon's new baby, that I wanted him to have with me. A tiny crack of pain spreads into a web across the glass case of me, at the sound of mine and Sheldon's dream playing out as his reality.

"I'll be ready."

Terminating the call, gathering my things, I start kicking myself. Now I've got to drive to the North Side through traffic.

"Eugenia—"

"Keenan, don't." I wet paper towels to wipe myself off in the car. I won't have time for a shower before Hadar calls. God, this will still look awful. "Don't call. Don't visit. Don't send flowers. Or pop up with a surprise. Stay away from my job. Don't contact anybody I know, or I will get a restraining order against you, Keen—"

Face forward, I go tumbling and trip over my shoe.

"You all right?" he asks. "You need me to help you?"

"No." After shoving it on, I peer around for the other. It dangles from Keenan's hand, in front of his naked chest, and above his open pants that partly reveal his underwear where he's barely shoved his dick.

His gaze follows me around the room. "The next time you're in New York, I want to take you to the beach—"

"No!"

"Push my dick into your body until—"

"Did you hear what I just said?"

"You can't feel anything else, not even the wind, just me—"

"What part of no don't you hear?" I yell, mid-hop, while I wrestle on a simple damn flat. "Stop *saying* that!"

He follows me to the door. "I'll walk you o—"

"No! I'll walk myself." I'm so fucking ashamed I surrendered to… a man-child. And worse, that he could fill my cup, like he turned me upside down and saw how life has drained me down to faded droplets stuck to the porcelain.

"Will you at least call me and let me know you got home safe?"

"I get home safe every night without you just fine."

Holding my blouse together, I grab my computer bag and place it over my messy chest.

"Then I'll see you in New York."

"You'll never see me again. Don't even think about approaching me, and if we happen to cross paths, you will walk the other way."

Amusement twitches at the corner of his mouth, as if he knows something I don't.

I'm out the door, marching to the hallway elevator. This next call I can't miss. With hustle in my legs, I'm especially quick to escape his magnetic hold, how our heat so enthralled me I missed four phone calls.

I strut onto the elevator. And then strut off.

Half-naked in the middle of the hallway, Keenan holds my purse.

"You could have told me I left it."

"I want you to come back and fight me again. I'm not ready for you to go, and you don't want to leave," he murmurs. With no warning, he grabs my face another time.

His entire tongue hugs mine, claiming my mouth once more, slow and deep, the suction licking my nipples, electrifying my nerves along my womanly canal that still tingles from his pressure. Around my neck, his fingers strum my flesh, massage away my protests.

"Take Hadar's call here and stay with me tonight."

I've lost all connection with the real world, all sense of my obligations. My obligations! Hadar!

I rip my mouth from Keenan's and take off, shoe still coming off as I hobble down the hallway with thoughts of how Sheldon will use these missed calls against me.

"See you later, Eugenia."

I don't respond, or create another opening for debate, or another pit of sexual volcanic activity for me to fall into. And I slay the urge to peek back over my shoulder at his coffee-shaded black godliness. Because he won't be seeing me anyway. Ever.

7

NO FLUKE

KEENAN

She had no idea how her tiny, clipped breaths in my ears, fluttering eyelids, throat muscles swallowing while excited spit gathered around the rim of her mouth, eyes laced with longing, all contradicted every 'no' her mouth threw at me.

Eugenia wasn't fighting me because she doesn't want me; she was fighting how she does. Nowhere was it clearer than in her body burying me so close and deep, so far in her darkest secrets, I couldn't tell where she ended and I began.

Yesterday evening was confirmation: Christmas was no fluke.

Months after I'd first laid eyes on her and passed up the chance to approach her, she showed up at Taste on Christmas Eve, beautifully mysterious and alone. Me holding down Explore by myself, all the other owners away, left no one to pry in our business and nobody to stop me, the way Desmond had when I saw her last summer. That night, her being in my presence a second time, under the perfect circumstances, was a gift in and of itself, not meant for me to ignore.

She doesn't fuck like chicks who want something on the other side of it—a ring, a commitment, a baby, money, the list goes on. No, Eugenia fucks as a spasm of her existence, as natural and unforced as Earth bearing fruit in spring. And hell, I drilled as deep in her as I could, in her hot, high-pressure core where that woman's raw bucking forges diamond rocks. This woman's wild state of being matches mine.

Yesterday was the gift that kept on giving.

Until Sheldon called.

Eugenia's innate glow she didn't even know she had faded to cigarette ash by the time she'd gotten off the phone with him. From zero to three-sixty, she morphed from a confident, soaring eagle to a cowering pigeon in a single breath.

And I got the answer to my questions of why she's so scared. He's her prison warden. He uses Hadar as leverage to make her jump through hoops.

I bet she can dance like Janet Jackson or Ciara. Last summer, her feet and legs twirled with some spice in their rhythm.

"Keenan?"

"Yeah, Laney, my bad. I'm multitasking." On the plane ride to Baltimore, in a meeting with the staff of Explore Adventures, I'm present for the video call but I'm clearly not paying attention.

"The insurance company needs more signatures for the concert next month," Explore's new office administrator, Chloe, reports. "Since we're adding new staff to sail the boats, help Desmond at the brewery, taking on new contractors and vendors for the supplies and ingredients, and Kevin wants new financial audit consultants, we'll need to report all this to our insurance carriers and to sign addendums. Also they want updates on all the traffic and events we're hosting at our locations, and the updated official event schedules."

"All right. I'll be back in New York this weekend. I need to take care of some things at home in B'More first."

Speaking of B'More, a text comes through from my boy.

Showtime: *What time you getting in, son?*

Me: *A few hours. What's good?*

Showtime: *We've got a kickback tonight. Come thru. It's going up. We need to firm up plans for August. You need to be celebrated. We big time now.*

Laney wraps up the meeting of my Explore staff.

"Thanks, everybody, I really appreciate you all's hard work, everything you're doing to bring this together. We see you. We've got a couple more months of elbow grease to put in, but you all know the big finale is worth it. A front row seat to history, and after we pull this off, we can write our own ticket to anywhere. You're helping engineer a new era of entertainment, where our destiny is sky-high and our potential is no one else's but our own."

Clapping and encouraged, we end our virtual meeting. Only Laney remains, her face wearing skepticism.

"How was that, Laney?"

"It was awesome, exactly what will keep them going."

"Glad to hear it. Anything else you need from me until I get there on Saturday?"

"No, I think that takes care of it." But a question lingers on her.

"Laney, spit it out, woman. What is it?"

"Your friend, Showtime, has been calling the office directly with all these requests for his party, asking us to provide difficult accommodations like customized meals sitting in his rooms before his crew arrives, having specific female servers deliver it, insisting on special privileges for his friends to be added to the guest list." It's obvious from the disdain on Laney's face that those are not the ends of her complaints.

"I'll talk to him and make sure he understands that anymore of his requests should run through me. Thanks for being patient, Laney."

Her pursed lips still convey she's not satisfied and I haven't fully dispensed with her issues.

"What else?"

She shakes her head. "Nothing. I'll see you when you get back. I've already booked your flight from Baltimore to New York. Please don't ask me to reschedule. That was really hard to book with these crazy airline cancellations."

"I promise, I'll be there. No rescheduling. Yo, Laney?"

"Yes?"

"Take off early and go have some drinks. On me."

She snickers. "I did that last night."

"So nobody has to tell you your worth, huh?" I ask with a laugh, and wrap up the call.

Back in my hometown, Baltimore, a few hours later, I stop through our family's company, McLain Construction, to handle my accounts there. I take the long way around the office, just so I don't have to pass my sister, Chaitra's, door.

She's already pissed me off to no end. The last thing I need is to hear her mouth about the occasional budget excess, which is necessary to earn us a ton of goodwill and new clients we're racking up. With all the Sasha Static promotions, and me serving as the head of one company while helping lead another, I'm up to my eyeballs with enough stress as it is.

The company secretaries sneak into my office the same way I did, so Chaitra doesn't see.

"Stunt Mannnn!" they sing quietly. All of them friends from high school and the neighborhood whom I've given jobs, we hug up now.

Though I'm from Baltimore, I now spend the bulk of my time in New York, where Explore is going full throttle and kicking into high gear for summer. So every time I fly home, it's like a little reunion. Overseeing my construction managers remotely, I return three to four times a month for major meetings and client engagements.

"Where did you fly in from?" Claudia asks.

"How long are you in town?" Tasha follows up.

"Yeah, what kickbacks you stopping through tonight?" Jewel adds.

They pepper me with questions and pump my head up, high on excitement for me that Explore is blowing up and projecting my status to mesosphere levels.

"Showtime is having a little something at his spot. Tomorrow night, it's probably Gina's. And Friday, I've got some, uh, private business to tend to," I answer with a wink.

"I bet you do. All the stunning you've been doing," Claudia gushes.

"Right? In all these magazines, on TV. Look at you!" Jewel half-sings.

"We always knew you'd be big time. Eh, Showtime's clubs are getting hard to slide into. Can you put us on the guest list?" Tasha bites on her lip and twists her hair, an apparent come-on.

Back in the day, we messed around some, and if I don't watch it, she'll try to fall on me again. Especially now, with all the Explore attention.

"I'll see what I can do, ladies."

"Aww, thanks, Stunt Man," Claudia purrs. "And what about VIP?"

These women are hilarious. "What are you trying to make happen in the VIP? I thought you were booed up with Chauncey now."

"My girls aren't booed up, though. And you can never have enough friends."

"Oh, I see. Well, each of you can bring one friend. *One.*

Okay? Don't show up with the whole damn block. I've got more folks to take care of."

Indeed I do. As I speak the words, my phone is jumping with texts and calls from friends who hear I'm in town.

"So what's going on with the Sasha Static concert? When do we get our tickets?" Tasha has worked her way to my side of the desk and drops her hands unprofessionally close to my butt cheeks as she rubs my back. She's wasting no time.

"Are you going to be partying with Kevin Middleton? Who's going to be in *his* VIP?" Claudia asks.

They must be a three-person investigation team the way they fire out these questions. It's back to Jewel. "Yeah, will we finally meet him? Did he really get married in secret like the tabloids say?"

At my door, an authoritative throat clears, and bodies go scattering.

No verbal commands are needed when Margaret McLain steps in. And drops a stack of newspapers and reports on my desk.

"Chicago, huh?"

"Yes, ma'am." I already know where this is headed.

"And what was such critical business in that city you missed an important status check for one of our largest accounts? One that you brought in. And you know they're expecting to meet with you personally."

Eugenia's naked, chocolate-covered body still rides my mind's eye. "I had a few meetings with performers there my friends wanted me to check out. People to perform on the boats and be cruise entertainment for Europe and the Caribbean."

My mother's long fingers spin the top newspaper so it faces me. The headline reads: *CEO of Explore Adventures Woos a Government Worker in the Middle of a Work Day.*

The vinegar of Mom's disapproval drips from her frowning lips. "That government worker didn't happen to be a certain ex-wife of a *very* powerful New York banker, who is well connected, whose former bank and current bank are investing in your concert. Please tell me you didn't go out and do some stupid shit."

Squirming under her psychological foot on my neck, I swallow. "Ma, come on now."

What I damn sure don't need, after Eugenia gave me her whole ass to kiss, is for my moms to trip. Still, I silence my frustration in a swipe of my hand over my face.

She brings her gangly body to bear down on my desk. "No, *you* come on. This is a pivotal time that could make or break you. You need to be focused. Not chasing tail. And you have plenty of tail to choose from. That English girl, Adella's sister, she's crazy about you."

"Ilyana is with somebody now, and I'm real happy for her." To say I'm relieved to be rid of Ill is an understatement, actually. I never thought I would get that damn girl off my nut sack. She was practically shooting her panties at me in a slingshot from the first moment our families met.

Ma points her long, crooked finger at me. "She's with somebody else because you messed her over."

"She wasn't my jam."

"Who is?" My mother's chastisement is already clear in her drawn-on eyebrows pinching together. "A woman who tried to drown herself less than a year ago? Get a woman who'll upgrade you. Who'll give you your *own* children and bring something to the table." Her index finger pummels the wood to emphasize her point.

"Ma, how could you say all this, or judge that woman, when you had your own problems starting in construction as a secretary coming over from working in a kitchen? Just as poor and broke as anybody, taking the bus from the projects? Now you're judging somebody else's value to upgrade me?"

Ma's pencil-lined eyes widen. "I'm not saying anything to you she won't say to her son in another twenty years. We do better so our kids can do better. Since she's Sheldon Rouse's ex-wife, I don't doubt she's a good lady he apparently saw fit to marry. And she didn't appreciate him enough to stay."

Am I wrong because it's precisely Eugenia leaving Sheldon and his money that intrigues me even more? She clearly wasn't with him for the paper chase or the status, which tells me I haven't even scratched the surface of her.

"That's not fair, Ma, you don't know her situation."

"I know I didn't work this hard, or come this far, to watch you be stupid," she says with a final side-eye on her way out.

The next couple of hours, I try to focus on McLain's reports, returning phone calls and receiving my assigned clients for meetings. I put on the smile, do the song and dance, but I hope I'm not overacting to compensate for me not mentally being here.

For the sixth time, I pick up my phone and hit the number to call the Chicago flower shop and then terminate the connection.

My PI swears to me he hasn't seen a trace of another man while tracking Eugenia, and she confirmed I was her last sexual partner. That revelation on its own was warm butter on a nigga's pancakes.

Instead of Eugenia's fierce wall scaring me, it forms a deceptive shroud of intrigue over her explosive spirit and conceals my Black Mystique.

"So Keenan," a client interrupts my distracted thoughts, "you told us you could get us the premium tile flooring at seven dollars per square foot, but the project manager is reporting ten dollars," the owner of a motorcycle dealership complains.

Dammit, Chaitra.

"Let me see what I can do on my end. We will try our best to acquire it for you. The problem is the rising cost of materials with inflation, and if you'll check your contract, there is a special provision for when the cost of materials rise through forces beyond our control that are neither your fault nor ours. I'm sure you're probably feeling this, too, with the prices you're having to list for your inventory there in your store. But," I say, holding up my hands for emphasis, "I'll see how we might accommodate you. The cost may not be quite as low as you were hoping, but we'll push it as low as we can."

I step out of the conference room and head toward one of my good buddies from earlier. "Tasha, can you put the floor guys on the line?"

"Sure, Keenan," Tasha replies.

"Oh," another voice screeches up behind me to confront Tasha, "I thought placing our individual calls wasn't part of your job description?"

My ears chafe at a sound worse than metal train wheels scraping on a track. Poor Tasha is caught unawares. But I'm well aware the secretaries around here do special favors for me that they would never do for my sister.

First off, she's mean. Second, I have a better rapport with these women who went to school with me and grew up in the neighborhood the same time I did. Third, they want hookups to kickbacks around the city, discounts when they come to New York for Explore, and access to my squad. So, of course, they're going to do tasks for me they wouldn't think of doing for Chaitra.

I speak on Tasha's behalf. "If you didn't antagonize the shit out of people, maybe they'd help you out every now and then."

Chaitra cuts her eyes at Tasha with that classic disapproving face that has made me cringe since I was a boy. It still does.

"A job description is a job description, regardless of who she's working with. It looks like male favoritism to me, in exchange for hookups. If somebody needs personal favors to do their job, or can't get their job description straight, we should look for people who can."

"Chaitra, cut with the drama," I say on my way to my office to take a quick call from one of the project managers. "What is it?"

"Don't call up the project managers and twist their arms to spend outside of budget. It's already been set. Stop promising clients favors you can't keep." She snaps my door closed behind her, and I'm certain she doesn't want the employees to hear us griping at each other.

I step around her big, overpowering ass. Chaitra likes to use her size to intimidate people, but she still doesn't understand that I refuse to let her do it to me. I reach around her and open my door, so the employees can hear me wipe the floor with her. Growing up, Chaitra had size and grit, and I had the personality.

"Chaitra, how many high-profile, million-dollar accounts have you brought in, year-to-date?"

She scoffs in lieu of an answer. "That's irrelevant. You can't go on stretching our resources by making McLain eat the costs for materials clients won't pay for."

"If we didn't throw in extras and take the occasional loss, we wouldn't pull the clients and referrals we're locking down in the first place. Large hotel chains, universities, and restaurants are rolling in. We're not just doing mom-and-pop's anymore. We cut people a break, they love it, and McLain showcases its best work, so we win the positive word of mouth that brings more traffic through the door. And I'll tell you how many millionaires you've brought in: zero." I hold my fingers in a circle to her fuming face.

Instinctively, I square up my shoulders. A corner of my subconscious anticipates her hand flying up to smack my arm, my back, or my head. I'm not little anymore. I swear to God if she tries it, she'll feel me like Sofia felt Harpo in *The Color Purple*.

I continue, "I've brought in *seven* accounts worth well over a million dollars, and I haven't done it by being cheap and stingy with resources. Our big hauls more than make up for the occasional loss. You clearly don't see the big picture and you just want something to hem and haw about."

"You can't keep moving like the math won't ever catch up to you, Kee."

"We just voted on this last month for Q2. The board is happy with the direction I recommended. So go back to your little rinky-dink reports and tiny braid shops and shoe peddlers who sell out of the trunks of their cars, with your small-minded ass. I don't have time." I couldn't be more sincere about that, especially after her betrayal a few months ago with my business partner, Solomon English. "Why don't you go find Solomon, and you and him make some giant babies and put together a damn basketball team or something? Just get the hell away from me."

The desk phone is already lighting up, and I pick it up.

Stunning the hell out of me, Chaitra places her hand over mine and shoves it back down. "Your behavior is getting real reckless, Kee. I heard you're going to Showtime's tonight, and you're planning a bunch of 'hood kickbacks with him in New York. You *know* how he moves. How do you expect people in the Hamptons to respect you as a CEO when you still roll with people like that?"

"*People like that?* Chaitra, they're the people we grew up with. Damn, girl. Just a little time with Solomon and Adella, and you've already forgotten where you came from. That sounds classist as hell. Fuck you. Get your hand off me, and don't *ever* touch me again."

I couldn't be more disgusted at the sight of her. If I didn't know any better, I would almost believe I see hurt in Shay's eyes. But that's just not possible. To emphasize that I'm dismissing her, I sit and take my call.

"Thanks, Tasha, put him through."

8

FLIPPING WITH NO BEARINGS

KEENAN

The parade of multicolored city lights marches across my tough-as-nails hometown in a congratulatory salute to that kid who conquered it, tooth and nail. From our bird's-eye view of Pratt Street, the black waters of the Baltimore Harbor do their job and reflect a resolute skyline, but they make no promises. Unlike New York or LA or even Chicago, my town offers no sleek sex appeal or fantasies of fame and fortune. Our nightscape does offer me a respectful nod for my perseverance. Puffing on a fat Jamaican spliff, I inhale, and let my mind blend into the lights.

"Let's give it to this nigga. Everything he said he was going to do, he killed that shit." My boy Rocio James holds up his drink for a toast with the rest of us. We call him Roach because he crawled around on the ground, between buildings, and under cars, like some insect before stealing and committing malfeasance.

"Hell, yeah, welcome home, bruh. You've been hugged up with all them Hamptons folks, I thought we'd have to send a search team for your ass," Showtime adds, pouring more

Cîroc in my glass. When I come to town, he blesses me with the best smokes, the best food, and the best women.

But the last few times I've flown home, it was between other business trips for Explore, and my meetings for McLain were packed in so tight, I didn't have time to hook up with the boys from the neighborhood. Handling two full-time jobs—COO at McLain and CEO at Explore—is starting to make a man second-guess if he really can do all the shit he once thought he could.

"Man, shut the hell up." I throw my arm around Showtime's neck and squeeze. "Don't hate because the rich white girls loved me at Georgetown and now their mamas love me harder in the Hamptons."

The boys crack up right along with me. Of the seven of us who ran together in Edmondson Village, in scrappy, bare-knuckled West Baltimore, five of us remain. Nigel was shot at fifteen covering his little brother's body during a drive-by. Aaron didn't make it out of middle school when he tried to steal a car, and several of the owner's bullets stopped him. After his death, I was the first to leave.

Ma's job as a temporary secretary when I was four years old had turned into a vice president position by the time I was thirteen. At that point, Ma could afford to move our family to quieter Bolton Hill. Even though Ma switched my schools, I stayed up with my boys and kicked it in the neighborhood, despite it pissing her off. I could never be one of those guys who turns my back on where I'm from— it was my whole thesis at Georgetown and my life thesis now.

Lorenzo raises his glass for the toast. As an information technology project manager, he's the only other one in the group who bothered with college. "Stunt Man, brotha, your ass is still alive."

We laugh into the clouds of smoke circling our heads,

some tragic irony in this grim reminder of how close we came to death.

"Y'all remember when this scrawny nigga used trash can lids to jump from the fire escape," Showtime starts and demonstrates with his hands, "onto the plumber vans in the snow and tried to ski off?"

The guys crack up, holding their guts and busting out laughing. "Like he really was on a mountain in the Winter Olympics and shit!" Roach rubs my mohawk.

I flip these high Negroes my middle finger and turn up my drink. "Fuck y'all, man."

"And shit, Nigel would get right out there with him!" Lorenzo adds. "He called himself skiing down some steps on a cardboard box!"

"This damn dude never met an obstacle course he didn't like." Kadeem cracks up too.

Our light laughter has erupted into uncontrollable chuckling. The memories are candles lighting up our faces, and they glow in my heart. But parts of the candlelight burn too hot once thoughts of Nigel hit me. Cooler than a fan, he might have been mayor of Baltimore.

"Stunt Man was the only fool who refused to die by getting shot, but by his own damn stupidity." Showtime laughs softly through the smoke.

My back against the railing, I hear myself chuckle. "Niggas like you only watched just to see me break my neck."

"And I would pay good money to see that shit again. You should have started a circus!" Showtime's been a hustler since he was a kid and parlayed funds from that into more cash profits as a teenager.

I grab Show and try to put him in a headlock. He throws his arms around my waist, and we roughhouse, spilling our drinks. Ashes from our blunts snow around us. It's Showtime's club, so he'll have somebody come and clean the mess.

"Y'all look like two damn slow, pathetic elephants," Kadeem observes. He plays professional basketball for the smaller American leagues and some international teams.

Show and I finally give up, refill our glasses, and make the toast.

One of the bouncers steps up to the velvet rope and motions for Show, but Show waves him off.

"To niggas in the Hamptons," Roach says. "Courtesy of a scrawny boy who started Explore in the hood first."

Roach details the hell out of some cars. But he's a hothead, and I always have to calm that fool down with jokes and a quick comeback, let him know how unreasonable he's being. He's got his own place and gets people's rides right, with skills so cold the waiting list for appointments is six months out. And my boy always has a person's back, no matter what.

"All the women downstairs are waiting for you. They see me all the time. Tonight, they came for Stunt Man," Show points out. "But first, the business." He reaches in his pocket, takes out twenty stacks, throws it on the table between us.

I stare at it, in no hurry to pick it up.

The others do the same, each taking out twenty stacks and sliding them to me.

"We're proud of you, dude," Show says.

"Be proud of yourself. We're still here, and we're handling our shit," I reply. "How many of us can say that?"

Into a safe deposit box, Show places the racks and hands me the key. For now, the box of cash enters his safe. "Come and get this before you leave."

"This B'More boat party is about to go off." Roach drinks down his liquor in a couple of swallows. "And I'm meeting Sasha Static, and after I put this dick on her, she'll be begging to marry my ass."

All of us share the same reaction, nearly falling all over each other at hearing this level of crazy.

"What?" Kadeem asks. "Nigga, she's going to marry you with all your ten kids?"

"It's eight, nigga, eight. And yeah, I think she will. Shit, Whitney married Bobby. How many of these women would gladly marry Lil Wayne, and how many kids does he have?"

"How much money does Lil Wayne have, compared to how much you have?" Lorenzo asks.

"Don't matter. I'll never know if I don't try. Don't be trying to dash my dreams and shit."

"Man, get your ass downstairs and find some women more suited to your reality!" Lorenzo shoves his head.

Unable to control ourselves, we go nuts cracking up again.

High as blackbirds sailing across an opal sky, we jostle on our way down the stairs, and Show grabs me again.

"I want to meet some of your Hamptons crew, man, the ones you and Desmond don't bring around here."

"For what, dude? You want to teach them the highlights of rolling blunts on a set of ass cheeks?"

"Those rich fools probably want to learn some things they don't teach y'all at Georgetown. What's up with that one cat you've been posing with in the magazines? Pretty boy who went to Harvard. Kevin Nickelson. That his name?"

"Middleton, Negro." High and chuckling, I'm only half listening. The ladies have already started waving. "You met him already, at the Valentine's kickback at Taste, remember?"

Whether I want to or not, I remember it too well. The night ended in Roach's temper almost getting him arrested, *and* he had snuck in some minors without me knowing. Kevin is the one who shut Roach down with one good pop in the jaw. I'm still lost on where that came from. But the fallout worsened an already tense business relationship between

Solomon and me, and we no longer meet unless our attorneys or other board members are present. I've always kept my squads separate—my Georgetown classmates, colleagues from the construction world, all stay separate from Roach and Show. Since the Valentine's blowup at Taste, now I keep it hush when inviting my childhood buddies to the Hamptons.

"I want to talk to him about his tech moves—Money-Cruncher. Costs ten G's to get in. Well, I joined it and I like it. I want to see how he feels about a partnership, to help me make that kind of social investment site for guys around here in the streets," Show says.

Now we've paused on the steps. I must parse my next words like rice.

This guy used to break me off candy money when we were age seven, and Ma was still robbing Peter to pay Paul. Every day, she or Dad would give me the exact amount of change for lunch—$3.75—not a penny more. Since they were both working, we weren't poor enough for food stamps or the free lunch program. If I wanted extras beyond a crap plate lunch, like chips and pop or a candy bar, or if everybody was hitting up a cookie sale, or stopping through the store after school, Show would pass me some of his drug money. Yes, he was doing that at seven.

There were also other times in the naughty teenage years when Show pulled strings for me—sneaking me into clubs, concert tickets, backstage passes, secret weekend trips to Atlanta and Miami when I was still in high school. Until Desmond was drafted into the NFL, Show was my underground hookup that kept me glowing like a million bucks. My connection to Showtime bumped up my stock value. Who am I to say no to him now that I'm in a position to pay it back?

"Kevin is a pretty open-minded dude, so I don't see why not, man. That sounds dope."

Happy as hell, Show nearly strangles my neck with his hug. "What do you say to me coming through next weekend for Memorial Day?"

"I'm in a bunch of meetings, so you'll have to find shit to do, but come through, bruh."

We barely make it down the stairs before the ladies start in. Show pushes me out front.

"Y'all, wear this boy out!"

I turn to horse around with him, give him a hard time, but he's disappeared. He's already off, with his bouncers behind him.

"You know he's still selling that shit, right?" Lorenzo asks, closing in on me.

I suspected as much but I only speak with Show once or twice every couple of months now. Besides, I've never been directly involved in his hustles, not even to make a referral to friends asking if I know where the good shit is. That's a police setup with bells on. "I don't worry about situations and people I can't control, man."

"You're making big moves now, and we're not kids anymore. Word is the pigs have started sniffing around. Careful, bruh."

Not right now. Just not now. A couple of girls jump on me, and I let them feel me where they want. For a little while anyway, I need to not think. Not a second thought has ever gone into clubbing and partying.

But a few minutes into it, even in my hazy state, I may as well be sitting in a colony of ants that I just want to flick off. I love women so I'm stunned as hell. In a lap dance that should be illegal, these girls grind on my dick and rub on my chest, clearly auditioning for after the club tonight. I rub them back, try to get into it. But the urge to go apeshit in their panties passes me up. Their faces, their thighs, waist-lines, do nothing for me.

"What's up, family, guess who finally decided to bring his busy ass up in here! Your brother and mine, we all love his no-sense-having ass." Showtime has taken the small stage. The audience cracks up, and quite a few are our longtime friends. "Here's the man who's bringing Sasha Static in from space, y'all. If you don't have your tickets to the concert yet, you'd better show him some love!"

Rapturous applause almost shakes the roof off, with hooting and hollering and bottles of champagne popping. Showtime definitely knows how to throw a kickback.

"Lacey, Sherri, bring y'all's asses up here." The place is going nuts, because they know what time it is at Show's spot. "These are our first set of contestants for the night. Thank you dope ladies for participating. DJ, queue up the music, please. Stunt Man, you want to do the honors?"

The diamond in his grill shining, he stretches his arm toward me with the microphone. He and I have done this so many times. But for some reason, now, I must be filled with lead on my way up there.

I reach out and take the mic. "Let's do it. What are you waiting for, nigga?"

Cell phones have already been removed at the front door. No snitches.

We go back and forth with the mic, jostling, like he's checking my strength. We're playing, but lately, I've started to wonder if we really are.

I snatch the microphone. "All right, ladies, show me what you're working with."

The DJ puts the music on, and the crowd hollers. Facing off, the contestants get to dancing, doing tricks with their butt cheeks and breasts to the pleasure of a hyped audience. They shake harder and harder, in each other's faces, before the clothes come off. Acrobats probably couldn't compete with these tough sisters who dive into the splits, pull their legs over their heads, twerk in a yoga pose, and clap what the Good Lord blessed them with.

They show out for me, and I know they're hoping to snag an invite to one of my New York parties. I point from one to the other, so the audience can rate them. This is demeaning as hell, but I've never been one to thumb my nose at how women hustle.

"So which one will it be, fam?" I ask.

The crowd hoots loudest for the queen who could roll her entire body real snake-like and pop while holding up one leg. "Looks like you're the one, baby."

All happy while she jumps up and down, her bodyparts flopping in the air, she does a little dance and hops onto me.

"Stunt Man!" somebody calls from the floor. "When are *you* going to show out? Let us see you cut up!"

"Yeah!" the audience eggs me on.

This energy of being back in my stomping ground, around the people I've known my whole life, who watched me come up from nothing, gives me a sudden rush. The hype fires through my veins hotter than rocket fuel, pumping them up until they're so full they're about to burst.

How many guys do they know like me? Whose entire family started at the bottom and is now taking over the Hamptons? Whose teachers told him he wouldn't be shit? And got a full ride to Georgetown, with a fellowship at Northwestern. In the hood, my brother Desmond and I are heroes.

Hell, I can't help myself. That kid will do anything for his people, no questions asked.

I turn my back toward them. Behind me, Showtime's boys line everybody up, and the crowd screams at the top of their lungs.

Plunging into a squat, I'm filled with diesel fuel and the energy springs my muscles off the stage. Fearless and formidable, the heart of that fourteen-year-old wild boy leaps, still not scared. Still dauntless. Still willing to defy gravity.

Feet off the ground, flipping in the dark room, that kid opens his eyes.

They see a blur, foggy and unclear. *Shit.*

What part of the somersault am I in? I don't see a beginning or an end. For the first time in my life, I wonder, what if I don't land on both feet? Is my mama right that this is the time I finally break my neck?

What started as exhilaration at some point converts to panic.

Hands reach around me.

Loud music and voices pound my ears.

I'm more relieved than a wounded man in the woods to see help.

Lifted and carried in the air, I still have no solid ground to plant my feet on. Strangers' hands grip at me, slide around my body, hands shove into my pockets like they're searching for cash, claw at my crotch. I left my wallet in the safe back at my office since Show always takes care of me. But did somebody just snatch a piece of hair from my damn mohawk?

The fellas stand me up. My heart raging in my ribs, it's not from adrenaline now.

Showtime throws his arm around me. "My boi!"

He brings me in and squeezes tight, until he's damn near choking me.

The room spins around my head, and the lights run tracks across our heads. I've never panicked in the middle of a back flip.

"Which one of them you taking home, dude?" Show asks.

I'm barely able to recognize he's talking about Sherri and

Lacey, both staring at me through hopeful eyes the size of silver dollars.

Lorenzo steps forward. "Look at this dude. He needs to take his ass to sleep. Come on, Stunt Man, your stunting is over tonight. I'll take you home." He turns to the infuriated women. "Sorry, ladies, another time."

"Why are you pissing all in this man's cereal, dude?" Show asks. "How often does he come home and enjoy himself?"

"'Renzo is straight, man. I'm good. I appreciate all the love tonight, dude." I grab Show in a bear hug so he doesn't take my leaving early the wrong way. But showing out for a crowd... busting a nut into another body I won't even remember tomorrow... reverses my mental rollercoaster tonight. Instead of propelling me to a climax, the activities tonight have left a nigga free-falling backward and can't see where he's going. "We'll hook up Memorial Day. D will be glad to see you. You still haven't hit up his new brewery spot, Slurp. I'll take you through there."

"And Kevin Middleton... you'll take me through his spot, too," Show reminds me.

"Yeah, man, fo' sho," I confirm, my chest tightening up at the thought. Kevin might deal with the occasional rapper of a certain net worth, but he does not fool with street guys like Show.

Lorenzo starts to escort me to Show's safe for the box of cash that will pay for B'More's Sasha Static boat party.

"Hold up, man." Before we go, I remember to address the last bit of business with Show. I've been putting it off all night. "About Explore and the concert. If you want changes to any arrangements in New York for August, just let me know. Hit me up, and I will address it with my crew."

Showtime addresses me with a long side-eye. "Dude, your little concierge is too good to talk to me?"

Laney is one of my best staffers, and I can't have her

feeling a way. She deals with Explore's official guests and patrons, as well as the owners. Technically, I have not placed Showtime on Explore's official event roster, because of his, uh, checkered history.

"No, man, but you know we're doing this under the table. Don't even trip. Laney doesn't know how to do things the way we like, so why are you overwhelming her and shit? I will take care of it myself. It's better for both our good times. Calm your ass down."

Show's attendance is not a formal arrangement through Explore's concierge office; rather, he is staying in one of my suites and sliding me cash to fund some of our personal yacht parties and hotel blowouts for our folks in the 'hood.

The more formal, corporate, swanky galas to be officially sponsored by the men of Explore, will be attended by the politicians, celebrities, and the "high society" types.

Can you imagine the First Lady of New York and her friends rubbing elbows with thugs from around the way? Or more specifically, highbrow women like Madison Rouse, my sister-in-law Dr. Adella English, or any of that Hamptons set rolling a blunt with guys who've been in the joint? They'll lose their over-manicured minds.

I add in a laugh so Show can see this is nothing major.

"All right then, boy, whatever. I'll see you Memorial Day, nigga, be ready to show your boy some love." Releasing me from his grip, he leaves to speak with some guys waiting for him on the other side of the room, who I've never seen before, who don't look like they came for the party.

In the car with Lorenzo, I'm half asleep when he arrives at my Bolton Hill brownstone. "You know he thinks your success belongs to him, right?"

"Hm, what?" I ask as he follows me up my steps.

"That dude thinks your come-up is his. He's been talking like he made you. I know Show helped us out as kids, and we're all boys. You're trying to stay loyal and act like things haven't changed, but you are moving in a different room than him now. You're still taking his money, and it's got him thinking he's a silent partner in your operation." He pulls me in for a grip. "Alls I'm saying is watch it, bruh."

"Thanks for the heads-up, boy."

I sink into the couch with that information swimming somewhere in the back of my mind, behind the questions of why this night ended so different from the others. My suede couch pillows surround me, high-quality leather relaxing my muscles. Firm and plush, it wraps around my mind and eases out my stress, almost like… Eugenia.

9

I DON'T GET TO RELAX

EUGENIA

Stress won't let me breathe easy. Tabatha enters my home in her second surprise visit this week. She was sitting in a car outside my building when I returned from my hike with Lus. She doesn't trust me.

Toward my bedroom door, she proceeds ahead of me. "Your friend who brought you the flowers the other day, how did that work out? Did you go on a date?"

If only you knew.

"We went for a bite after work. All the flowers and the boat were a nice gesture, and I appreciated it, but I told him a relationship, or any other complications, are not my priority right now."

"So you and him didn't do anything else? He didn't come back to your place? I saw his photo in the paper. That's a yummy one right there," Tabatha notes. "A lot of women back at the admin building were talking about throwing him on the grill. Nobody would blame you, Eugenia, if you took a small moment of space for yourself… after you've worked so hard all these months on your classes."

After she throws back the doors of my walk-in closet, her

chest freezes as if she's expecting to find a man hiding in there.

"All these months are dedicated to my son. That's it and that's all." My own heart must hang suspended; either that or it beats so fast I can hardly tell it's there.

I have no clue what Tabatha knows already, so I keep my answers short to reduce the number of lies I have to tell.

As her fingers graze the hangers, her head tilts to the side, and her feet take us into the bathroom, where her eyes continue to scan for hints of evidence—boxer shorts, shaving cream, a razor, Jordans, a watch, chain, cologne, extra toothbrush, any whiff of male presence that could show I'm weak and tip the outcome of next week's hearing in Sheldon's favor.

The outcome is already heavily leaning in his favor, or she wouldn't be here. Though I'm confident she won't find anything, her presence still arrests my breathing. I'm relieved when she heads for the door.

With no warning, she dashes to the trash can, pops it open, and gives it a little looksie. My vitals hit the roof. My torn blouse, dirtied with chocolate.

I remember I already disposed of it, in a trashcan out in the alleyway, and took the pants to the cleaners.

"Have a good afternoon, Eugenia," Tabatha closes out with a professional smile I use with my clients, and which I now loathe being used on me.

I don't get to relax yet. Next up is the obligatory family barbecue.

Lus offered to hit a movie with me instead, or do a spa day, maybe some mani-pedis, but I've ignored the family long enough. The last time I saw them was when I returned from New York over the holidays. And I'm not jazzed to see them now, but Tabatha might call them to collect statements on my compliance for her report, so I need to make nice. Lus also offered to come with me for moral support, but I don't want her meeting them. One way I manage to forge my existence into one imitating sanity is by keeping the few positives in my life separate from the mess.

Once I enter Aunt Amy's backyard, the tall brown paper bags, rolled-up joints, and the smell of wild grass, greet me first. I'm already calculating the shortest amount of time I can stay before I excuse myself for "other errands" without coming across as this being the last place I would want to take a piss.

"Well, well, smack me down with a feather. Look who decided to bless us with her presence," my cousin, Valuable, starts.

"You could have just said 'hi' and kept it moving, Val." I turn to the others at the dominoes tables. "Good afternoon, everybody."

"Hey, Eugenia, girl, it's good to see you," my older cousin, Shawn, says with a hug. "We don't see you around these parts too much no more. Can't say I blame you, sweetheart."

"Don't pooh-pooh her like she's something special," Val adds.

"Yeah, she gave up her special status." My cousin, Koi, shuffles a deck of cards. "Genie, why don't you come on over here to the regular folks' table and throw down some spades?"

"Hey, Aunt Genie!" My nephews run to me, their arms wide open.

"I haven't seen you in a long time!" Rashad says.

"Yeah, where is Hadar? When are you bringing him over here?" Marshall asks.

"Is he still in New York?" Charnley asks.

"Yes, he's with his dad. I'm going to see him next weekend."

Charnley, my middle nephew, holds on to me while we walk toward the spread of food. "Can we go with you?"

"Yeah." Rashad jumps in. "And what about the Sasha Static concert?" His eyes peer up at me with sparks of longing that strike in my bones. "Is he going?"

As I wrap my arms around my nephews, I can't miss the unkempt, overgrown hair beading up against their scalps, nails dirty and bitten down to nubs, their oversized shirts sliding off their shoulders, and their dusty sneakers flopping from their feet that have no socks.

"Hadar was supposed to call us after his party the other day. Why ain't we heard from him?" Marshall asks.

In their faces, the melancholy of being left behind mirrors the abandonment of my reason for living. "Don't you mean, 'why *haven't* you heard from him'?"

"You know what I meant, Aunt Genie," he replies.

I can't bear to tell them all Hadar's doing when Sasha Static goes to New York. "I don't know yet what Hadar's plans are. His father and I will have to talk about it."

"Why ain't Sheldon told you your own son's moves?" another voice cuts in. Still sober but tinged with alcohol, he won't be sober for long. "You *are* still the boy's mama, ain't ya? Or did Sheldon buy Hadar a new mama, too?"

"Gene, hush your mouth!" my mother hisses, approaching us and staring everybody down. "Get out of your sister's business. Let's everybody just have a good time while we're finally together."

"I'm just telling the truth. What did I say wrong?" Eugene, my older brother, feigns innocence. "We're glad you finally came by, sis. Good to see ya."

"Hey, Genie." Nelson, the third sibling after me, comes over and plants a kiss on my cheek. "Can we slide over and talk for a minute?"

"Yo, dude, she's not doing it. I don't know why you're even bothering with her," Gene says to him.

"I'm not doing what?" I ask.

Nelson puts his arm around me as we walk to the drink area. "So, um, you think you could spare a little change? Me and Elise real tight right now."

I suspected that's why he invited me. "I noticed you were on the family chat the other day. It would have been nice if you'd opened your mouth and had my back."

"Come on now, G, what you talkin' 'bout? And for what? I was quiet for the same reason you was." He smells like he worked on cars before he and his family walked here to West Washington Boulevard from a few blocks over, where he lives on West Adams. "Arguing with them is a dead end and will probably have us fighting. Like you need that. Besides, we're forty. Who listens to them anyway? Just like Zenaria said in the text, they ain't got nothing close to what you do."

I just wish sometimes my brothers, somebody, *anybody*, would speak up for me. "So why are you and Elise behind?"

When he laughs, his chipped front tooth reminds me of a fight he had in his twenties. "You know how it is, sis." He thinks a moment, scratches his head. "But then again, I guess you don't know. Not anymore, huh?" The rest of his thought appears in his eyes but doesn't exit his mouth. "Our car broke down, and we had to get the carburetor unclogged. Plus, one of the pipes is busted, and we've been putting off getting that fixed for a while."

"She really making you stand here and explain what you need, dude?" Gene breaks in. "Genie, the man wouldn't be asking if it wasn't legit. Shit, we your damn family. Why all these questions like he's filling out a credit application? You sitting on the money so why are you pressing him?"

I cock my neck back, feeling old Eugenia hyping up. "Why don't you give it to him since you've got so much to say, huh? And if you don't have it yourself, stay out of my purse. Don't tell me how to use mine. Please, and thank you."

Eugene, the oldest of our parents' four children, two years ahead of me, side-eyes me and blows off my attitude with a loud, dismissive cackle. "Girl, bye. If you don't give that boy the money, you ought to be a damn shame of yourself. You're living up in that high-rise, working a fancy county job with good government benefits, riding around here in luxury, and you can't give a second thought to your family? We ain' seen you all year. That's fucked up, Eugenia. If *we* struggling, then *you* struggling. None of us is straight until we *all* straight. And that's on some real family shit right there."

"You'd be straight if you went and found a real job. She doesn't work for you. She's not your employee, and you're not her damn ball and chain Genie has to drag around everywhere." Even now, seven years after I first heard those words, Sheldon's fury still rings clearly in my ears.

This principle Gene just uttered—what's mine is yours and what's yours is mine—has been the fuse to our ongoing battles for years. It drove Sheldon up the wall when we were married, to the point he and Eugene almost came to blows one Thanksgiving. Sheldon hasn't returned to my family home since. *They're too lazy to get off their asses and make something of themselves.* One of the cracks in our marriage I couldn't repair—my family attaching themselves to my opportunities—Sheldon spurned as less than scum.

As I open my mouth to rebut Eugene, I already know what his response will be. If I tell him my education or arrangements with Sheldon don't concern him, he'll come back with how my family putting food on the table allowed me to attend college in the first place. Like I said, a never-ending battle.

"Gene, man, go somewhere," Nelson pleads. "She finally came through, and here you are, beefing."

"Her being here ain't some kind of reward. Shit, she s'pose to be here."

I turn to Nelson, ready to just see Mama and chill. "I'll put it in your account. That good?"

Nelson's chipped tooth shows up again in an embarrassed smile. "Um, I can't use my checking account right now. Got some issues there, too. Can we run to a bank or something for a hot minute?" And we can't wait either. Nobody in their right mind should be on some of these streets after certain hours, let alone withdrawing cash from a bank.

Once we make the run and ride back, I head toward the family room. Surrounded by my uncles, seated in a recliner and watching basketball, Daddy nurses his classic bottle of Crown Royal. It seeps through the wrinkles in his worn-down, sixty-four-year-old flesh.

"Genie, how you doin', girl?" Uncle Manny asks.

"I'm good, sir. Nice to see you."

"We don't see much of you, so yes, it is nice indeed."

My father hasn't looked up from the television, his blatantly loud silence an admonishment that he's not pleased.

"Hey, Daddy."

He turns up the bottle, and I watch the brown liquid flow past his lips, the sight of it bringing back too many memories of the increasing hellfire with each of those sips. "Hey, Eugenia," he says, eyes still trained ahead.

Reaching to pat his shoulder, I may as well be reaching for a pipe bomb under his button-down, short-sleeved, city utility worker shirt. "It's good to see you. How've you been?"

Again, the bottle turns up, seeming to provide him more liquid tolerance of me. "I finally see you. And I've been better."

I won't let the conversation end on that note. "We

shouldn't discount our blessings. We're usually doing better than we think. Things could always be worse." I lean over and kiss his forehead that doesn't move.

So far, I've made it through half the battle—my cousins and my daddy. With a tiny breath, I head to grab a plate and sit with Mama. I'll do an hour of time there, with her and my aunts, and then flee. The exit to my uncle's family room is so close.

"Where's that boy?" his voice asks behind me.

More than a question, it's an accusation.

Why ain't them dishes washed yet?

Why's the window open? You been sneakin' out it?

Why's it dirt all across the front door? What I tell ya 'bout goin' in and out?

One would think such simple questions wouldn't spur so much terror.

I close my eyes, think of Hadar's joy last summer on the boat. Of his handsome father spinning us around and dancing with us. Sheldon was relaxed, finally focused on his family, instead of his work at the bank. In that moment, where my heart chose to remain, I breathe. And open my eyes.

"He's with his father."

"Still?"

"For now."

The chains around my chest rattle while I fix a small plate with enough food to munch on so I'm occupied. Same greeting for Daddy's sisters, just so I can sit with Mama. She won't raise up right away to talk with me privately since it would be too obvious we want to converse on affairs that are none of their business. Leaving as abruptly as I would prefer would look rude.

"How you doin', honey?"

"I'm fine, Mama." Aunt Amy's dry baked beans and

coleslaw stick to the roof of my mouth while I force myself to chew.

"You look good."

"So do you. What's been going on? How's everybody in the missionary at church?"

"Well, Ms. McGruder's foot is still bothering her, and Mother Jeffries's house got flooded. She has to stay with her daughter. They ask about you all the time. We read in the paper where you met somebody. Real handsome and nice, huh?"

"No, Mama, he's just a friend. He's the man that runs the company that put on Hadar's birthday party. Those big displays, boats and all that, are no big deal. The government workers just don't have anything better to talk about."

"Speaking of Hadar's birthday party, it would have been nice if we could have seen him," Aunt Amy notes. "We saw him on all his other birthdays. Sheldon wouldn't let you invite us, huh?"

I stop myself from firing back with, *And who would have bought your plane ticket to New York?* After spending half the night tossing and turning, thinking of smart aleck comebacks to combat their questions, I'm just waiting for any one of them to bring up my open DCFS case.

"Actually, it was Hadar's first time in years having a birthday in New York with Sheldon's family, after his last few were here. He's loving it, and that's most important." I peer at my watch. Fifty-one more minutes.

"Boy just shouldn't forget where he come from is all," Aunt Amy retorts.

After nearly an hour of sitting on an electric pole in the middle of a lightning storm, I say my goodbyes.

"Maybe next time you come, you'll bring Nephew with ya," she practically spits.

I know her and her daughters well enough to understand

that's not a happy tiding. She's insulting how I don't have my child in my care.

"How many times did you lose your kids, and how many different daddies do they have again?" I snap.

She had that coming. I'm damn tired of being "respectful" as I'm scrutinized by people who have zero moral authority to judge me.

While I'm deciding how far I want to take this, my mother grabs my arm.

"Come on, G, I'll walk ya out."

"She's got a lot of damn nerve," I fume under my breath.

"I don't know why you let them get under your bra. You know they're just jealous and resentful they didn't try to go nowhere or do nothing." She follows me to my SUV. "The social worker called me this week."

"I figured as much. She's putting together her final report for the hearing in a few days, and I don't think it's going to go my way. What did she ask you?"

"About that man in the paper. She wondered who was it and if we know him."

"She sprung up on me twice this week looking to see if I was hiding him."

"I told her I've never seen that guy and you've never brought him up. But tell me now, Genie, who is he? And don't give me no lies, girl. Ain't no man gon' do all that for somebody he don't know." A wall of concern glares at me through her probing side-eye.

"Mama, I swear I've only met him twice. The man and I had dinner on Christmas Eve, and I saw him again at Hadar's party. Then he shows up here in Chicago." That is mostly— okay, partially—true.

"Dinner? That's all?" My mama's stare hardens.

My millisecond of hesitation is too long.

"Oh, hell, Eugenia, how could you? I knew that man

didn't come here and put on that big show just over some damn dinner."

"Mama, please don't. Not now. You have no idea what this is like, being alone all the time."

"You only have a little longer in this case. You can shut them nosy county people out of your business and take Sheldon's foot off your neck. Don't be *stupid*, Genie," she mutters through pinched, worried lips and throws her arms around me. "Be stronger and smarter, girl."

"I'm trying, Mama." But no matter how strong I am, I'm fighting a losing battle.

Sheldon's suave presentation—a handsome banker, standing in court at six feet and two inches with a clean record and Ivy League education, who's never missed a child support or spousal support payment—knocked the senses right out of that middle-aged, black, female judge overseeing our case. That, and his high-powered Manhattan lawyer squad, led by a black woman who attended Spelman with Madison Rouse.

In this court case, since the hearings are state-sanctioned, Shel didn't have to pay my lawyer fees. Without him footing the bill, I was given a scrappy, court-appointed attorney who knows her stuff but is no match for one of the top law firms on the East Coast. His lawyer, Tazima Beasley, is annually named to the coveted list of Top 100 SuperLawyers of New York.

With an unlimited budget for medical and psychological experts to evaluate me, assigned investigators to dig into my past and old boyfriends, and years of medical records to throw in my face, Sheldon pulled the rug from under me.

On the drive home, fighting tears, all I see clearly is the triumph on Shel's face as he stood over me in court a year ago.

The moldy festering corners of my life were exposed to

harsh light, and my family's raggedy drawers hung out for the world to inspect.

He couldn't have made his point any clearer—I don't have the emotional intelligence, social clout, or financial savvy to give Hadar what he deserves from this point onward.

10

THE WORLD HAS SHIFTED

EUGENIA

"So, Hadar, how was your school year?" the judge asks from the bench.

"It was good," he mumbles. Buried in his coloring book, he looks like he's in jail at counsel table, next to his court-appointed lawyer, Sheldon on one side, and me on the other.

"Good? Just good?" the judge prods our son. "Your therapist tells us you've had an outstanding school year. You've gotten *all* A's, toured the Kennedy Space Center, seen a spaceship take off, met astronauts, gone camping with your brothers in Colorado, built your own video games. Your social worker says you love to make things. What do you want to be when you grow up?"

Without daring to venture a glance left or right, he mutters, "I want to be a computer scientist who makes programs to grow food in space."

My heart is full with pride… and heavy with pride.

What must be my pain blows out of Sheldon.

"Wow, that sounds incredibly smart. I know your parents are very proud of you. Tell me, what will you do this coming weekend to reward yourself for all your good work this year?"

He shrugs as an answer.

"Son, what do we say about looking people in the eye?" his father tries.

The crayon stops. Hadar pushes his gaze up. "I… I don't know what I'm doing this weekend."

The judge leans farther over the bench. "Hadar, can you tell us why you're so quiet right now? All the other times you've come to see me, you've been happy."

He peeks at his lawyer who nods him on.

"I'm worried."

"About what, honey?"

The words lock up his throat, and my terror of them locks up my soul.

"That you'll make me choose my mom or my dad, and I don't want to choose."

The judge's gaze turns tender. "I'll tell you what, my friend? How about you not worry about that today? You've got a whole three-day weekend coming up. Time to have fun after all your hard work."

The judge turns from my son to me. She could sharpen metal with her side-eye, and the veins in her fingers ripple underneath her skin. I'm certain she'll step down from that bench to personally wring my neck.

Her face a stone wall, it's too familiar. It's the same sharp-ironed dressing down I catch from other older women when they're hit with a whiff of Sheldon and then they find out I left him. I'm done. I won't be awarded my son back. I could attend all the parenting classes and counseling sessions, and she'll punish me just for leaving what everybody else judges as a perfectly happy marriage.

"Hadar, why don't you and your mother go eat ice cream

and play at a park, ride some bikes, see a movie? Just you and her."

Oh my God.

I still don't believe what's happening, or even realize it, until the shrill voice of Sheldon's lawyer brings me back to my senses.

"Your Honor, may I be heard?" the indefatigable Tazima Beasley's lethal calm asks.

"No, you may not. I've heard from you and Mr. Rouse a great deal over the past year, and now it's my turn to be heard."

Oh my God!

The judge continues, "Mrs. Rouse, I'm sure I don't have to tell you how critical this is, me trusting you."

The words shake from my mouth, "No, ma'am."

"I've read your entire file, including Mr. Rouse's records on your… past. The psychiatric evaluation, the doctor's notes, medical reports, all of it, still concern me. Gravely." The iron of her unsmiling mouth grinds on me. "But you've done everything I've ordered. Your therapist tells us you're very honest and have made great strides, including an unforeseen temptation you experienced in Chicago just a few days ago—"

"Your Honor, that's what Mr. Rouse wishes to address. It's a concern for him also. This man, Keenan McLain, has dangerous friends and is obviously a romantic diver—"

"Ms. Beasley," the judge chastises with the birchwood switch of her side-eye, "do not interrupt me again. Aside from that, you have no proof. None. The social worker conducted surprise home visits and interviews twice after Mrs. Rouse received a visit on her job from a man who is clearly smitten with her. She gave credible explanations for how they met—over Christmas while she was in New York to see Hadar, and then once again, when she was in New

York for Hadar's birthday party earlier this month. Chance meetings are not events she can control, but what she could control, she handled incredibly well. The man rode up on a boat in the middle of the street, filled with flowers, and instead of falling weak and letting him sweep her off her feet, she politely informed him she is committed to her son. Her fortitude in such a spontaneous moment is what eased my concern."

The judge stares at me.

"She is self-aware and recognizes that her family structure, upbringing, and the settings in which she grew up led to disastrous relationships that took her on a deeper downward spiral. Mrs. Rouse refused to let it happen again. Her laser focus this past year on the need to parent Hadar has been her utmost priority."

My blood pumps so hard in my ears, I can't hear my own sobbing, let alone the judge's question. "I'm sorry, Your Honor, what was that?"

"How long will you be in town?"

"U-until T-Tuessday."

The bailiff walks over with tissues. I barely register my lawyer's hand swiping my back repeatedly with congratulations.

"Good, you and Hadar have three full days together. What are your plans?"

Joyful waves of disbelief rumble out of me in an indecipherable exhale. "I don't know. I wasn't su… wasn't sure you would grant me…"

Is that warmth on the judge's face? "I understand. I'm sure you and Mr. Rouse can reasonably coordinate the exchange times and locations. Mrs. Rouse, I also don't have to remind you that your unmonitored weekend visit is to take place here in New York, and you are not to leave the state, and must be accessible to the social worker at all times. Please inform her once you've figured out your plan. And Mrs. Rouse?"

"Y-yes, ma'am?"

"Do not prove my concerns to be accurate." With a stern final warning, her gavel comes down and concludes the hearing.

A nervous, surprised wreck, I'm hardly able to mount these wobbly legs. But I can always find energy and strength to hug the best part of me, the part of which I'm most proud and actually got right.

After months of my personal bond with my son being supervised by Sheldon's mother, Sheldon's wife, or one of Sheldon's siblings, Hadar and I can finally talk alone. We won't have to walk on pins and needles around one another, and he no longer has to behave like somebody's strapped him to an electric chair. Sheldon's intimidation can be subtle but effective, and he's worked it on our child. It's not victory I feel when we all exit the courtroom, or even validation, but just a smidge of liberation.

My ex-husband holds open the door; the silent stoicism on his face couldn't signal his objections any more clearly. Still, he's a gentleman, and pulls himself together with the discipline and civility on which his Southern parents raised him.

Even now, five years after I left our home, the scent of his cologne, and his perfectly chiseled torso under his dress shirt, still makes me wonder what-if.

"Thank you," I say to him.

"Hadar has a weekend bag already packed in the truck. We prepared it just in case. I'll bring it to you."

"I appreciate that."

My imagination starts to dally in the better times between us, until a figure approaches in the corridor. As if she's a crutch that holds him up, Sheldon nearly stumbles toward a waiting Chrissy, who's holding their two-month-old daughter. At hearing the words he whispers in her ear, her eyes widen with catastrophic shock before she remembers to correct her face.

Shel is no longer mine. Last summer, he made it abundantly clear, as he does now with his arm thrown around her, planting consoling kisses on her forehead.

To stop torturing myself, I face my son, the one who still is mine, and throw my arms open wide. We never had a celebratory hug! We're walking out of here, just him and me. No more ball and chain, even if just for three precious days.

"We did it!" I gush. Hadar and I have finally been freed, at least partially, from custody jail. "Baby, what do you want to do first? Y-you hungry?"

The wind is knocked out of me when my ecstatic embrace of Hadar is met with a limp pair of arms that barely circle me.

"I don't care." Instead of the glee and excitement we've shared over ice cream sundaes, chili dogs, bikes, Transformers, and roller blades, I'm smacked with my child's stony politeness.

I touch his fresh haircut and tilt his chin to me and throw him a mental rope so he can start swimming back to me. "Honey, if you're not..." I fight not to become a deflated balloon. "We can go to the park, or the zoo if you want, or..." Too late. My lungs are already malfunctioning.

"It doesn't matter, Mom. Can we just go?"

In his eyes, I search for my honeybun-eating baby boy, my bestie who can't play basketball to save his life but likes to say he's on the team. Instead of us telling inside jokes with our eyes, or him looking to me for approval or agreement, Hadar's attention turns to his new little sister. He walks toward her now.

"Bye, Krishna," he murmurs.

The baby responds to his voice, giggling while he plays with her in Chrissy's arms. The heaviness on his face breaks my heart to witness that he has other objects of his affection now.

Maybe he just needs—I pray all he needs—is time to adjust.

Chrissy makes her way over. "Genie, if you need suggestions on his favorite places to eat and what he likes—"

"I *know*... what my son likes." That might have been a petty, bitch way to react, but call it my frustration with her possessing my child for the past year.

Deeper than that is my frustration with myself, and how I stupidly walked away from Shel. Now she lives in a shiny palace on a hill, where she and Shel teach Hadar perfect manners and etiquette and go on expensive trips where I can't always talk to him. That was the first reaction—the *only* reaction—to spring into my head. The most instinctive, natural, animal response imaginable is that I am *still* his mother.

Hadar rolls his eyes.

"Young man," I snap as his father comes back with his things.

"Hadar, come here, man."

Walking behind the two of them and their lanky legs, I manage to catch pieces of what Sheldon says.

"Don't worry about anything else. Your mom is here to be with you. Show her around, and you and her have a good time. You have the rest of the summer for Great Escape. Your cousins will always be there. They're not going anywhere."

"Yes, sir," my child replies, trudging ahead with leaden feet. He may as well be using them to walk right over my heart.

Sheldon squares his own shoulders. "We'll be in Sag

Harbor for the weekend, but I'm just a call away if anything comes up or you need me, G."

"I don't need an instruction manual, Shel." Why are they treating me like I didn't bring this boy into the world?

"Fine. Just offering. So, meetup at four o'clock on Monday?"

"Six," I counter.

"Since he left school early today, he has makeup work, in addition to his homework for Tuesday. He'll need time for all that on Monday evening."

"I'll handle his homework," I insist. "Does he have his books?"

Sheldon swallows. "They mostly use laptops and do it digitally."

"He and I can knock it out. Can't we, Hadar?"

"All right. Son, your computer is in the truck. Be careful and don't drop it."

"Yes, sir," Hadar mumbles.

Sheldon, Chrissy, and I are left alone. Though I had a brief conversation with her last summer, in my effort to reclaim Shel, the three of us have never breathed the same air. One would think we could at least conjure up some polite pretense to move past the tension, but I can't front as if Sheldon didn't use every resource he has at his disposal—private investigators, computer hackers, and psychologists—to go to war on me. And I suppose Chrissy has her feelings about me after my last-ditch attempt to reclaim my child's father last summer.

"Sometimes, he struggles with complicated division," Sheldon says to fill the screaming silence.

"I'm sure we'll be fine."

"It takes a while to slog through traffic, have dinner, and settle the kids for school the next day, so, five o'clock?"

Of course, Sheldon's so strapped down with his perfect

family that I need to cut off my time to accommodate him. "All right."

Hadar comes back with his laptop case.

"Just call me, and I'll come scoop him wherever you are. Have a good Memorial Day, son."

The three of them—Sheldon, Hadar, and Chrissy—seem to tear themselves away from one another. The "beautiful couple" of New York high society act as if they're sending him off with a stranger.

My son walks to me as if that's what I am now. I'm unsure if he's putting up a front for them or if he is just agitated he's not at a theme park. Still in shock at this third degree he's giving me, I load his things in my rental car and give him his space, just like we learned in parenting class and I've taught my own clients to do in my profession. I just never expected that I would be the one who needed social work techniques.

I rented a hotel room near Central Park, where there's lots of activities and takeout food. His silent treatment toward me in the car is punishing and loud. Though we're only separated by a few feet now, it may as well be the Gulf of Mexico. But I allow him his few minutes to let out whatever mood he's carrying.

Since it's three o'clock in the afternoon when we arrive, after taking his things to the bedroom, I walk him back downstairs.

"Why don't we go for a horse carriage ride? You still like those, right, or is that something else you don't do anymore?" I know I should be careful and subtle with my digs. His therapist will interview him afterward and so will his social worker and lawyer.

"That's fine," he mumbles.

"Look, Hadar," I start once we're in the carriage. I've pointed out several landmarks to him so he can explain to me what they are, and I try other techniques to redirect his attention from what he wants. But an hour later, he is doing what his father did to me during our marriage—blocking me out mentally.

"I know you wanted to go to Great Escape, and you will go. But there are other ways to have fun when you're not doing what you want at the moment."

"Okay," he answers simply.

On what should be a scenic ride through Central Park, the horses may as well be riding us to Hell. The last time we did this was a year ago in Chicago. We pretended to be on a magic carpet riding through the clouds. He loves make-believe and using his imagination. But it's been an entire year, and the chasm between us is a wake-up call that I've missed out on a lot. Now my ten-year-old gazes into space, tuning me out, as if I bore him.

All out of ideas, I watch him pick at his chili dog two hours later over dinner.

"Why aren't you eating?"

Instead of answering me, he raises his hand and signals for the server.

"Yes, young man, what can I do for you?" she asks when she comes over.

"Is this grass-fed meat?" my son asks.

Since when does he care?

"I'm sorry?" Vexed, the server tosses a confused expression at me.

"Grass-fed?" Hadar continues, in a sophisticated tone that sounds a little too grown-up and informed for my comfort level. "Raised in a pasture instead of a coop or pen. Are these turkey dogs?"

After blinking a couple of times, the waitress manages, "I believe they're pork, son."

Hadar frowns at his food. "I'm not hungry."

"You haven't eaten all day, and chili dogs are your favorite."

"New studies show that hot dogs shorten your life span, Mom. They increase the risk of cancers like stomach, breast, and co… colo…" He closes his eyes, as if he is drawing from some inner power, and reopens them. His head bobs while he concentrates on his next word. "Co… lor…ect…al. Colorectal. Processed meat causes cardi… cardi-o-vas-cu-lar disease and death." He scratches his nose, just as Sheldon does when he's being condescending on the low.

Infuriated, I pick up our trays and dump them. Phone in hand, for a fraction of a second, I sweep my finger over the screen to call Sheldon and ask for food options. Then, I chuck it back in my purse. I won't allow Chrissy the satisfaction.

"All right, Mr. Food Connoisseur, tell me where you'd like to go."

Hadar taps his finger along his chin. "Dinosaur Bar-B-Que?"

"Dinosaurs? I suppose dinosaurs are grass-fed, huh? You mean the chef actually cooks and grills prehistoric animals while we watch?" I reach across the table to see if he's still ticklish in his neck, and hopefully to push us past the awkwardness of having to learn my own child all over again. "I don't know where the dinosaurs are in this town."

He pulls out his phone his dad bought him. "Don't worry. I've got you. I'll call out the directions while you drive."

My laugh is a tiny sigh of relief. "This has disaster written all over it. You never give good directions."

"I've gotten much better helping Ma… Chrissy." Panic jumps from his eyes and right into me.

A slew of competing thoughts—whether I should address this, what have they been discussing with him, just how close she and him are, what has he told her about me—crisscross through my head like a hundred intersecting train tracks all going in different directions.

Pretending to check a noise on the other side of the restaurant, I turn my head so he doesn't see me subtly swipe at my burgeoning tears. Then I swing my gaze back to him. He's staring right at me, and his eyes fall.

"It's okay, honey. Come on. Let's go."

At the restaurant he chose, he tries to put up a good front, but his energy is lackluster. He finally eats his food and answers my questions about school with all the excitement of a prison inmate.

"Hadar, we've had fun on all our other visits. What gives?"

Hesitant, squeamish, he peers across the table at me like I'm fire he's scared to touch.

"We were all together. My cousins, Rome and Isaac, were at the visits, too. Blake came. It was fun with more of us to play. And sometimes Granny came or my uncles. Now all of them are in Sag Harbor together. Rome and Isaac aren't even Blake's real cousins. They're mine," he whimpers jealously, tears filling his eyes. "But he's having fun with them, and they're doing a big Memorial Day cookout and a beach bonfire, football, boats, water skiing, without me." His head sags toward the table.

"You and I are going to do fun stuff tomorrow, too, Hadar. We can go to the Statue of Liberty, to ride bikes, to the arcade," I hear myself near-pleading. "We'll finally kick it by ourselves and do stuff without people watching."

He nods. "Okay."

Just a little more time to blow off steam and he'll be fine.

Back at the hotel room later that night, he falls asleep watching *Ready Player One* since he said no to the movies. "I just want to go to bed," he'd told me, as if he simply wants to get this weekend over with.

Lying in bed next to him, I search for activities we can

book for tomorrow. Some of them cost hundreds of dollars, and while I can manage it, do I really want to spend all that for a boy who's not having fun?

Suddenly, a light flashes in our dark room. Next to a sleeping Hadar, I realize he still holds his phone. A new text message has popped up.

Dad: *It'll be over before you know it. Next weekend, we'll all be at Great Escape and you'll have your reward for all A's this year. Love you.*

I scroll up the message thread to see the texts Hadar must've sent while I showered.

Hadar: *Please, Dad, come over here so I won't be by myself.*

Dad: *I'm sorry, son. The judge said it's just you and her this time.*

Blake: *Go to bed really early, and when you wake up, it'll be the next day. Keep doing that and play some phone games. It makes the time go faster.*

Chrissy: *Blake, don't say that. Honey, no, just enjoy your mom. She loves you and has worked hard for you. Don't be hurtful.*

They're on a family chat? And Chrissy is… having to encourage *my* bond with *my* child.

Tears blurring my vision, I stumble to the balcony. I sensed over the last few months that he was becoming more distant, but I would have never imagined him not wanting me at all.

I've lost the one person on Earth who was in my corner, who was worth fighting for. Why did I work so hard?

What do I *do?* The world has not only shifted, it's fallen apart. What else do I have without my own son? Sheldon may not have won the hearing the today, but he has *won.*

In near paralysis, I spend the next half hour shriveled up in a patio chair. I'm not the only one to blame for losing my family. But Sheldon's so good at painting our failure like it's all on me.

At the end of my rope, I don't think I can take another day of Hadar's disdain and scowling while I jump through hoops to win him back.

I scroll through the contacts on my phone, for the one person in the world who doesn't take sides. She's kind to everybody, even at our worst, the one person I could always tell *anything* to, and my business never traveled.

"Hey, sweetie, congratulations. I heard the judge gave you and Hadar your time," she whispers when she answers the phone.

I hadn't realized it's now 12:15 a.m. I've been on the balcony sobbing longer than I thought.

"Princess," I squeak.

"Baby, what's wrong?" My former sister-in-law coughs a bit, and her voice turns concerned.

I wipe my face, not wanting to hear myself admit I'm unable to keep my son. This was not how my fantasies of besting Sheldon were supposed to play out. "Can Hadar come play with Isaac and Rome? I can stay in a hotel."

"Girl, absolutely not. Come on over here. Ma loves having Hadar," she says, referring to my former mother-in-law, Sheldon's mother, Professor Verona Rouse. "Nobody's in the guest house right now. You can sleep there while the boys do night tents."

Something is off about Princess's voice, like she's been eating sand. But still, it is an oasis in the middle of arid desert land.

"But I... I think I would rather drop off Hadar and I'll stay in a hotel." I can only take so much of Sheldon and Chrissy and her rich Hamptons friends sashaying around together, with their new husbands and babies.

"You most certainly will not. I'm feeling under the

weather and sometimes I'm a little tired to be chasing these kids on boats and water skis and swimming. While the family takes the children out, I'd love some company." Princess then mutters, as if she's walking away from her husband and Sheldon's older brother, Roland, while cupping her mouth. "And *you* can tell *me* what you did to Explore's CEO that's got him riding into Chicago on a big boat for you."

I half-cry with joy to hear an understanding voice, and she and I break into giggles the way we did years ago.

Early the next morning, we barely drive inside the gates of the Rouse family's new compound when the scowling Hadar disappears. A whole happy other kid grabs my neck and gives me the fat kiss I never received yesterday.

"Thank you, Mama!"

I'll try my best not to take that as me losing him. I know I'll need all my emotional strength for Sheldon's family.

Hadar runs toward his stepsiblings and cousins, and I hang back at the car, unsure I want to do this. Already, I can hear Roland snickering and Mr. Rouse scrutinizing.

But the angel who is Princess steps forward on the wrap-around porch and holds her arms open in a sign that I won't have to face them alone.

11

NOT SO CAREFUL WITH YOU

KEENAN

"*H*ey, Stunt Man!" the black women shout from the pier.

"Stunt Mannnn! Over here!" Another chick beckons to me from a boat.

Oh, shit. My laughter is automatic as I throw a thumbs-up at the woman who flashes me her naked breasts.

"You shouldn't encourage their behavior," Laney fusses while she directs our staff and security to take their positions among a growing crowd of admirers.

"It's all part of the fun, Laney, lighten up."

"I don't want to give our critics and competitors any leverage to call our brand unfit for kids."

"Point taken, Chief."

"I know you're the chief, Keenan," a nervous Laney replies, "I'm only in your ear because Explore is important to me."

And her commitment is important to *me*. For a good minute, I study our concierge. She was desperate for a job after graduating college over a year ago. Since then, she's been far more than a concierge. "I know that. Calling you Chief wasn't a dig, it was a compliment."

"Thank you," she says.

On my windsurfing paddle board, it's the ocean and me now. A few docks away, Kevin agreed to take on swimming in the ocean. Solomon is giving a tour of Taste's premium chocolate reserves, which draw far more intrigue from foodies, food critics, and chocolate lovers than we could have ever imagined. Rocky is handling Sights Unseen and leading a private group to a nearby island for lunch.

"Can I go with you?" one of the groupies shouts to me from behind the security rope.

"Sorry, there's only room on here for one. Maybe next time, baby."

The mild waters of the Atlantic splash on me. Today I personally came to oversee Adventures myself, making sure we're all visible for photo ops, social media selfies, and the groupies and fans who flew here from around the world hoping to meet the men of Explore Adventures.

After this, I've got nine meetings to cram in today, but this is necessary. Last year's summer and fall promotions, along with our grand opening of Taste in the winter and New Year's, is paying off this year in dividends. Word of mouth has spread like wildfire, and with this being Memorial Day weekend—the official kickoff of summer—the company is firing on all cylinders.

Summer has always been my medicine. Hoisting the sails, pushing out toward the oncoming waves, I wade farther into the ocean. Wind blows me along with the currents, and I soak in the sun. Windsurfing over the murky green ocean waters, I'm hyped by the thrill. Pulling down on the bar that steers the sail transports me through the wind gusts, and I let them carry me for the next hour.

A damn good workout, but unfortunately, those nine

meetings await me.

One of the staffers hands me a towel and security pushes back onlookers. I throw the deuces at all the snapping phones aimed at me.

"Mr. McLain!" a group of black kids call out.

"Boys, calm down," a mother shushes.

I head toward the black families. "Gentlemen, what's good?" I ask, taking their cameras.

Excitement dancing in their feet, they jump up and down. "Mr. McLain, are you really from Baltimore?"

"Did you grow up in the 'hood?"

"Did you really used to pretend to be Batman and Superman and fly off your roof?"

I laugh at some of what they've obviously been reading online, grab their camera phones and snap selfies with them. "I don't think your parents want me telling you this, but yes, I grew up in Edmondson Village in Baltimore, and yes, it is true that I broke my leg at age eleven. I was trying to fly to my friend's building on four kites I glued together. I also got in trouble for breaking my neighbor's window on the way down."

It's always cool to tell these stories to little brown boys and watch their eyes light up.

When I turn to the crowds again, the Rouse family walks forward, led by Roland. Approaching the back of Explore's line, he holds up his tickets in the air.

"Vincent, those tall guys back there," I instruct a staffer and point them out, "could you escort them up here?" The Rouses are important. Since they'll be helping with Explore's business, and their companies are sponsors of the concert in a few weeks, they shouldn't be at the back of the line.

I motion for Explore's security to let them through.

But I'm disappointed at the absence of the one Rouse I'm hoping for most.

"Mr. McLain," Roland greets me with his hand outstretched. "Good to see you, man."

"A pleasure as always, bruh." Both of his brothers are present, Sheldon and Jerrell. "I understand you all will be helping Explore clean up our financial and corporate act."

"Actually, I'm assigning my sister, Kamilah. She knows everything I know, and I'm always just a phone call away. But I will stop in periodically."

"Glad to hear it. We appreciate you all's help."

"The appreciation runs both ways. Explore is hot right now, and we're glad to be part of this, especially before the big concert. Thanks for the hookup on concert tickets by the way. The kids are ecstatic." Roland turns to the other two. "You remember my brothers, Sheldon and Jerrell, right?"

"Of course," I reply. "Jerrell is friends with my brother, Desmond. What's good, bruh."

"What's happening, man."

Sheldon offers me a firm hand, *very* firm. His vibe is not warm, but civil. "Keenan, congratulations on all this." He grips my hand and sizes me up with the infrared lasers of his eyes scanning to see through me. He must've heard I was in Chicago…checking in on his ex.

I return the stiffness and remove my hand from his so this Negro knows he doesn't intimidate me. "Thank you for letting Adventures host your son's party the other week."

"It was so much fun!" a kid bellows next to him.

I recognize the skinny little twig that is Eugenia's son, and his blue glasses, from us hosting his birthday party a couple of weeks ago.

Sheldon shakes his head at Hadar. "It's not like we had a choice, man. He wouldn't stop asking, and he loved it, so job well done. Explore has a lifetime fan in this one."

"Kevin says you're helping us with all that complicated tech stuff for our digital financial payments and our hookup with MoneyCruncher," I point out, trying to make this chitchat go as smoothly as possible.

What I really want to ask Sheldon is can I get in Eugenia's guts without him cockblocking, but I refrain.

"That's correct. We'll be starting up in a few days."

"We'll be happy to have you. So what brings all you fellas here today?"

"Windsurfing!" Their sons clamor over one another at the same time.

"Ah, one of my favorites. Now that's fire."

"Will you be teaching us?" Hadar asks.

"Do you want me to teach you?" I reply.

"Are you skilled?" Sheldon interrupts.

He stands a few inches taller than me in height only, not in confidence. I meet him, eye to eye. "Yes, I am skilled." My attention is diverted back to the hyped-up boys. "But I have a full schedule today. I'll hook up with you guys soon, though. Next weekend's a little lighter, and I should be around. For today, Vincent is one of our best guys, though."

"Wait a minute," another voice pushes through our conversation. "I thought you guys were riding jet skis, not windsurfing."

The sun's warmth finally reaches a man's air sacs.

Sharp and demanding, unleashing all her protective lioness, she's here.

When she notices me, her face freezes, struck by the same lightning bolt that hits me.

"The boys came and saw the line for windsurfing, and they want to try this," Sheldon explains.

"No," she blurts, arms crossing her chest the way she did with me a few days ago. "What kind of protection does that provide? Who will be with him? Sheldon, I thought you would be riding with him on jet skis, the way you have before, not him standing on open water."

"Mom, please?" Hadar pleads.

"This is something new he wants to try," Sheldon insists.

"What about his eyeglasses?" she presses.

"I brought his headband," Sheldon snaps back.

"No. Will you please just stick with jet skis?"

As she says this, I remember our talk over Christmas Eve about her terror of being on a boat, of going in the water.

"You mean the others are going out there without me? Dang, Mom! Why do you always do this?" A frustrated Hadar is on the verge of tears, but his tone still borders on a little too much disrespect.

"Son, apologize to your mother. I don't want to hear you talk to her like that again," Sheldon mutters, obviously irritated with her also. "G, can I see you alone for a minute?" He's already marched off before he's finished asking.

I step to the boy so he doesn't see his folks doing what mine also did. "Hadar, how would you like it if I gave you that one-on-one lesson today?"

His teary eyes brighten before they go dark again. "My mom will never let me. She's too scary and doesn't let me do anything. Thanks, though, Keenan."

"Let me handle your mom, and you go with Vincent to pick out some gear, okay?"

Hadar wipes his face like he still doesn't believe me. "Okay."

Passing throngs of folks who shake my hand, I find his parents outside a boating and surf shop.

"You can't keep doing this, Genie. He's a boy, not some toddler." In Sheldon's clipped tone, he seems to speak to a child.

"He's not a good swimmer," Eugenia argues.

"Why do you think that is?" Sheldon hisses at her. "*You* don't swim! Your family doesn't swim, so he's never spent time learning. But you can't project your fear of water or thrill rides onto him. He feels left out when he's not doing what the others are doing, and it makes him feel weak. You're screwing up his confidence."

Sheldon towers over her, almost like she's a poorly performing student he scolds, instead of a concerned mother.

"Excuse me, sorry to interrupt, but if it makes Eugenia feel like he's safe, I'll take Hadar out on the water."

"No, it won't." She glares at me for even thinking to touch her son.

"I thought you had other commitments today," Sheldon challenges.

"I'll push them back so Hadar can join his cousins."

"And why would you do that for him?" Sheldon throws a skeptical side-eye between Genie and me.

"Your boy is out there crying, man. Your family is working with my company. Consider it a courtesy. Just trying to help."

Sheldon still drips with suspicion. "And you say you know what you're doing out there?"

"I wouldn't be the CEO of an adventure company if I couldn't handle every activity we offer. I know what I'm doing." I don't believe that assures him, but he clearly wants his son to gain some independence.

After Sheldon leaves Eugenia behind, I approach the woman who tussled with me the other day, the strong and feisty Black Mystique.

I want to ask how her week was, what she did, who she helped, to feel her fingers play in my mohawk while she pours out the contents of her mind.

Hair in a simple ponytail at the back of her head, no makeup or frills, she gives no fucks for appearances. In the midst of all these dime pieces out here yelling my name, the sun crowns Eugenia.

Instead of asking all I want to ask, I stay focused. "He needs space to be a young man. The tighter you hold him to you, the more he'll try to break away. Come out here with us. It'll help to see his mom trying it with him. You know I won't let anything happen to you or him."

She's tough and soft at once. "Why are you doing this?"

I move to close distance between us. She's quick to sneak a glance at Sheldon across the boardwalk and she steps back.

"You know why. I'm still high on the drugs between your th—"

"Stop it," she pushes out from her chest. "Don't you *dare* in front of my son."

"Don't you mean in front of your son's *father?*" I push back.

Deep in the diamond mines of her high-pressured eyes, Eugenia's shocked I said it, that I see through her, to the real source of her torture. Facing each other down in silence, we're nearly snarling bulls. My street sense challenges hers. That tough shit only ignites my dick. I swear if she throws a punch, I'm throwing her against the wall and I don't give a damn who sees.

"Be careful with him."

"Fine. If helping your son is the closest you'll let me get to you, so be it."

Chewing her lip, Eugenia takes a final peek at Hadar, the same look my moms gave me when I left home for summer camps. "He doesn't normally do stuff like…" She knocks the emotion out of her voice and reasserts her toughness. "Be careful."

"I will." With my eyes, I take a sweep over her breasts, and though they're hidden under a tank top, they're not hidden. It hugs her D-cups perfectly, damn perfect, better than girls half her age. "And when I'm finished with him, I won't be so careful with you."

12

ALL THAT ENERGY

EUGENIA

The oxygen in my chest bursts in flames.

"Heyyy, Stunt Mannn!"

"Mr. CEO, over here!"

"Say, where's your big yacht? I can help you park it!"

"If Eugenia don't want to ride that big boat of yours, I got you, boo."

Wrapping their arms around him, their claws scraping his back and slipping down to his ass while he makes his way through the crowds, these women may as well be grabbing at leather on sale half-off.

The flames in me erupt as he stops among them, starts accepting their business cards, takes their cell phones, holds them up for selfies, lets them hug him and play with his mohawk. Every touch, smile, and overly friendly embrace bubbles up in my volcanic pipe. I try to force my eyes away but am too infuriated.

He receives all their cards and shoves them in his pocket, which I shouldn't give a second thought. After all, I suppose I did tell him to pursue younger women who are single.

But here I stand, digesting ash.

Those women are my co-workers. Here in New York. The very ones Lus told me were trying to read Keenan's card that came with flowers, now they put extra energy into swaddling him with their titties.

Their faces come so close, I wait for Sharae to kiss him.

He snaps away, continues onward, toward Hadar and the boys. And I release the flaming breaths I hate I'm holding.

On the boardwalk now, I brush aside my co-workers and revisit my terror of water, the memories of me splashing in a pool full of kids during a shooting, all of us scrambling to escape.

I wait for how Hadar will handle the water, if he'll get out there and freeze up—so vulnerable, not knowing what to do, and panic. I fear how his little body will handle being out in the ocean with nothing else around him, and how he'll perform, especially compared to Roland's more athletically gifted sons, Rome and Isaac.

"Ma'am, come with me." Princess appears from nowhere and sneaks her arm through mine.

"P, I can't. I need to watch—"

"*You need* to come with me." She pries me from my little boy. "And explain that whole earthquake we just saw."

"Girl, you're being dramatic. There was no earthquake."

"You haven't lied to me all these years. Don't start now." She prods me away with her. A tiny cough escapes from her gut that she tries to hide.

"You want me to grab you some water?"

"No," P snaps, wrangling her purse. "I want to grab slushies and spike them with this gin." Her grin is devious.

Confused, I crack up at her unscrewing the top of her bracelet.

She concludes, "You need to calm down so we can discuss important current events."

I'm dead at her shenanigans. "Is that a flask you're wearing as a bracelet?"

We grab slushies and huddle together while our kids play out in the water.

I stop her hand when she tries to pour gin in mine. "I can't, Princess, not with my open case."

"You're not in Chicago, and your social worker's not anywhere around."

"But the New York social worker might drop by for a surprise check-in, and I just got him. I can't mess this up."

"All right, fine."

"But I do miss our old days. And remember our edibles before we found out we were carrying Isaac and Hadar?"

"How could I forget? On New Year's that one time, Sheldon was wondering what was wrong with you," Princess laughs. "You fell asleep on Jerome's rocking horse, you were so high."

Holding my belly and laughing, I walk with her down memory lane. "I forgot all about that!"

"But I didn't. And I've still got the pictures. I'm showing Hadar when he gets older, the first time you ever jump on his case for using…" Her voice fades, joy in her eyes evaporating.

"P, what's wrong?" I ask.

I'm a little taller than she is so it's hard to capture her face.

"Nothing. I just had… something in my throat is all."

"And what's going on with this dry voice of yours?" From her parched throat comes the voice of a woman who's either been stuck in a desert or doing hard drugs. I've been a social worker long enough to know.

"A summer bug. Nothing serious." She checks for our sons and their fathers before continuing, "but stop deflecting from Keenan. I saw the energy he was serving, like he could've taken you right there on that pier if you'd let him."

I allow her to pretend like she's not the one deflecting.

Over my shoulder, Keenan guides Hadar on the water, under the watchful eye of Shel and his brothers. Now that P has helped lower my stress level, I actually notice parts of Keenan I didn't see at Christmas. And the other day, I was so freaked out and panicked and horny and rushing that I didn't fully process what he was putting on me.

I'm processing now, though. At about five feet and eleven inches, he's two or three inches taller than me, with a layer of meat on his eight-pack. The water may as well be his home, he's so comfortable on it. Not quite as thick or tall as Sheldon, but then again, Charles Rouse spawned a set of Louisiana linebackers. Keenan is athletic in the sense of a track runner or javelin thrower.

"Ohhh, I see," Princess teases, breaking up my daydream. "So when did that go down?" Her suspicious eye dares me to lie.

This is Princess. She's never shown a second of ill will toward me, not even last summer, after the games I played in a last-ditch grab for Sheldon. Through these lips that don't want to tell, the truth slips out.

"Christmas Eve, when you all were at Sheldon's wedding."

Chuckling in her gut, P turns up her bracelet flask. "Mmhm. I'm listening."

Her chuckling is contagious, and the little bursts of joy snuff out my anger.

"And the other evening in Chicago," I whisper.

"Oh!" She snort-laughs, and her spiked slushy flies up her nose, choking her up.

Her hand flies to cover her mouth, and I remember why I love and trust her so much. On our way down the board-walk, the sun beating down on our faces, we're more unruly than schoolgirls.

"My visit with Hadar didn't start until Christmas morning, but I didn't want to be in Chicago with my family asking me questions about the wedding and being jerks. So I came to the Hamptons a couple days early to be alone. Keenan was managing Taste by himself while everybody else was at the wedding. He saw me hanging out alone, and I think he figured out what was up with me. He invited me to spend the night with him and his friends on a boat."

I'm stunned at how good it feels to finally let that out with somebody. That night, I couldn't believe somebody actually persuaded me to relax on a boat.

"And?" Princess tugs on me.

Now it's me whose humor is a snort. "He definitely delivers all that energy he's carrying." Our night inside a glass elevator near the ocean floor was so intense I can still feel him smashing me, my titties, and face against the glass.

P keeps pulling on me. "So you had a part two in Chicago."

"Oh, I tried fighting him off. You know Shel has his ways of finding out everything. But I have zero discipline with that boy. I tell him no, and he blows me off like he owns my secret codes."

"So let him unlock you then, heffa," Princess insists.

"I don't have time for that, P. Didn't you hear me say Shel is looking for any excuse to keep me from getting Hadar back?"

Princess sips her spiked slushy. "Genie, I can't tell you your priorities, but life is short. These kids have their own lives now. They're not worried about us. It's time for you to reclaim yours."

"But I've missed this last year with him."

"You also had a lot of good years, and you have more, ah…" Her voice breaks.

Again, she disappears. Her throat seems to choke on a

sadness only she tastes. But Princess has never been sad and has no reason to be now. No reason I know of.

"P, what is wrong with you?"

The next time she faces me, it's with a boatload of tears. "You and Hadar have so many more years ahead of you, Genie. His life may be different now, but that's not a change you should resent, only one for you to adjust to. It's a chance to grow and not sit around being bitter."

"I'm not bitter."

"I would be," my former sister-in-law insists, her gaze glued to me. "If I had a perfect marriage that wasn't necessarily perfect for me, I'd be frustrated and mad I couldn't make it work." Her hand is firm and yet consoling on my arm. "Sheldon is incredible, but he wasn't for you. He didn't bring out the best in you, nor you in him, and that's what love should do. That doesn't mean you don't deserve love at all. Stop punishing yourself."

Now it's me who chokes up at the potency of her words that seem to hit the bull's-eye of my darkest insecurities. I failed to "keep a damn good man" as my aunts and cousins say. And I've lived with it every day since.

We walk back to see the boys coming in from the ocean. My little heartbeat jumps up and down and waves his skinny arm at me from the pier, like he just conquered a mountain. I'm a mix of melancholy and uncertainty as I wave back. I'm not ready for him to have his own life.

While Sheldon preps Hadar to go out on jet skis, a bigger crowd has built up around the pier. Spectators hold up cell phones, and younger black women, ten and twenty years my junior, whistle and call out. Emerging from among his admirers, a black statue moves toward me.

"Hi, Keenan. I'm Princess," she says, sticking her hand out, "Roland's wife." She nods toward me. "Genie's sister-in-law."

"Pleasure to meet you, Princess." He turns to me. "Your

boy did well for his first time. He's kind of nervous but he's determined, a fighter, like somebody else I know."

"You don't have to be polite. Hadar is awkward at sports."

Keenan shakes his head. "Only because he doesn't play them often enough, and water sports are new to him, so he's self-conscious. If he did them more often, his confidence would grow. I can work with him more." His eyes surf over me. "I can also work with you, give you a private lesson. Maybe tomorrow morning, before I start up with Explore?"

Now I glare at him. "Keenan, I asked you to stay away from me. You have more than enough options standing over there." I motion toward the crowds with my head, and some bitterness that surprises me. I'm remembering my co-workers' business cards in his back pocket.

He wipes ocean water from his glistening body with a towel. "And I told you that's not happening. But maybe I will check out some of those options," he replies and winks.

"Good for you. I hope you and them enjoy."

P rolls her eyes at me and addresses Keenan. "What she meant to say is she would love a private lesson. I'll personally make sure she gets there."

Keenan's teeth grip his bottom lip like he wishes it was me. "Excellent." He turns and points toward a hill. "That side road right there will take you to the point of that hill up there. I'll be waiting. Seven-thirty?"

"What's up there?" I interrupt him and Princess making plans without my input.

A mischievous grin spreads across his face. "A surprise."

"I don't like surp—"

Princess jabs me in the ribs. "She *adores* surprises. Seven-thirty it is."

Keenan has a baby face when he's amused, as he is right now with P. "I like her. A lot. All right then, Eugenia. I hate I have to go, but I do." His voice lowers, and he takes a gander at my mouth, as if assessing whether to snatch me up and do something crazy I'm learning he has a tendency for.

"Don't you even think about it," I warn him.

"You'd better be glad your son is over there. I don't give a damn about Sheldon seeing," he mutters and struts off.

"Oh, *shit!*" Princess cackles. "That must be some damn good riding y'all are doing."

He can barely leave the boardwalk and enter the Explore shuttle, so many girls and kids clamor for him.

Now it's time to take Miss Princess to task. "I can't believe you did that. I'll never hear the end of Sheldon's mouth when he finds out."

"I can't believe you're standing here acting like you don't want him. You let me worry about Sheldon." P finishes her spiked slushy. "We're going to the club tonight."

Already, I'm at nope. "Tonight, I'm spending time with Hadar. Maybe he'll make cookies or cupcakes with me."

"Girl, please. Hadar and the boys will be playing the new *Fallout*. Hadar's not worried about you. Once we square away the kids with their grandparents, and the guys go out on the boat, we're heading for the club. And you're getting a surprise."

"Why did I let you talk me into this?" I ask Princess.

From wall to wall, Taste is bursting at the seams, totally different than the snowy ghost town I stumbled into at Christmas. Now it jumps with young black professionals, more urban and rugged cats who might be from the same rough places I'm from. Mixed in among them are white guys in expensive grunge and cargo shorts who clearly love black culture, and white girls licking their chops for a successful brother.

"You wanted to be talked into it."

"And since when do you party?"

She doesn't need to answer. It's apparent. She is now Princess *Rouse*, Mrs. Roland Rouse, the wife of the President of the Audit Division at New York Bank.

Her being in the know is a testament to how far Sheldon's family has come up since I left it. As the wife of Roland Rouse, sister-in-law to Sheldon Rouse, and now sisters with Madison and Chrissy Rouse, Princess is practically royalty and can go anywhere she wants, sit anywhere she wants. It's a far cry from ten years ago, back when our kids were babies, we were stuck at home, and our husbands worked all hours of the night to turn the Rouse name into a brand.

Now they've indeed arrived. She's living the high life we once joked about. But one would never know P has become one of those rich wives. She's so kind and soulfully breathtaking, one would think she's only been gone from her native Baton Rouge one day. The only giveaway of her changed social and financial status is our premium seating in a corner booth in the heart of the Hamptons.

Everybody who's anybody is here at the MoneyCruncher Summer Opener, to officially kick off high-traffic season.

A few celebrities are present on the scene, seated behind VIP ropes and on the balcony.

Kevin Middleton enters the dining room to applause and catcalls, but no camera flashes because we turned over our phones at the door. He reaches behind him and wraps his arm around a gorgeous, tall woman who surely must pose for *Vogue.* I vaguely recognize her, but apparently, she knows me.

In a fleeting moment of her owning the room, and me surviving it, I'm stunned when her eyes pause on mine. Her glare of disgust levels me and doesn't leave me when her eyes pass.

"Who is she?" I ask Princess.

Princess offers my knee a firm squeeze. "Doesn't matter."

"Glad to know I've got fans in high places," I mutter.

"*You're* in a high place," she says with a rattle of my arm.

Across the room sits Sharae, Leddy, and Niara. I can only imagine how much money they combined among themselves to pay for that booth in one of America's most popular restaurants at the start of summer.

They hold up their drinks to me in a mocking toast, giggling and snickering, and point their server in my direction.

He comes over with a tray of liquor-filled cocktails and sets the drinks down right in front of me. Every social worker in Chicago knows I have an open case and that I don't have my son. Taking a drink is anathema in an open child safety case.

From her perch in the opposite booth, Sharae blows me a drunken kiss. They all bust up laughing and take off into the dancing bodies.

"Friends of yours?" Princess asks.

"You know me," I say with a sip of my Shirley Temple. "I've got friends everywhere."

"Forget them."

"P, I know you meant well bringing me here, but I really would rather curl up and be al—"

"What's up, everybody!" a familiar voice blasts over the speakers.

At recognizing that voice, I cut a hard eye at Princess.

A smile sneaks around the corner of her lips. "You know you wanted to see him."

"Like I want those drinks." Dangerously delicious. The cruelty.

"I want all of you to give a fat show of love to my favorite rich guy, Kevin Middleton." The clapping and hooting is almost unbearable as the two of them raise their glasses to one another across the room. "All you Silicon Valley folks who've invested in Explore over the past year, been a friend to MoneyCruncher, and brought your friends along with you, on behalf of Kevin, the Explore family, and myself, we can't thank you enough. All the good banking people here in New York, the Los Angeles and Atlanta entertainment heads in the house with us tonight, who've been writing checks and spreading the word, from Explore, we want to say thank you. This summer is going up, and you've all got front row seats!"

Like he plugged himself into their sockets, the entire restaurant feeds off Keenan's hype energy, and he charges up from theirs, all of them jumping and yelling. A little of the wattage might make my kinky hair stand on edge.

I crane my neck to peer through the bodies and view him on the small stage.

"While I'm up here, also say what's up to my boy, Showtime, who's visiting from my hometown of B'More. He's got a sweet club down there, so when you're passing through, show him some love. You'll be seeing a lot of him around here because he's making moves out here. Him and me, we go way back, and we have a little tradition from when we were kids throwing parties at the pool in Edmondson Village."

The cheering starts up again.

"What's the tradition, sexy?" Sharae calls to him from her booth.

Keenan's smiling baby face gazes at the crowd. Awash in stage lights, he's super young, enough so that I almost feel guilty for hitting him with a bowl the other day. But not so young the thick calves peeking from under his shorts and lean steaks in his arms don't give me flashbacks of the other day.

"Why don't you come up here and find out, sweetheart?" Keenan flirts back.

Howls erupt in the audience. She bounces her overly eager ass to the stage, and an animal tears through me.

He turns to his friend, Showtime. "You want to do the honors, my guy?"

"I'd love to, bruh, but we need one more," his friend says.

"Me!" College-age white girls scream and swat one another's hands out of the way.

A splash of cold liquid shocks me, hitting my neck, crawling down my back and ejecting me from my seat. "What the—?"

"Oh, my bad! I don't know how that happened!" An animated Princess feigns innocence underneath an extreme spotlight that finds me.

"Do we have a candidate volunteering back there?" Showtime asks.

Hooting and hollering fills my ears. Wait.

"No!" I cross my hands back and forth in front of me, that I'm not a candidate for anything.

"Here," P says in my ear, and slides a stiff shot in front of me. "Drink it now."

"P, it's alcohol and—"

"The social worker is not coming." She speaks straight into my ear. "I talked to Sheldon. He called her. And there are no cameras in here. Take it to the head, sis."

Grabbing the glass after a year of no alcohol, I down every drop and cringe at the burn.

"So what do you say, gorgeous?" Showtime asks from the stage.

With a shove, P sends my feet tumbling into the bright-white light. "Now go up there and check her ass."

An excited crowd pushes me and my doubts forward, with me kicking myself the whole way.

Above my head, Keenan's infatuation rocks him back and forth on his heels, the glow in his eyes shining spotlights on me. Maybe, inside me.

Fucking Princess.

His friend, Showtime, pulls me up. "All right then, sweet lady, what's your name?"

"Eugenia."

He turns to my coworker, her chest out, chin up for a competition.

"Sharae, big daddy."

"Oh, damn," Showtime says to Keenan. "She called me big daddy. So who you got, man?"

Keenan rubs his hands, his face full of mischief, and bites down on his bottom lip. "I haven't decided. We'll see."

With a hard glare, I remind him I'll take all those business cards and shove them down his throat. He's having too much damn fun. But the alcohol is creeping in, and I turn to face Sharae's twenty-five-year-old ass for having the audacity to test me.

WE COULD BE DANCING

KEENAN

*A*stonished is not the word to describe me reading the text several times earlier today, to make sure I'd read it right.

Princess Rouse texted that she didn't have reservations for the kickback tonight and asked for a space. I would have taken care of her anyway because she's Roland's wife. But once she wrote she would bring Eugenia, I ensured they would have one of the best spots in Taste. After mine and Solomon's earlier fights over guest priority, we now plan out space for high-profile, last-minute requests.

Princess promised I would be in for a treat, but hell, I had my doubts on whether she could actually bring stubborn-ass Eugenia in here.

Now I'm flabbergasted, tickled at Princess shoving Eugenia from their booth. If she convinces her sister-in-law to come up, from here on out, that woman can have from me *whatever* she wants.

Black Mystique is even more beautiful when she glowers at me. Like there are a hell of a lot more important things she could be doing than dealing with me. With those tight, track-running curves teasing me from underneath her black strapless jumpsuit, she crushes every single chick in here. Caramel smooth skin, and a crown of woolly, sandy-brown hair, wild and slicked back into a bushy ponytail, *shit*.

"So this is a dance contest," Showtime explains, chuckling. "And it gets a little… spicy. We'll leave it to our guests here which one of you is most creative."

The moment she hears this, my Black Mystique takes off, led by the appall on her face. And drags the tenderest half of my chest with her.

Damn.

But Princess waits at the edge of the stage as if she's coaching a boxing match and pulls Eugenia down to yell in her ear.

I can't decipher what all's being said, but it sounds something like, *Don't you dare leave her up there with him. Here. Take another shot.*

And I'll be damned. Eugenia actually guzzles it.

This woman must be to Eugenia what Mickey was to Rocky Balboa. What my brother, Desmond, is to me.

I'm tickled when she resumes her position on the stage, nervous and determined, with new liquid courage. Though I know exactly what I want, I'm not saying a word because I'm on the hunt for Eugenia's *other* side.

Showtime cues up the music. "Now the two of you will face off with each other for three minutes. Anything goes. We won't stop you. Winner gets tickets to Sasha Static. And maybe, *maybe*, her choice of who she'll kick it with this weekend—Keenan or me."

She doesn't dare throw a look my way, but her quite-endowed co-worker, Sharae, eyes me and flicks her sizable breasts in my direction.

I hope I didn't calculate this wrong.

Beyonce's "Baby Boy" blares on the speakers, and the crowd gets hype.

Sharae breaks out, twerking in her heels, her tiny skirt flopping over her butt cheeks. Her hips jerk slow and on beat, speed up, and she turns, drops it all in a deep squat, and pops on the floor. She's pretty good, but it's typical freak stuff we've all seen.

What I see next shocks the shit out of me.

Eugenia's head lowers, eyes close, in some withdrawal from an inner well that must dive down to a fountainhead of moxie she rarely touches.

She drops into the full splits, in all three ways—left leg, Chinese, and right leg—and breaks it down to the crowd's sheer delight.

Showtime's mouth falls, and waving the mic up and down, he encourages her.

I'm at a loss. Not missing a beat, her every move syncs to music that must live in her bones even when it's not playing.

Sharae steps it up and takes off her top to reveal her busty bikini. Struts over to me and jiggles them on my chest. I've had plenty of it.

Instead of competing head-on with Sharae, Eugenia somehow elegantly springs up from the floor. She doesn't remove a single article of clothing but raises a lean, muscular leg over her head, turns to the audience and starts pumping. With precision pops, her booty firm and yet supple in that jumpsuit, she lets herself go. Out comes a woman who loved life at one point, to the fullest. Perfectly balanced, on one leg, the woman I first saw on a boat last summer has made her grand return.

I fucking knew it.

Back in school, she must have been Chicago's state dancing champ or some shit. Kicking off her heels, she's in the moment. Her bare feet shift onto her toes, out dashes a foot. Pirouettes? She can spin on her damn *toes?* Raucous energy in this restaurant, the crowd jumping and cheering, must be the permission Eugenia didn't know she needed.

Princess was not lying when she said a treat. Show and I swap impressed grins, and a nigga's got to readjust what's going on downstairs. I'm not sure I want her throwing out the same stamina she puts into humping.

I think about pulling her back, but a dead Eugenia has clearly come alive, and she's swinging and feeling and popping like she needs this life. So I hold off, and stand here in the radius of her unbottled fireworks, for her electricity to charge me up along with everybody else.

Finally, me and my dick are thankful as hell when she stops, turns to the side of the stage, puckers her butt out, and *finishes* with twerking.

Oh, *hell*, nah. White boys pat her butt, spanking it while she throws it out a little too sharp for my comfort level. I move to go put a stop to that nonsense, but Show's laughing ass blocks me. This setup was a bad damn idea.

An out-of-breath Sharae is still trying, damn near breaking herself while jerking against me half-naked. I look past her since my only concern is making sure those dudes don't put their hands *any*where else on Eugenia Jackson.

I signal for the DJ to cut the music. Once he does that, the amped crowd still sings a cappella and Eugenia's still feeling herself. Now I'm going to pull her ass back because *that's* enough.

But a dogged Sharae is determined to attach herself to me one way or another.

Some drunk guy grabs Eugenia and picks her up, and I'm ready to blow once he swings her from the stage and into the crowd.

I nearly punch Sharae to push her off.

Beside me, Showtime makes it a light moment. "Hell, I guess the winner's been declared then."

"Put her down!" Off the stage I leap with my whole being and start throwing bodies out of the way. "Put her down!"

A gaggle of women in the front row pry Eugenia away from this dude, and I shove him back.

"Get him out of here!" I bellow at security. "And get his picture so he doesn't come back!"

Eugenia in my arms, holding her to me, I'm all "concerned dad" and shit, weighed down with a ton of guilt for putting her in that situation.

"You all right, baby girl? My bad, Ma. I didn't expect that. It shouldn't have happened." Shaking in my bones for what almost jumped off, how this could have been worse, I can't remember the last time my heart pumped this hard. Or that I was terrified, because being scary isn't my thing. All the stupid stunts I've pulled, they've never scared me. I've never feared for anybody's safety like my oxygen supply was being cut off.

But Eugenia wipes the sweat off her glowing ass skin, an exhilarated smile on her features, and no panic anywhere on her. To the contrary, a grown woman, flawless and relaxed and in her element, now glares at me.

"What are you doing?"

I'm stumped. "Protecting…l-looking out for you."

Her eyes squinted in a hard chastisement, she presses her index finger against my chest and backs me off her.

"Who said I needed you to do that?"

She moves around me and back to the stage. Showtime doesn't have to ask. The crowd already loves her. Hands cocked on her hips, Eugenia snickers without an eye in Sharae's direction.

Show asks her the question he always does. "So who you

got, queen? Keenan or me? Although I'm pretty sure I can guess."

Eugenia could pin me to the wall with the darts of her ire, and she answers into the microphone, "I haven't decided yet. We'll have to see."

"Ohhh!" Showtime joins the audience in crowing as a chorus.

Whoa. If this isn't foreign territory, I don't know what is.

"Where's my Sasha Static ticket?" Eugenia asks.

Okay, so, I definitely calculated this wrong. I got it right but for the wrong reasons?

At my side, Kevin appears. "Well, that was stupid."

Never one to mince words, it's why I respect him.

"She was down for it. She was having a good time."

"I don't mean her. I'm talking about him." Kevin nods his head toward Showtime. "We need to talk."

"Fine," I mutter. Can't wait to hear what that's about.

But right now, Eugenia jumps from the stage and heads off. I weave through throngs to catch her. "Eugenia!"

I'm careful not to grab her arm, only cupping her elbow gently. The fire she breathes justifies why I use caution.

"What is it, Keenan?" she asks. The music starts up again.

I must be a glutton for punishment. It doesn't make sense how I chase this woman to see her scowl.

"Dance with me."

"Why didn't you just ask me to do that in the first place?"

"Because it's like anything else with you. Asking you directly is a guaranteed 'nope', so I have to rope you out of your comfort zone." I can't help my damn laughter. Even though she showed me up with her stage performance, her schooling me is still attractive as hell.

Now she swings her hand in my face. "And who do you think you are, playing me against my co-worker?"

My motives today when I plotted this have me smiling. "I knew you would win."

"How did you know that?"

I ease her hand down. "Like I told you before, I just know you." Wanting to smell her, touch her, suck her, I tilt my head toward hers.

She pulls her head away. "But you thought I needed to earn you?"

"I thought you needed to earn yourself. Your *true* self, who's not all shriveled up and cowering from Sheldon."

Tired of this back and forth, I slide my arm around her waist, draw her to me, breathe the coconut and vanilla emanating from her skin, gather in my fingers the luxurious fabric separating her body from me. For a fraction of a second, her muscles relax and begin melting with mine, like damn, we can finally rid ourselves of these tough pretenses.

"If she had won, would you have gone home with her?" Eugenia murmurs into my neck.

"You're asking because you care who I take home?" I bury my fingers in the lush forest on her head.

"I'm asking because I care about you playing me."

Embers of disappointment flutter out of me, blowing toward her, as I flow back in a single step. "Eugenia. I halted my schedule of major events, pissed off my staff who are here busting their asses, went to Chicago and put in a lot of work so you *wouldn't* think I was playing a game with you. For you to accuse me of playing you?"

It's true. I didn't expect Sheldon Rouse's ex-wife, a woman who married as high up the "available black male" food chain as one can go, to look at a young buck such as myself and take me seriously. Hence, the overblown show of interest to steal her attention.

This might be the first time any effect resembling remorse or reflection dawns on her face.

"You openly flirted with women who clearly are not my friends."

"Over a dancing contest that was meant as a *joke*. And only so you would relax and I could be closer to you." I won't tell her that her sister-in-law helped me set this up. That's neither here nor there. "If you were going to be mad about it, why'd you get up there?"

"Free Sasha Static tickets." The overhead lights dance in her eyes, a universe of stars where a tiny sliver of a playful Eugenia shines in them.

"Mm." Jealous of her jumpsuit, irritated I can't sneak underneath it, I rub her hips. "No other reason?"

"Should there be?"

I have to wrap this up. Even with me slightly annoyed at this woman, I don't want to leave her. But over her head, a stone's throw across the restaurant, Showtime is in Kevin's ear and probably pitching his case for a street version of MoneyCruncher. Kevin is a pretty open-minded guy, but I haven't had time to set that up. I'm also slightly concerned about the guys Show brought with him who I don't know too well.

I remove the stack of Eugenia's co-workers' business cards from my back pocket. And place them in her hand. "These are all thirteen women you need to watch out for when you get back to your office."

Her eyelids flap with surprise.

I continue, "But you don't need me to protect you, or look out for you, or tell you that, because you're older than me. And I'm younger than you, so automatically, I'm playing you, huh?"

The fine battle lines of Eugenia's internal war argue with me across her forehead, where I lay a kiss.

"The time you spend making me say things you already know, we could be dancing. I'm not forty, Eugenia. And I may be a little flagrant. But my age doesn't make me altogether ignorant. Or insincere. I'll see you at seven-thirty."

I kiss her forehead again and wonder if that's now regret on her face that I'm leaving her.

A few moments later, I slide into a seat in Kevin's booth. "What's good, gentlemen? Cher. Brett."

His wife, Chenera, and longtime friend, Brett, are also present.

"What's up, man," Brett says.

Her scowl reminds me I'm still in the doghouse with her. "Keenan."

I start to ask how Ilyana is doing, just so Cher knows I do care about her childhood friend who was my sneaky link for nearly a year. But Cher's gaze cuts from me to Eugenia in the booth below, and back to me—a stern warning for me to proceed with caution.

All right. Point taken. I might have said some fucked-up things a few months ago to Ill's brother, Solomon, while I was hot. But I won't give up completely, because I could use Cher's help. I'm not ignorant to the fact she's related to Sheldon now by marriage. My brother, Desmond, also told me there's beef between Eugenia and Chrissy from last summer, which might add a drop of vinegar to Cher's side-eye. That animosity might not be a bad thing. I'm kind of counting on it.

But it's not the priority right now.

"So," Show explains, "I was just telling your boy here how cats where we come from want a piece of that Money-Cruncher action, but more specific to black business owners. And I could base something like that in DC, or Baltimore, you know? We could start up, like a Black Silicon Valley and shit. You know I'm good with the seed money."

Kevin laces his fingers together, in that way Kevin does.

"We need to discuss more specifics and flesh it out," I say, to defuse the unspoken concerns already apparent on Kev's face. I turn to Show. "It's my bad, dude, we haven't had time to get into it. I've had all these meetings."

Kevin wields a slick smile. It disarms the uninitiated, makes them think he's giving them whatever they want, that he's their friend. "You drinking good, bruh?" he asks Show.

"Hell, yeah, the best. My boy here hooked a nigga up tonight. I've met all kinds of folks. Now I'm sitting here talking to you. They say you're the coldest in the tech game."

Kevin's green eyes and curly hair are equally deceiving. It leads strangers into thinking he's another rich, mindless pretty boy, and he plays on that. "I don't know about the coldest. But being black, I *am* the one with the most to lose. I'm sure, as a business owner yourself, you know how that goes."

"Oh, absolutely, bruh." Showtime wags his head up and down, rubs his hands together.

"And how about the accommodations around here? Our boy, Keenan, set you up right, yeah? Where are you staying? The Water Lily?" Kevin's fingers spin his drink glass, signifying the wheels of his mind turning.

"Steele Towers. It's dope. Real nice. I could see myself staying there a lot, you know, for our future meetings and shit. Hell, maybe I'll even buy me a spot around here, start up my hustle, too, you know?" Showtime laughs, but not easily. It's loaded. He rules the streets. He's not used to having these conversations in a more formal context, and I'm certain he believes that's where I come in.

"And this guy really can get it done," I add. "Since we were kids, he's always built something out of nothing. Three clubs back home, two clothing lines, a couple of cigar lounges, and now a workshare space for black professionals. My guy's the street version of Kevin Middleton."

Kevin reaches for another bottle of Beluga Russian Gold

Line, refills Show's glass. He doesn't need to top off mine since I haven't touched it.

Down below, a couple of guys approach Eugenia's booth.

The actual fuck?

Kevin raises his glass to Show. "Respect, bruh. It takes hella focus and brains to build profitable businesses from the ground up."

We all drink to Show.

Beyond the rim of my glass, Eugenia takes the hand of some random who leads her to the dance floor. The whole idea of me telling her I would see her at seven-thirty was that she would go home.

"Appreciate that, man," Show replies. "But my focus got me here to this table—that and my friendship with this good dude—to meet with ballers like yourself. That's a hell of a come-up, right? So the hustle was worth it. My friend here tells me you're a hustler, too. So would you fuck with a street collab? We're not exactly the Hamptons, but B'More's got money."

"I'm glad to consider whatever it is you're aiming to do. I'm all for black elevation," Kevin reassures him.

The concrete streets of Baltimore weigh down my chest with uncertainty for what Showtime really wants. I've never had to pay attention. We've never done anything formal, always cash, and I never asked questions. Show always made sure not to do his dirt around me, a college-bound dude who straddled the line between the library and the streets.

We were friends, and our run of high school and college parties was lit. But it has never fully resonated for me why Show didn't really ask anything of me in return. Until now.

That dude thinks your come-up is his. He's been talking like he made you. I was half dead the other night when Lorenzo brought it up, but not so out of it that I forgot.

Over the years, one of us had to stay clean, so I could

open the door for Show in legitimate settings.

Across the table, Show's grin says it all. Kevin eyes us both.

"How about Monday evening? When some of these activities are winding down? We can flesh it out more."

"I'm down," Kevin says. "We would need to discuss the legal particulars of how that would work—ownership, participation, corporate structure, my intellectual property for my trademark-protected algorithms and processes, how much your friends are willing to pay for access to all that. The last offer I received to be bought out was seven-fifty," Kevin states.

"Seven hundred and fifty thousand?" Show adds a whistle.

"Million. Seven hundred and fifty million." Kevin is unsmiling now. He doesn't drop that figure aimlessly. "I know you want to copy MoneyCruncher, not buy it outright, but that's just to establish an idea of what it took for *me* to build my hustle."

"Much respect, bruh." Now Show raises his glass, to which Kevin nods.

"Are those men down there who you brought with you your lawyers?" Kevin asks.

Show chuckles. "Not exactly, man. Much smarter. More useful."

"I look forward to meeting them and finding out how they'll be useful to me." Kevin will use the security cameras to scan their faces and learn their identities and backgrounds by morning. For now, he offers an unsuspecting Show his hand. "I hope you don't mind my enjoying the rest of my evening with my wife and best friend. Until Monday evening then."

I walk Show down the stairs.

"Damn, man, I'm good for about five mil, but *seven-fifty?*"

I'm really hoping that figure will make this the end of

whatever he wants. He asked for face time with Kevin. I provided it.

Behind him, Kevin eyes me and makes his way to Solomon's back office.

On the dance floor, some dude I see around from time to time is all hugged up on Eugenia. That fool must want my foot to hug up on his nuts.

"Yeah, dude is cold," I say to Show. "I really had to be on my shit to bring him on board." Between my mother's credit and finances, Solomon's connections and finances, my own longtime savings and Georgetown connections, we came out with around eighteen million dollars. That brought Kevin to the negotiating table last year. The strong concept of young black money and its promise for MoneyCruncher kept him there.

"What do you have going on tomorrow, man? Come kick it with us. You've been so busy with all your little groupies screaming your name, niggas can't find you. Let's pop some bottles, boy."

I shake my head. "Can't, man. We've got too much going on. It's do or die time around here. No sleeping at the wheel. You know how it is. You just make sure you have your script ready for Monday. Kevin doesn't miss shit. Any questions, text me." I offer a grip.

"Oh, I see how it is. I can't get no play, huh? Why don't I slice me a piece of all this action?" he asks, his gaze skipping across the custom-designed ceiling of Taste. He's been here several times, so he's not seeing anything new. "Maybe they could use some threads around here. A Taste Chocolatier line of shirts or silk scarves. Explore fedoras."

"Bring us the proposal, and the board will discuss it."

His eyes examine me over the gleam of his diamond grill. "Since when did you and me start using 'proposals' and shit?"

A heavy-ass thud rocks across my body with every drop

of my heart. "Since this got bigger than me, Show. Stop tripping. You know I'll help you come up in any way I can." I throw my arms around his and give him a squeeze.

"Thanks, homie. That means a lot," he says in my ear. "But nothing is bigger than you and me."

His arms locked around me, when I attempt to pull back, I can't separate myself. For a moment, this embrace is a little too damn long and it almost seems he's making a silent point. Finally, he lets go.

For a moment, I'm too miffed at what the hell just happened and can't walk off. Instead, we stand here peeping each other a couple of extra seconds.

"Nigga, what the hell was that?"

"I'm just fucking with you, dude. You know that. 'Til Monday." He laughs to break up this weirdness.

But on my way to the back, in my head, he still grips me. I take that with me to where Kevin waits in Solomon's office. He's freeze-framed on the security screen the image of Eugenia being carried off the stage.

"That right there is called a liability," Kevin starts. "He won't even wait until he returns from Alabama. You know we're getting a call about this from his lawyers, probably sometime tomorrow. Miracle will not waste time. She's probably already sent it to him," Kevin says in reference to Solomon.

"It wasn't supposed to go down like that. Usually, when we do it, it's cool. It was cool this time with Eugenia."

"Because you know her, which we'll address that part later. But for now, do you know who that guy was who picked her up? The mayor's grandson. The mayor's grandson tried to carry the ex-wife of a prominent banker out of the building." He stares at me. "What if that had been uglier? We know Eugenia, and she seemed to take it in stride. But what if next time, it's some chick we don't know? And she goes running to the press talking about how somebody in our establishment assaulted her and we didn't do enough? Or what if one of our security had roughed him up? Do you know how that headline would read? Not 'Explore Kicked Out a Guy Who Assaulted a Poor Lady'. No. It'll read 'Precious White Boy Got Battered at a Black-Owned Establishment.'"

This Negro pulls no punches, and for that, I respect the hell out of him.

"Kevin, I feel you. But this could have popped off with anybody, anywhere. Are you making this bigger than it really is?"

"I wish I was, man. But we literally just dug you out of the shithouse a couple of weeks ago after all that business from Valentine's night with your friend, Roach, and the underage minor thing. I crossed the line my damn self by punching him out. Now I'll have to explain this dance contest thing to Solly. Twice in six months, Kee? This shit only happens when you bring your friends. And who the hell is this Showtime dude anyway?"

"He's got a record. But we can do something with him."

"What he wants sounds like a money laundering operation. Tell me he doesn't deal."

Kevin waits.

I swallow. Like I said before, I never asked questions. Doesn't mean I didn't know.

"So you're standing on the stage with a drug dealer, and what happens when the papers catch wind of that? You're not in B'More anymore."

"I built Explore, and I appreciate you two doing it with me. I understand your concerns. We can make sure our activities stay kosher. But you and Solomon can't dictate who can and can't come into the Hamptons, man. That's some bullshit."

"Bruh, I get it. You love B'More the way I love New York, and you want to bring your folks with you. But you're not in a strong enough position to do that yet. And even when you are, you *still* can't fuck with D-boys who are active in the streets."

"The whole premise behind black adventure is more exposure for *every*one, Kevin. Not just the ones with college degrees."

"Keenan, you're smarter than that. This doesn't have shit to do with college. And everything to do with liability, which he is one. We can have a damn good party, but no more off-script, last-minute anything. Everything from here on out is planned and by the book. Tell me, why did you come to Solomon and me for help getting Explore off the ground?"

I rub the area over the sinking sands in my chest. "You know why, man."

"Yes, I do. But apparently, you forgot. You didn't start a company with Showtime, or Roach, or any of your other friends from the 'hood, and you didn't start Explore *in* the 'hood either. And we all know why you didn't. You brought your ass to the Hamptons and asked for our help, so you could play on another level, which means you're playing by new rules. *We're* your partners. And we chose you. Not them. Remember that." He raises up from where he sits atop Solomon's desk. "As for Sheldon Rouse's ex-wife…"

"Man, don't start. Why are all of you so scared of that Negro?"

Kevin spins a world globe at the edge of Solomon's desk. "It's not fear. It's shared interests. Yes, I've beefed with Sheldon in the past, and with his wife. But things change. Our interests change. Yours have changed. I can't tell you what to do or who to fuck," he says, as the world turns beneath his fingertips, "but I'm starting to wonder if you understand where your interests lie."

14

I LEAN IN

EUGENIA

I'd forgotten.

It's been too long.

Motherhood and divorce and work and the devastation of losing yet another baby drained me of life and shut off the music of me. But even before then, Sheldon would question why I was dancing so raunchy in public. He loved my "sophi-stiratchet" side in closed quarters, but not in front of his family and banking colleagues. He would chastise me under his breath as uncouth and "inappropriate" when I got buck at his family reunion. So I toned it down to become the classy, contained wife the banker wanted. It still wasn't enough.

For now anyway, I shut out those memories. Tonight, the rhythm and the beat have found and revived Old Eugenia.

My eyes closed, sweating bullets, whipping my head, I'm in my zone and dancing by myself. Suddenly, arms slide around my waist and pull me backward. He's flipped on a switch, and now I can't stop grinning and dancing. He left whatever he was doing and came to dance with me now, and this song is perfect. My hands up over my head, these hips keep thrusting.

Snatched out of my little stupor, I'm hoisted off my feet.

"Yeah, that's a hard fucking no."

At hearing Keenan's irritated voice, I'm shocked. It wasn't him behind me. Slinging my arms around his neck, I start cracking up.

"Say, mane, did you see me dancing with her! You're being real disrespectful!" some other guy bellows.

Still carrying me, Keenan glares at the guy. "Do you see where she is right now? She don't have any other dancing partner than me, buddy! Keep it moving. It's plenty of 'em 'round here. Just *not* this one, bruh."

Keenan smacks my ass hard.

"Oow-ha-howw!"

"You just got in some heat with a random, and now you're on somebody else?"

"I thought it was you!"

"Mhmm. All that lip you just gave me about your co-workers…" He brings his hand back and spanks me again.

I bolt up. "You've got one more time!"

"Girl, don't threaten me."

"Stunt Man!" women call from behind velvet ropes.

"I want a whipping, Stunt Man!" another yells.

"Do me!"

"My turn!"

"Lucky bitch."

Princess appears, beaming at me as she trails us. Once upon a time, in our late twenties, when we could all go out, we were closing down these Saturday nights with our husbands. But things change. Time to turn the page.

Keenan marches out of the dining room, through the lobby, bouncing me over his shoulder. "What are you still doing out this late? You are somebody's mama." He tickles me between my legs, forcing me to squirm. "You ought to be ashamed of yourself."

"That's not what you were saying the other day in Chicago."

"You weren't splitting and spinning like that either." He approaches the valet. "Folks, please bring these ladies their car. She's had enough for tonight."

Crisp Atlantic air floods my nostrils, flows into my lungs, circulating through me. Unlike the Hamptons nights taunting me in my loneliness last summer, full of satiated couples and unattainable parties, this night embraces me.

Keenan sets me down. "For the last damn time, good-night." He turns to Princess and hugs her. "You're my new best friend." Over her shoulder, he stares at me. "I'm keeping your sister-in-law in my back pocket."

Tonight, despite all the excitement, I've still noticed how Princess's laugh wavers between dry and creaky, and dry and gutsy, as if she's scraping the last bits of her soul for whatever laughter is left in it.

"I doubt you'll need me anymore, Keenan. Looks like she's finding some act right."

"Shh, don't jinx it." Keenan takes P's hand, kisses it.

Soon as he does, Princess breaks into gagging, and her lungs whine, seeming to claw her ribs to escape.

"Princess, woman, what is going on? Why do your lungs sound like that?"

"Do I need to grab some water or some help?" a concerned Keenan asks.

"No. No big deal. I'm fi…" She punches out a few more coughs and stifles the rest that still knock on her trachea.

"That's not true." I've heard that cough. "Let's get you to the house."

The SUV is brought around, and our cell phones are returned to us. Keenan and I help her into the passenger seat of her Range Rover, with her pushing us off the whole time. I hop behind the wheel to drive.

"If you can't make it in the morning, I understand. But I'll only accept the excuse you're helping her. Nothing else," Keenan says.

I'm shocked when I turn away from checking P to find Keenan reaching over me, strapping me into my own seatbelt.

"She'll be there," a raspy Princess answers for me.

"Apparently, the two of you have a way of communicating," I say, "so we'll be in touch if plans change."

"All right, gorgeous. Take care of my wing woman over there." He withdraws out of the truck only partially. Half of him lingers in front of me, his mohawk giving off its scents of rose water and almonds, eyes filled with expectation. Him pausing at my mouth forms a question.

"Go ahead. Get it over with," Princess mutters.

"I can't," I murmur. My hand against his chest, I press him away from me. My court case. Sheldon. The judge. There are cameras out here now.

We must be in *The Matrix*, the way I seem to punch out several layers of him.

"Keenan—"

He hauls the rest of himself away. "In the morning then. You only have a few hours. Rest up." He closes the door on me.

"What was that about?" A dissatisfied P fusses between giving me directions to the house and coughing. "You couldn't kiss the man goodnight?"

"One of my core issues I'm addressing in my case is poor relationships and choices in men. My therapist says—"

"Aaggh," P retorts, half-gagging, half-disagreeing, "that's bullshit. You're scarrrre..." She hacks in a way that has me suspicious.

"It's not bullshit! Keenan just showed up on my doorstep days ago. I can't start gallivanting around with some stranger while I'm showing the judge I'm more responsible. On top of that, he's young. He's into me now, but he'll move on to someone else tomorrow, and he'll leave me looking stupid. Oh, that'll show the judge how mature and wise I am. No, ma'am."

"Did he not just march you past all those women? Make a left up here." She clears her throat a few times to continue. "Genie, I know you have your custody situation, but Keenan is feeling you. That's not a hit-and-quit. If you were just ass, he would wait until you get home and text you *after* the club. I peeped him peeping you last summer. You remember when I told you?"

"I do." I recall thinking he was a handsome guy, but my mind was on another life raft swimming back to Sheldon. "He's smart but immature."

"What you consider to be his immaturity does you a lot of good. You look and sound way better than you did last night."

We ride through the wrought-iron gates of the Rouses' property and park in the circular drive. I shut off the truck and turn to Princess. "You don't."

Before she can stop me, I grab her purse, thrust it open, and immediately find what I'd hoped not to.

In my hands, the lightweight fabric is a heavy gravestone.

"Oh, Princess." Realization shovels dirt onto my chest. "You shouldn't have been out there tonight. God, no."

This explains the drinking from a flask today, skipping out to a club, leaving the kids with Roland or their grandparents, and doing the kinds of things we haven't done much of in years.

"I'm going to spend every minute being alive." That's the steadiest her voice has sounded all night.

My gaze stumbles to hers, and I step into her inevitable tomb of acceptance.

Not her.

I don't dare ask how much longer she has. I wouldn't want anybody, friend or doctor, putting a period on my existence.

Heaving her bloody handkerchief from my hands, she places it back in her purse and covers my hand with hers. Our heads fall against each other, and we clasp for dear life, in this quiet space, the last twelve years of babies and marriage and laughter and hope, gasping and gulping for every yesterday we lived and every tomorrow we still haven't.

"I'm glad you called this weekend. I needed this," she whispers, on the brink of what might be a breakdown.

"Me, too."

"Well, obviously." She snorts. "Only Roland and Ma know. He refuses to accept it. He's still taking me to experts."

I nod my understanding. "Whatever I can do…"

She shoves our joined hands into my lap. "Do it for yourself." The iron of her eyes sharpens me. "I'm fine. I've had an amazing time. Roland and I have had a storybook life from when we were kids. I'm at peace. You still haven't found yours. Yet."

Just like that, I'm stunned at the disappearance of her hands from mine and she gets out. As if she has decided there is a cutoff to the amount of sadness she will allow in one night.

Inside the guesthouse, still reeling from the devastation, I peel off my jumpsuit in the dark and take a quick, hot shower. The last person in my life to die of lung cancer was one of my favorite clients. With no parents left, and no eligible family, her child wound up being placed for adoption. Before that, it was my grandmother.

At 1:38 a.m., I want to do a little journaling and write

down these thoughts, but my body is shutting down. Onto the bed, I throw myself and land on a body part.

"Ow!" my son's voice cries out.

I switch the lamp on. "Hadar, what are you doing in here? I thought you were in the tent."

"We watch shark movie," he mumbles. "Mm, bad dream."

"Baby, what have I told you about watching those movies too late at night?"

He's already sound asleep again.

I half laugh, half pout. I'm exhausted, and Hadar is a horrible sleeper. But this might be one of the last times it'll ever happen. In what must be a laughable symbolism of our relationship, he hogs the entire bed, and I make a tiny space for myself on the edge to squeeze in.

Terror awakens a fifteen-year-old me.

"What time you get in here last night?"

"I was home at 11:30, Daddy." My eyes strain in my head while they discover his gun against my cheek.

"You's a lie. You just creeped in here. I heard ya."

My chest is a torture device with it wrenching out each one of my breaths.

"Get that gun off her, Gene," my mother attempts cajoling him from the door. "She's been in that bed all night."

My brothers wake up.

"Daddy, stop," Nelson pleads.

"You're scaring them," Mama joins.

"Come on, Daddy, let me make you some grits and biscuits," my older brother, Gene, Jr., offers to distract him.

From my eyeball to Daddy's, I make no sudden moves, and ease off the barrel of his shotgun. Then, I sink to my bed and hide under the covers. Next to me, another smaller body lies down and circles his arm around me, my youngest brother, O'dell.

Light rapping on my door frees me from the torment of sleep. Twenty years later, my worst nightmares and memories still haunt me. My biggest regret is still a prison cell. No amount of therapy has liberated me.

"I'll be in the kitchen with coffee," Princess says from the other side of the door. Her voice ropes me back to the present. It's 6:30 a.m.

How on earth does she do it? She's *got* to be tired. I'm tired. My pooped-out muscles drag from all the activity yesterday. Every inch I move reminds me I am definitely not in high school anymore.

And still, a new energy burgeons at the core of me.

Am I excited? Nervous, even?

How many years has it been since I've gone on an actual date? Not a hook-up. Even last summer, pregnant by my on-gain, off-again lover, he and I didn't exactly "date." A construction contractor with good dick but who has older children of his own, he agreed to give me his sperm for a baby, and I would absolve him of any obligations and take on sole financial responsibility. It turned out to be ectopic. Not exactly the stuff of swooning romances.

But still, I tote all my previous failures out of bed with me. A thread inside seems to pull me through it all, onto my feet.

He didn't tell me what we were doing for this "private lesson," so I throw on jeans and a Hensley over a black bikini from way back when that I'm shocked I can still fit. Wrestling my bird's nest of 3A-type wavy Afro, I pull it into a messy topknot.

"You look perfect," Princess says at the kitchen table. She closes a book in which she writes and picks it up.

Seeing her so serene, so seemingly unbothered now by things the rest of us worry about, sends shudders through the walls holding my heart. "So do you." I shove some cash, my phone, and my ID in my pocket. Nothing else. "I'm not putting on makeup."

"I don't think he went all the way to Chicago to see your makeup."

Sheldon's mother enters carrying the morning paper. "Good morning, dear." Her hug and kiss on my cheek are warm, as is her gentle chamomile scent. Always has been.

"Morning, Mrs. Rouse." I kiss her cheek.

She's never made me feel unwelcome and has always been lovely, has offered me whatever I needed. And during this year, she has been a godsend, joining Hadar and me for days-long visits and acting as a mediator between Sheldon and me. But I am not ignorant to the fact she didn't think her son should have married me in the first place.

"Where are you ladies off to?"

"Morning walk at the lake," P answers. "We should be back in time for church."

"That sounds good and relaxing. I'll get the kids' breakfast. They'll be ready when you come back."

"Thanks, Ma."

The embrace between the two of them is completely different. Princess is indeed one of Professor Rouse's daughters now, her *first* daughter-in-law. There was a time when I would have given my right arm to have that approval. The unfilled chasm of never receives it still lies open in me.

I'm grateful that Sheldon and Chrissy absented themselves yesterday evening. They leave the boys here at the Rouse compound, while Chrissy's and Princess's daughters go to the Page residence. Chrissy's mother takes her baby so she and Sheldon can go be alone. All this house-hopping among the well-to-do isn't much different than back home in Chicago.

"What were you writing?" I ask P in the truck on the way over.

"A book to Halle. All the things she'll need to know… that nobody ever told us." She lets out a dry chuckle.

The humor of that gets ensnared in the bramble bush of despair and doesn't quite make it out of me as a laugh. "That's a whole lot of book right there."

P smiles. "If she were to ever publish it, it could be a bestseller."

"Isn't that the cruelty of life? Famous and well-known once we can no longer benefit from our exertions?"

"My daughter will benefit and that's the wealth for me," she reminds me with a glance that's playful and stern.

She's handling this too well, too strong.

Droves of questions flock my mind, a sea of blackbirds all flying in one direction. I'm not brave enough to ask a single one.

"Thank you, Princess." I'm unable to say that without the reason for my thanks squeezing emotion up my chest.

"I'm glad you called. Thank you."

At the sight of Keenan, I'm forced to take several breaths.

Behind him is the rising sun that already blazes over an endless ocean horizon in the east. Down below the cliff where he stands lies miles of sprawling, lush, lazy Hamptons trees and marshes along beaches, boats, jetties, docks and the trappings of an existence that has, somehow, always evaded me.

Perfectly relaxed, he dons a pair of aviators, cargo shorts, and his kinky mohawk. I'm just now noticing how ink curls up his calf and along his thigh in the form of a flaming sword, Keenan awaits.

"Why does that boy want me and all my issues?" I ask, more to myself than her.

P scoffs. "That *man* wants the crazy ass from last night who forgets all her issues."

Next to him sits a giant parachute, waiting to take us off the edge.

"I'm not riding on that."

"Yes, you are." Princess removes her seatbelt and grabs her book. "Let him reintroduce you to the woman you are, instead of who you struggle to be for everybody else." She gets out.

He comes and opens my door. "Princess, woman, you're the gift that keeps on giving."

Ignoring him, I point at the parachute. "I'm not doing that."

He reaches in and unfastens my seatbelt, his spirited aroma of salty ocean, cool cologne, hair gel, and new clothes almost nullifies my objections. "Don't knock it until you try it."

I start to reassert what I just said when he places his open hand between us. His face brushing mine, the spearmint gum and morning coffee on his breath greets me. The coffee beans in his eyeballs speak to mine, and his thick, luscious lips move against mine. "Don't knock *me* until you try me."

I'm still hesitant, but that cocky gleam in his eye has a conversation with parts of me that don't hesitate. I give him my hand.

One of his Explore staff comes out to help him prep the gear.

"Hadar will probably be looking for you after church, when the family meets at Sharon's around two," Princess says, dropping multiple warnings.

"I'll make sure she's there," Keenan reassures her. "Discreetly."

A tickled Princess yanks me to her and whispers, "You'd better enjoy the hell out of this. *Discreetly.*"

She takes out her book, a pen, her coffee tumbler, and a blanket, lays it all out under a tree.

"You're going to hang out here?" Keenan asks her.

"If I may." That throaty, ashen voice, so full of resolve, upends *my* resolve the more I hear it. "This is perfect."

Keenan turns to his employee. "Vincent, will you hang out and make sure Mrs. Rouse has whatever she needs?"

"That won't be necessary, Keenan. I'd prefer the alone time."

With a vexed expression, not quite understanding what that's about, his nod is slow. "Okay."

"P, call me if you need anyth…?"

Her resolute eyes slice through me again, and her perfect peace meets my naked terror. "I will not."

I fight not to fling my arms around her and hug P back to me, to all our innocence and ignorance and foolishness of yesterday, from this stark and aged mountain of wisdom where she stands today.

"Um," Keenan starts, clearing his throat and reaching for me, "I'm guessing you've never paraglided. It's not hard at all. We'll be seated in those harnesses. I'll steer us." Right now, he slides his hand around my hip, where his thumb hooks into one of my jean loops and steers me. "You look good."

"I wasn't sure if I dressed appropriately. I didn't know what—"

He circles my throat with a hand, and Keenan pauses, eyes parachuting into my own.

Again.

My every breath traverses my airway underneath his thumb at my throat's base.

And I'm trying to figure out why he stands here staring at me like this, expectant.

"No cameras now," he finally murmurs.

I also hear the rest of what he doesn't say: No Sheldon.

In my chest, the fist of my heart opens and closes between us. The next time it opens, I reach for him, stand on my toes, and lean in, press on his mouth my failures and disappointments and devastation and heartache and hope and fearlessness and fear. Pull his lips onto mine, taste his confidence and adventure and passion and sensuality, suck his tongue, let my hands rest on his chest, over his heart. And I come to him this time.

He cups my head. His tongue circling mine, existence encircling me, he inhales me. Until I fly off the cliff, my body and soul soaring, on fire, my innermost parts screaming for him.

"Good girl," he murmurs into my mouth. "You're perfect, as always."

His voice dismantles my electric fence, however thin it is.

An Explore employee walks up and holds out a harness.

In my mind, I try to maintain some semblance of control and not get wrapped up in this. He's a thirty-two-year-old hot-blooded black man, seven years my junior, with his pick of any woman around here. There's no telling how many of those overeager girls he's brought here for his little "thrill rides."

"I remember you telling me over Christmas you didn't like water," he says.

"So you decided to torture me by bringing me to more of it?" I ask.

Shaking the belts on my harness, he chuckles. "Yes and no. When I torture you, it'll be the good kind."

"There won't be a 'when,'" I correct him playfully.

Keenan's solid arms wrap around me and finish connecting belts to one another. "If there wasn't a 'when' you wouldn't be here."

"I came because you were nice to my son yesterday." We're back to talking shit.

Those eyes are back to undoing me. "You came because you're still thinking about Christmas Eve and Chicago."

"Smart-ass." I try to peer through the cords, over my shoulder, for one final glance at Princess. "P, I'll call you la—"

Keenan kicks something around us, and suddenly the ground disappears from under me.

"Oh my God!" The water, the earth, safety, and comfort are suddenly so far from my feet that dangle in the air. "I can't look!" I slap my hands against my eyes. "I'm about to die!"

Starting with my heart that nosedived out of me soon as we flew off the edge.

15

YES, SIR

EUGENIA

His laughter is filled with genuine amusement at me. "Put your hands, down, Eugenia. You'll miss the view."

"I can't believe I let you do this to me!" Helpless, my legs swing in the air, precious Earth so far away, the morning winds carrying us.

"You're going to be up here for a while. May as well enjoy it." He reaches from behind me and tugs at my hand over my eyes. "Come on."

Through a tiny crack of my eye, morning glory stretches below us, slow and tranquil in the tall, full trees and swaying marshes, so peaceful and inoffensive it seems to laugh at my panic.

"So what do you think?"

"I might enjoy it more if I wasn't afraid I'll die."

"The best views are up high. That requires some risk and fear, but don't you think this is worth it?" His voice is low, sensual, in the same cajoling tone it was Christmas Eve night on the boat, when he put me on an elevator and told me to close my eyes.

I open my other eyelid slowly and peek around, at a vast, endless Earth, so picturesque, my panic feels foolish. "I suppose it's not so bad once you get used to it."

"Not much different than hiking up a mountain and scoping out the three-sixty view. Do you hike? I know you run, and I learned for myself you're in pretty good shape, so I don't see why you wouldn't hike."

In my peripheral vision, he tugs cords on either side of us.

Now I'm laughing at the memory of him a few days ago, how my veins almost jogged right out of my skin at the sight of him running next to me. "Did you really follow me all the way from my apartment?"

I relax and realize this aerial view of Hamptons' compounds, manicured properties, and sailboats, I've only seen one other time—when Keenan flew me on a helicopter.

"I did. Hadn't come ready for a chase, wasn't wearing the right shoes, but like with anything else, it wasn't going to stop me."

I can't see him in the tandem seating behind me, but his voice is relaxed, his arms maneuvering the parachute, as if nothing holds him down and he feeds off this weightlessness.

"Why did you put that much energy into somebody who asked you not to? Who has other obligations?"

"Are you using your obligations as excuses?" His arm shoots out suddenly, over my shoulder, and he points ahead of us. "And while you make excuses, are you missing out on the world?"

We sail over tiny sailboats and yachts that float atop sparkling water, reflecting the sun's ascension over the ocean. We must be at least two or three miles out from where we started. All of it is a stunning dose of nature I didn't realize my depression needed.

"Why do you care, Keenan?"

"Honestly, Eugenia, I won't bullshit you. I'm not sure.

What I am certain of is how I like showing you things you're afraid of. Your surprised breaths you take when you come across a new situation, and your disbelieving ass struggles with it, but then you like it and forget to be scared. It tells me there's a whole lot of woman in you who's clawing to escape but you're too chickenshit to open up and let her out. I like opening you up."

"Don't you mean you like the good sex we have?" I huff. "Just call this what it is." May as well not be dumb.

I'm wearing a helmet, and suddenly, his hand slides underneath it, along my scalp to grab the roots of my hair.

"So my touch doesn't throw your red blood cells for a loop? That's what you're saying? That when you pulled up this morning and saw the parachute, you didn't feel one iota of adrenaline? And when you heard me outside your job last week, your heart didn't jump one inch? You mean us hanging here in the air together, the whole world right under our feet, doesn't make you wonder what else we could put beneath us and conquer?"

His fingers massage as much of my scalp as they can reach, sending my eyes rolling up to my brow bones, the juices between my pussy lips tickling me before it puddles up in my panties.

"What else I can do to you." His fingers release my scalp, slide to my neck, and rub out the tension. "You know the sex wouldn't be good if you weren't feeling all this in your chest right now."

Gliding over marshes and dunes, large houses, and countryside, the emerald landscape bordering the coastline, my bones, muscles, and body give in to the weightlessness. It's so relaxing after a while, nowhere to go, nothing to possibly worry about way up here, where the world has stood still and I could probably fall asleep floating.

"I see how this has its benefits. You started doing these

outdoor stunts when you were young, pretending you were the Dark Knight," I smile and recall.

"You remembered."

"How could anybody forget that?"

"Ma would finally send my brother or sister to come find me, usually on the roof of our projects, where I could see the stars and airplanes better."

That's not all he told me Christmas Eve. "And you never joined sports or the military because you don't like discipline or rules."

"Shit, all right now, girl, I *can* figure out how to snatch you up before we get off this thing," he threatens between laughs.

"You'd better not!"

"So where'd you learn how to do all that ballet shit you pulled out last night? While you were letting guys spank you."

Now it's me who chuckles. "Next time, don't start what you can't finish, player."

Our laughter comes so easily way up here, far from it all.

"I did any and every activity I could as a teenager so I never had to be at home—ballet at the Y, drill team, student council, debate." I don't want thoughts of Daddy and my brothers or Mama to darken what's been an unexpectedly bright weekend. "Soon as I entered middle school, I signed up for everything I could. Turns out, dancing came natural to me. I could do it in my sleep. A few minutes of learning a move or steps and I picked it up fast. So I was dance team captain in middle school and high school."

"Why didn't you keep it up?"

"I tried to in college, made the varsity dance team at Northwestern. But it wasn't my passion. Helping my people was. My grades and internships were more important to me.

Plus I had to work so I could afford extras. I quit the team in my second year when I didn't have any more time."

Keenan has fallen radio silent.

We descend closer to Earth, and noisy, hectic reality.

"How will we land? How does this work?" I ask.

Still, nothing.

I can't see behind me, but his hands still grip the cords.

"Keenan?"

"L-lean back before we approach the ground, use your running legs to stay up and not tumble forward," he says.

We don't move as fast as a plane landing, but the anxiety is similar as the world comes closer. Ahead of us, a jetty juts from a forest into bay waters.

Faster, we hit the ground running. In our seated position, we fight to stay on our feet, for the parachute not to drag us.

"Pull back. Pull back," Keenan instructs.

I follow his commands, using every shred of strength I didn't know I had, to pound my legs against the earth so the speed of the parachute doesn't drag us forward. Leaning backward, pounding my feet on the grass, pressing against the force of gravity, an energy of strength shoots through me.

Yeah, I'm still on my feet. I'm damn strong.

Into the damp marshes, we skid, the parachute collapsing ahead of us.

"Whooo!" he howls, his powerful legs slowing us down. "Damn, that feels good! How'd you like it?"

The exhilaration is a shot in my heart and accelerates my brain cells. Heart thumping, adrenaline pumping through me, that trip injected me with a dose of natural vigor coffee can't touch.

"Haaaa," I exhale. "I can't describe that."

The serene setting of high grass and clusters of trees contrasts with the meteor shower still spraying through my body. Ahead of us is a clearing. This time, no Explore staff await us. No businesses in sight, just a stretch of soft grass lining marshy saltwater, tall, wide trees, and a small clapboard cottage. Not far away is an in-ground fiberglass rock pool connected to a steaming jacuzzi. This area seems exclusive and private.

"Would you do it again?" he asks while freeing himself from the harness and safety belts.

"Maybe. If I were put in the situation again and I didn't have a choice."

He begins unfastening me. He's in no hurry to move his hands that casually linger above my butt cheeks, slide over my stomach, brush over my chest, effectively challenging my wall of discipline.

Keenan straightens and stands erect before me, close enough for his chest to sweep my breasts. "And if you did have a choice?"

Before I can answer, he pivots and grabs the parachute, folds it up.

"Can I help with that?"

"You can grab the harnesses and helmets."

We start walking inland, toward the cottage, down a narrow dirt path.

"The view was breathtaking."

"The view still is breathtaking." He shoots a glance at me. "It's cool to be far away from all the grind, isn't it? To feel like you're on top of the world, where you see how small our problems and hang-ups really are. It's like I'm capable of rising above it all. I don't know of a better feeling than that."

I scoff. "Wait until you have your first kid and he or she smiles at you for the first time."

Again, he seems skeptical while examining me from the corner of his eye. "What happens when your kid starts smiling at somebody else?"

The thought fills me with horror. "I'll worry about that when I get to it."

"I'm nobody's daddy, but even when I have kids, I'm not sure I want them to be the whole of my life. I would not want to be the whole of theirs."

He throws the parachute, helmets, radio, and harnesses into the back of a jeep and starts toward the pool where large food baskets wait on a small table.

"Why do I feel like you're addressing me?"

"Not just you. I'm addressing all Black parents who keep their kids held in so tight they don't have any experiences. Then, out of nowhere, at eighteen, push their kids into a world they don't know squat about. Meanwhile, wealthy white kids learn to explore and be curious before they're ten. And by college, they're running circles around us."

"Your mother didn't hold you in so tight?" I ask.

"She was too busy with her new construction executive job, which suited me perfectly. Allowed me a lot of freedom. My older sister tried instead, and she was always too…"

Genuine curiosity places me on edge in my wait for him to finish.

"Come on." He seems a smidge agitated now.

"And what if some Black parents just want to protect their kids from a cruel world as long as they can?"

We arrive at the little cottage nestled in a cluster of trees. I leap at the surprise of his hands landing on my hips.

"Cruel for who?" he murmurs. "The child, or you? And are you really protecting them when you deprive them of their sense of freedom they'll need to thrive?"

He lifts one of the food covers, and I cover my open mouth with my hand.

"I wasn't sure if you would want breakfast or lunch. It's still kind of early, not yet ten."

I stare down at the chocolate pork chops, the same meal I ate on Christmas Eve when Keenan approached me at Taste.

"You were sitting at a booth by yourself reading the news, and you wouldn't stop ordering this chocolatini with no alcohol. It was annoying me."

Our light laughter joins the early summer wind rustling the trees.

"I wasn't there to get buzzed. Just to enjoy a good meal and a quiet evening."

"From the moment you walked in, the evening was anything but quiet. The bus boys in the back wouldn't stop talking about how pretty you were. I had to go out and see for myself, so I used the drink thing as cover. Then I remembered seeing you that summer with Hadar and Sheldon."

Our chuckles continue.

He takes my hand and flips open the other baskets that reveal breakfast—chocolate chip pancakes, chocolate waffles, chocolate bacon.

I crack up. "Wow, chocolate bacon."

"Hungry?"

"Actually, not right now." I stare at how heavenly the scenery is. "In Chicago, even on hikes, I rarely go into setting like this. I want to walk around. Do you mind?"

He shakes his head. "We can do whatever you want, beautiful."

We start off down the narrow dirt trail again, in the opposite direction, leading way from the marsh and toward the woods.

"So your love of risk and thrills drove you to start Explore Adventures, Mr. Invincible."

"I suppose in my head, I'm still Batman, the Dark Knight. Leading our people to new life adventures, exposing them to new things so we're not always relegated to the same shit."

He pushes up low-hanging branches that block our path,

clearing it for me to walk underneath. "What about you, Ms. Eugenia? Tell me more about you wanting to help your people."

"What more is there to say? The highlight of my day is pointing my clients in the right direction. Especially when I run into them months or even years later and they call my name in Target or at a food stand." I reminisce now and savor the warmth flooding my chest. "They wave me down and go, 'Hey, Ms. Rouse, I just wanted to say thank you. I earned my GED.' Or they tell me their kid is graduating soon or won a full ride to school. Or they found a good job. Or they bought a house. I didn't do all the hard work. They did. But I was the person they needed in their life at the right time, who pointed them in the right direction. It's not the sexiest job, and I'm not jumping from cliffs—"

"But in your own way, you are. Throwing yourself into other folks' problems every day, giving up your emotional energy. Our community needs the selflessness of people like you."

He has a way with words and metaphors. "Thank you for that."

"It's true. And you should probably also be praised more often, swept off your feet more often, spoiled more often."

What does that even feel like anymore?

Maybe he didn't hear me the other day when I told him I can't have kids, and he just said he wants them.

"Keenan, I appreciate all this, but you really need to know—"

My feet tumble aside, and I'm yanked into his arms. "No, I don't need to know shit."

Those perfect lips take mine again. Not soft, not hard, but insistent. Nipping and sucking my lip, pushing his tongue in my mouth to find mine, he sucks me into him. The pressure of his mouth defies me, *dares* me, to come out of myself.

Deeper, more intense, we bite harder, tug longer.

"And fuck your appreciation." He nibbles my lip, clutches it—clutches me—and lets go. His teeth move to my jaw where his tongue licks, and the sensations tingle in my nipples and underneath my belly button. With his head, he nudges mine aside to access the valley of my neck. And grips my skin.

"Ahhh…"

This man does, in fact, work me like I'm his toy. My titties and womb flutter like those leaves hanging over my head, every time his tongue samples me.

"No!" I suddenly snap back to my senses. "No!" I push on the hills of Keenan's chest. "No passion marks."

He rises from my neck, sweeps his tongue up my lips, sweeps my brain clear of all else. The band holding back my messy knot slides off, and his fingers fist all my wild crop, snapping my head back.

Keenan's eyeballs examine mine. "Come to Europe with me. Give me ten days to put anything on you I want."

Fuck. "No."

"Eugenia."

"*No*, Keenan, this is a temporary thrill for you, and I'm too old for that shit," I whisper against his lips, under the shade and dancing shadows of these trees. Unable to turn from his magnetic mouth, I defy my own damn words.

He grips my nipples through my bra, thumbs them like they're remote controls to my womanhood. "You don't believe that. If you did, why did you come here? So I could play with you some more?"

More of me dissolves in him every time his teeth grab my lip.

"My sister-in-law—"

"Bullshit. You like how I play with you." He sneaks his hand under my shirt and pushes up my bra. "Your 'hood ass likes it rough. You're wild. And in your heart, you want a wild boy. You try to cover it up with that little 'mommy' act, but you can't hide from me." Keenan drops to my bare breasts. He sucks me the same way he kisses, making demands of my body while he takes it hostage. Spontaneously, my chest thrusts out for him to put more of his mouth on me.

Keenan wastes no time hoisting me up, and I sling my legs around his waist. One of my nipples between his teeth, his breaths shallow and quick on my skin, he carries me back to the house with all the intensity of a panther carrying meat.

"Inside or out?" he asks, a glint in his eye hinting he already knows.

"Outside."

As soon as we hit the jacuzzi, with none of that romantic pretense, he gropes at my jeans, and I jerk at his cargo shorts, both of us barely breathing.

Down my butt crack, and into my folds, he slips his fingers.

"Mmph. You're ready for this dick."

I pull out his fingers, and they're fully soaked with my essence that he slides over his tongue.

"Have you been with anybody else?" I ask. Reminding myself I'm not twenty anymore, I stop him from entering me. At forty, what am I doing out here? One of many, another notch on his belt.

"No, baby." He carries me into the jacuzzi and lowers us. "I've been waiting for my boxing champ. And before you ask, no other woman has been here. Not in this tub, not in this pool." The sunlight bouncing off the water illuminates the seriousness in his eyes.

Naked in steaming water, he turns me around, leans me over the top step.

"Don't wet my hair up. I won't be able to explain it."

"You won't be able to explain that limp in your walk either, baby girl," he murmurs, kissing me on my back before he punches into me with a vengeance.

"Uh!" Sharp, sudden, my diaphragm can't snatch in air fast enough.

"Mhmm." His hand on the concrete to anchor us, he slides his other arm around me, up to my throat, locks me in position. "So I'm too young?"

His dick was a superyacht the other two times. But this Negro's got something to prove today.

Stunt Man shoves that thrill ride into me violently.

"Call me too young one more time." On the jacuzzi steps, hot water snakes around our knees and thighs. He lets none of it interfere with him and my pussy. Arms clinging me to him, he yanks me up and down.

"Keenan, no!"

"You love tellin' a nigga no. That's your favorite goddamn word, isn't it. Move ya hands." He spreads my knees wider. In my back that's already sore from last night, he presses a deep arch. *"Open this motherfucker."*

"Ah!"

My pussy parachutes and she's feeling the wind beneath her wings. Those forceful centimeters of his manhood depriving me of my control, I now sail the skies on Keenan's dick. This Negro's got me soaring.

Arms weak, they balance me against Keenan's nuts slapping my ass cheeks with no mercy.

Through clenched teeth comes a mutter. "I'm too young? Listen." His strokes splash in my canal, louder than the jacuzzi's whirling. "Your wet pussy don't think so."

He grips my throat, winds his hips, the head of his dick marking every inch of territory. "Ride this young nigga dick."

"Ah…" My hair loose, wet and hanging over my eyes, titties bobbing, like a fiend, I buck. My thighs clap against his muscles. Holding onto the edge of the hot tub, I open wider for Keenan's shaft to beat my cervix. "Mmm…"

Spasms dance through my womb that creams on his wood.

"That's it. Good girl. Now Imma train your fightin' ass."

"Keenan—"

"No, no, baby. It's 'yes, sir.'" He plunges up and into me like he's unstopping my pipes.

"Nnno…I'm notttt…"

The head of his dick drills close to my heart and crosses my eyes.

"Yes, sir!" he insists.

"*Fuck* youaaah!" I scream, even as this Negro expands my universe.

"Oh, ha-ha, fuck me, huh?" Still anchoring me to him by my throat, he mutters in my ear, "We'll see if it's fuck me when I tie your ass up, baby."

The lift of his pelvis, with me on top of it, hammers that stiff log into my guts and rearranges my perspective.

"Grrr!" I'm disabused of any notion I still have some control.

"Stop wiggling." He yanks my head back. "Yes, sir."

The bang of his pelvis beating on my ass, no mercy, slaps water everywhere.

"Haaa…"

Keenan rolls his hips, feeding me his dick my canal worships. "I can't hear you, what?"

Caging me with one hand, he whips my pussy, and she dances at every lick. I don't want to sing for him and blow his head up.

But my body betrays me. He's awakened my womanhood, broken up my cobwebs, and now he's taking me to glory. Those high-energy thighs pumping, Keenan burrows in, delivering left and right uppercuts in my stomach.

"What you calling this young nigga, Eugenia?"

His dick attacks my G-spot, and doesn't let off of it. Everywhere I squirm, he chases, grinding on my womanhood.

Thighs wide open, no more defenses, him wearing me down, my existence erupts. "Haaaaah! Yes, saaarrrr!"

Electricity explodes across every nerve in me. But he pulls out.

"Keenan!" What the hell?

His tongue in my folds, he starts licking my pink meat.

"Haaa, Keenan!"

"Your pussy taste like chitlins. I'm eatin' it."

"Nno...aaaah!"

"What did I tell you about 'no'?" He proceeds to hold my legs out, and pushes his face and tongue on the pearl of my clit, circles around it, sucking and tonguing it. My legs tremble at his soft taste buds weakening me. He drags his mouth up and down my chitlins, where he digs his tongue in both my openings.

With me facing the ocean, immersed in this Heaven on Earth, Keenan delivers heaven between my thighs. I've dispensed with all the pretense, and now squeeze my legs tight around Keenan's head so he can feast on me. In the folds of my womanhood, dipping and licking, his relentless tongue action takes me on a trip once again. He may as well be shucking corn off a damn cob, the sensations exciting every layer of my womb until my flesh is so tender, and I'm so gone, I can't take it.

Whimpering, I slap behind me, at his shoulders. "Kee..."

Keenan grips tighter, and I swear I hear him whisper, "That's it, Mommy, come on my face."

His nastiness stokes my ecstasy and I convulse. "Fuck!"

He's right.

This buck-wild version of me, he forces her open.

Lifted above the water, my hips and pelvis in his hands, I balance on the concrete and ride his tongue plugging my pussy, charging up every power line of my nerve network, from my cervix to my brain, and release a guttural Sunday morning scream into the trees.

"Asshole." Tremors and sparks still shoot through my being.

Biting my butt cheeks, he kneads my flesh, massaging away my objections. "You didn't like it?"

My legs trembling so hard from overexertion, I lay my head on the wet concrete. "No."

Keenan laughs behind me. "Right. Take time off work and come to Europe with me next week."

I shake my head. It would cut into the next weekend I have with Hadar in a couple of weeks, and I'm not missing that. But also, as good as this has been—the best since my son's father—one of us needs to apply some damn sense.

"Keenan, I can't have kids. You just said you want kids. Where is this going besides good fucking?"

"Who told you that?"

My blocked fallopian tubes, in both sides, and all my fibroids, maybe? My despair last summer when I finally managed to conceive, only for it to be ectopic, leaving me empty in more than my womb? All the universe that has pretty much determined my destiny is to be empty?

A sigh rumbles out of me. "It's complicated."

"Explain it to me."

"No. Besides, I live in Chicago. You live in New York. I have baggage. You don't know me. This has been a lot of fun —I can't tell you how much—but let's stop while we're ahead."

I would never want Hadar to be in this situation, with a woman who can't fulfill his desires. Reaching for a towel, I reach through my hurt and upset that I have to say this, but it's the right thing to do.

I start out of the jacuzzi. Keenan reels me back in.

"You were also homecoming queen," he says behind me. "Twice. Middle school and high school."

No.

"You played basketball and ran track in high school." He slides his hands around my waist and presses his nakedness to mine. "In your yearbook, you said you wanted to be the head of Chicago social services so everybody could have equal access to resources. You graduated from Northwestern with honors. Where you were president of student government."

Tears parachute down my cheeks for that lost girl who now buries that past in the towel.

"When you were young, you lost a few friends who were killed, two of them right next to you, at the community pool, while all of you were swimming. I'm guessing that's why you don't like the water."

Gently, he lowers the towel, circling to the front of me in the water, kissing my forehead, eyes, cheeks, and ending at my nose.

"How did you find out all that?"

"One of my boys in Chicago remembers your brother from middle school. My private investigator did the rest."

"Which brother?"

"The one who's locked up."

Odie, my youngest brother.

"You hired a private investigator to spy on me?" I ask. "The way Sheldon does."

A surprised Keenan takes a moment. "Spy is a strong word."

"What would you call it?" I stare straight at him.

He rolls his eyes and thinks of how to spin that right.

"Intrigued. Figuring out the best way to come at you. And it worked, so I don't regret it."

"Don't do that again."

His eyes trained on me, they don't waver, and he nods. "Yes, ma'am."

His attention drops to my hips, stomach, and thighs, where his fingers play on my flesh in the warm water. "I don't know what the future looks like, or kids, or us living in different cities or any of that. All I know is you take up hella space in a nigga's head. And last night, when ole boy carried you off the stage, I almost lost my fucking mind. That's some new shit for me. Let me see you again before you leave. When do you fly out?"

"Tuesday." Sheldon heads back to Jersey with Hadar on Monday evening. It's possible.

"Take a later flight or something. We're having a kickback Monday evening. Why don't you come through? Kevin and Show will talk some business, but it'll mostly be games, food, and music. Spend the night with me. Let me at this pussy again, make you say shit you don't want to say." He's cracking up before he finishes.

Our laughter is summertime-in-the-Hamptons easy, too easy.

The mellow ocean breeze kisses my bare breasts too easily, tousles the loose curls and kinks of my hair too easily, frees my mind from all rational thought, until my arms thread around his neck and legs connect along his waist, too easily. "I'll think about it."

Keenan tilts my chin so he can gaze through the windows to my universe. "I know what people say. And I don't care. Your crazy is lightning in a nigga's dick."

I press my eyes closed. That hits too close to home. Digs too deep into my graveyard of bones.

"Eugenia."

That word still clangs through my mind.

He must feel its reverberations because he clasps my head with both hands and brings our heads together. "Eugenia."

I can't. The only person who's ever been stuck in my fucked-up world of depression and PTSD with me is me.

"*Look* at me." He licks up my lips and shoots a flamethrower up my body.

Scared as hell, I dare to open up for him to see me, all of me.

"You're a flawless mothafucka, every part of you, at every level, in all your many facets, every fucking glorious one. A diamond, Eugenia. My Black Mystique. Shine for me."

16

EUGENIA JACKSON

KEENAN & EUGENIA

KEENAN

"**D**amn, boy, you can't lift more than that?" my older brother, Desmond, asks in a grunt that night.

"I'm tired, fool. Be grateful I made it here to help your ass."

"Tired from what? Posing for pictures, running around with your shirt off, girls jumping all over your little wee wee?" He eyes me hard.

I thumb my nose a couple of times and hide my damn grin.

"Oh. Okay," Des continues, "that's what it is. You've been fucking, and that's why you don't have any legs tonight."

Moving over to the bags of barley, we squat together again.

"One, two…"

Over our heads, we hoist this big ass bag and pour barley

into the tank for soaking over the next two days, before he processes it for his next brew of beer.

"Shit." Sweat collects on my brow that I wipe off since I've been helping him all evening. Filthy and sweaty, I take a swig of his craft beer, and for a moment, it crosses my mind about where Eugenia is. I didn't want to let her leave earlier. Not even to send her back to her son.

Her body glistening with hot water droplets and steam rising off it, my wood drilling in and out of her, my fingers clutching her throat, gripping that wild, woolly-ass hair, her tongue drooling spit, I almost arrested her and told her she wasn't going *no*where.

Paragliding will never be the same.

And I've done it with the best, most athletic chicks. But the carnality of all my previous sexual adventures does not compare to how Eugenia nearly jumped from her skin, how her eyes almost sprang from her sockets, when we jumped off the edge.

Vulnerable, afraid and yet curious, she was an unwilling inmate being freed from prison.

Between yesterday's meetings, windsurfing, paragliding, partying last night, and Eugenia this morning, I'm an active dude, but this weekend is dragging me by the tail.

Still, everything was worth it. Had I not been out there, I wouldn't have known Eugenia was in town. Wouldn't have had another shot at seeing what's between us.

"Negro, are you doing some work, or will you just stay over there grinning like you won the lottery and shit?" my brother asks.

I almost start to tell him I may *have* won it.

"Haha, she put it on your ass, too," Desmond teases, tousling my mohawk. "So which one of your little groupies was it?"

"Nobody, dude." But hell, I can't help the smile that keeps creeping up.

Desmond shoves me in the chest. "Nigga, spill it."

Again, we squat to lift this heavy bag of barley meal and pour it in.

"This one's not just a link-up." D checks me out over the tank. "The volleyball player who does threesomes? The lawyer who gives good head? The actress who was a beauty queen? The weightlifter?"

This boy's rundown of the coldest women I've had since I started kicking it in the Hamptons has got my stomach shaking.

"I said it was nobody."

"And I said you're a liar." He keeps ticking through the possibilities. "For you not to even say who it is? Since when do *you* keep shit quiet? You usually want everybody to see your trophy case." He strokes his chin before we lift the next bag. Realization shudders his face. "Wait a minute. Don't tell me..."

Maybe if I turn my back and walk away, he can't read my face. "I'm *not* telling you."

"It's not who I'm thinking. You wouldn't be that dumb."

Aw, hell.

"You're not banging whatshisname's wife."

"She's not married."

He snaps his fingers. "Sheldon Rouse!" he blurts. "You are not laying with his crazy ex-wife who tried to drown herself in the ocean, man. Especially not when I warned your ass."

So I don't get pissed at how he talks about her, I take another swig of brew.

D walks around to face me, scrubs his hand down his face. "Rouse is helping you with Explore."

Hopefully, my shrug and cavalier attitude are enough hints that I don't care. "And? Why is he such a big deal?"

"The Hamptons 'hood stick together, just like we all did back home. And if I'm remembering right, she did some fucked-up shit last summer and nobody around here deals with her. These folks only tolerate that woman because she's Hadar's mama. What do you expect to gain from being with her? Man, I thought you were kicking it with somebody dope."

The beer bottle hangs from my fingertips. "She's not 'that woman.' She has a name."

"Her name is Dirt around here, as far as you're concerned."

Flexing, I say it with my whole chest for that gorgeous lady, inside and out, who's been through some shit and yet stands tall like the Statue of Liberty. "It's Eugenia Jackson."

But D also remains firm. "I'm pretty sure she still wears Rouse, for obvious reasons. That ought to tell you where her head is. Tell me it's just a one-and-done, dude."

My mouth remains shut.

"And your face is looking straight fucked-up too, all puppy dog and shit." We lift another bag and pour it in. "Ma called me and asked me to talk to you, but I refused to believe it. Like, nah, not Kee. He knows better. Life is good for you right now. Explore is all you've wanted your whole life." His gloves still on, he falls onto the tank as if I'm pouring out *his* life, and glares at me over the rim. "You can have all the pussy you want. *Any* pussy you want, Keenan."

I've thought about that, for the past six months. "And it was all good and fun, until I climbed in hers. I tried to move past it, get back to the old routine and… she's got layers. Every time I ask a question, I need more answers. So many places in her mind for me to go. She's not on some silly, immature shit. And it's so much she hasn't been exposed to. Yeah, she's older, but still innocent and virgin in a lot of ways."

My brother processes. Hell, I process.

"So what will you do about that whole child she's raising with somebody else? You ready for that?"

The gears in my head have already started turning. "I was hoping I could get a word with Adella."

D scratches his head, and the surprise bulges through his eyes. "Excuse… what?"

"Chrissy and Eugenia have a beef over what went down last summer. You just said it yourself. Adella and Chrissy are friends. Maybe Adella can arrange a sit-down so I can talk to Chrissy. Adella can help smooth things out."

"Keenan, dude, you know I love the hell out of you, but after the way you showed your ass this spring with Solomon and Ilyana, why would Adella do that for you?" D asks.

"Yes," a third voice cuts in. "Why would I do that?"

My sister-in-law peers up at me from the bottom of the ladder, hands laced together so daintily underneath her pregnant belly, in that way high-end women do, while her eyes drip fire.

From the burn of her side-eye, there is no room for politeness or pretense.

I lower myself down the ladder to face her straight on.

"Because Sheldon might be an asshole, but he crosses me as a solid man. Which means he looks out for Eugenia as the mother of his son, even if he doesn't want to, and even if Chrissy doesn't like it. He won't have to do that anymore if I'm looking out for her. And I'm pretty certain, as the new Mrs. Rouse, Chrissy won't mind being rid of Eugenia."

Adella closes in on me. "How does Sheldon know *you're* not the one he needs to protect Eugenia and his son from?" Dr. Adella McLain's low voice does its job, spitting syllables through clenched teeth. "Everybody around here knows you're brazen, crude, and ignorant. And the *only* reason you're operating here in the Hamptons *at all* is because of *my* brother. Not because you merit any modicum of respect. You and lowdown Eugenia probably deserve one another. But nevertheless, you are correct—Sheldon is a good man. A real man. He is not simply going to entrust his family, not even his ex-wife, to the likes of *you.*"

"Adella, I'm sorry about Ilyana. I was always honest with her, though. Never once did I promise her a commitment. And Solomon can be stingy and conniving. You know it's true. You went through it with him yourself."

"Which still doesn't answer my original question of why I, or Chrissy, should talk to you." She turns to my brother. "Dinner is in your office. I'll see you at home."

D walks over to me, squeezes my head and shoulders. "I ain' never seen you take a lashing as humbly and quietly as you just did, so this shit must be real."

I scratch my head with the lip of the beer bottle. "How did you do this?"

"Do what?"

"Become her husband." I recall a time when Adella couldn't bear to look at Desmond.

"Priorities. Remember last year when Del and me were first married and none of y'all could find me for months?"

I do. "Chaitra got pissed you weren't answering your phone, and she came for Del." It was the beginning of my sister and us falling out.

"I had a wife now. Del and me were complete strangers, and I didn't know the first damn thing about commitment. I kicked the hoes and homies to the curb, boys I've known my whole life. Real women won't give you a second thought if you're still about that bullshit." He turns his bottle up, sucks his teeth. "And neither will any of these people around here."

My lungs fold in for Showtime and Roach.

"Your heart is in the right place, Little Brother, but you can't bring everybody with you."

It's strange. I've gone through my whole life preaching against the fucked-up politics of respectability—of sororities, fraternities, titles, honors, awards, and clubs we black folks love to cloak ourselves in so we feel more special than the next person. For that reason, I've never given two fucks about what anybody thought of me, or my brash, in-their-face conviction.

Until now. The flashbacks won't leave my head of Eugenia snatched off the stage, how terror almost froze a nigga. Or of how last night, Show's arms locked me to him, like a man separating himself and going his own way wasn't an option. The claustrophobia shuts me down and has me rethinking politics versus peace of mind. And my new priorities.

EUGENIA

"You put him up to it," I say to P on Monday morning about the dance contest. How else would Keenan have known I would win?

The ocean breeze drifts across the portico and eases the morning humidity.

"I plead the Fifth." She parts her daughter, Halle's, hair for ponytails. "But how is your little pet feeling today?" She peeks at me through a corner of her eye, and her lips tuck in a slick smile.

As do mine.

"You have a pet, Aunt Genie?" Halle asks.

Immediately, I snuff out that chuckle.

"Mmhm, sweetie," P replies, "It's a cat. Aunt Genie's got a big, nappy, thirsty cat."

Our stomachs quaking, I shake my head at her.

"Mom!" Hadar shoots out of the boys' tent and onto the portico, throws his arms around me. "You're up. I'm hungry."

"Mm, good morning to you, too. So what are you going to do about being hungry?"

"Mmm, I think I'm going to let you fix chocolate chip pancakes," he says.

Princess and I chuckle.

"Ha! He's going to *let* me make him pancakes. And what did I do to deserve that honor? Besides spend eleven hours giving birth to you and three years wiping your nasty butt."

"Can I have pancakes?" Halle asks.

"Does your grandmother have chocolate chips? Flour? If she does, *you're* cooking all of us pancakes, and I'll sit and watch you do a good job while I talk you through it."

Of course, I wind up helping him and the kids and their messy selves. Isaac is on cleanup duty, Halle is cracking eggs and measuring flour and milk, Blake is mixing and pouring, Hadar is at the oven flipping, and Rome sets the table.

"What is this?" Mrs. Rouse asks, coming in. "We've got a new restaurant?"

"Don't speak too soon. We haven't tasted them yet." I stand next to Hadar to make sure he's paying attention and doesn't burn them.

"If these taste good, though, and Granddad actually eats them, I'm getting the recipe patented and we're selling these in stores as a stream of income, like Dad always talks about," Rome says.

"They will taste good, though, because it's my mom's recipe. And you can't patent it, because it's my mom's," Hadar replies.

I help him flip, and a little piece of joy flips inside me.

"It's okay, Rome," I tell him. "We can always enjoy them around here whenever we want. I'll give you the recipe."

Hadar's big eyes look up at me. "Does that mean you'll be here a lot more cooking us pancakes? And we'll all be together? You, me, Dad, Chrissy, Blake, Kara, and Krishna?"

I suppose that's the page of my life turning as I rub mix from his face. "Take these pancakes off. They're done, so Blake can pour in another set."

My son pulling me around the beach with him is a fullness I can't describe. It's not just him and me the way it used to be, and his joy doesn't arrive the way I wanted it to. That's an adjustment. But he still reaches back for my hand to show me his "inventions", or checks for my reaction when he does something, to see if I'm impressed or if I'm proud. He's happy.

And Sheldon, Chrissy, and I manage civility. Even Roland and Mr. Rouse play nice. As well as their sister, Kamilah, who nurses hard feelings about me after my divorce from her brother. Can't say I blame her. I'm certain Princess and Mrs. Rouse had a lot to do with that.

I'm glum near the end of Memorial Day when they're packing their cars to drive back to Jersey.

The silver glow along the cloud of saying goodbye to my son is that I'm packing up for my own… night away.

"Eugenia, you're welcome to stay here as long as you want, sweetheart, since your flight doesn't leave until tomorrow," Mrs. Rouse offers.

"Thank you for that, but I've actually been invited for a boating trip. I'm trying to get over my phobia. I might even book a massage." There is no point in me lying. All these people know each other, and Sheldon can easily check. Clearly, they all know about Chicago.

"Well, take care, hon. Have safe travels to Chicago. When will you be back?"

"Weekend after next. Every other weekend until the judge says otherwise."

Her face is only mildly pleased at hearing me say that I will fly out here every alternating weekend until the day I die, if that's what it takes for me to be in Hadar's life. I will not just give up or disappear.

"So, Mom," Hadar starts as he carries my bag, "where are you going? Whose boat are you riding?"

He's getting old enough to be in my business. Or maybe he's been listening to Sheldon and any assortment of his wife, mother, or siblings.

"Ugh, nosy. Why? Who have you been listening to?"

He lowers his head and whispers so no one else hears, "Are you going to see Keenan?"

"What makes you think I would see him?" I'm careful with the way I ask my question to elicit information.

Popping the trunk, he puts my things in. "The other day, you and him were arguing, the way you and Dad used to argue. And how Chrissy and Dad argue now. Only you're not mad for real, and you look like you're about to kiss. You and Keenan play-fight."

God, it seems only yesterday, this boy couldn't even form words. With a chuckle in my soul, I press my lips on him. "I love you, baby."

"I love you, too, Mom. I like Keenan," he whispers. "Dad and Chrissy don't, but I think he's nice. If you see him, will you tell him I said hi?"

"You can tell him yourself. He says he'll take you on the water any time you want."

"Son." Sheldon stands on the other side of the trunk. "It's time to roll out. Will you give your mom and me a minute?" He turns to me. "Appreciate you driving him out here when it was your first weekend having him to yourself."

"Thanks for letting me hang out around here."

"You know you don't have to thank us for that. If he's here, you're welcome, Eugenia. Even if he's not here."

"Thank you."

His nostrils inhale and tell me there's more coming, confirmed by his arms settling across his chest. "So, there's a camping trip coming up, starting next weekend, soon as the boys get out of school. It lasts a full week. They'll be going upstate, to the mountains with the boys' fraternity, Blade and Key. They'll learn wilderness techniques."

A ball of my nerves already clogs my throat. "Will you or Roland be chaperoning?"

"No."

"By himself out there, Sheldon?"

"He won't be by himself. He'll be with Blake, Rome, Isaac, other boys, and camp leaders."

"Why didn't Hadar say anything about this to me? How long have you been planning this?" There goes my perfect weekend. I should have known this was too good to be true.

"We only learned about it yesterday at church, but the boys heard and were excited. I think it would be good for him. And he didn't tell you because he knows how you get."

"Sheldon, he just had a nightmare yesterday and crawled into bed with me. How many of those nightmares does he have that you aren't telling me about? What if he has one out there and we're not around?"

Panic now thumps in my ribcage at thoughts of my son searching for me and I'm not there. The same way dread hits me when I imagine my little brother, Odell, innocent and locked up in prison without anybody.

"His mom won't be there this time, and he'll have to use his coping skills he's been practicing in therapy. It's what he needs."

I rub at the area of my breasts where, it seems like only last week, my baby rested his head. "That also cuts off my weekend visit."

"We can double your make-up visit when he comes back,"

Shel offers. He doesn't seem callous or mean-spirited in this, as if he genuinely is pushing Hadar to grow. "Blade and Key helps young Black boys form bonds and connections long before they ever leave for college. High-profile men from the Hamptons were in it. Kevin Middleton was president back in his day."

But that doesn't quell my worry for my only child in the woods with people we don't know, who won't protect him the way I can. "Hadar has never been away from his parents or family for any time longer than one night. It could be traumatizing to wake up and not know where he is."

"He needs to gain more independence." Shel is more insistent.

"You mean more independence from *me*," I snap.

"That's not what I mean, Eugenia. I want our son confident and strong. Not weak and babied."

"I can't agree to that."

Sheldon's face ices over and freezes up my insides, and I know what's coming when winter hits him. "Let Hadar go on this trip, and I won't mention to the social worker anything about Keenan McLain."

Now, on this deceptively sunny day, we trade shade.

"You're fucking him," Sheldon concludes. "Whatever. That's your personal choice. But what happens if the judge finds out you're not as responsible as you led her to believe in court?"

The brick walls of my heart collide in an avalanche. "What are you talking about?"

"I'm talking about Keenan's drug dealing friends, the people he surrounds himself with, the wild parties he has, the underage minors he got caught with at Taste a few months ago that subjected Taste to almost losing its license, and let's not forget his temper. Earlier this year, Solomon had him served with a restraining order to keep him out of Taste.

Keenan may be innovative and brilliant, but mentally and emotionally, he has never left high school. You wouldn't recognize this, since you never did either. The judge didn't want to hear any of this a few days ago. Maybe she'll be more willing to listen now. Especially since something almost happened to you a couple of nights ago, *at Taste.* So that dude hasn't learned."

Buried underneath the rubble, I claw for an opening to breathe. "Nothing happened to me! We were having fun and it was fine. You'll never be satisfied unless I'm alone and miserable, so you can feel vindicated for the divorce. You're not protecting our son. You're using information to manipulate me."

"And since you still make poor decisions, you need to be manipulated. I don't enjoy watching you screw men who aren't good for you. But I'll be damned if I let you teach that poor decision-making to Hadar."

Sheldon stares down at me over what must be my wintry grave while he finishes burying me.

"I'll email you the permission slip for Blade and Key, so you can sign and send it back. Have a safe ride back to Chicago."

Barely standing, I shoot my hand out to the car and balance myself to make my way around it. How did he know?

As the thought crosses my mind, Princess rushes over and throws me in an embrace, whispers in my ear, "I have no idea what he just said or did, but I didn't breathe a word. He and Ma have been talking through the weekend, about what, I don't know. I promised I'd pull him back, not that it would be easy. Call me if you need to. Love you, girl."

"Love you, too, P," I manage through my ribs already rattling.

Roland waits in their truck with the kids to drive them

back to the city. P's sweet and she tries to be supportive, but just as years ago when she was overwhelmed and I was depressed, I know better than to think we'll have time or space to be that close again. Especially with what she's going through now.

Driving out of the gates of the new Rouse Hamptons compound, I turn onto the stretch of country road, past all those emerald-green stretches of Heaven on Earth, over which I soared so high, so freely, a day ago, now every bit a torture chamber, with its mocking illusions of tranquility that laugh. Silly me for thinking it could actually be possible.

Why did I not know all that? I looked Keenan up and saw a couple of articles about a fight and underage minors at Taste in February, but nothing was attributed to him directly. I blew it off, too easily. Scuffles happen at parties and clubs all the time. But Sheldon also tends to paint every little misstep as a travesty. And because I've tried to kill myself three times, people listen to him.

No tears fall from these dry, crusty eye ducts that lead to no well of water in me. From the arid, dustbowl in my throat, no scream erupts.

There was no way I was remaining at the Rouses' for another night of forced cordiality. So now I drive down the highway of this Heaven that is really prison.

17

SOMEBODY I CARE ABOUT

KEENAN

"Try it again," I instruct the deliveryman over the phone.

Through the large bay window of the library at the Middleton property, I watch people on Explore's board amble in from the circular drive outside. I showed up here early, just so I could have a moment alone to check on this, what's become my obsession.

"Sir, I'm sorry, I can't. All deliveries are being rejected by the front desk. They will not accept anything or allow us to even leave it at the building door."

"Donate it to the first homeless person you see. Or give them to your lady or your mother."

I refuse to believe my only option is standing here and pressing my storm into this windowsill. I'm not a "stand around and do nothing" kind of man.

It's crossed my mind several times to go find her.

From the moment the boat set sail on Monday evening, hauling me farther away from land while I realized she seri-ously wasn't coming, I started to jump off that motherfucker, straight into the ocean and swim to go get her.

But I had to deal with Show and Kevin and ease the blow of Kevin refusing Show's offer. Kev is elegant in the way he does it, but it's a refusal, nevertheless. Now as far as Show goes, there's that to deal with.

Me sitting on the road outside the Rouses' property most of Monday night, once we got back, didn't turn up anything. Most of the cars there were gone. But I still sat out there praying Sheldon Rouse's big country ass would ride up and I could run him over. Thankfully, God doesn't like me enough to answer my prayers. Or, maybe to my fortune, He detests me enough to ignore me.

There is not a doubt in my mind Rouse is the reason she didn't come. And I've spent every minute of the last six days stopping myself from going to address him personally. She would only hate me, whereas now she only distrusts me.

I booked two flights to Chicago. And then canceled.

I already tried the bold, direct approach; if I do it again, I have no doubt she'll call the police and slap me with a restraining order, simply to appease Sheldon where their son is concerned.

So once again, Stunt Man is flipping in the air with no bearings, unaware of where he is in the backflip—no clue what he's doing or what to offer her or what to say—or how he'll land.

If I make the wrong move, I really could break my neck this time and lose Eugenia altogether.

Behind me, people enter the room for our Saturday meeting.

Solomon takes a seat. On the other end of the table sits his new significant other, and the woman who stabbed me in my back, my sister, Chaitra.

Kevin and I swap quick loaded expressions.

At the top of the meeting, Solomon cracks his knuckles, glaring at me. "So last weekend, things got a little out of control at Taste, *again.*" He whips out the freeze-frame image Kevin showed me, of Eugenia being carried off the stage. Of the wind being knocked from me.

As my lungs are already strapped tight, I'm unable to take a deep breath. "I apologize. It won't happen again."

"You've said that before," he snaps.

"That's somebody I care about." I don't want to put Eugenia's business in the street by saying too much. "I would never want to put the p...people in my life in harm's way. It'll never happen again." My voice cracked under the weight of that.

Solomon noticed.

He and Chaitra exchange stunned glances.

"In addition to that," he continues, "I perused the guest lists at some of our booked hotels for August, and I notice you've booked a lot of rooms in your name. But many of your guests from Baltimore are missing from the lists. Yet, they call Miracle at Taste, Laney at Adventures, and the clerks at hotels, asking for special services and meal reservations when their names are not on the guest lists. They say they are personal guests and friends of yours. *Several* Explore employees have complained about this."

"I'll take care of it," I say to a fuming Solomon.

"Not good enough." His energy headbutts mine. "The whole point of this Sasha Static concert is to make money and establish our luxury brand. We could benefit so much more if you'd stop giving hookups to your friends who don't want to pay."

"They *are* paying. Some of them just can't put their names on anything official because they have legal complications is all. I will write the checks to the hotels and vendors to cover it."

Solomon snorts, "Legal complications, huh? You mean felons with warrants who want a piece of the action but are scared of getting arrested, like your boy, Shonathan Harper, or 'Showtime' as you call him."

I probably would have still made it out of the 'hood without Show, but my success would look way different. I would not have the street credibility back home that I do, or the massive social following and popularity I do from all the years throwing events, events his money paid for. So I can't sit here and simply not speak for my 'hood.

"I understand you want the audience to be picture-perfect. But plenty of these rich, white boys around here have records, Solomon. The only difference is money and name. You just don't want them from the streets and black. The whole *point* behind Explore Adventures—since I *am* the one who founded it—is to introduce thrills and luxury to people of color who've never been exposed to this kind of thing. *All* people of color, not just the Disney ones."

A few seats away, Chaitra squirms while listening to the two of us.

Solomon leans forward. "Keenan, you just said you don't want to place people important to you in harm's way. How do you reconcile that with the threat that Showtime and his friends want to sell drugs in random goods during the week of events?"

I have no idea. I've never piloted my life during an oncoming plane collision between one side of my heart and the other.

I am still very much of Baltimore and I wouldn't even know where to begin to start shedding my hometown roots.

Kevin speaks. "I received a call the other day from the First Lady's office."

"We already have New York's First Lady booked, and the First Lady of Jersey," I remind him.

"The First Lady of the United States." His green eyes that look eerie as hell at times, especially in the sunlight, now bear down on me with the magnitude of just what this is. "Keenan, you did it. This has become everything you wanted. You brought us all together."

"Not quite, Kevin." Across the table from him, I'm sure to make this clear. "Not if we're leaving people out."

"Not people. Just criminals."

My mind flips back twenty years, to Show passing me two hundred dollars for a pair of sneaks that Ma refused to buy and Pop couldn't afford.

"Criminals are people, too."

"The Secret Service will be there. We don't need anybody's *legal complications* affecting Explore's bottom line," Kevin finishes.

"We've got security at every event, metal detectors everywhere, and constant police patrols at—"

"There won't be security or police at your *private* hotel parties and boat parties I'm hearing about, parties you're setting up with your friends," Solomon interrupts. "This isn't about picking on you or discriminating against our own people, Keenan."

"It's about liability. None of our friends are legal liabilities." Kevin shuts off his tablet and laces his fingers on the table.

Solomon crests his fingers, cannon guns ready to fire, the war zone of his face anticipating *my* fire. "No private parties with your buddies. None. Whatever you've planned with your Baltimore folks at this point, you'll cancel. *Everybody* who holds a ticket to the concert will register for their own hotel rooms and services, and *all* the money stays above board."

The room waits.

And they are right to, because every time they push me, I bring the roof down on their asses.

I nod.

They keep waiting, as if surely, it couldn't be that simple.

Chaitra blinks, a lot. They're all sitting at the table, anticipating the other shoe to drop, like maybe I came here with a bomb in my shoe or something.

But this is my company.

And more than that, the freeze-frame picture lying on the table, the proverbial writing on the wall, its ink scraping painfully across my vital organs, illustrates why Eugenia didn't show up.

"Good." Kevin breaks the ice. "It's time we brought in financial consultants to tighten our operation. Explore's organization needs a makeover, and we still have a supply situation with our ingredients we already bought from Europe held up in containers on ships. I don't think we should trust that to just anybody. The Rouse family has agreed to head up organization of the corporate structure, and I'm working on my brother, Lion, for operations and supply chain."

I tune out and miss the rest of that discussion, because as much as I love Explore, I'm not present.

At the end of the meeting, somebody raises our work with inner city youth here in the Hamptons.

"Speaking of youth, Keenan, how's it going on getting those European deals?" Rocky asks.

As many times as I've traveled overseas, loved every escape and expedition, lived for every minute, I look forward to this trip now about as much as a trip to the dentist for a root canal.

"I leave for Switzerland, Greece, and Italy next Monday and will return two Thursdays after that. While I'm there, I'll negotiate and sign more travel contracts for Sights Unseen and Adventures, and specifically, creating a schedule for youth. Hopefully, starting next summer, we'll offer youth voyages also, with full-time instructors and counselors taking Black kids to Europe for swimming, mountain climbing, survival skills, the whole nine, all paid for by the Middleton Foundation, courtesy of Mr. Lionel Middleton."

I sweep my fingers across the table. Just a few weeks ago, I could say all that with my chest. Seeing my dream realized, of marrying adventure and Black community, now feels like an inflated hot air balloon that's not taking off.

"I'll continue to take meetings for the concert en route and while there."

"The Black Business Council is continuing the program it started last fall," Kevin adds, "and they're also asking us to let the kids help with concert activities where possible."

"I'll help, on Solomon's behalf," Chaitra volunteers. Isn't that cute.

She may as well twist my intestines with a wrench.

After the meeting ends—finally—as everybody clears out, Chaitra comes to me and has the nerve to put her hand on my shoulder.

"Keenan—"

I knock it off. "Move, Shay. You could have helped me out. A lot of our folks they call 'those people' are the same neighbors who ate at our table. We ate at theirs when we didn't have shit. Now you act like you don't know anybody, because 'these people' around here have started accepting you?"

The broken stones on my sister's face crumble, almost convincing me she might actually care this time. But I know what's behind those raggedy eyes and twitching mouth— guilt.

"Keenan, I'm sorry."

I reject it. With my head and hands and the pieces of my heart Eugenia didn't take with her, I refuse.

"No. You're not. You feel guilt, but you're not sorry. You're hoping I'll just get over it so you can feel better and look yourself in the mirror." The weight on my mind loads down my eyes enough that I don't bother lifting them for her.

"I was young."

"So was I."

"You would never stand still, always hiding, and moving and jumping off buildings and cars. I literally had to fight people for you." Now she throws out too many excuses to count.

"And you made me pay for it by beating the hell out of a kid with ADHD." Those memories choke me up, and have my blood running at what feels like a thousand miles an hour. "With your *fist*, Chaitra. You took out every ounce of frustration you felt at Ma and Pop because you weren't out playing sports, and you put it into me. Why do you think I was hiding and running away from you all the damn time? And if you were truly sorry, you would have supported me when I first came to you with Explore, instead of going behind my back with Solomon and Taste."

Tears emerge from behind her heavy-ass stones. "I didn't want to support you after you grew up and spent years laughing at me around your friends, acting ashamed of me."

"And yet you still followed me wherever I went, because you're not creative enough to come up with shit on your own."

Her cheeks and mouth shake, and that's how Shay gets when she's pissed. "I didn't have time to come up with ideas when I was always busy helping Ma, and you and D were having all the fun."

"That's your problem, not mine. I didn't invite you into my company, or onto my board with your backstabbing ass. But I did just ask you to move."

She sits. "Yes, I love Solomon, but I also love you. And

right now, you don't look too good, Keenan. You've never apologized for *any*thing. What is going on with you today?"

"None of your business."

"I want to help you. So how do we make this right?"

I manage to shake this anchor that is my head. "We can't. Because I don't give a shit about your apologies, or your crocodile tears, or your money. Your actions have said it all."

Mashing my fingers into my eye sockets, I sit here on top of the world, achieving my lifetime dream, and sinking to the bottom of the Dead Sea.

18

NOT JUST SOME RANDOM

EUGENIA

"This report is missing critical information. Updated counselor statements? She's been going to counseling for months, and your last therapy letter is three months ago. What's happened since then? The judge will want to know." I close the report.

"I called the therapist several times with no response."

"Call the therapist's supervisor. Ask him. How many times have you called him?"

Sharae sucks on sour grapes in front of me. "You don't have to throw your weight around to pay me back for New York. I'm reporting you to Ms. Darcy."

I pull the remaining reports out of my leather shoulder bag and stop myself from slamming them on the table. Instead, with calm and poise that give no hints of distress, I set down my hand as if I'm carrying a feather. "While you're at it, show her your other lazy efforts where your recommendations are not backed up by sufficient evidence because you didn't complete your investigation and I had to cover for you." I slide them across the table at her. "I will not sign off on a single one until they're complete."

After she stomps out in a tantrum and I'm left alone, I don't dare allow my head to collapse in my hands, at the risk someone might walk in and see me crumbling. Every sin and error constructing my psyche rises with me when I stand from this chair.

Back at my desk, I rip off a printed photo of a naked Keenan they've taped to my computer. I can't help my moment of pause, in which I notice a large dragon tattoo inked down his back in exquisite detail, that breathes fire down his butt cheek to the flaming sword on his thigh. In the photo, a woman's hands curl around his cheeks. He's obviously receiving a blow job at some party. The image is grainy since it's been pulled from the internet and, of course, some smart-ass in my office took a marker and drew a stick figure of her tongue licking his butt crack. I trash it before heading to my SUV.

A Monday evening spent in a hotel, balled up in a bathtub crying, and the following days staring at reports I don't read and nights staring at television shows I don't watch, have not cleared my head.

"But you had a fantastic weekend, so why are you down?" Lillian asks during a phone therapy session I hold in my car.

"I miss him." Construction workers hammering on the concrete outside the garage may as well be hammering me to pieces.

"But Hadar was happy to be with *both* of you. That was such a wonderful idea, Eugenia, to not be selfish or vindictive and keep him from his other family, but for all of you to be together. And you wound up having fun. It was a win-win. You and Sheldon are building a solid foundation of working together once this case closes. If that's not the goal, what do you envision for you and Hadar?"

Although I miss my son terribly, I wasn't talking about him this time.

And Sheldon's "solid foundation" is not my vision. But I have to frame this answer carefully. This is not really a therapy session. "My son's happiness, however it happens."

"What if it's not in Chicago with you primarily? Will you continue to be sad, Eugenia?"

If I can't have Hadar, and I can't have a man who adds to my life, what will I be? "No mother in their right mind is ever happy to be away from their children, Lillian. So I'll focus on ways to secure my own happiness, other purposes to live for."

That's the best and most honest way I can say I'll try not to end my life again.

"And what are those? What do you have to live for? Maybe you should think of them to pull yourself out of your funk today."

Nothing. I have nothing to live for. "My work. The promotion I have coming up in a few months." Which means nothing to me. "The children's series I've always wanted to write. Traveling." I don't know where that one came from. It hasn't crossed my mind much before. But after paragliding over the Hamptons…

"Have you started working on it?"

No. "Here and there. I've started putting notes in my journal."

"There you go. I'd love to read it as you work. Maybe you can also start a website or blog and share your process of healing while writing it."

No chance in hell would I give these bitches the ammunition. "Ha. There's an idea. Hadn't thought of that."

Before I exit my SUV, I stare into the cupholder at all the flower cards Keenan sent this week I haven't opened. Despite me leaving the flowers for the front desk to donate, I still smell them in my mind.

"Ready for lunch, girl?" Lus asks, meeting me in the lobby.

"Sure, why not."

"So how many of them were in the Hamptons again?" she asks once we're out on the street.

With a glare, I warn her not to go there. It's bad enough I have to deal with their salty attitudes, and wonder if he did anything with them. "It doesn't matter."

"Genie, you know they only act like that with you because they're jealous it's not happening to them. Why don't you ask to be transferred so you don't have to put up with this?"

"To hell with them. I wouldn't give them the satisfaction of thinking they can run me off."

"But you're unhappy. When you came back on Wednesday, you looked a little down but you still had a relaxed vibe to you. I actually caught you smiling to yourself a few times. Whoever this dude is, you're feeling him. He's clearly not just some random."

It's been a long time since this ocean gushed through my veins so strong, and at the same time, brought with it the dreadful threat of my ship wrecking.

Last summer, with Sheldon and me being alone at times, I tried to force that rush to return, and it wouldn't. Any romantic tempests between us had long subsided, and I was only torturing myself trying to stir them up again.

Now, here I am, with waves rushing through me and no idea where they're taking me. "No, he's not just some random."

"Why don't you call your social worker, Tab, and explain it to her, so you can bring him into your life?"

"Because Keenan and his friends are trouble, and my son is young and impressionable. No."

I didn't need Sheldon to make that clear. I already had my own anxieties about him.

"Excuse me!"

A heavy voice spins me around, and I face a tall woman

I've never seen in my life but whose features still appear somewhat familiar.

"Yes?"

"Hi. Eugenia, right?" The woman approaches.

My street sense ratchets up. "Who's asking?"

"My name is Chaitra McLain. I'm Keenan's sister."

Lus scratches the back of her neck. "You know what? I'm going to pick up something and take it back to the office. Return some calls. Genie, I'll see you back in there."

"Can I buy you lunch?" Chaitra asks.

"No." As much as my chest drags this sidewalk, and I haven't closed my eyelids one time without the fiery sword on Keenan's leg flaming behind them, I won't win my son back entertaining fantasies.

In her jeans and one-shoulder t-shirt top, her laidback style isn't all that different from mine. "Then will you give me five minutes?"

"Why? I've made up my mind."

"I understand why you would. He is an asshole. Pompous and," she pauses to roll her eyes to her brow bone, her gaze dancing between her thoughts, "insolent. Prone to impulse. But he has a heart of gold. And he's the most brilliant person I know. I'm not just saying that because I'm his sister."

"Sure you are."

"No. Kee and I are not close. We've been at each other's throats for years. I have no reason to come lie for him."

"What kind of man fights with his sister?" I genuinely need to know. Because my brothers aren't the greatest either, and if their treatment of me is any example, then I'm right in my conclusions of Keenan.

She sighs. "It's complicated."

"From what I hear, he fights with everybody. And my life is complicated enough." Today, I'm in full mental armor and will not be deterred.

"I think you're un-complicating him. That's why I'm here." Emotion seems to redden her eyes some. "Even if you decide to stay by yourself, I at least want to meet the woman who managed that. And you're still listening and asking questions, so you must feel something."

I throw the door open to the restaurant. "I'm grabbing food. I can't stop you if you want to be here, too."

"You're older than Keenan. I get it."

"Do you have children?"

"No."

"Have you ever been married?"

"No."

"Do you work in a public service profession with vulnerable adults and children that requires your conduct to reach a high standard?"

"No."

"So then how do you get it?"

"You're age what? Thirty-six? Thirty-seven? About the same age as me?"

"What difference does my age make?"

"Come on, Eugenia, age makes all the difference. You're asking me all those questions to avoid humiliation. By now, you've probably picked up a few battle scars and you'll be damned if you let a piece of dick give you anymore. At this age, despite career or man history, we're not all that different with our intolerance of bullshit. At one point, Keenan came with a lot of it."

I order my kung pao chicken and Thai tea with boba. She does also.

"Your brother is incredible. He is going to make somebody a damn good man one day, when he grows up."

"But he's making your eyes change like that today." She sips her Thai tea and stares at me. "And you're growing him."

"Hmph." I don't deny the twitches in my stomach.

"I don't know what's going on between you and him, but the last time I saw him a few days ago, he wasn't moving like my ludicrous little brother who has nothing to lose. He was moving like somebody's damn good man. And I'm saying that as somebody who's been on the receiving end of his arrogance."

"I don't have time to raise somebody else's son."

"Or are you scared to open yourself up again to somebody else's son? *Especially* now. After you've probably already been hurt by somebody else's son and are extra nervous with a son of your own." She takes a breath. Her chest might be shuddering. "And it doesn't help that all this is going down in the Black Hamptons, where they're not the kindest to outsiders." On her trembling face, she must feel those memories personally.

With my food in hand, instead of carrying it out, I take a seat. And extend my hand for her to sit.

"No, they're not."

"I'm the sister-in-law of Adella English, who is Chrissy's childhood friend. I didn't exactly act my age when Adella married my brother last year, so I ran into trouble with them all."

I almost spit out my kung pao chicken, choking on it and swallowing more Thai tea to wash it down. We sit in the restaurant laughing our asses off for a minute.

"Te-he. That was good." I'm still chuckling. "I didn't exactly act my age last summer either, when I found out how serious Sheldon was with Chrissy."

Last June, I walked into the beautiful home he bought me for the first time, and realized just how much he loved me, how I'd allowed my family into my head. It slammed a hole right through me. And to see Chrissy's panties scattered in places where they'd obviously made love... her living my dream... him putting on her what was once mine... I clawed like hell to reverse time. The world caved in on me as I realized I couldn't, and I needed to numb myself from the dead-end reality.

"Yes," I murmur, remembering the ocean closing over my head, "that crowd can be a tough sell."

"Kind of like a rich gang."

I snicker. "More like a pack of wolves. Wondering who to tear apart next." I swallow my chicken and rice. "I appreciate you coming here, Chaitra. That you did, despite your issues with Keenan, makes clear how much you still care."

"No. Not how much I care. How much he's *grown*. Despite me caring for him, I wouldn't have done this six months ago." Chaitra wipes her mouth, sets her hands on the table. "I've never seen Keenan as humbled and calm as I did a few days ago when he saw a picture of you."

"A picture of me?" I wonder. Oh, goodness. Where?

"Yes. The security cameras at Taste snapped you being carried off the stage."

Lord, that must be how Sheldon found out. Nothing I do can stay private.

Chaitra continues, "The Explore Board discussed it at a meeting. Now, normally, Keenan is defensive and confrontational, dismissive about issues that come up." She studies me the way one studies an out-of-the-ordinary event unfolding. "Not this time. He was cool, rational, hell, *agreeable*. He actually apologized like he gave a damn. After the meeting, I asked him what planet I'd landed on, where he cares about another person. He wouldn't tell me. So I started looking for you, to ask you myself."

The food now sticking in my throat, I stop eating. "I didn't mean to make myself the subject of Explore's conversation." Me out partying, having a careless weekend tryst, will likely be the subject of conversation at our next court hearing.

"I think the real conversation is how we're all grateful it happened. It was unfortunate, and I'm sorry you went through that, but Keenan finally sees this isn't all partying and games. I saw the full video of him going after you when they picked you up." She falls back against her seat. "It's the only time I've ever seen him jump for anything other than some stupid stunt. My brother rushed into that crowd ready to lay his life down for yours. The real subject here is how my little knucklehead brother… is not a knucklehead when it comes to you."

"You're pretty good at this."

She shrugs. "I'm a CFO in construction. I spend a lot of time convincing stubborn people to do what they don't want to." A smile over her tea. "I may not be a social worker, but we both deal with children, in a sense."

Tah. Cute. "I'm glad I helped Explore, and Keenan, but I've got my own issues."

"If you stay caged up and scary over there, and never open your heart again, you're going to live with your biggest issue for the rest of your life."

Okay, so I might like her.

I'm already living with it, from the time I wake up to the time I go to sleep. I no longer reach for the photo album in my nightstand, but rather, those thirteen business cards. Not because I give a damn whose names are on them, or the nasty notes they scribbled to him on the back. The cards still carry his scent. Nor have I dry-cleaned the jumpsuit I wore to Taste two weekends ago.

"Why didn't Keenan come say all this to me himself? If he's growing into the man you say, why send his big sister?"

A flash of lightning strikes her face, twinges her lips. "He doesn't know I'm here. He'll kill me if he finds out I interfered in his private life."

Coming to speak for her brother with whom she fights, at

the risk he would disapprove… is a whole lot of mountain she's trying to move.

Do I love my own brothers? Yes.

Do I respect them enough as men to do something like this for them? Only one of them. Odell.

The afternoon lunch crowd fills in the little dining room around us, chairs scraping and workers chattering, as she and I suck up boba balls and hold the silence.

"I won't betray your trust," I reassure her.

"Thank you." She plays with the straw. "So, will you go back to my brother and take him out of his misery?"

The amount of risk that requires weighs on me. There is no amount of romance worth the risk of losing my son. "No."

19

WHAT THE...?

KEENAN

I button my suit jacket. Take a sip of water. Shift positions in my seat. Unbutton my jacket. It should definitely be unbuttoned. Buttoned up is too stuffy and wooden, says I'm trying too hard.

I go over all my arguments in my head, every possible line of reasoning, every one of my worst fears, positives and neg—

"Mr. McLain."

Anxiety locking my fingers together must spring into every other limb.

"Mr. Rouse will see you now," the secretary informs me.

At 2:30 exactly. I figured he had that kind of personality. Why I was twenty minutes early.

The rise from my seat affirms my purpose.

Entering his massive corner office on the top floor, I don't give a fuck about the trappings or that I've never had anything like this at McLain Construction. Never wanted Wall Street.

I don't bother offering a handshake. Neither does he. He crosses me as the type who thinks I need to earn his respect.

"Thanks for seeing me."

"Thank Middleton."

He motions with his head at the couch facing away from the city, toward him. So whoever's talking to him focuses solely on him and doesn't get distracted—positioning of furniture in a business setting is Power Dynamics 101. I perch everything I have on the edge of this cushion. I'm extra focused.

He takes the chair directly across, reclines lazily, crosses his legs, laces his fingers. As if he's seeing a fucking student.

"I'm never going to do anything to place your son in harm's way."

"And I'll make sure of it."

"You don't have to do it by torturing her."

"Eugenia tortures herself."

"Allow her to liberate herself. What are you going to do? Keep treating her like a child who can't make decisions for the rest of her life?"

"No. Just until my son turns eighteen."

"Trust her to do it now. She makes damn good decisions for him now. Hadar's a good kid, and since he's spent most of his life with her, that's proof of how she raised him. That's also proof you're not keeping him from her to protect him but as revenge. You're on some domination and control psychotic shit."

"You have no idea where Eugenia came from, who she spends her time with, her state of mind, or what she's capable of when she enters that state of mind."

"But I do know you stayed with her for several years, and *she* left *you*. Not the other way around. So she must not have been that bad. And even after she left you, she restarted her career in a different city—a violent city—while holding it down as a single mom, and Hadar turned out just fine."

"She did the basics. Not that I owe you any explanation, but my son deserves better now, and he'll get it."

"That's what this is really about. Not that he's unsafe with her. You just want her out of the way while you turn him into some prep school snob."

"Like I said, it's none of your business. But what's the alternative? That he turns out to be like you and your friends?"

"The alternative is that Hadar lives his life and becomes whoever he wants. That he's sharp enough, exposed enough to a range of experiences, and well-rounded enough to stand atop the mountain of all his achievements, survey all his choices from a three-hundred-sixty-degree angle," I say, paragliding in my mind again with Eugenia, when we literally sailed the skies of New York, "and choose which way he wants to fly in the world."

"He certainly won't get that three-sixty on West Washington Boulevard in Chicago."

"Anybody can get that perspective from wherever in the world we want. It doesn't take a perfect parent to raise a good child. And you really should stop parenting Eugenia. You're not her daddy."

He doesn't flinch or move a muscle. "But I am the closest to one she's got."

Shit.

"Then support what every parent wants for their children —happiness. It's time she had hers. You're right. I can't tell you what to do with your son. But I came here to address you, man to man, so you'll see for yourself I'm not playing about his safety. I'll do whatever I have to so it's never jeopardized."

He finally moves and tilts his head. "*Whatever* you have to?"

I know what he's asking me—the entire immense, scary fucking weight of it.

Slowly, I lift my head and nod. "Whatever."

He switches positions, uncrossing his legs. "My turn. Why Eugenia?" He shrugs. "You're young. There are a lot of women your age who don't have her... history."

I refrain from telling him it's none of his business since, after all, I brought my business to his office. "There are no other Eugenias. What other people see as flaws on a diamond gives it character. Her history shaped her to be exquisite. You damn well know it. Or you wouldn't have married her."

Behind his eyes, he assesses. "Is that all?"

"That's all." I stand. "Take care." Having no idea whether he's convinced, I head for the door and the rest of my errands here in the city.

"You rejected your invitation to Harvard."

I stop in my tracks.

Kevin told him.

Hanging on to the door handle, without turning around, now it's me who shrugs. "I love my city, and status never meant shit to me. I'll leave all the Ivy League jockeying to you prep school boys."

"I KNOW it's not easy. Explore is better off. You're better off. You had to. For a few reasons."

"Yeah." The third shot of whiskey does its job in my throat. I've got them all lined up, as many as the flight attendant would let me have.

"And you think these contacts of yours will give you solid arrangements for hotels, meals, transportation, sights, all-inclusive?" Kevin asks through the video screen.

"There is no better time to do this." Unfortunately. "We need to leverage this concert before it happens—all the hype, promo, celebrities, cash flow, banks—to secure as many deals as we can, and lock in friendly discounts, while we've got all this fuel in the tank. Our position is strongest right now. Not after the concert, once the bubble pops."

I sure as hell don't feel like doing Europe, especially when there's so much work remaining stateside, and not when being overseas is akin to jumping several universes away from Eugenia.

But I still possess enough of my right mind to know I can't drop the ball on Explore or all the opportunities this concert presents for us.

"Agreed. And by next summer, Sight Unseen should be going up."

"With all this madness right now, I think bringing in an outside company to toughen up our corporate game and finances, plus putting your brother on supply chain, is a good look. Has Lion said yes yet?"

Back in LA, Kevin shifts at his desk, a not-so-sure half-grin over his button-down. "He's working his way around to yes."

We bust up chuckling. This nigga is so slick; why he has my respect. We came from different backgrounds but have more in common than most dudes I've known forever. He doesn't totally approach the world like a rich guy. As a matter of fact, Kevin's more street than a lot of street guys I know, but can cover it up with the pretentiousness these corporate types love. We're both the youngest sons, both renegades, both gamblers with life. Only he's smarter with the politics, and I've always struggled with that shit.

At this point, we're more than business partners. He's become almost as much of a brother as D, which is the only reason he could have possibly convinced me to do what I just did. Well, one of two reasons.

"We should also start considering our next major event," he says, "and what that looks like—a talent showcase, an expo, a South by Southwest kind of thing, what exactly."

"Fo' sho. That's the next move." I down another shot, because despite this Scottish whisky being some of the toughest in existence, this liquor is not doing what I need.

A tiny piece of my eye wanders over my shoulder, with this stupid hope that leaves me feeling dumb every time I shift back to my tray. I don't know why I bothered looking. Of course, she didn't show.

"You sure you'll be straight, man?" Kevin stares at all my shots. "To handle all those meetings yourself, you know you'll need to put that down, right?"

I nod. "Yeah. I will." Eventually.

"All right then, man, I'll see you on the T-Mobile video call for integrating all the wireless that week, and the check they'll write us." A hand over his chin, Kev peeps me out one more time. "You sure you're good?"

"As good as I can be, dude. See you in a few days."

How in the hell do people do this? Walk around with somebody else owning you—the air you breathe, how hard you laugh (or don't), the thoughts you think, how you digest food, when your body is ready to receive nourishment, how the retinas in your fucking eyes convert the light into electrical signals and affects the way you see the world?

Thirteen hours past the dread of meetings, reading reports and spreadsheets, and emailing, I wake up from a liquor-induced, unstable sleep as I land in the Swiss Alps.

Without her.

Since it's 7:30 p.m., I freshen up real quick in the airport bathroom and get my shit together. No matter how many cars I jump in or corners I turn, I do so with the pitiful hope that a sliver of light shines through the darkness in my retinas and I will visually process her.

The Swiss send a "welcome party" to pick me up in a jeep and drive me to a restaurant called Barenstobe. The baked sole is killer. Any other time, I would sample the entire menu and see what I'm missing. Tonight, I just need to get through this presentation sober enough.

"I wanted to check that you arrived safely. You look like you floated there on an ocean of liquor," Ma says to me in a video call once I've checked into my "hotel."

"Would have been more fun." I turn up a bottle of Scotch I placed on reserve to be waiting on me when I arrived. "I'll be good."

"I'll call you again tomorrow to make sure."

"Doesn't mean I'll answer."

"I'll send a search team if you don't, so it would be in your interest to do so." Back in her B'More office, Ma folds her arms. *"Keenan."*

I stare at her.

"You've endured worse. And you've made it. Lo and behold, surprise, surprise, adulthood comes for us all eventually. This too shall pass, and you will be fine."

There's nothing I can say to ease her worry, or my misery. "I'll talk later."

Finally, after a few more sips from this bottle, my bones and muscles dissolve through my skin. Not a single thought remains in my head, and I'm grateful I've had enough liquor to temporarily sink them all. But I do not want to sleep in this bed, not when I booked it with other ideas in mind.

The scenery blurs like I'm underwater, and as I try to take my clothes off, my limbs stunningly do not cooperate. I have to toil hard as hell to pick each button through a hole, wrestle off this shirt, and then thread my body through the needle of these pants. Somehow, I squirm to hit the floor with a thud and close my eyes.

I open them again, and it's still dark.

Damn, this floor is cold and uncomfortable, so I move to climb back into bed.

"Mmph."

What the…?

Again, I wiggle to move, pulling on my arms. But they're raised above my head, where my hands seem to be…

Shit!

I jerk again and I'm hitched up in a body clutch I can't escape. Blindfolded, I can't see!

"What the hell is th—?" My mouth is stuffed.

Fuck! Like a motherfucker sprinting from the apocalypse, I'm fighting and squirming like hell to break free, to see, yell, something. I've heard of people being kidnapped overseas, held for ransom, sold into slavery, and I guess I always took for granted it just wouldn't happen to me. This is the first time in my life when I actually regret I'm high up in these rural mountains, where nobody can hear me, in the first damn place.

"The last time I saw you," some goddamn electronic voice says over my head.

Oh my God. This is some crazy-ass groupie or fanatic!

"I don't fucking know you." But the words don't come out through this towel stuffed in my mouth and sound more like, "Aarf daah fog owe yaa."

"I can't understand what you're saying." This person is talking above my head but using some kind of voice changer to disguise their voice. Fuck! "Would you repeat that?"

"Take this goddamn towel out of my mouth, and I'll tell you, crazy bitch!" Comes out sounding like, "Taa thah gaada taa owaah aah ta, ya craw bah!"

"I still don't understand you," the voice says. "But don't worry. We'll understand each other soon enough."

This *cannot* be how I die.

God, please don't let this be how I die. I know you don't like me that much. And I deserve some of that. But if you let a nigga live, I swear I won't cuss out anymore old ladies or dare 'em to try to wet their mouths enough to suck my dick. And I pray this in the name of the Father, the Son, and some damn good weed.

I always promised myself I would die like in the *Revenant* or *Legends of the Fall*, living in the wild and fighting off a bear or some shit. Not by a crazed groupie selling me to hairy, musty-ass men who don't take showers.

My soul almost ejects from my body at the slam of something next to my ear, and all I can do is wriggle around like a pissy-ass worm.

"You talked a lot of shit the last time I saw you," the voice states.

"Mah, aapojaah." Damn. I was trying to say, "Ma'am, I apologize."

"Do you remember when I told you to go fuck yourself? You recall what you said?"

Hell, how many people have told me that? "Nnn maah."

"I can't understand you. I asked if you remember what you said."

Helpless and groggy, I shake my head.

"How many women have told you to go fuck yourself?"

I shrug. A lot.

A stick slams so close to my head, I almost missed its draft on my ear through the banging in my chest and eardrums.

"Good thing I brought a little something to help you remember."

I'm totally naked. But my dick is now in her hands. Oh, Lord, I don't want to die that way either.

"I'm going to remove the towel from your mouth. When I do, you'd better not scream. I've got your dick in my hands."

I nod.

"Now I'm pouring something on you," the voice changer says, "and you still can't scream. The only way you can make it stop is to say one thing."

Shit, my chest is all tight. I'm having a fucking heart attack. I wish I hadn't been so indifferent to my mother. If only I could call her back and tell her I'm grateful as hell she's concerned and still worries about my insolent ass.

Hot liquid hits my dick. "Shaah!"

"You'd better not scream! I only want to hear 'yes, ma'am'!"

She yanks the towel from my mouth, pours more hot liquid on me.

"Fuck! That's hot as a pot of grits! Your ass is *crazy!*"

The voice speaks, low and creepy, "That's what they say."

More hot shit hits my flesh.

"What'll it be, Mr. McLain?"

"Yes, ma'am! Goddammit, yes, ma'am! Will you please *stop* that shit!" I'm hoarse, and she must have put something in my liquor, because my energy is sapped.

Wait a minute.

"Very good, Mr. McLain. Now, I'll ask you again," footsteps approach my head, and this might be my wishful thinking, but I swear I just caught a whiff of coconut and vanilla, "do you remember what you said when I said, 'fuck you'?"

There it is again. That heavenly coconut and vanilla mixes with her natural, sensual mystique. I'm probably hallucinating. Though it's dark as hell underneath this blindfold, and the boy in Edmondson Village is flipping in the air, unaware of his bearings, lost as fuck, I still hope my retinas will process the light from her.

I'm sure everybody probably hallucinates and thinks all manner of fantasies when they face the end, conjuring up their loved ones, reliving that last fuck or imagining all the ways they still haven't fucked. I've fucked a lot, so no problems on that front. But I am imagining all the ways I still haven't fucked her.

The smash of that whip next to my ear again sends me damn near a foot in the air.

"*Now*, Mr. McLain!"

"I-I said, I can't wait to get your ass tied up. That's what I said!" I can't think of anybody else who told me to go fuck myself but Eugenia. Despite me saying it to other people, she's the only one on my mind.

Slowly, the blindfold lifts from over my eyes.

My breath leaves my body, and what fills me is the oxygen of her, and shit, it's the most sustaining gas I need to inhale. Nectarine, primrose, and coral streaks of light stretch across the skies over her head. Behind her the early dawn peaks over these open, green Swiss mountain ranges.

No walls surround us, no building, and I'm not in a room. My bed sits in the middle of morning dew on blades of lush greenery, covering long stretches of sharp-edged peaks that slope down to serene valleys and villages, for as far as the human eye can see. Nothing stands between Eugenia's exotic nakedness and the majestic work of God.

Black Mystique is just that, in her leather straps wrapped around her titties and barely covering her ass, with dark smoky makeup on her mouth and eyes. Even while she's unsmiling and stern, a streak of mischief plays in the light of her irises.

She stands over my head, a shapely leg at either side. I twist as hard as I can in my imprisoned position to reach her ankle and lick it. Her pussy drops to me, and her thighs spread apart over my chin, all that moist pink meat opens and shines for me. Inches from my nose, pearly cream pooling around her opening, the salty sweetness is killing my dick. I try to rise, and push my nose in it, tongue in it, but can't quite reach. That shit is worse than drugs within arm's reach of a fiend.

Her essence mingles with the fragrance of daybreak and vegetation, intoxicates my brain and almost sends me back into unconsciousness. "Baby, bring it here so I can taste it."

"If I say you really showed your ass these last few weeks and I'm making you pay for all that shit you did, how do you answer?"

All that waxed grown womanhood stares down over me.

"I'm guiltier than a mothafucka. *Please,* torture me."

She leaves me weak as a hurt animal when she rises and takes it away from me.

"Not like that, though. You wrong for that shit."

Even though she's being coldhearted as hell right now, there is no place on Earth I would rather be.

"Now," she starts, lifting a little metal pot off some warmers.

I brace myself because that doesn't look too safe.

She brings it back and holds it over my dick. "You remember when you wrote in your note a few weeks ago *you* wanted to make *me* scream on top of an open mountain range? How do you plan to do that in your current predicament?"

I crack the hell up laughing.

She pours that creamy shit on my dick standing as tall as these mountains now at the sight of her. "Okay, okay! I don't know how I'm doing it tied the fuck up!"

"Wrong answer!"

More hot cream spills on me.

"Yes, ma'am! Yes, ma'am!" I'm half laughing, half squealing, and this morning goodness nourishes a man's whole existence.

"Very good. You're a fast learner."

"You're so goddamn beautiful."

The whip slaps down on my chest, and I grind my teeth, but I'm not flinching now because that shit makes my dick jump.

"Focus. Now, did you, or did you not, fuck any of my colleagues Memorial Day weekend?"

"No."

The whip cracks air and stops over my eye. "You sure?"

"Yes."

She brings it back in a threat.

"Yes, ma'am!" I chuckle and grunt. "I'm sure."

Eugenia nods. "Did you fuck anybody else since Chicago?"

The whip pulls back.

"No, I couldn't."

"Since Christmas?"

"Three."

"You sure?"

"Yes, ma'am." My heart's so full.

A drill sergeant couldn't dog me harder than she's doing. "Why three?"

"After Christmas…" The days after I dropped off Eugenia in Alpine flood me all over again. "My head was all screwed up. You stayed with me. The sex wasn't just a transaction. You sitting across from me on the couch, by the fire, hiding from me was… that was the sex. Your body and your mannerisms—you thumbing the cup, breathing all slow and careful, eyes filtering out what you would let me see and what you wouldn't—your body was saying what your mouth wouldn't."

I keep remembering.

"We were making love before we touched each other. I was still making love to you after we finished. I thought the feels would pass. Tried to kick you out of my head, for all the reasons you keep spitting—you've got a kid, you live in another city, you've been through a lot, you're older and probably got a whole world behind your eyes I'll never understand. So I went back to this other girl I messed around with last year."

"Ilyana," she murmurs.

My head lifts from the ground. "How did you know that?"

The whip clips the side of my face. "I'm the one in charge here."

I snatch her whip between my teeth. "I like it when you're in charge."

"The others?"

I think back over the last six months, how I tried my hardest to forget Black Mystique. I attempted going back to regular sex, regular conversations, regular emotional exchanges. But no female wields Eugenia's ferocity, or rides my dick like it's a rocket, or launches my soul into take-off.

"I wasn't feeling Ill, and I knew she wanted something permanent, so I cut that. I called up a couple other baddies I have in rotation, to keep me preoccupied. But that didn't work either. I had already caught feelings for the baddest one."

"What do you want with me, Keenan?"

"Something permanent." What the hell did I just say? That came out of nowhere.

A cloud of pain floats across her face now. "Even if I can't give you children?"

Though I hadn't thought all this out, there is no doubt in my mind. I've asked myself this since she told me in Chicago, and reflected real hard on it, because most men want to continue their family name and legacy. But my life and all the things I love are a gray mass without Eugenia. Kids aren't even worth having if she's not there next to me worrying about them. "Yes, ma'am." I swallow. "But I still plan to bust a couple in you, though."

She lowers her head.

My eyeballs skid nearly to the top of my white meat from disbelief.

But I don't want to miss a millisecond of her spitting on my log, watching her saliva slide down my hard-ass shaft until my dick glistens in the morning sun. Eugenia dives down and makes some of my tree disappear in her head.

I'm mesmerized at how slow and pretty her tongue rolls up and down; from my balls, she wets up to my head, where her teeth nip on my skin.

"Ah! Shit!"

"*Shut* up." Her tongue eases the sting, and that contradictory sensation heightens the softness of it massaging and caressing my head. She is patient. Not in a rush. Mouth so moist, head game so methodical, twisting out of the blue and alternating rhythms, and then blessing my manhood with repeated bobbing and licking. Then I go inside her mouth again for her continuous sucking, bobbing, and twisting. The sun is coming up in a nigga's dick, hot and lit. Summertime cracking all through the veins in my wood. Birds singing over my head and shit, and Eugenia's mouth blowing me raw.

I try to keep looking because I don't want to miss her leather-clad body hovering over me and her mouth spread over my log, but she's stirring up a heat wave in my scrotum, and I'm squirming toward the edge, and she pushes me off this time.

"Fuuuuck!" I hear some maniacal fool scream out of me as his soul crests these mountains.

She sucked all that hot cream glaze off me.

In a single leap, she gets up and hops to my torso, unchains me from the steel post of the bed, and though my wrists are still bound, I loop them around her neck and bind her mouth to mine. Eugenia sucks on my tongue like she does everything else, with fearlessness and fire that's just naturally in her. My erect need is blessed with her wetness slipping onto me, and it gets better every time I'm in her.

So goddamn good, the sensations eclipse my respiratory system and clutch my breathing, and the feel of her womanhood galloping on my dick outweighs my life.

She goes fucking nuts. That beast from Christmas Eve night rears her head, and that ass tears my manhood in pieces every time she yanks my dick head.

Eugenia twirls her pelvis, contracting them damn muscles, and riding while she peers down at me through vicious eyes. My wood in her pussy, all heated and soaking me up, it's a whole new world. My heart in hers, my soul in hers, I drop my cuffed arms around her back and chain her ass as far onto me as I can get her.

Inhaling and clawing and sucking and biting, she drives me to the edge again, to the point I'm no longer breathing.

At the edge of the world, we scream and moan into each other.

If for some reason this doesn't work out, I'm never fucking anybody under the age of thirty-five ever again.

20

A WELCOME ESCAPE

KEENAN & EUGENIA

KEENAN

"So, now I have to go tell Show."

Lying in bed next to her before my first set of meetings, I'm glad we scheduled them late in the day to adjust to the time difference. But my ass is hung over and I haven't seen a wink of sleep.

I've never lain in bed with a woman and talked after sex. Never. Every other time, as soon as I did the deed, my purpose was served. Even for the filthy ones who really put it on me, it's always been transactional and I checked out after the nut. The couple times I was feeling a chick, I wasn't so far gone that my mind stood still long enough to know what to say to her after it was over. Like any person with my neurodevelopmental challenge, my head has always been preoccupied and ready to jump on to the next event or goal or focus.

"What will you say to him?" Eugenia stares directly into me.

Underneath an azure sky, we face each other. The duvet covers only our bottom halves, and our fingers play. These majestic mountain peaks complement Eugenia's naked perfection, her almond skin in the white bed cover easily blending into this pristine nature. I hate I need to go anywhere.

"The truth." Happy as I am to see her, every time I remember the task ahead of me, a piece of me plummets to Earth again.

"Will he ever find out about this list?"

I shake my head. "Probably not. But I've still betrayed him."

"He's betraying himself if he insists on living that life."

"You know that's not how friends and family see it."

"Do you think he'll do something unreasonable?"

"No. He doesn't do physical stuff, just underground dealing." Showtime has been inside for transportation, sales, conspiracy, and other drug-related crimes. He's too smart for assault or battery or any violence. I know he has other folks take care of that so his record never looks violent.

"He doesn't sound like a fool. He'll know why this is necessary and he'll have to understand. If he's your friend, he will."

I just don't know who else he's been associating with these last few years I've been working and haven't rolled with him the way we used to. I'll cross that bridge when I get to Baltimore.

For now, conversation with this woman soothes me, like my worries aren't disappearing in the void of somebody else's head, but they land on fruitful territory and return to me in spades of wisdom. Eugenia doesn't just nod politely; her responses confirm she's processing my situation along *with* me. My female friends from Georgetown—women I don't sex but do call for advice—are smart and intellectually on point, but brains are still different from the depth and solidness of life experience. Eugenia has both, and that is food nourishing a man's soul.

"Right now, I'm trying to understand you." Still unable to believe she's lying here and what I've wanted for months is real, I pull her to me.

I'm excited and nervous to climb over her, with all my thoughts climbing over me. What am I doing? Am I ready for this? Wanting a woman worth her value is one thing, but can I handle it?

This Negro, who's never cared two shits what a woman wants, has never been so scared to ask, "What do you want from me, Eugenia?"

The breaths tripping out of her throat, quick skip of her pulse in the hollow of her neck, and her mouth parting tell me that caught her off guard.

"Nothing."

I slide my arms underneath her back to bring her closer. She winds her legs through mine, and my dick is already excited to do these jumping jacks. But deeper than that, my gut and heart will leap off this mountain, over and over.

"That's a lie. You want something, too." I push inside her, enter her contracting womb, hear those shallow gasps in my ear, feel her fingers trace the tat on my back. "Or you wouldn't have gotten on the plane."

"Free European trip."

I love her throaty, chesty laugh, wide array of perfect teeth, supermodel-sleek skin.

Breaking up our giggles, I start stroking inside her. "You came here for something."

I've always hoped no woman would ever want anything from me. I ran away from women's hopes the way hoes run from VDs. Now my big fear is this grown-ass woman truly may want nothing from me. And my feels and heart may be left leaping out there on their own.

At first, it attracted me. Her independence and detachment was part of her allure. Now that I'm jumping off the cliff and looking down, I'm terrified she may not meet me on the way down.

With her wet and creaming all over me, and me driving into the depths of her until I'm mentally lost, her ass meeting every one of my thrusts, it's hard to know why she came. Is it the sex? I press my fingers on her clit, and she arches more, pussy drenching my wood. Her fingers stroke my balls at the same time she catches my lip between her teeth. Is she just nasty, or is she trying to fuck a nigga up for life?

It's hard to tell as the second coming descends on my nerves, and I ascend these heavens.

Not only do I want to talk to her about everything, I almost go to sleep inside Eugenia, content to just lie here for the next few days and not do shit.

"They're coming to get me at one, and I should get up and look at emails and numbers. But I can ask the trip coordinator to set you up a massage or at a restaurant, a village tour or something. What do you feel like doing?"

"I feel like coming with you," Eugenia answers. It shocks the hell out of me, because that's not what I would be doing if I was in Europe on somebody else's dime.

I stare down at her, and again, Black Mystique stares back at me, serious as a heart attack which… enthralls me and horrifies me.

"Woman, go relax and soak in a hot spring or something. Do some nice things for yourself. When was the last time you just kicked back and enjoyed life, no worries?"

"I'm about to kick it now, with you. I want to learn the man who produced Explore, what makes him tick."

Fuck a nigga up for life. That's definitely it.

Once we're ready, I can't give her the time I wish I could. Back when I first asked her to come with me, it was on a whim and I hadn't fully figured out the particulars of how I would actually romance her amid all these meetings.

But like the woman she is, Eugenia doesn't want for attention and takes it in stride.

"Good afternoon, this is Eugenia Jackson, and she'll be joining us."

Never once do I look up and find her bored. In jeans, a silk tank, and a light blazer, she wears her hair tousled and out in a curly, thick bush forming a halo around her head. Leg dangling over her other leg, arm thrown over the back of her wooden chair, she eyes me with a goofy grin every time I peer over my shoulder.

"So what do you think of this schedule?"

"What do you mean?"

"You've been sitting there listening. Does this lineup sound okay for Black folks? Learning about these Swiss traditions and history?"

"Some of it. Not all of it. I think you can strike the mazurka, foxtrot, and polka. Keep this as rich for them as you can. For sure, the bookstores. The architecture, hiking, education on the earth. Especially the part about Africa colliding with Europe to form the Alps, and how one day, they'll be one continent. Eurafrica? I had no idea. That is really cool to know." Eugenia's eyes light up as she describes that. And it filters through my retinas.

"So you think people would be willing to pay for a demonstration of that?"

She nods. "I would. I think other parents wanting to educate their kids would."

I look over the numbers and costs for the overhead, hold some calls with lawyers and insurance contacts to talk about covering those activities. A number of touring companies have showed up to make their pitch for their tour. Eugenia is pretty clear about telling me which experiences may work and which she's not too crazy about. By that evening, the representatives have figured out they need to win her over more than they do me.

That night, sitting by a window past sunset, we're at a restaurant nestled on the side of a steep mountain. I'm on a call running these options by some of the guys back home. I do a double take at seeing two little girls playing and skipping around her. My knee-jerk reaction is to jump up and go see what that's about.

Black women don't like for anybody to touch their hair, and Eugenia is well within her right to stand up and say something if she so chooses.

But Eugenia breaks out laughing. The girls pluck flowers in her kinks, leaning forward to smell, pulling it out to see its elasticity, and comparing it to their bone-straight locks. But nowhere on the social worker is there a hint of stress, not even when the girls grab teacups from empty tables and sit for imaginary tea. My lady pretends along with them, tickling the shit out of me while she plays with their little ponies.

"All right, girls, come on. Come! That's enough. Thank you so much. I so apologize," a harried mother comes from the kitchen in her apron. "You're far too kind for watching them, ma'am."

Riding in the jeep back to the bed an hour later, we intertwine our fingers on her thigh. In pitch-black darkness, I can't see beyond the headlights illuminating the tiny mountainside road. Though her profile is barely visible, through her silence, she must be taking it all in.

In bed, after I send a few more emails and wrap another couple of video calls, we lie naked again at the end of our day together. It's so dark out here, our only light is the stars in the sky and tiny village houses below. The scene resembles miniature model villages.

Exhausted as dogs after a dogfight, we only have enough energy to curl into each other for the first time since Christmas Eve night. But it's even more comforting because tonight we're not strangers and she's not on edge. Lying down without sexing? Hell, something big is happening for a nigga.

The long day and the time difference are killing me, as well as waking up early to her, so I'm snoring before I even close my eyes. But I still find energy to place my hand on her abdomen.

"So you *do* still want kids."

EUGENIA

"I wasn't ready. Sheldon's parents groomed him and his siblings for privilege and influence. Dealing with those types of people, all their little microaggressions and power plays, takes a certain mental stamina. Neither of us knew that I didn't have it."

The lonely cave I lived in five years ago is dark and twisting, echoing with voices of Daddy and Odie and gunshots, painful enough to shut my eyes now.

"It felt like I was thrown into a den of wolves. It was my hell to deal with while he was overseas."

I'm brought back to the tranquility of the Alps by Keenan's rough hand, cupping my cheek and rubbing off my tears.

"I'm sorry you had to go through that. He should have

been there for you, and you should have been his first priority."

"As far as he knew, I was. It wasn't my time."

"He wasn't your man."

I don't know why I got on the plane. Was it to hear him tell me that?

Since it's still daytime in the States, but the middle of the night in Switzerland, our sleep is uneven, so we lie awake talking under this blanket of night sky. Not in a million years would I have ever thought to put a bed outside on a mountain. But the openness of all this nature is a welcome escape from my cave walls. It's more therapy than any superficial phone conversation with Lillian.

Beneath us rests the quaint, picturesque village of Appenzell, with its rolling green hills, shops, colorful houses, cows that provide the milk for Swiss cheese and its history dating past the Middle Ages. The scene is a mountainous, still-life photo or an Alexander Babich oil painting, and this art and nature aesthetic relaxes me completely.

What do I want from him?

What does a woman want at this point, after she's had all the things women usually work hard for, and managed to lose them all? Big time. Where do I find the courage to want anything again, for fear of losing it? Or fearing that I may hurt him, without even trying. How do I grow past the fact I've trained myself not to want or hope, so I'm not disappointed when I don't receive? Or that if I do receive, I'll screw it up.

I can't look at Keenan and fix my mouth to say all this. Not when he makes love to me as if he's trying to join every fiber of himself to every fiber of me, and I'm scared my hopeless ass doesn't have any fibers left for him to connect to. Or he turns to me, holds out his fork for me to eat a bite of his steak and he sucks off the sauce remaining on my mouth. Or he takes his time lathering me in a copper bath filled with whey.

I'm stunned in the afternoon as we are led to a cliff and shown to some small round, wooden tubs that cowboys once used for bathing in Westerns, the tubs that are so small your arms and feet hang out of the sides. Beyond them lies endless valleys between elegant mountains so breathtaking I could live here forever.

"What is this?"

"What does it look like?" That baby face of his breaks into chuckles.

"Welcome to the Swiss cheese bath, my dear." The attendant brings us a stack of towels and soap and starts explaining how the bath works. "Not to worry. The curds have been removed."

I peer into the disgusting yellowish-green milk. "Oh. What a relief."

The attendant sets down fruit, cheese, and champagne, and the moment he's gone, Keenan comes to me. "It's non-alcoholic."

"I'm not stopping you from drinking."

He lifts my light sweater over my head. "I'm only drinking when you are."

"You don't have to do that."

Our fingers fumbling, us staring at each other, we wrestle off one another's jeans.

"Don't tell me what I don't have to do. You're not in charge here. Get in the tub."

He turns me around and guides my arm.

"We're both getting in here? There are more tubs over there. Only one person should go in here."

"Why don't we try this out? Being one."

Squeezed inside, I'm sandwiched on top of him, which I suppose was his goal. He can't stop laughing with a gigantic smile that he pulled me into this, at us pressed together in this tiny tub of foul-smelling cheese byproduct, him circling my breasts with soap, and me soaping over his chest, washing between one other's thighs. It's the most uncomfortable, and nothing sexual is happening, only goofiness and pranks.

"I don't want to leave." The words slip out of my subconscious while I'm immersed in the long lines of greenery ascending to the sky. I doubted it was possible for me to be so relaxed. "That tiny village is Heaven on Earth."

Some of my sadness seems to evaporate in the peace and stillness.

"I don't want you to leave," his voice whispers behind me. "So you think people would rather spend more time here than in Rome?"

"You should give them options. Some tourists may want nothing but to relax their entire trip, and a village-based excursion in mountains with food and quiet baths and hiking may be it for them. And then a combination, like you're doing. And just a cities-based trip for the people who only want to run around and party and sightsee. There should definitely be at least three packages for people to choose their pace and experience."

He listens intently before making notes and going back through spreadsheets, working to build his enterprise, the same way Sheldon used to. What happens once Keenan has built his? Who does he become?

Rome is packed with people, and the food is hit or miss, which I have plenty of time to taste-test with him in meetings.

"What's the word?" he asks once he exits a presentation.

"Open up."

With suspicion, he does so, his face scrunched and cringing. The entire kitchen crew observes, all smiles and giggles.

His mouth slides open like I'm sticking in a bomb. Fear in his eyes that gaze at me, he gnashes his teeth the way Hadar used to when I fed him black-eyed peas. "What is this shit?"

"Jellyfish."

He spins around in desperation for a trashcan.

"Did you get that?" I ask one of the hosts.

"We got it," she replies with my cell phone in hand.

My shoulders and gut shake along with the others'. "We'll see how all your little groupies like that on socials."

The Colosseum, Pantheon, Trevi fountain, the Forum, thousands of years of Roman and European history and architecture in one of the oldest cities on the planet, all require five days, and that's still not enough time to learn and digest. I almost don't believe my vision, that I'm really seeing old stone slabs and ruins lying around the city from structures built hundreds of years ago, or even millennia.

"Unfortunately, the beautiful statues that once stood here were stolen through the centuries," our tour guide explains. "The metal was often taken and melted down for somebody else's statue, and the slab bases left behind. That's what these are." We stare at myriad dusty stone slabs with deep cracks telling just how much they've endured. "These impressions in the ceiling overhead once contained iron clamps."

Then there's the Curia of Pompey where Julius Caesar was stabbed, how this senate meeting site from the early B.C. period was buried under other buildings for millennia, and then unearthed in the 1900s at the direction of Italian dictator, Mussolini.

"What do you think about this for kids? About Explore bringing an inner-city youth trip here?" Keenan asks me.

"This city is huge. So many distractions and ways for a kid to get lost down these alleys, tunnels, and cobblestone streets." Rome is literally a network of beautiful bridges, waterways, and giant historic buildings that a teen could easily think they're wandering off for a moment and lose the group. I shake my head at the preposterousness of a bunch of children running around in Europe with no home training, kids who can hardly make it through an American mall without fighting. My social worker instincts kick in as I descend the list of safety hazards that promise to wind up in assured disaster.

"You'd need a *lot* of professional staff, Keenan. Two kids to a dedicated monitor. I'm not talking about lightweight parent chaperones either, who'll only be halfway watching. A trip like this requires professionally trained child psychology and secondary education instructors. You need people who are serious about youth, not just casual camp counselors looking for a free trip. Then there's the insurance. The kids and their parents would need a couple of orientations about conducting themselves in a foreign country, with foreign laws, and all the adequate warnings, what to do if they get in trouble or engage with police. In fact, you probably should only take youth who have a proven relationship with Explore. Whichever kids performed well the year before, who can follow rules and—"

"Troubled doesn't mean incompetent, Eugenia," he reminds me in a tone that evidences his sensitivity on this subject.

"You think I, of all people, don't know that?"

He sucks his teeth and smiles a little as he remembers who he's talking to.

Normally, Keenan is defensive and confrontational, dismissive about issues that come up. Not this time. He was cool, rational.

Chaitra's insights are not lost on me. But he hasn't blown up at me a single time when I've pushed back or voiced my concerns. I've seen none of the behavior I also read about online. None of the conduct Sheldon was also sure to point out.

I do love how his caring about our community reflects my own.

"Don't be offended. We come from the same place. What you want still requires heightened safety," I explain. Our driver delivers us to our second hotel in Rome. "What if somebody has epilepsy, high blood pressure, diabetes, asthma? You should also probably keep a couple of nurses close."

We enter the Hotel de Russie Rome for the first time. A miniature palace is where we're laying our heads for the next two days. We're staying in the Valadier suite that's $4,600 a night, with soundproofed rooms and marble walls.

"Oh, God, can your tourists afford this?"

"This is for the business types and executives we're courting, who'll bring their clients to Explore for their company retreats. We'll arrange mini-adventures for them with some Black flavor to it. But like you said, I'll make sure we have different packages and options for people on different levels. That way, everybody feels included and it's not totally outside the reach of professionals not established yet." He stretches out his arm and wraps it around my waist, guiding me in front of him and threading me through the gardens and tables to sit for a massive dinner with the Roman team of vendors.

In the middle of a presentation of the offerings and pairings, I'm sampling every type of dish imaginable—oxtail stew, tripe, grilled lamb.

But I look over to find Keenan's gaze drifting. Underneath the table, his leg stabs the patio floor beneath us.

Subtly as I can, I slide my hand over his thigh, and give him a couple of squeezes to bring him back from somewhere else. As soon as the travel executive gives him a break to eat, I'm still offering him silent support.

My tone is easy and comforting between us. "Do you take medication?"

His eyes flicker, with part surprise and part shame. He nods. "Yeah."

"You forgot it? Which suitcase is it in?"

Back in the suite, I rummage through his messy bag as he directed and find it exactly where he described, in a leather case with hygiene products and condoms we haven't used. We've been humping for the past few days, sometimes from the moment we open our eyes to the time our heads hit the pillow. Bringing the bottle with me, I'm subtle in passing it to him under the table.

"How about we take a walk to see the grounds?" I suggest to sneak him away from the group.

"Oh, let us show you the details and designs," the tourism official offers.

"We would love to hear about that tomorrow. We hope it's all right if we just steal a few private minutes for ourselves tonight, just to walk and take it all in? We won't be long," I explain.

A shaky Keenan pulls out my chair, and I clasp his hand at my backside.

Behind a bush, his back to me, he swallows one of the pills I hand him. "Thank you."

Easing my arms around him, my fingers on his chest, I lay my cheek on his back. "Don't hide from me now. It's not anything to be ashamed of."

He turns and draws me into his arms. Around my back and along my scalp, his fingers are tight and grateful, such that my feet leave the ground for the moment he lifts me. I'm not sure I'll ever get used to the sticky warmth in my center matching the balmy humidity of Rome. Or how he holds nothing back when we start tonguing each other and his energy demands one hundred percent of me, even the parts I think I no longer have, that he seems intent on proving to me that I still do.

In the shadows of this real life Van Gogh painting, outside the gold glow of romantic lamps and hanging string lights in the bushes, nobody can see me nearly come undone as the backs of his fingers stroke my nipples over my dress. Though I spent hours last night digging my nails into the dragon tattoo across his back, and I'm sore from all the action this week, I still leak into my panties at his touch.

"Don't go back to Chicago."

At the thresholds of his humanity—his eyes—he's not laughing.

"Chicago is my home. It's where my family is, my job. You knew that."

"What I knew is you were miserable when I came to see you in Chicago. You were miserable at Taste last Christmas. But you're not miserable now."

I cut my eyes at this silliness and turn to walk away. "Of course I'm not miserable here. I've been on vacation for days."

He hooks his finger through the open cutout of my summer dress and tugs me back.

"Then how do you explain your happiness Memorial Day weekend?" In the dark, behind hanging vines that conceal us, his handsome face breaks me down the way he tends to do. "Or when I first got to your city and you pretended you didn't want me there, but we both know you did." His arm swings over my shoulder and cocoons me inside it, until all else disappears but his neck and his athletic, cool cologne. "You're happy when we're together."

His voice drapes around my heart and nurtures my thoughts of trying again, hoping again.

"Keenan."

"So you're going to front like you're not feeling this, too?"

"No, I'm not going to front. But are *you* fronting like you don't know my history? My last run in New York didn't go so well." As much as my heart sinks under those words, it's true. I tried to kill myself and I'm only setting myself up for failure if I don't acknowledge my weaknesses. "You should be offering your home to a woman who—"

"To the woman whose air I want to breathe every day, whose pussy I want to eat for breakfast every morning."

I push my fingers over his mouth.

He wags them off. "You said it yourself. Your marriage wasn't your time. You weren't ready. But that was years ago."

"And how do you know *you're* ready? You're giving up all your crazy parties and women and sex now, Keenan?"

The doubt twitches in his eyelid.

I shake my head. "No. I won't be your test subject."

He combs his hands over his mohawk and grips it. His stare grips me. "This is some scary shit for me, too. I ain' never gave myself to any woman. But I also don't want to inhale another whiff of New York air in these lungs without you there breathing it, too. Chicago is not your home anymore, Eugenia. It's your comfort zone, where you run to when you don't have anywhere else to run. But it's not where your son is, and it's not where I am. Spend the summer in New York with me, and Hadar, and the Explore youth."

21

THE MAN SHE DESERVES

KEENAN

Touching down in Baltimore, there's a light trimming the clouds, and I'm marching toward it. I have a big task tonight, but the reward is worth it.

Once again, the time difference when I land in the States is kicking me in the gut. It's morning time here and evening time in Europe. Eugenia and I worked on the plane ride and only slept a little.

Though I'm exhausted, I still have the burst of energy to shoot her my first text.

Me: *Good morning, gorgeous.*

I've had her number for months, but this is my first time using it. Before, I was too nervous and didn't know what to say that wouldn't freak her out. Had I been outrageous with her over the phone, I definitely wouldn't have gotten an audience in person. So I did it the other way around and dropped in on her, face-to-face.

Black Mystique: *Good morning, sir. I'll be thinking of you today.*

The wait was well worth it. It was hard to watch her keep

walking toward the gate for Chi-Town while I headed to my leg for B'More.

Morning it is, in a lot of ways.

Me and my heart enter the office at McLain Construction, and the secretaries from high school all parade in. Normally, this is cool, but so much weighs on my mind. I only have forty-eight hours in town to cover a lot of ground.

"Heyyy, Stunt Mannn," they sing in whispers.

"You getting our B'More boat ready for the Hamptons?" Tasha asks, her hand reaching for my back.

Her face freezes when I stop her.

"I promise you, ladies, the Hamptons will be lit. But for now, you will have to excuse me. I have a lot of catch-up work and a ton of meetings today."

A joint earthquake must hit all of them at once.

"Ha. Wow, okay then, Stunt Man. Bein' all serious," Jewel observes with smacks of her gum. "Can we at least holler at you in the club tonight? Show's spot? VIP?"

I shake my head. "Got other business to tend to this trip."

For the next eight hours, business is what I do, to the best of my ability when I'm not thinking about what goes down tonight. I pick up the phone and remind myself of why I am making this move in the first place.

Me: *How's your day going?*

Black Mystique: *How many pictures have been taken of you getting screwed or blown?*

In my office, I can't help cracking up, the laughter busting out of me and releasing some of this stress on my back.

Me: *My bad. College. If I'd known Black Mystique was coming, I would have saved my virginity.*

Black Mystique: *Bullshit.*

Staring at the phone, remembering waking up to her on a Swiss mountain, now I'm sitting at my desk giggling like a little kid and shit.

Me: *Don't look. There won't be anymore... new ones.*

Me: *I miss you, baby.*

Faster than I typed them, I delete those words.

It's too soon. And I just saw her a few hours ago. *And* I'm still scared as shit.

Finally, the end of the day comes for me.

Lorenzo: *You straight?*

I massage the sharp pains in my chest. My moms comes to stand at the door of my office.

Me: *As I'll ever be.*

Lorenzo: *I can meet you over there.*

Me: *Nah. Stay out of it.*

"Call me when you're finished?" Ma asks. She tries to be tough, but there's no mistaking the fear in her unsteady walk to my desk.

I nod.

"After that, when do I get to meet this Eugenia?"

At the mention of that, a nigga's full hundred watts of light fills him up and comes out across my lips.

Ma's eyebrows express surprise. "Oh, well now. So D and Shay weren't lying."

Hold up. *"Shay?"* I haven't confided anything in my sister.

Ma's mouth snaps closed. "She just noticed you acting different at the last Explore meeting is all."

"You sure that's all? Did Shay do something?"

Come to think of it, she hasn't come into my office today trying to swing her big stick around, beating my nerves about budget and excess spending. It's been awfully quiet. Maybe she's with Solly.

Ma shakes her head. "No, don't worry about her. This will probably be the only time I tell you to just worry about yourself."

Down in the garage, she walks me to my BMW, and Pop appears.

"So the last one leaves the coop, huh? What's goin' on around here? What's this I hear about you trying to be a real man?" he asks.

He grabs me in a long, tight grip.

I shake my head. "Not trying to be. I am."

"That's it. What I want to hear." He slaps my back, still holding on to his youngest. "You'll be fine. Just fine. I'm proud of ya."

"Thanks, Pop."

I don't hate him the way Shay does, nor sideline him like Desmond. I used to go hang out at his barbershop all the time with Show, 'Renzo, and the others. He didn't have any money, and that never mattered to me. It didn't even really faze me that he left before I was ten, not the way it pissed off Shay. She felt robbed and stuck with Des and me. But because Pop wasn't in the house and Ma was too busy, I had way too much freedom as a teenager, and I loved it. My teachers and counselors invited me on hikes around Maryland and Virginia, which turned into boating and rafting expeditions in Colorado, Wyoming, and California, which then landed me in front of Congress testifying about the benefits of nature for kids from the 'hood, especially us who were neurodiverse.

My imagination opened doors to summer programs and camps, and relationships with adventure-seekers who funded me going abroad. And finally, admission to Harvard, USC, Duke, Vanderbilt, Xavier, and Georgetown.

But behind the scenes, even after Ma moved us away, I still made it back to Edmondson Village, to my crew. If everybody else couldn't afford to go global, I would bring the world to them. And we threw down. On Show's dime.

I was never going to leave them all behind the way D did when he started playing football or Shay did when she started making money.

I *always* chose my 'hood. Even when it came to the college I attended.

Heavy feet carry me straight through the door of Show's.

"Stunt Man!"

"Stunt Dog!"

"Stunner!"

"Hey, sexy!"

My childhood buddy comes toward me with outstretched arms and pulls me to him in a firm embrace. Bottles pop around us, hands slap my back, squeeze my shoulders, express their pride in a native son that I'm not sure I deserve.

"Player, welcome home, son," Show says, releasing me. "How was Europe? Everybody can't get that passport privilege, you know?" He references how, as a felon on parole, he can't leave the country.

Sometimes I wonder if I should have convinced him to stop selling.

"Show, let's find some place private, man."

"Damn, dude, somebody serve this man a drink." He waves over a server. "You look like you just ate your last meal and you're going to the electric chair or some shit."

Exactly how it feels.

Show's easy grin and crinkling eyes worsen my guilt. "So you handled your business in Europe? And now you're back where you belong? Where'd you go? Sweden? France?"

"Switzerland, Italy, and Greece." Heart banging harder than the Bose stereo speakers, I sink the whiskey the server just set down.

"Damn, you want another one of those? Get him another before we start up tonight, so he can loosen up some."

Any possibility of a kickback diminishes once my hand goes up. "That's okay. I'm straight, man."

Show's easiness evaporates. "Why don't you come with it,

Keenan? What are you doing here looking all tight?" His linked fingers come down on the table in a heavy fist.

"Explore has decided there will be no unregistered guests at the hotels for the concert. There'll be no individual or private boat parties that aren't arranged through Explore's approved vendors or—"

"Cut, man, cut." He puts his hands together in perpendicular form. "Say that shit in English."

"I'm not holding any parties separate from the ones hosted by Explore. Explore's official boats will be the only boats on the water that week."

Thirty-three years compresses into what must be a full ten seconds that passes between him and me. Judging from the glitching of his eye, I swear he's about to punch me out.

"You mean we're not having *our* parties?"

I nod. "Right." I wave over my armed security who totes the suitcase, and he flips it open on the table. "There's all of it, everything you've passed me over the last year." $675,000 cash to contribute to several Baltimore-themed parties the week of the concert. "The others are getting their cuts returned to them."

"Tuh." He motions for the security guard to close it. "So my money's not good enough for you anymore? I had a lot riding on this. On *you*. I invested in you, financed your come-up, but more than that, I've always had your back. Have mine now."

"I can't, Show."

"Don't give me that shit. Yeah, you can, man. Where is this coming from? Huh? Your high-yella rich friend?"

I shake my head. "It's me. I'm the CEO. The buck stops with me."

"Is it that lady you were hugged up with Memorial Day weekend? The one you almost broke your neck for onstage?

Maybe we ought to pay her a visit. She doesn't like me? Maybe I can change her mind."

Immediately, I see fucking fire. *"Don't… put her name… in your mouth."*

"Ha." Across his face—the flaring nostrils, glazed-out eyes, curling lips—he's pissed, even if he knows how to keep it in check. "So that's who it is."

"Show." My fists curl into bombs. "This doesn't have shit to do with anybody else. I will support you, and anything you want to do—*any*thing—when your business is legit. Clean. I've always been clean. My partners are clean. My company. Is clean."

His fingers hug the table. "And it'll stay that way. *One* party. Just have one blowout with me. I can't believe you're making me—" He pounds the table. *"Beg* for this shit!" he finishes, sputtering.

"You don't have to beg if it's all on paper."

I square my shoulders, because I am prepared to do *whatever* it takes. Explore will have the CEO it deserves, and Eugenia the man she deserves.

I can't say sorry. I'm not sorry for this, but in hindsight, I am sorry I failed Show. That I kept putting off the inevitable and didn't address this with him sooner, as I kept coming home over the years, carefully walking the line between our diverging worlds.

So it looks like I'm cutting him loose now that I'm making a name for myself, when this might have gone down a whole lot different if I'd started spitting truth in his ear years ago.

"Now that you're bigger than me, will I even see you for the concert? Those backstage passes still good?"

"You'll have to purchase them through MoneyCruncher and book your hotel through Expl—"

He slaps his glass from the table. I don't flinch. A man of conviction never should.

I'm not telling him about the list I agreed to, of people who have already fallen out with the hotels for being too demanding over the phone, or gotten confrontational with Explore staff, and now they are forever shadow-banned from any of our events or locations. The best way to make clear to the Hamptons community and all our sponsors that we're a worthy, safe investment starts with me. And *my* conduct and choices.

He opens up his hands. "What do you want me to tell all our people?"

"I'll tell them. I'll put the word out."

"Get the fuck out of my establishment."

As I walk out, I carry the disappointments and loss of friends and homies with me. But I also recall twisting in the air the last time I did a backflip, and landing. How their hands clawed me, felt inside my pockets, groping me like I was a damn circus performer.

Tonight, I didn't valet my car so I wouldn't have to stand around while they brought it. Instead, it sits where I left it across the street.

Lorenzo waits there. He lights up a joint and passes it. Shit, I take a deep hit, dragging into my lungs the high of memories long past.

"You're only doing what you need to protect yours. This was a long time coming."

I blow out the smoke of our yesterdays. "A long time could still come for me."

One thing is for certain. Whatever happens from here on out, the boy from Edmondson Village is not flipping in the air, lost or twisting with no sense of his bearings, not anymore.

WHAT ARE WE DOING?

EUGENIA

"*Odie, no! Put the gun down!*"

"Ma'am, please, come forward," the correctional officer says to me, his voice removing the bullet from my chamber of memories.

After hours of waiting in line at Stateville Correctional, I'm finally passing the metal detectors. Displaying my driver's license and having the correctional officers verify my identity, I haul my twenty years of guilt through these lead doors. They slam behind me and lock me into a sepulcher of the walking dead.

At the slab of table sits my baby brother, Odell.

"Sis." His eyes crinkle up, and he grabs my hands. "It took you forever to get here. What's it been? January?"

I nod. "Sorry about that. Between my job and my court case and the classes, it's been crazy. But I've been putting money on your books."

Until January, I was visiting him once a month. But the last visit here, right after Christmas, right after I left Hadar behind in New York, after so much had gone down last year… ripped up my delicate emotional fabric. Barely holding it together myself, seeing my sweet, amazingly talented Odie in here alone reminded me again of another failure.

"Are you all right? Is anybody messing with you? How are you holding up?"

He wouldn't tell me if he were in trouble. But the bumps on his forehead and aging cuts on his cheek and arms disclose the answers he won't.

He lifts the weight he's carried on those shoulders for nineteen years. "Same. Food ain't got any better." Some semblance of a smile attempts entering his lips. "What about you? Hadar? You've seen him? The job?"

I pull out pictures on my cell phone from Memorial Day weekend, and he scrolls through them, getting lost at the beach in Amagansett, his eyes soaking it all in. This tiny slice of joy for him is an anchor of guilt hanging around my neck.

"Check out you and him swimming in the Hamptons now." His lips manage a wan smile that sinks under the wistfulness. "Marrying the banker was a good move. I know y'all are separated and he's married again. You and him had some beef. But you gave him a kid, and look at where it got you. You meeting him wasn't all bad…" He takes a moment to tap the photo of Hadar and me.

I've never brought Hadar here to meet Odie. Sheldon would flip.

"Who is this?"

"Who is who?"

He spins the phone back in my direction.

Hidden among the many photos of Hadar and me, or Hadar playing, is a picture of Keenan and me kissing on the edge of the cliff Memorial Day weekend. A small laugh kicks from a corner of me that must be growing by the day. Princess must have snapped that with my phone while I wasn't paying attention.

Odie is injected with a shot of my humor, and the crinkling around his eyes deepens, his smile turning genuine as he nods. "Aww, okay. That's who he is."

Mountains of joy rise in us both now as my fingers scroll to the photos of Europe.

"Damn. Switzerland," he murmurs. "All this perfection." Its fresh air seems to enter his head that wags up and down underneath the heavy concrete walls of this place. His finger taps my phone screen repeatedly. "This here is what's up. I'm real fucking happy for you, sis." Swiping through the mountains, caves, footpaths, villages, food, and odd hotels, he seems to live all the wonders for himself.

"Odie." A geyser of emotion gushes up my airway as I prepare to tell him. I remember the last time I delivered this news, after Sheldon proposed. Odie cried. "I may be going back to New York for a while." And abandoning him all over again.

Today, his hands reach for mine over my phone.

"It's what you need to do. You shouldn't have left. Ain't shit here in Illinois for you. Don't come back this time."

I had my interview with Roberta and Lionel Middleton via videoconference a couple of weeks ago, and then with Lion and Kevin, to work at the new Middleton Foundation, the charitable funding arm of Explore.

With me as Acting Executive Director, we'd do a trial run for a few months while I help them get it off the ground, organizing the Middletons' entire center for youth that would coincide with a potential book and documentary on Blacks in the Hamptons. I'd hire staff to help map out all the logistics, hazards, and legalities of bringing inner city youth to the Hamptons, and then ultimately, sending those who thrive on to Europe. I'd also integrate it with their Explore activities and the Black Business Council's youth business program. Meanwhile, I'd take unpaid leave from my job with the city of Chicago, not formally ending my position right now.

It's a chance to social work in a new way, outside the rigors of the city bureaucracy and everyday monotonous grunt work. Doing what I love, I'd build something new and special from the ground up. Alongside seeing my son more often, and Keenan, my life is taking on actual purpose I don't have to lie about now.

"I'll come and see you when I come to see Mama."

"Just make sure I keep getting these," Odie replies, tapping the photos. "I want to see it all."

He buries his face in my hands, and I hold him in the closest way this facility will allow, for as long as we can. He was fifteen when he went in for manslaughter and was tried as an adult. Wherever I am, I'll come and fight for him.

He's the only brother I would fight for.

For now, I have to go. It's a long drive back to Chicago, and my condo isn't quite packed. Plus, we're having a family barbecue this weekend, and I have an interview with Tabatha who'll transfer my file to the social worker in New York. Keenan's flying in to help me finish packing and to meet my family. I absolutely did not want that, but Keenan being Keenan...

The next morning, Tab sits with me in a near-empty space I've lived in since the last time I left New York. Sheldon's name is on it, and he's agreed not to sell it from under me until I know for sure what I'm doing next. Then he'll likely put the sale proceeds into my next home or a trust for Hadar. I have my own savings and retirement accounts now, so I'm inclined to buy my own place at some point.

"You look different." Tab didn't have any house items to search today, so she perches on a sofa I'm leaving behind for now. "There's a glow about you."

Hands shoved in my jeans, those words resonate in my wiggling toes. "I feel different."

"You went to Europe, and now going to the Hamptons for a new position?"

"It's all temporary for now. We'll see how it goes, but yes, the Middleton Foundation will be a change from the grind at the city of Chicago. And Hadar is there, so it makes sense."

"Wow, so much happening at once. How exciting for you. I was blown away when you called and said you were breaking out for Europe. How did you come across all these opportunities so fast?"

Very carefully, I fish out parts of the truth. "Friends and associates who have connections. The Middletons are doing a lot with their new youth work, and they need help. The Europe trip is to start planning youth activities for the Foundation to take kids there next summer." My conscience whips me and leaves stinging welts all over my insides.

She nods. "Good for you, Eugenia. A chance to try it again."

Keeping my words few so as not to give away too much, I keep my smile on autopilot and wag my head. "Yes."

Instead of relief, I'm beaten with an electric cord of guilt as she holds out her hand. "Congratulations, and I hope it all goes well for you. Contact your new social worker with the number for your new therapist and information so she can start up your file there."

An hour later, Keenan throws his overnight bag in my Lexus at the airport.

"Baby," he says in my mouth, sucking me up before I have time to greet him back. His fingers buried so deep in my hair they loosen my bun, our faces pressed so close, all that restless energy charging at me, I can hardly breathe.

Exhilarating and… overwhelming. His electricity excites and startles me. I know I shouldn't compare him to Sheldon, but what other standard is there to compare him to? Certainly not my father or my brothers, or the guys at the office, but the highest standard of man I know. Keenan does not fall short of Sheldon. He's just different in ways that shake me.

I pull back a little. "Mr. McLain. We have to go."

"Yes, ma'am," he whispers with a final tug of my bottom lip. Telltale deviousness crisscrosses his face. "Two weeks is a long-ass time, you know?"

Two weeks of nightly video calls, of falling asleep on the phone, masturbating while the other watches… I've even relearned how to text pure silliness, about nothing at all. It's been forever since I've felt comfortable enough with some-body to do that. But our last text exchange?

Dark Chocolate (I know that's the nickname my cousin Koi gave him, but it stuck): *What kind of panties you got on?*

Me: *The kind your daddy likes.*

Dark Chocolate: *Shid, don't fuck around and get hurt. My daddy'll tear your ass up.*

Me: *If his son is any indication, I doubt it.*

Dark Chocolate: *Ooohhh, damn! Black Mystique got some heat on her.*

Now my guilt-riddled nerves twist around one another.

This too shall pass, Genie.

"So what's the latest on concert preparation fiascoes?" I ask him.

He swipes a hand down his face. "Shit, how many damn different kinds of microphones are there? How many places can you put 'em? I swear she'll have one hanging out of her ass."

Cracking up is another thing I'm doing a lot of these days. I forgot my own little thuggish sense of humor. Sheldon's is kind of stiff, and in squeezing myself into his life, I let that piece of myself go.

But the laughter subsides in front of my aunt's house.

Before I can give him any warnings, he's already out the door and coming around to open mine. Totally relaxed, Keenan holds out his hand, and I place mine inside it. He brings me to him, and when I lean to kiss his mouth, he rises to kiss my forehead, gentler this time. His fingers in mine are reassuring and protective. Like he's reminding himself when he can be too much, and the time to be just enough.

As we enter the backyard, all the heads turning are an orchestra.

First up are my brothers.

"What's good, bruh?" Eugene asks. "So you're the one who's taking our sister away again, huh? Like the last dude. And when will you be sending her back here, tail between her legs?"

"Eugene," I mutter.

"So you're Eugene? The oldest?" Keenan asks. "Let me ask you something, man. How many times since she's been back have you taken her out and done something nice for her? Even a scoop of ice cream?"

"Eugenia's got enough money to buy ice cream for this whole block, for *years*."

Keenan shakes his head. "That wasn't my question. Until you can say how you supported her, don't talk about what some other dude did, man."

"What's up, man? Nelson. My sister is over there grinning ear to ear. Let me shake your damn hand. You want some food?"

Keenan leans against his ear. "Is it any good?"

The two of them bust up.

"Nah, not really."

"All right then, kill that. Why don't me and you do ribs or something later, okay? And make sure they're fire. A nigga's stomach is killing me." Keenan slaps two hundred dollars, more than enough for ribs, into the hand of a shocked Nelson.

Keenan's swagger makes its way to my mother, who's a little taken aback at how he lifts her from the ground to hug her tight and plants a long kiss on her cheek.

Without hesitation, he goes inside the house, where Daddy is. I start after him, to make sure it goes okay, but Mama's arm swings around my waist.

"Tell me all about this New York thing you're about to do."

Her contentment is lined with wistfulness while she listens to the arrangements. The worry lines on Mama's face deepen, and her fingers spin her simple gold wedding ring around and around. "I'm happy for you, baby." We sit by ourselves in the den where the only noise is children running in and out. "I'm sorry, Eugenia."

I don't need for her to elaborate, not on a sunny day with no clouds in the sky. "Don't be, Mama."

"But I am." Her mouth twitches as it forms the next words they've been holding for years. "We shouldn't have told you to leave Sheldon or put our noses in your marriage. I was only worried about you. You were so sad, and I hated hearing you talk like... you were on your way to an early grave."

My eyes close and reopen, and for the first time I've ever relived my marriage, I don't feel the fingers of death squeezing my throat at the memory. "We all go through our night."

She presses me hard. "I hope now it's your day."

"Me, too."

"Genie," Gene calls from outdoors. "You coming over here to slap down bones or not?"

"Yeah, *Genie*," Keenan repeats mockingly, devilishly. "Come take a seat."

On the other end of the table, I squeeze in next to a salty Koi and a bitter Valuable.

"Good afternoon, cousins."

Silence.

Am I wrong for enjoying that music to my ears?

"You want something to drink?" one of my cousins asks.

Keenan's head swings in the negative. "Eugenia first. And non-alcoholic only. I only drink when my lady drinks."

Not a chance passes that he doesn't reinforce for every ear in the yard that I am to be respected.

"He is definitely not your ex," Nelson mutters and throws his arm around me.

In the truck on the way back to my place, Keenan's fingers hug mine. "So what time is my interview with the social worker? We leave tomorrow, and I still haven't heard from her. I want to knock that out so I can enroll in the parenting classes and we can push past the hard part. Is she calling in the morning, before we go?" He squeezes my thigh.

Anxiety squeezes my lungs while I squeeze his fingers. "Oh, I met with the social worker this morning."

The news ricochets across him. "I thought we agreed we would do that together. But you met her while I was on the plane?"

"We can meet the new social worker in New York together."

All the screwed-up things I've done to Sheldon, and yes, the hurt I intentionally caused him, was slightly different than this tsunami unfolding on Keenan.

"Did you at least tell her about me, Eugenia?"

"Keenan—"

He slides his fingers out of mine and sits erect in the seat. "Don't Keenan me."

"All I want is to get one step closer to my case being closed, without raising any new alarms. I just want to be home free. With one less person in my business, nosing around and digging up information, coming up with reasons the court should stand in my way."

The prolonged silence is arresting on the way home. He grabs for the door handle. "So you didn't even mention you were in a relationship."

I meet him outside in the garage. "That's not fair. You don't know how it is, with her combing through my house and my life for the past year, making up problems where there aren't any. I'm doing us a favor. Let the case end, and then we can shout it from the rooftops."

On the elevator, he's not reaching for my hand and places his overnight bag between us, his eyes waiting for the door to open. He follows me to my condo since he's never been there before. Each time I look back to check on him, my whole existence rides the elevator down his face.

"What boxes still need to be moved?" he asks.

"The bedroom, bathroom, and closet," I answer while I call for takeout. For the next few minutes, my only option is to give him space so we can talk it out once he's calm.

I place the order for food and check the kitchen drawers one last time for any important material I might be forgetting.

"So is this the real reason you didn't tell her?" Behind me, Keenan stands holding my old photo album.

"What are you doing with that?"

"It was out on your nightstand. Not in a storage or packed up already in some box. It's one of the last things you haven't put away." He lays it on the island. Staring back at us from the cover is Sheldon, Hadar, and me. "So you still look at it."

My truth out of his mouth cuts deep. I can't bullshit him.

"From time to time."

"Why? This dude abandoned you and left you by yourself while you struggled, but you still worship the ground he walks on. Sheldon's not even that special. He's just like any other Negro who's family pointed him in the right direction. Anybody can follow directions. But what is a man when he has no compass and no direction, but he can still figure out the right way?"

Keenan pinches the bridge of his nose, clutches the flesh over his ribs like I hooked the machete in him.

"You know, I thought if I tried hard enough... tah... to show you I can be the man in your life, that if I changed my ways, you would trust me... or at least stop telling me to go find somebody my age."

The knife of my baby's anguish twists and digs deeper, into us both.

"Keenan, it's not for the reason you think. Every now and then, I reflect on who I was then and who I am now, how I've changed."

"Bullshit, Eugenia. What are you and me doing if our future is constantly in the shadow of your past? If I'm always walking behind Sheldon and you're always dwelling on what you lost? I don't even consider your marriage a loss; it's what you willingly gave up. But you act like it was your biggest mistake. And if that's the case, then what am I doing here? Am I your little brother? Your fuck boy? What? Clarify it."

I reach out to touch him, and his body is water evading oil.

"I'll finish stacking these boxes for the movers and then I'll sleep on the couch."

"Is that necessary?"

"You tell me."

His eyes blinking, his body swaying, each of his realizations, all his pain, pounds on me. And forces me to my final cliff.

23

JUDGMENT DAY

KEENAN

""**W**e appreciate you working with us. Welcome to Explore." I extend my hand toward the chief of another company, and our staff clap for our newly minted endorsement agreement.

My whole body probably carries more weight to the next meeting than what's in these beer tanks.

Black Mystique: *Keenan, where are you?*

Me: *Good morning to you, too, Eugenia. I'm working. Everything good?*

So this is what that relationship tension be like? She's been here all of three days, and I have missed her every night I can't lay with her. Despite me being irritated.

Black Mystique: *If it was, Lionel Middleton wouldn't have been the last man I said goodnight to.*

Her sparks of humor always pop Fourth of July sparklers through me.

I won't be mad at her forever. I'm not truly mad now. Even the night I slept on her couch, I laid awake fighting myself not to march to her room and make her properly scream her goodbye to Chicago. During our cab rides through the city, the two hours on the plane, I had not been so much pissed at her as frustrated with myself.

I chose to go after a divorced woman with a kid and a shaky mental history. Not to mention my own colorful personal life that's not as easy to disconnect from as I anticipated. I didn't fully appreciate what the hell I was jumping into back in Rome, the moment I leaped all the way off the fucking cliff and asked Eugenia to come back to New York. She's already failed here once, as she reminded me. Now her safety and success, I'm at least partially responsible for.

And since everybody tried to warn me and I didn't listen, it's not an issue I feel like discussing with Desmond, or Kevin, or Ma, or any one of the myriad people who told me not to put myself out there like that.

Me: *I'm sure Mr. Middleton was real grateful for that.*

Another woman, with no strings, would have definitely been simpler. But my fool ass needed complexity.

My hand sliding over my mohawk as I head to a video call, I turn the corner of Slurp.

And slam right into a body.

"Excuse—"

She's standing here, the prettiest, sweetest way a man can start his day, even with us at odds. Eugenia shoves her hands on her hips, with her eyes holding the kind of fire that really could burn me. My instinct to leap in her mouth is a knee-jerk, but I ignore it. She probably wouldn't let me anyway.

When we arrived in Southampton the other day, I dropped her off at the Middletons' and didn't pick her up or explain anything because I was still annoyed.

"I have an emergency and I need you to come with me. Send somebody else to your meeting." Now panic tightens her mouth and eyes, and she's breathing heavy.

Her upset spreads to me and flushes out every other little petty concern. "Is everything okay? What's wrong?"

"No." With the palm of her hand, she mashes worry into her forehead.

Showtime's threat crosses my mind, and I motion for security. "You haven't heard from anybody I know, have you?"

Eugenia shakes her head. "No, it's my issue, but I don't have time to explain, and we need to go."

"Tell me what it is, and I'll help you deal. I can't just leave with all these meetings. There isn't anybody else."

"Lion agreed to take your meetings until you get back this evening."

"Until I get back?"

Kevin's older brother, Lion, comes toward us, who's been overseeing Explore's operations the past couple of weeks. "What's up, man. Your little lady here told me you could use a stand-in. I can spot you until around four. I know I'm not the young, dashing Explore CEO, but your sponsors and vendors shouldn't have a problem meeting with somebody named Middleton."

Well, he is an oil exec; it's not like he doesn't know how to do this.

A wide-eyed strain has overtaken Eugenia that I only see on occasion, when she confronts a big internal decision—when we stood on the cliff and she was figuring out that I wanted her to kiss me, a few days ago as she stood over me in Switzerland and tried to figure out what I wanted from her, when I shocked her at her job, and after I surprised her again in the Chicago condo with the chocolate fight.

"Please."

I don't know what I'm expecting, but the fact that I'm still expecting something with her, and I've never expected so much as a rat's ass with anybody else, leads me to follow Eugenia to her Lexus and open her car door.

"So what is this about and where are we going?"

She seems to breathe for her life, bordering on hyperventilating. We strap in. "My rights to Hadar…"

"What about them?"

Diving into a mental zone, she quakes through the words. "I could l-lose him."

Since I'm lost on the first thing to say and have never been in any situation involving spouses or kids, I reach for her hand. But she's so wrapped up in her thoughts, she may not even realize I'm here. I'm confused on how this concerns me, so I sit here and nurse my worry for her and give her space without asking anymore questions.

In New York City, we turn onto Lafayette Street and pull into the courthouse. Outside of it stands Hadar and Sheldon.

"Hi, Keenan!" Hadar bubbles out, apparently clueless about whatever is happening.

"Hey, buddy, what's up?"

In the background, I hear Sheldon ask her, *"Why didn't you say anything? I thought you were going to tell them."*

"Mom says I can practice windsurfing but only when you have time," Hadar says to me.

"Your mom is right. I'm pretty busy readying up for the concert, but we'll find some time." My mouth speaks to Hadar, but my eyes search a tight Sheldon and antsy Eugenia for some sense of what's popping off.

"Eugenia, what's going on?" I whisper to her on our way through tall, massive double doors.

On the opposite end of the courtroom, a hard-looking Black woman sits behind a high bench and glares like she's about to throw all of us in jail.

"Baby, just be patient. I have to fix this." That's her first time ever calling me that.

"Fix what?"

"So, Mrs. Rouse," the stern Black judge begins.

Eugenia raises her hand and speaks in a trembling voice. "Uh, Ms. Jackson, Your Honor."

The judge is not the only one taken aback at that correction.

"Oh. It was Rouse when you were here a few weeks ago," the judge notes and perks up my ears.

Eugenia scoots her chair to the main table. Kind of still perplexed, I take a seat behind them, in the audience.

"Things have changed since then."

"Yes, they have, haven't they?" Apparently, the judge is pissed and holds up a piece of paper. "We are here for an emergency hearing, based on a Last Minute Information report I received from your Chicago social worker with statements of your co-workers at your old job who have reported you."

The woman's angry eyes could pour out hot tar on Eugenia.

"Enlighten me on what's changed. Mrs. Rouse—now, Ms. Jackson—before Memorial Day weekend, you allowed me to believe you were not in a romantic relationship, and you sat there and said nothing when Mr. Rouse tried to voice his concerns. You told the social worker you were not seeing anybody. But come to find out, you partied that very weekend, purportedly with this man. Because of your lies, why should I trust you, that you are a caring mother, devoted solely to Hadar and your mental health? Why should I not revoke your unmonitored visits right now, grant Mr. Rouse full custody of Hadar, and close this case *today?*"

Shit.

"Your Honor." Eugenia rattles harder than guys I've seen with guns to their heads. "First of all, this is K-Keenan McLain."

The judge aims the rifle of her finger at me. "And this would be the gentleman on the big boat in Chicago, whom *you* claimed you weren't seeing the last time we were all here. But that was another one of your lies. Is he the one who took you to Europe a few weeks ago? When you told the social worker that trip was part of your work with the Middleton Foundation?"

"The Middleton Foundation?" I blurt. *The fuck?*

Eugenia squirms in her seat and shoots me with a beggarly side-eye.

She brought me here to find out she lied about who paid for her to travel?

"That money came from me personally. Not the Middletons. I don't need to hear this." To hell with it. I'm out.

I am definitely a fucking idiot. I threw myself off the mountain as a blind fool who didn't know shit, wouldn't listen to shit, and now must eat shit.

"Keenan, will you *please* sit?" Eugenia pleads, wild-eyed. "Please."

The judge's ire sharpens. "You have a lot of explaining to do, Ms. Jackson. The only reason I haven't closed the case already is we have invested *a lot* of time in you over the past year. You came in here a year ago, a broken woman who'd just lost a baby, and tried to commit…"

The judge's eyes peer down at Hadar, who sits frozen between his parents.

"I saw a mother with a troubled history and a promising future. And I wanted to believe in you." She targets Eugenia with her gavel. "So for the last time, I want to hear why I still *should* believe in you. And then I'll make my decision."

"Your Honor," a tiny little woman who must be Eugenia's lawyer snaps forward, "please allow me to explain."

"No! I want to hear it from Ms. Jackson. She owes me that much." The judge casts an eye at me. "Young man, seems to me you have every right to walk out of here and never turn back. But if you're joining us, take a seat."

Eugenia's red, watery eyes beg me.

As much as I don't want that to fucking stop my blood circulation, I do still have one question she's never answered. My need to hear it outweighs my fury at myself for being so dumb.

She turns to the judge. "Keenan is my significant other. My boyfriend. *Now*. A month ago, no, he was not."

The judge stiffens.

Eugenia's hands shoot up in a mea culpa. "Yes, I've known him since December, as I told you before. But we did not start dating, because I was focused on my son, Your Honor. I cleared my life for the past year, for my son. And yes, Keenan showed up at Hadar's birthday party, and I immediately pushed him away—as I pushed away every other temptation —because I just wanted Hadar back. I wanted to show you that my son and my mental health have been my *only* priority over this last year."

Her lungs seize air.

"I have not been seeing anybody the past year. Before Memorial Day, I didn't drink, I didn't date, I didn't go out. But I *did* I attend every therapy session, social worker meeting, class and group activity. And I put up a front with my therapist and pretended those activities made me happy when they really didn't, so I could get my son back."

"So you lied to her, too?" the judge asks.

"Yes," Eugenia states with energy. "But I complied with your orders. Every. Single. One. To tell you the truth, Your Honor, I hate number-painting, and I don't like cooking with other people. It's only relaxing with no noise and I do it by myself. But I attended group cooking because you ordered group work, and I wanted my son. Yes, I told the therapist everything I knew she wanted to hear—I'm happy, life's great, I'm growing—because I wanted my son. But I managed my real thoughts of loneliness, failure, and depression—not by any classes or court-sanctioned therapy—but by finding happiness in my own small ways. My favorite coffees, journaling, running every morning, hiking, and confiding in a co-worker at the office I trust. Because I *want* to live, for my son."

Eugenia convulses, seeming to pause between her truths, not hunting for words but for strength. The bailiff brings her a box of tissues.

"When Mr. McLain came to Chicago, I pushed him away, because my past relationships have been an issue and I wasn't going to start up a new one. I told him this. I intended to keep showing you, Your Honor, that I am strong, and my priority wasn't a man or a baby or a fantasy, but my mental health and my son."

I can swear I almost hear Eugenia's lungs wheezing through her sobs as she fights for her life.

"But K-Keenan *saw* me. He's one of the only people who saw through my charade, that I was putting up a front and being strong. When I came to New York for Memorial Day, you granted me unmonitored visits, but Hadar still wanted to be with his cousins, and I only want to see him happy. So I took him to Sag Harbor. While I was there, my sister-in-law meant well by setting me up with Keenan."

Spreading her hands in front of her on the table, she seems to lay out her soul.

"And, Your Honor, since then, I've gotten more therapy in the past month than I've had my whole life."

"Explain," the judge orders, seemingly invested now.

"Mr. McLain nudged me into some activities I would never do, which I'm grateful for. Paragliding, dancing, tasting other people's food, weird mountainside…" She clears her throat. "Accommodations. Bathing in… cheese."

The judge's eyebrow rises. "Cheese?"

"Yes, Your Honor." Eugenia's throaty, breathy laugh is

nervous but alive. "That really is a thing. Go figure. But being taken out of my comfort zone has been eye-opening, transformative, and life-giving in ways I could not have imagined. I have spent years punishing myself for walking out on a so-called 'good man.'"

Eugenia clasps her fingers together, presses her eyes closed.

"Sheldon *is* a good man. But when I left him, I may not have been leaving something good, so much as running toward a life that's good *for me.* What I needed wasn't being cooped up in his home, networking with bankers' wives with whom I had nothing in common, or waiting for him dutifully and wrestling my own demons while he worked overseas. And I've been seeking my own life for years—a life where I am whole, I am enough, and I don't feel powerless, the way I did during my marriage. That's not his fault. It's just that his life was not mine."

Fuck.

She and I both take a long-ass drag on that life weed.

"Over the past year, as I have found my strength, I have become all those things. I *am* disciplined, I *am* focused, and I *am* balanced, and I am capable of deciding who belongs in my life and who doesn't. This wasn't always the case, when I was weak and insecure and reaching for happiness everywhere, but it's the case now. And I am more discerning so I maintain my sense of peace."

She stares at me out of the side of her eye.

"I didn't keep Keenan a secret to mislead you, Your Honor. I did it because the last time you saw me, I genuinely was trying to keep him out of my life. Both he and my sister-in-law saw that I needed a break from being strong, and from all the hoops and court orders and constantly performing for everybody else. He and I have grown closer over the past month, yes.

That's what my old co-workers are reporting to you. But even now, I've exercised discretion where it concerns Hadar, and I've made it very clear to Mr. McLain that I will not tolerate his old lifestyle, if we were to continue in a relationship."

"Why didn't you tell your Chicago social worker about him the other day when she asked you about your trip?" the judge asks.

"I should have. But I'm a social worker myself and I know how these cases can unravel fast. All the work I've put in over the past year, all the sacrifices, would be undone so easily, if she makes the wrong judgment about Keenan. I just wanted to get out of Chicago and close that part of my life, to deal with whatever happens next. It was wrong and I am sorry. But I brought him here to lay it all out, so you can see I'm not trying to hide anything. He's the only man I've dated in the past year, and not until recently. And only once I concluded he's safe for me."

The judge strokes her chin and clicks on her computer. "So you're saying that you're still on the straight and narrow, and that Mr. McLain isn't some random who'll take you off focus. What is he to you then?"

As Eugenia's breaths stumble from her subconscious, so do mine. I need my answer.

"No, he's not some random." She clears her throat. "I love him."

In front of her son *and* in front of Sheldon.

Ohhhh, fuck.

The judge shifts her examination to me, motions for me to approach the main table. "And Mr. McLain, not that it's any of my business, but just because I'm nosy, do you love her?"

I stand and stare down at Eugenia, her eyes waiting. "Y-yes, ma'am, I do love Eugenia. With my whole heart."

The judge chuckles. "You look a little green around the gills there, Mr. McLain, you sure?"

The entire courtroom busts into laughter.

"I've never said that to any woman. Hell... My bad! I-I mean, I barely even say it to my own mother. So this is kind of new. But, yes, I'm more than sure."

A sly grin on her face, the judge continues, "I've looked you up on the internet while Ms. Jackson was talking. Very... interesting."

My stumbling ass manages to reach the table where I sit next to Eugenia's lawyer. The women in the courtroom—court clerk, bailiff, women sitting behind a counter, the lawyer representing the city of New York—all pass their phones around, staring at me and chuckling.

"Ms. Jackson, you believe Mr. McLain has changed since these photos?"

Eugenia eyes me. "Based on what I've seen for myself, yes, Your Honor."

"Mr. McLain?"

"I have definitely changed over the last few months I've known Eugenia. And I don't regret those changes at all. She, and the other people around me now, make me a bigger and better man."

"Hadar, what do you think about the time you've spent with your mom?"

"I like her happy. She's more fun now than she used to be."

The judge grins at him. "I'll note for the record that Hadar has a very large smile on his face, a big change from Memorial Day weekend, when he looked like I was sending him to jail. So you think we should give this Keenan a shot, Hadar?"

Hadar nods. "Yes, ma'am."

"Well, how can I punish Ms. Jackson on a technicality when her son is sitting there beaming and I've got a table full of happy people? Rare. But that's the whole point of this court. Mr. Rouse, I haven't heard from you. You want to take this chance to say you told me so?"

Now it's my ribcage cratering as I wait for him to go all in.

"No, Your Honor. Mr. McLain came to my office and addressed my concerns, man-to-man. And I've been hearing about his positive changes through our mutual connections. As long as that continues, you'll hear no objections from me."

"Well, on that note, I'll keep this case open two more months. Mr. McLain will submit to the social worker's authority, make himself and his home available for interviews and inspection, take a parenting class, and anything else I require for Hadar's safety. Understood?"

"Yes, Your Honor," Eugenia and I answer at the same time.

"Ms. Jackson, do not cross me again."

"Your Honor," I speak up. "Since you want us to be honest, there is one situation I'm dealing with. Not everybody is happy about my changes. I'm letting you know for the moment, I'm keeping Eugenia at a secure place while I make sure none of my former associates target her out of revenge. I don't think it'll happen, but we're still using every precaution, and I'm telling you so you know I'm not continuing to surround myself with bad people, but I'm letting them go. I don't want any of this to reflect poorly on Eugenia."

The judge nods. "Understood. Thank you. In that case, I'll make an order Hadar may spend time with Mr. McLain only in the company of his parents, or in a public setting, for now. We'll have an update when we come back after Labor Day. Mr. McLain, Ms. Jackson, Mr. Rouse, Hadar, good luck to all of you. Now excuse me while I look up these cheese baths."

Outside the door, Sheldon turns to me. And holds out his hand. I take it.

"You'll keep me updated on your situation." It's more of a demand than a question.

"Sure."

He addresses Eugenia. "Tomorrow, I head to California with Blake and Kara. They're having a visit with their dad's side of the family, and Chrissy and I are going, too. That leaves Hadar here with you for the next week. You good with that?"

Eugenia nods. "Of course."

"Where will you and him be staying?" Sheldon asks.

Eugenia looks to me.

"The Middletons'. They've agreed to have both Eugenia and Hadar for as long as they need."

It goes without saying Sheldon approves of that. "Eugenia, if you need to take him over to Mom and Dad's, they're around. As well as P and Ro, Jerrell and Maddy and the others. Kam is also around for a new assignment with Explore. There's a number of people you can call if you need help or start feeling overwhelmed, G. We're all in the same community now, and you don't have to do it all alone this time. There'll be no judgment."

Again, Eugenia nods as the two of them seem to be having a clarifying moment between them.

Sheldon is almost gone, and his heels spin to me. "Don't make me regret this."

"I will not."

He leaves me with an excited little boy and his nervous mother, my heart.

"Li'l dude, come here." I pull Hadar to me, cover his eyes with my hand, and tug Eugenia to me with the other. Everything inappropriate I wanted to do to her for the last seventy-two hours, I express in my tongue action. Her head motions, locking her hands on my face, her mouth on mine, her destiny to mine, express that no doubts remain in her about this man.

Hadar giggles. "I can still see you two."

His chuckles are infectious and kick into me.

"Don't worry, homie, Imma work on my stealth game."

"So why are you putting me at the Middletons'?" she asks on our way to the SUV. Sheldon is bringing around Hadar's things and they'll say goodbye.

"It's Showtime," I say without going into detail. "I'm just being careful for a minute. Kevin's folks already have thick security, so it's perfect to keep you safe."

"Have you heard anything?"

We talk in vague terms while Hadar plays a video game in the backseat.

I recall the rumors I'm hearing from B'More, about Showtime making a deal with some hardcore types we don't know. "I think something's going down there. I haven't heard it'll come here, but I'm not taking any chances." I don't want to freak Eugenia out, especially not now when it's turned into such a good day for her, and me. "Sorry about the pics." I turn out a joke I know will get her worked up.

It does the job. She rolls her eyes. "No, you're not."

Over my shoulder, I check for her son before I stick my tongue out, lick air, let her know I want to fuck. My thumb sweeps her shoulder. Scooting my legs open, I grab my wood.

She pulls her eyes real quick from the road, sneaks an eye over at Hadar, and peeps my bulge in my pants. Her teeth clutch her lip, with a lethal side-eye warning me she'll bite my shit again.

"You two need to work on it," Hadar mutters from the back.

Eugenia kisses her teeth. "How did I go from having a kid to a drill sergeant?"

Once we get our laughs out of the way, I kiss her hand. "I don't want you to worry."

"I'm not worried. You keep forgetting I'm from Southside of Chicago."

Cracking up down the freeway, holding hands, I actually relax. "Yeah, I forgot you might be more 'hood than me."

24

I MIGHT HAVE YOUR MUSIC

EUGENIA

"Wow," Hadar murmurs, inching forward, one step after another, his eyes nearly the size of Coke bottle caps.

We stand in the Grand Foyer of the Middletons' breath-taking home. Simple and still so elegant in country Hamptons decor, it's a more of a museum boasting treasures, antiques, and precious papers. After a week on the job, we're all still feeling each other out, and the last thing I need is Hadar to shatter a timeless piece of Black history.

Brendan Middleton joins us with his son, Braelan, and wife, Kendall, and his mom, Roberta, who is herself incredibly stunning enough to hang from one of these museum walls.

"Be careful, honey, don't break anything. I can't afford to replace any of these pieces," I instruct him.

"I won't." But instantly he spins toward Lionel Middleton. "I saw you talk at Slurp on Juneteenth about Black people who were not slaves."

The handsome patriarch of the Middleton clan smiles at

my boy. "All right then, son, what did you think of my presentation?"

Hadar strokes his chin. "Well, it was pretty good. Your information was amazing, but your delivery needs practice."

The adults bite down on their laughter.

I saw the viral video of Mr. Middleton's Juneteenth talk a few days ago at Slurp brewery. The man was clearly emotionally distraught and on the brink of a breakdown. But leave it to my son to share his father's manner of critiquing literally anybody.

A curious Mr. Middleton places his hands behind his back. I wonder if I should intercede and try to explain this away.

So far, I haven't run into them much, since I'm staying in one of the guesthouses with my own key, separate entrance, and its own small kitchen.

"So tell me where you think I need some help." Mr. Middleton takes it like a champ.

"My dad says you're not supposed say 'uh' a whole lot while speaking formally, and you did it enough times that it concerns me."

Oh, my God.

"Is that right?" Mr. Middleton asks. "What else concerns you?"

"You use your hands a lot, and you were looking down at the floor some. If you speak publicly again, you should push that chin up, shoulders back. Yours were hunched."

"Huh. Your dad sounds like quite a smart man. What do you say about helping me prepare my next few speeches?" Mr. Middleton asks.

Hadar lifts his chin, strokes it the way he's seen the judge do. "We might be able to work something out. For a small fee."

The adults break into raucous guffaws as I direct my

child to my side. "Mr. Middleton, Hadar would be honored to take part in your Hamptons history work."

While Kendall escorts the boys out to the tennis court, I turn to my attention to the task at hand.

"You're doing a pretty good job of pulling this together on your own, on an informal basis," I begin. "But if this is to become an ongoing camp where you're rotating out kids, taking field trips, placing them on Explore boats, and allowing them around heavy equipment at the brewery, eventually flying them overseas, we need a lot more legal and safety structure in place, not to mention staff. As well as a computerized system for tracking their medical, mental health, and behavioral needs. That should be priority number one."

Mr. Middleton's lawyer, museum curator, videographer, biographer, and charitable adviser, all sit up and take notes. This is our first day having a real meeting after the last few days of me touring Explore, meeting with the Black Business Council, and observing the hodge-podge way they've been managing their youth program, which is an off-the-rails train wreck waiting to happen.

For the next two hours, I unfurl my concerns about the weaknesses of their inner-city youth program, in which they currently host a handful of youth, maybe ten, for a few days at a time.

"I'm glad you're here, Mrs. Rouse," Mrs. Middleton says at the end of the day. "We need your help in a lot of ways. Our family is working to redeem our name and reputation, and we've been searching for somebody who cares, who isn't just looking to climb the Hamptons social ladder or build their résumé. You have genuine passion for what you do."

"It's Ms. Jackson now, and you all aren't the only ones redeeming your reputation. I needed this help myself, and I appreciate you extending it."

In her emerald eyes that match the pine and moss mountainsides of Switzerland, she offers vast openness that doesn't judge me. "You are quite a change from what we're used to around here, and that's a good thing." She pats my hand in this intimate way that must make people feel she's their best friend. "As well as Mr. Keenan."

The mention of his name always cajoles a laugh from me.

"Why don't you come to a meeting of the Madames this Saturday?" she asks me, her fiery-green eyes pouring into me.

"The Madames?"

"Yes, a girls' club we have. I'd like to introduce you around, have you share some of your insights with us. It's a private group, invitation only."

Now it's clear what she's saying to me, and the door she's opening. Through that doorway, the rays of gratitude enter me. "I can't tell you what your invitation means, Mrs. Middleton. But I'm afraid I'll have to decline. Sororities and clubs and all that stuff are not what I'm after at this point in my life. Been there, done that. My work and my son are my only focus." I roll my eyes. "*And* Keenan."

"I am admiring you more and more by the minute. Tell me whatever we can do to help you."

Only a single mountain remains sitting on me now.

Other than that, I now fly the freest that I have my whole life. "You've already done it. Just by letting me be here."

A thought pops into my mind. "Although… if I could trouble you for one small favor, I'd truly appreciate it."

"Come on, Mom! Stop being a chicken!"

"That's okay, I think I'm good, son. You and Keenan, you two handle it, and I'll stand over here and cheer you on."

I turn away from Explore's activities dock, filled with paddle boards, surfboards, water skis, and other water equipment. Ahead of us, ocean waves rush toward us too fast for my comfort level, rising and crashing with teeth ready to drag me under and swallow me whole.

"Hey, Stunt Man!"

"Stunt Man, over here!"

I don't care about all the women howling and whistling at him or flashing him in the water. I'm not going in there.

On the sidelines, Keenan's partner, Rocky, and his friend, Lorenzo, crack up as I make my escape.

"Girl, stop being so dang scary. It'll be fine. You're not even going in that deep!" Lus calls out from the water.

"Mom, you promised!"

"I changed my mind." In bare feet, I scurry down the wooden dock.

"Baby, come here."

Behind me, I hear his feet coming after me.

I'm so close to the boardwalk.

"Genia."

These legs take off running.

His run faster.

"Keenan, put me dowwwwn!" My screams and laughter swing in the air with my body.

"I know you didn't think you could outrun me. It's easy. It'll be you and me the whole time," he murmurs, toting me back to the paddle boards at the shoreline.

"Why can't you and Hadar paddle, like you have all the other times?"

"Hadar needs to see *you* do this," he whispers. "Like we talked about, remember? We'll all do it together."

He sets me in the sand and walks me toward what has

always looked like a watery graveyard to me. Inhaling as much ocean air into my lungs as I can, I face Hadar. His eager eyes light up and confirm that Keenan is right.

With my son as my main focus, I sweep aside the flashbacks of me as a girl, thrashing in a pool full of panicking kids, all trying to escape a bloody shootout.

Keenan drags the paddle board into the water, slips the paddles through the loops, and then reaches for my hands.

Big breaths. My rapid heart strum fear on my ribs. Still, I get on my knees in the sand and lay on the board. Despite the summer humidity, we may as well be in the North Pole the way I shiver. In my hands, the paddles keep shaking.

"Hold on a moment, baby, first your hands. Put them in the water." Keenan's body disappears in the ocean water where he sinks deeper the further out we go. Floating, he directs my paddle board.

All my fear and anxiety I place in my trust of him, and lower my hands in the warm water.

"That's it. Feel it and don't be scared of the water. Cup your hands and push the water behind you. I got you." He directs the board. "Now kick. Use your hands to keep cupping the water back and propel yourself forward."

"That's it, Mom! You're doing it!"

We push out farther into the water, into the deep, and salty ocean starts to swallow me. But I focus on Hadar's face and keep cupping and kicking. The rush of waves through my fingers doesn't eat me as it does in my nightmares.

"Okay, now the paddles." Keenan lets me grab them and do the work on my own, with him directing me how to turn them and use them. "See," he murmurs, kissing my shoulder, "I told you you could."

It's been a long time since I've waded into any body of water to swim. The only other time I've entered water as an adult is with Keenan on Christmas Eve, and even then, we were still in a container. Why I got on his boat that night, I don't know. I can't think of any reason other than he met me in my hour.

Before long, once I wade through the anxieties and terrors that have haunted me for twenty-five years, I can stand on the paddle board and propel myself some alongside Hadar.

"Next time we do this, we're racing." On our paddles next to each other, he's all smiles.

"You can race all you want, but I'll win. You're in big trouble now, buddy." I'm still a little shaky with my paddles, but decades of angst are slowly washing away.

When we come back to shore, Sheldon waits and claps. He lets out a low whistle. "For a minute there, I almost thought I needed a new pair of eyes. Congratulations. I never thought I would see the day."

"Not like I had a choice," I complain.

"Mom did really good for her first time, didn't she?" Hadar asks.

Sheldon checks out Keenan and me. "She's doing a lot of things really *well* for her first time. I'm proud of you, G."

During our marriage, my fear of the water and refusal to get in it, irritated him to no end. Keenan dips out and gives us a minute, as he has a tendency to do when Sheldon and I have our moments. Thankfully, Kee is starting to understand we have another kind of relationship now.

"He just needs to get the saltwater off him, but other than that, he's good for the Fourth of July parade. You'll drop him off in a couple days so he can see the concert preparations?" I ask Shel.

"Yeah, is it okay if Blake, Rome, and Isaac come, too?" Shel asks Keenan.

"Sure. Explore can use all the little worker bees we can

hustle up. Bring your elbow grease, Hadar. You'll need it," Keenan says.

"You can't handle all this muscle," my son replies. They do their complicated hand grip that makes no sense.

"More like we can't handle all those twigs," I crack.

"My twigs can paddle faster than you," he says, walking away with his dad.

"For now!" I call back. "Love you."

"Love you, too."

Lus strolls over to me. "You and Kee are cute."

On the Explore dock, Keenan puts away the boards and directs his employees.

"We aiight." I try to ignore my elevated blood circulation every time I peep him out. "You ready to head to Slurp?"

"Actually, we're heading somewhere else."

I'm confused. "We are?"

Lus's head swings toward Keenan's childhood buddy, Lorenzo, and a sexed-up haze enters her eyes. "No, *we* are."

"Op…*oh*. Well, all right then."

We swap hugs.

She winks. "We'll see you guys tomorrow."

"With a fiery update, I hope."

Keenan slides his arm around me. "Where do you want to watch the fireworks?"

"Your place."

"Genia." That's what he calls me. He doesn't want to call me "G" like Sheldon does or "Genie" like my family. "You know we can't go there."

"Now who's afraid to face their fear?"

"I'm not scared, but I'm not slipping up when it comes to your safety either. Show's been to my spot a couple times, and I want to make sure he's good and I'm not hearing any blips back home." He opens the door to the jeep for me to get in it.

"Have you heard any blips at all?"

"I have not, and I want it to stay that way for a minute before I bring you home. But Lord knows, I'm tired of beating my meat over the phone."

We ride to the cliff where we paraglided Memorial Day weekend, a perfect spot to watch Fourth of July fireworks spray over the skies, across several Hamptons towns. Lying over the hood and windshield of his jeep, we pop a couple of sodas.

I'm somewhat taken aback that he keeps checking me out.

"A year ago, I first saw this bad-ass, sexy-ass, grown-ass woman who was dancing on a boat. She wasn't some typical dime piece. She carried a load on her face, on her shoulders, but it didn't scream pitiful. In her, I saw fire and determination, like the flaming sword on my leg. Her son pulled her to the dance floor, and she didn't move much but she had some cool footwork, like she could crush the scene if she was dancing for real. I started to step to her. But my brother stopped me. Told me she was nuts, problematic, disrespectful, nobody wanted her around here."

His arm hugs me tighter to him. "All the things they say about me."

Every word from his mouth is a small Fourth of July sparkler firing up my heart cavity, firing through my nerves, heating the blood rushing to my womanhood and up to my brain. Under his t-shirt, my fingertips dance over his abdomen. The fireworks pop off in our mouths, dangling off one another, our tongues pirouetting.

"I kept thinking about you." He talks against my mouth between kisses. "Then I saw you again at Christmas—just you and me this time. Nobody around to stop me. My soul kept preaching it was no accident. But I doubted I had a shot. What could I offer you that Rouse hadn't? You'd already had money, houses, cars, status, the whole nine. So when I came to your town, I rode a big boat to your job, filled with flowers, to show you I'm none of what you had before. I wasn't coming to you on some materialistic shit, but I might have the music that lady on the boat can dance to."

Tears squeeze from warm springs of emotion spiraling in me, even as I laugh. "And here I thought there was no rhyme or reason to you."

"Sometimes there wasn't." His soft chuckles roll from his stomach muscles that contract under my fingertips. He fingers my nipple under my bra, holds my titty, bites it through my t-shirt. "I haven't had a chance to tell you yet. It's been so crazy this week with our schedules. But all that stuff you said in court the other day was dope, almost had a nigga ready to marry you right then and there."

For the past week, since the court hearing, Hadar has been with me at night, and on the phone, he talks to Keenan more than I do.

I meander to the button of his shorts, manage to undo it, sneak my hand inside, and cup his bulge. The mere promise of ecstasy arrests both our sets of lungs at the same time.

"Thank you for seeing me," I tell him, "and what I needed from you, before I knew myself."

We roll off the hood of the jeep, and his mohawk lowers down my body where he peels off my t-shirt. His lips taste my titties and stomach, his eyes focused on the task at hand. My jeans come undone under the expert precision of his hands, and in the process, Keenan seems to take down the rest of my barbed wire.

"Keenan, baby, seriously? We're doing this here?"

"Yeah, why not?" He scrapes my bikini bottom down my ass, clawing me naked.

"But we haven't showered from the ocean."

"I like my pussy salty."

Though I'm concerned we're parked at the top of a cliff

overlooking all the Hamptons and might be discovered by some wanderers who could report us, the thrill of mischief squirts from my pussy. And an eagle-eyed Keenan snatches my cream on his tongue.

"Ah."

Right where I still stand, my thigh slung over his shoulder, his wet taste buds light up my folds. Eyes drunk with sex, his mouth stays open and displays my juices mixed with his spit.

Once I'm yanked down to him on the grass, he slides my nectar into my mouth, swirls our bodily fluids together, for me to taste myself on him. My whole womb clamors for him while I shove off his shorts.

The first round of fireworks burst across the sky.

Keenan lays me on the grass. His manhood entering me sprays the fireworks from my canal to my brain. My legs open wide for him to cradle my butt cheeks and lift me from the grass, filling me up. Until the tip of his dick must feel my heartbeat. One of my legs he raises over his shoulder, and he must want to drive his dick toward my throat.

The pressure whips up my back, sends my head against his shoulder.

But he eases my head back, forcing me to see his lips curled over his teeth and the fight between his eyebrows. In his high-energy stroke is a vengeance. "Who's your mother-fucking man?"

In my canal, he hooks up, stealing my air and stroking my soul. The dick whips me until I'm delirious, clawing the grass. "You."

"What's my name?"

Fireworks thundering over my head, him fucking me senseless, I can hardly breathe. My answer limps out of my intoxicated brain: "Keenan McLain."

With every stroke, he drags his dick all the way out, dips

his hips and punches his girth all the way back into me, drilling my body into the grass.

"Who?"

My nectar sizzles on his strokes, pussy begging for mercy. I'm gripping him for life, and can hardly speak. "Keen... McLaaaaa...."

Our fireworks blow our pelvises into the ground. He takes all of me, and I give it all. Screaming and kicking the whole way off the orgasmic cliff.

THE MAN HE WAS

EUGENIA & KEENAN

EUGENIA

Dark Chocolate: *You wearing my favorite thong?*
Three weeks away from the Sasha Static concert, I'm tired of sleeping at the Middletons' and of Keenan and me screwing in his jeep or my truck because he refuses to do the nasty on the property of Kevin's parents'. And he's determined that we should wait for any signs of potential mess in Baltimore to clear out before I move my things to his spot.

The delay isn't necessarily bad, since the extra time allows Hadar and me to do more. Princess, Etta, and I can take out the kids or hold summer swim parties and sleepovers. I turned down Mrs. Middleton's invitation to attend the Madames functions, but I do enjoy her brunches and dinner parties where I meet her colorful friends and they pick my brain about child psychology and what might be wrong with their grandkids.

Also, Hadar can adjust to me being romantic with

Keenan, and Keenan can find his bearings with Hadar. Plus there's the whole shift for Hadar of having two sets of parents.

But still, I started my day a little while ago with my nipples aching for Keenan's mouth, and the punch-drunk way his eyes glue to me when he's slowly pulling on each one with his teeth.

So, grabbing my morning coffee at Sharon's, I'm sexually frustrated. Now I have to go meet a group of kids and camp counselors at the Sag Harbor firehouse and pretend my clit doesn't need a hose.

Me: *I'm wearing your daddy's favorite thong.*

Dark Chocolate: *Girl, I can't wait for you to meet my daddy and I want you to say that shit to his face.*

Me: *Whatchu gonna do if—*

"Eugenia Jackson."

Before I can fire off my next smart-ass response, I'm interrupted. In front of me hovers a somewhat familiar face that closes in. From Memorial weekend at Taste.

"Showtime."

Behind him, in a large black SUV, sits a car full of guys.

"You remember me. Keenan must've told you to look out."

"No, you're the only person I've met named Showtime, and at six-foot-two, with a full grill of diamonds, you're hard to forget."

My phone vibrates, most likely with a message from Keenan.

But my eyes don't divert from Showtime's glare. Fear is the last thing this guy needs to smell on me, and calm is the vibe I'm keeping. No sudden moves, I don't touch my phone or do any of the things Keenan told me to do if this were to happen.

The handsome young man with a couple of scars on his face examines me. "So here's the woman herself, who turned my boy around in a full one-eighty since he's started up with you."

"I'm disappointed."

His eyebrow rises in a question. "How so?"

"First off, you're late. Second, as his friend, *you're* the one who should have turned him around, if he was ever what you thought he was at all. And I'm pretty sure you knew he wasn't."

"How do you know what he is? You just met him."

My phone vibrates, and I'm certain that's Keenan calling after he saw the three message dots for the message I never sent.

"What should worry you more is why you *didn't* know who he really is. You've known him longer. Or were you so focused on your own ends you weren't concerned about Keenan?"

Show's glare tightens through slitted eyes. "You talk real fancy with all that psychology shit. What if I just say you're responsible for fucking me over? Plain and simple."

"First, I'd say you're a fool for thinking that. Second, it doesn't seem like you're fucked over, Showtime. And third, if you think I'm responsible for the high-achieving man your friend is becoming, that's not on me, but I'll gladly take credit."

My phone rings now, repeatedly.

Showtime motions toward it. "You're not going to get that? Tell him I'm here? Cry for help?"

"Is that why you came to me and not him? You expected me to cry?" I shake my head. "You barked up the wrong tree."

"Answer it."

"No." And I don't bat one eye. "Be a man and call him yourself."

He spends the next few seconds evaluating who he's

talking to. "You're a tough nut to crack. I give you that," he mutters.

"Tougher men than you have tried it." *Daddy, put it down!* The memory rises in my mind as fresh as if it happened yesterday. "One of these days, I'll tell you about the first time I ever tried to kill myself. You're talking to somebody who's not afraid to die. Like I said, wrong tree."

A shocked Showtime eyes me. Apparently, he's reeling that this didn't go how he was expecting. I'm not some delicate girl cringing in his presence.

"Why don't you believe I'm fucked over?"

He cares about my opinion.

"You're still breathing. And you're only what? Thirty-two, thirty-three? Whatever you might have gotten yourself into, you can get yourself out of it."

Behind me, car tires screech to a halt and doors swing open.

"Show." Keenan races up and steps between us, placing me behind him. Desmond and Lorenzo, move to his side. "Why didn't you tell me you were here? And why are you talking to her? Stepping to my lady is a bitch move, dude."

I examine Showtime. "Showtime was just getting ready to call you. And apologize. For not coming to help with your concert preparations sooner."

Keenan mutters at me over his shoulder, "Why didn't you answer my calls?"

"I'm a social worker. It's my job. I had it."

He hits me with the side-eye that says he's pissed and he wants to fuck. "We'll talk about this when we get home."

KEENAN

D and me look inside the SUV's and see Show's brought dudes from B'More with him.

D starts cracking up.

These are dudes we know, not the unfamiliar guys who've been at Show's right flank in business establishments.

But my heart pounds my chest faster than prey being chased.

"Show," I start, "what the hell are you doing riding up and scaring my woman?"

He shrugs. "She didn't seem too scared to me. You look scarier than she did."

"Looking out for her is my job."

"I wanted to see what you were working with, if you had some little crybaby, or a real one."

"You could have asked me." Breathing like I just ran a marathon, my lungs labor for oxygen.

"I didn't want you prepping her and whatnot, which you probably tried to do anyway."

"Damn right, I did. Genia's my woman and what you just did proves I was right to get her ready. The way you just pulled up on her is damn disrespectful. You've been on some crazy shit lately, running with dudes we don't know, rolling dice at a table where I don't sit. I ain' never questioned your moves. You're a grown ass man, but when you bring it to my front door, we've got a problem."

I confront him right here and now, in the parking lot. Straight, no chaser. On my fucking life.

Show sizes me up and his eyes cloud over, the same look he gave our enemies back home when I knew he would have them handled. He never says anything, but his face always promises a reckoning.

Roach and Kadeem get out of the SUVs and come stand

next to us.

"What's your move, Show?" I ask.

He holds out his hand between us for a grip. "I know you're clean, Keenan. And I know you didn't take your ass to Georgetown and put in years to come over to my side. You made yourself clear. I ain' gon' fuck you over after you came this far."

A fat wave of relief leaves my lungs that's been holding it in forever, and I accept his hand.

"Gentlemen," a police officer says from his patrol car. "Everything good here?"

"Yeah," Show answers, with a kind of melancholy grin I can't really interpret. "We were just standing here discussing what we're having for breakfast." He turns to me. "So how about them pancakes?"

For the next two hours, we all sit and laugh about old times—Nigel, Aaron, Kadeem, Roach, Show, 'Renzo and me. But the energy is not legit, like we're all sitting on a razor-blade or something.

Since I have no time to spare this close to the concert, Show and the homies from home offer to help with the grunt work for the next couple of days. Since Desmond especially needs the hand over at Slurp with getting his brews ready, we accept the help.

"Your lady is fire though. For real, mane," Show says to me.

I just can't make out this vibe he's giving. "Dude, you know the minute you go legit, all you have to do is say the word and you can have any part of this you want. Right?"

His hesitation, that uneasiness on him, is a brick wall standing between us. "Yeh, son, I know. And Imma hold you to that shit too." His lazy side grin, eyes that barely open, communicate a different message.

Why the fuck did he come here?

26

CLAWING THEIR WAY BACK
TO LIFE

EUGENIA & KEENAN

EUGENIA

At the Rouse compound, I arrive a few minutes early to pick up Hadar. His Dad hasn't brought him here for the drop-off yet, which is perfect to sneak in a few moments with Princess.

"Hey, you." My voice must drag the ground with my feet. This is my first time seeing her since she was released from a three-day stay in the hospital a couple of days ago.

Her weak, dry laugh surprises me again. No matter how many times I talk to her, I always expect the hearty, confident warmth to wrap around me. And I'm stunned when feeble mortality greets me instead.

"Keenan let you go long enough to see daylight?"

"You, Hadar and Mr. Middleton are the only people he lets me see." Through my tears, I smile. I don't bother taking her hand, since I know she won't let me. Too overtly comforting and final. Since she won't allow us to talk about the obvious, I try to think of other subjects that don't require talk of future plans…

"How are you?" I ask.

"Blessed." She's not too tired to serve up a silly smile. "Judging by how you limped in here, I see your pet is still blessed too."

As we crack up, I forget she's weak.

"How are the Middletons treating you?" she asks.

I don't ask why she's on the terrace, instead of the bed. No part of me would want to be there either—one step away —as long as my muscles are still able to move.

"Very interesting people. I think Mr. Middleton is glad to have his family history project to keep him busy. He runs sections of his book by me, and it blows my mind. How many Black people do you know who can recite their family history even fifty years, let alone five hundred? They must appreciate having company on the property, since their sons are all grown and live out of town. Lion is back from Texas, but he's busy working on Explore."

Princess's expression takes on a certain naughtiness. "Yes, that and he's also been 'busy' with other pursuits." She forms air quotes with her fingers.

My eyebrow rises in a tacit question.

She flicks her head toward Kamilah, out in the backyard playing with Ro and P's kids.

"Really?"

"Really. They're public knowledge now. Lion was over here the day before Juneteenth, to have Sunday brunch with us. They stayed under the gazebo for an hour." P sips her tea.

I'm well aware Kamilah hates me for leaving her brother. But I also know Kamilah is in her late thirties, only four or five years younger than me, and finding love gets harder as we grow older. If she's found hers—especially with some-body as wealthy and prominent as Lion—good for her.

This conversation lights up P's mood. "I saw Lionel talk at the brewery during the Juneteenth celebration. He is a phenomenal man. Their family is very different. It's like their only goal is to gain more wealth, more power, and it's awesome to watch a Black family do that."

With a nod, I agree. "And they're kind, giving."

P shrugs. "Most people are kind and giving when they're old, trying to get right with God, to make up for all the shit they did when they were younger."

We burst into spontaneous guffawing out here on the porch.

All my love and gratitude for P pours into my gaze. "But hon, you don't have to get right with anybody. You've always been right. I admire that about you."

"Girl, nobody is right. But speaking of that, I'm glad you're here." She slides to the edge of the wicker chair.

My instinctive reaction is to circle her with my arms and pull her up, but her warning glare knocks me back.

"I can walk." She goes inside the house, slower than she once did, but her strength persists.

A couple of minutes later, she comes back with a book I've seen before. It's the book she was writing in the morning she drove me to Keenan.

"Your journal."

"Halle's book." P places both her hands atop it with finality, like it's the Ten Commandments. She opens the cover and takes out a business card, and I'm shocked at her reaching toward me with it.

On it, I read the name of a lawyer—Duncan McPhee. "Why do I need this, P?"

"You won't. My daughter will." The only evidence I've seen of P's future now crystallizes in her stare. "I'm turning this book over to an attorney. Legally, it will remain in trust with you as trustee, Eugenia, for the sole purpose of giving it to Halle. When you think the time is right."

Immediately, I'm shaking my head. The tears come back. My many brushes with death return, as a casket closing over my chest. "No. That's...I can't..."

"Eugenia." Her voice may be dusty, but more firm than ever. "You can. And you will."

"Why can't Kamilah or Etta..."

"Because they'll do what Roland tells them. He's her father, and he'll read it first. As any parent should. I don't want him to. This is womanhood in here. Doesn't have a damn thing to do with him."

A lone tear flees from her body, and escapes to the large bound book, a baptism of every word she wrote.

Her womanhood lays into me. "I can't think of a person more suited to recognize a girl's pain than you." Her fingers sweep the cover. "When you see it on my child, you call that lawyer and instruct him to have this book hand-delivered to Halle. I don't care how young or old she is. If *you* feel it's time, will you do that for me?"

Why would she trust me with this?

"P, but how do you know I'll..."

Live.

How does she know I won't hit another mental cave and try to take my life again.

"I just know, especially now. You appreciate life more than you ever have." The blades of her words shouldn't cut so pristinely.

She's right. I do.

Having to claw my way back to life after all these months, my joy today is the real thing. Not just an imitation of joy. As Keenan would say, I'm not just fronting. That I wake up next to Keenan in the morning, watch my son make me breakfast, and go connect youth to successful people is a fulfillment worth living for.

"Promise me." Guttural, final, she demands it.

This is one bonding event with Princess I would gladly reject. "Yes, I promise."

In the background, her lively kids scream and play while chasing their aunt, Kamilah. The Rouse yard brims with activity, love, joy and future, as P and I sit in quietude, saying goodbye to the past, and future.

"Mom!" my son calls from the front foyer.

Jumping around, like we've been conspiring on some foul shit, we swipe our hands over our faces.

"Yeah, baby?"

"Are we going to see Keenan and the concert stuff?" he asks, flinging his arm around my neck.

"Yep. I'm ready when you are." Before I forget the lawyer's card, I stash it in my cross-body bag. I give Princess a nod. "Drinks next week?" Like all this is normal and we've got all the time in the world to goof off.

"You'd better."

Outside, I head toward the car and I notice Chrissy is still in the driveway. Pacing around with her phone, she argues with somebody and Shel is nowhere around.

"Blake, that's not the agreement. Stop using your kids to get a hookup for Sasha Static. We are *not* negotiating. Stick with your court-ordered agreement. The answer is no!" She's clearly worked up.

Her kids have run in the house, and Hadar still lingers inside with them, but the baby remains in the backseat and is getting fussy.

The social worker in me kicks in. I point to the baby, to see if she needs help.

Her fury with the phone call increasing, Chrissy nods.

I swallow my tiny bit of angst and do what I never thought I would—reach to hold Sheldon's baby. Tears are welling up in her eyes from where she's trapped in the car seat and on the verge of screaming.

From all Hadar's talk, I recall her name. "Hey, Krishna. Don't be upset with Mommy. She's coming. She's almost here."

I start making funny faces, as I've done when I've detained parents' children. To coax a child into trusting me as I remove them from their home, I quickly try to become their friend. Parents yell and scream at me, and at police, and I focus on reassuring their kids. As I do now.

"Krishnaaaa, why are you making that silly face?" I ask her in a soft voice. I try to drown out her mother's frustration and stress. The baby giggles.

Yes, it's bittersweet to see her with Sheldon's eyes and intense expressions. But she's precious, and exactly where she's meant to be.

"Thank you, Genie." A seemingly rundown Chrissy comes over, but she doesn't reach for her child. Instead, the young mother might still be stuck in the throes of her argument with her ex-husband.

"Chrissy, if the kids want to come over with Hadar and visit sometimes, they're welcome to." So she can catch a break.

I may have fished her from her fury. Her eyes focus on me now, and she blinks like she now realizes it's me standing in front of her.

"Okay."

She reaches for Krishna and I hand her over.

Now it turns awkward while she's probably questioning my sincerity.

"Chrissy, I'm sorry. I was wrong to interfere in your relationship with Sheldon last summer. I had no right. In a sense, I still considered him mine to claim. And," I pause a moment, "he's amazing. Your presence in his life startled me, and I wasn't ready. But our sons are brothers now, and it looks like I'll be around for a while. I hope one day, you and I can move past what I did." I shrug and try to make it light a moment. "Besides, you did throw up on me, so you definitely give as good as you get."

She lets out a half-chuckle. "Thank you for that. For what it's worth, I'm sorry about you los...what happened with your baby. I lost one myself once, with Blake." A shade of heartache darkens her eye. "I hope things go better for you next time." She peers down at Krishna. "Thanks for keeping her calm while I handled...issues."

"See you later."

"See ya."

KEENAN

"Genia, sweetheart, this is real nice and all, but you know it's not changing anything, right?" I ask her.

Ignoring me, she shoves a platter of beer-battered chicken wings in my hand. "Can you go set this on the table, bae?"

I tuck it with the other dishes she's made, between all these damn candles she's lit and spread across the house. I'm complaining, but they're lighting up my world.

I'm just skeptical and don't want her getting her hopes up.

Our first guests arrive at the door.

"You invited *them*?"

"Are you letting them in?" Genia shoots back.

I open up for Solly and Shay.

"What's up, bruh?" He looks about as happy to be here as I am to have him.

"Hey, baby bruh," Shay says. She holds up a box of dessert from Taste.

"Shay, what's popping?" I want to hug my sister as much as I want to hug an anaconda. I turn to Eugenia and make the introductions. "I don't think you two have met Genia yet, but this is her, my queen."

Eugenia extends her hand to Shay, and the way these two interact, some aspect of this feels contrived as hell. "Pleasure to meet you, Shay."

"You, too, Eugenia. I've heard you're making heads spin with the Explore youth program."

Eugenia is very warm toward Shay, a little too warm. "The kids won't stop going on about your basketball practices."

Behind them comes Kevin and Cher.

"Eugenia," Kevin says with a smile and holding up a bottle of some real expensive liquor he always brings back from crazy-ass places around the world. "The woman of the hour. How much do I owe you for making my folks happy?"

"They're a joy, and so is the work. The pleasure is mine."

Kevin looks over at me. "Keenan McLain." He motions at Genia. "She's smarter than you."

I give him a grip. "So? She's here next to me, so I must not be that dumb."

"Cher, thanks for coming." Eugenia extends her hand to Kevin's wife. "I know your cousin, Chrissy, and me, we've had beef."

I'm astonished as Cher shrugs it off and takes Eugenia's hand. "My husband has also beefed with my cousin, so I guess we'll have to leave it under the bridge." Cher eyeballs me. Hard. Like she still wants to cut me for not proposing marriage to Ilyana, her childhood friend. "Keenan."

"Cher."

While Kev, Solly, and I catch up on last-minute to-do's for

the concert, I peep Genia across the room chopping it up with Cher and my sister.

My woman and my sister are laughing a little too hard, like they've already talked at some point.

Before I can ask her, Lorenzo shows up with Genia's old coworker, Illustrious.

"My boy." I offer him a full-out hug and press into him my gratitude for a lifetime.

"Sir." He speaks in my ear. "You've got a hell of a lot to be grateful for. I hope you know that."

"Damn sure do."

After I greet Lus, I slide over to Genia and pull her aside.

"Bae, who else you invite to the house? Who all comin' over here?"

She can hardly talk through her big-ass, goofy grin. "Why don't you just enjoy the surprise?"

"Why all this secrecy, though? What's going on with you and Shay? Why are you and her over there giggling and shit like this isn't your first time hooking up? She been talking noise about me?" I follow her around the kitchen. "Genia."

I'm glad she thinks this is so funny.

Finally, she turns and nestles her hand between my chest muscles. That shit calms me instantly. The candlelight glowing in her eyes illuminates a nigga. She can always tell when I'm getting worked up.

"Stop ignoring your guests. If they really hated you, and didn't want this to work, they wouldn't have come. It's time you and your partners did something together besides argue." Black Mystique commandeers me to her and sucks my lips.

"So are you telling me what all my sister said or not? You know she's treacherous, right?"

Her eyes all animated, Genia stares at me with some

mischief to her. I'm not going to like whatever comes out next.

"I once heard a wise man ask, 'When was the last time you took your sister out and did something special for her? Even just a scoop of ice cream'?"

I roll my eyes and she pats my cheek.

"Genia, you been doing shit behind my back?"

"Come on. Grab the game."

After we welcome in Lion and Kamilah, we go to stand in front of everybody.

"You guys, thanks for coming and kicking it with us tonight," Eugenia starts.

"Yeah," I join in behind her, turning up my beer, "we're real happy you're here. I attended by force, as I'm sure you gentlemen probably did, too."

Kevin throws a wine cork at me.

My baby elbows me and continues, "You guys are about to pull off one of the biggest shows the world has ever seen, in just a couple of weeks. Some Black men. You've worked together this long, through hell and high water, and lifted five companies from the ground. You've had all the accolades, the magazine covers, and the ritzy affairs." She grins. "Now it's time to do something you clearly don't know much about—chill."

Eugenia spins the card game between her hands. "We're going to play a little game called 'New Phone, Who Dis'?"

"I *love* that game!" Cher calls out.

Lus nods. "Me, too. That's dope."

I kiss my teeth. "This sounds like some campy shit."

Three hours later, with some Marvin Gaye on the vocals, every person in the room is sprawled out on the floor. Shoes off, drinking and lining up their cards, we're trying to come up with these damn phrases. Especially me.

To be so stingy and stuffy, Solly's got a little humor to

him. His phrases have been pretty damn funny through the evening. Him horsing around with my sister kind of brings out a playful, relaxed side of her I've never really seen. She doesn't look all resentful and bitter with him next to her.

Full of liquor and laughs at the end of the night, he approaches me.

A few steps away, Genia throws me a warning glare.

I give him a grip. He *is* going to be my brother-in-law soon. "Thanks for coming, bruh. And thanks for… doing this whole Explore thing. I might have been an ass a couple times. My bad."

Solly's tall ass brings me in for a half-hug. "Eugenia does it for you. Hang on to that."

Behind him comes Shay.

"Appreciate you coming through, Shay."

"I appreciate you for actually letting me into your house." She's half joking, but it's more truth than joke, and she doesn't move in to hug me because of our history.

So I initiate the embrace we haven't had in a minute, and her eyes grow.

"Hit me up, Shay. Maybe you, me, and D can eat lunch at Slurp or something."

The others help Genia and me clean up, and once they're gone, we collapse on the couch.

"All right, I know you're not going to tell me what you and Shay been up to. At least tell me how did you get frosty Cher to lighten up?" I ask her on our way to sleep.

Genia snorts. "I got in her mother-in-law's ear."

Curling up with her, I'm liking this relationship situation.

But still, one item of business takes a seat in the back of my mind. Or rather, two items.

"Baby, you invite Show?" I ask her.

Maybe he didn't come tonight because, after what went

down the other day, Genia felt uncomfortable and didn't ask him.

The couple of days he was here, we talked it out and him and the fellas really did pitch in. It was almost like old times. Got me thinking he could come here to the Hamptons and link up with me. We'd be off the rails.

"I did, baby." Genia tucks into me. "I pulled his number out of your phone, but I didn't hear back."

He mentioned he's busy with a lot of stuff back home. Maybe he's even closing out some hustles, so he can line up to become legit for real. I'll just check in on him tomorrow.

But I'm so fucking grateful for this woman. She is the nuance my life needs.

"Baby?" I want to ask her about something Show told me.

Her eyes closed, she's almost asleep. "Hm?"

I want to let her sleep, but this has bothered me all week. "Can I ask you something?"

Eugenia opens her eyes and turns over.

I feel like shit for bringing this up. But when will the time ever be right?

Tomorrow, I'm buying a ring. I asked Kevin to refer me to his jeweler the day I confessed I loved her in open court.

"Show said you mentioned...the first time you tried to.... He said you're not afraid to die. He was impressed with you. But you and me, we've never talked about any of that."

EUGENIA

No, we haven't discussed it.

Not that I hide it or run from it. Since I'm focused on

living, it's not too helpful to think of death. I don't fear it, but I also no longer go looking for it.

Yet, this man who pumped life back into my heart is worried. These past few days, the weight of the world has tarried at Keenan's brow. It may be the pressure and stress of the concert, concern for the tension with his childhood friend and our safety, and that a lot of major changes are occurring for him very fast.

But I don't want a day to pass where he worries about my mental state. Or for him to be stuck in a relationship in which he doesn't have all the facts or know every risk. Particularly, with him being younger than me, he'll have enough time to find somebody else if he chooses.

Odie, no!

So clear in my mind it could have happened yesterday…

"You don't have to talk about it if you don't want to," Keenan whispers.

"We should." Still lying in front of him on the sofa, I stare directly in his face. "Keenan, the first time I tried to take my life was the day my brother was convicted for manslaughter."

He's only the third person I've told this to, who wasn't a police officer or a judge. The only others are Illustrious and Princess. I never told Shel. And he never asked. He just wanted me to move on.

"After bailiffs took Odell out of court, I went home. Went inside my daddy's gun cabinet. Grabbed a gun like the one Odie used. Placed it in my mouth. Pulled the trigger."

Only Keenan's breathing disturbs the silence.

"Odie was defending me. Daddy always took out his guns when he got drunk. I was twenty and studying for a college exam. Daddy started bothering me…"

"You been whoring with that boy? That why the winda open? Huh, Genie?"

"The window is open because it's hot. Will you leave me alone? I have a test."

"Come here, Genie! You's a lie. You been sneakin' and I know he in here. Where he at?"

"Daddy, nobody's—"

"Get off her! Damn! How would you like it if somebody was shoving a gun at you all the time, huh?"

"Odie, no!"

My fourteen-year-old brother is up in height now and just big enough to confront Daddy. The man is caught off guard when Odie snatches the rifle, shoves it under Daddy's chin. "How you like that? What you got to say now? You ain't so tough now, is you?"

"Odie, put it down!" I scream.

"No, I want to hear what he says now!" Fourteen-year-old Odie demands.

I push the barrel away from Daddy's throat, and at the same time, Odie stomps his foot.

The gun fires.

Through our wall, the bullet enters the next house.

And kills the eleven-year-old girl next door.

Living it all over again, I stand inside my mental furnace and burn.

Rivers soak my face that I'm too distraught to wipe. "I killed that girl."

"No, the hell you didn't," Keenan murmurs.

"Odie didn't say a word. I watched him like a lamb taken to slaughter. Police took all our statements, and I told them what I did. They arrested him because he held the gun. The prosecutor went for the highest charge. Odie pled out so he could at least have a chance at the second half of his life. He sits where I should be sitting." I say with my last bits of oxygen, "Sleeps where I should sleep."

"Baby, don't say that."

"I didn't want to live. Didn't deserve to. I tried to tell the judge. He didn't care." My chest convulses and collides with my trachea, causing a traffic jam in the center of me. "The prosecutor and public defender were going to… do what they wanted anyway. When I got home and put the barrel in my mouth, the trigger jammed. My brother…"

I go on to tell Keenan about the loneliness while Sheldon worked overseas. And then last summer, when I saw how happily Shel and Chrissy were in love, I had lost the only chance I would ever have at the "good man."

"And you still graduated Northwestern with honors," Keenan says between his own tears.

"If I hadn't, Odie would be in there for nothing. If I die, Odie would be doing time for nothing. But being alive can sometimes be too much weight to bear. Before Hadar and Sheldon, he was the only reason I had to live. Hadar being out of my custody gave me a new goal to strive for."

I don't tell Keenan the rest. That he is one of my new reasons. He doesn't need that pressure. He should have an open pass to leave and go live his life any time he's ready.

But being a man who has endured his own trials, Keenan wipes my face. The harness of his arm secures me against his chest. Just as he did the first night I laid with him and he tenderly took care of me, no strings attached.

Before we drift off to sleep, he mumbles, "We're going to get your brother out. And Show out of the 'hood."

In the same spot on the sofa the next morning, Keenan's vibrating phone awakens us from sleep.

He peeks at the screen through one eye, and then, bolts up on the couch.

"Bae, what is it?"

He's reading.

"Keenan?"

The life drains from him. "Show is dead."

27

MY NEW REASONS

EUGENIA & KEENAN

EUGENIA

The five partners of Explore open up the show, walking out to greet a still audience.

"As we stand here right now, the world's first Black private citizen is flying in space," a tearful Kevin Middleton reports, to our thunderous applause.

The Black families of the Hamptons possess priority seating alongside major celebrities and executives on the main U.S. Navy fighter carrier where Sasha's shuttle will land.

Hearts exploding with pride, we all stand to our feet. Emotion brims in our eyes, pours from our souls, and we let it out in the clap of our hands until they sting.

This is a different kind of Freedom Day for Black people on Earth. That resonates for every mind with the audacity to dream and aim bigger. The whole concept behind Explore Adventures.

"All my crew and team members at MoneyCruncher,"

Kevin continues, "thank you for all the elbow grease you've put in this past year. I told you we'd get it done and we did. Now, the sky is the limit. And with all this success and acclaim, guess what waits for us tomorrow? That's right. More hard work."

The audience laughs.

"No, but really, I want to thank my wife, my mom," he pauses and looks over at Lionel Middleton, "and my dad, and brothers. My family gave me a playground in the Hamptons where I could dream big. Back when I was taking apart computers and coding in our garage, little did I know a young explorer from Baltimore would hit me up one day, and our destinies would link up and take off."

Kevin passes the microphone to Keenan.

My love opens his mouth, and all that comes out is the strain in his throat.

The microphone falls to his side, the world comes down on his head and his shoulders start to shake. Of all his grand visions and far-reaching accomplishments, he now hangs limp, as if this small speech seems to be the one thing he can't do.

From my seat, I clutch my chest as if my hands can remotely open my baby's throat. A couple of seats away from me, Chaitra does the same. Next to her, so does Keenan's mother. Desmond and Keenan's dad rises and starts to go for him.

But the men of Explore join around him. Their arms link together, and they huddle to hold Keenan up.

Once again, the audience is on its feet.

"I...I want..." His gut sucks in a sob. "...to dedicate this concert to Shonathan Harper, Aaron Valley, and Nigel Green." He finds me where I sit. "And Odell Jackson. And every other young Black man who n... who never got a chance to explore."

Not a dry eye remains on the boat.

I am no longer a dry, parched desert. The waters of emotion overtake me, and I am no longer afraid to swim in my vulnerability and humanity.

Lost in his moment, Keenan drops the microphone to Solomon.

"We also would like to thank all our longtime neighbors, friends, college classmates, fraternities, sororities, people who signed onto this vision from the start. We especially are grateful for the families in the Hamptons that we could set aside our differences, put our heads down and work together. The Rouses, the Pages, the Townsends, Englishes, the Middletons, families who were exploring and advancing Black excellence before Explore even existed, we thank you."

Martin and Roccard say their remarks.

"So without further ado, let's see where our space traveler is now," Kevin says and signals to one of the tech staff.

"Oh, my God," my former client from back in Chicago, Victoria, gawks next to me. On the other side of me sits my former co-worker, Lus.

Not a single eye closes, not even to blink. And our eyes don't fail us.

Sasha Static becomes the first Black female private citizen to fly outside Earth's atmosphere.

On the jumbotron, we all watch her float around in weightless suspension at the perimeter of Earth's atmosphere. Fifty-three miles over the Atlantic Ocean, she waves at us. All of us Black folks sitting out here on multiple yachts, wave back at her. But the cameras she's got on the space shuttle project images of us, so she can see us here supporting her in the Hamptons. And not only here, but viewing parties have been set around the world, and the concert is only being broadcast exclusively via Money-Cruncher. Only in MoneyCruncher's contracted venues can people watch back on the Hamptons streets and in businesses.

She gives us an update of her flight, and we watch her float. "I wore my natural Black hair just so I could see my Afro floating on a spaceship," Sasha jokes, to which we Black women laugh.

For the next hour, we all fidget and wait for her shuttle to make its descent.

"Mom," Hadar starts, "She is not the first Black woman in space though, is she? That was Mae Jemison, right?"

"Right, honey."

"Mom," Hadar mutters, lowering his voice. He's been moving back and forth between the Rouse seating area and my area with the McLains. "Blake and Rome said you're hotter than Sasha Static." My son's nose wrinkles up. "I didn't like it, and I told them to shut up."

Behind me, my brothers Eugene and Nelson, along with my nieces and nephews, crack jokes. I throw a side-eye over my shoulder to silence them, and my eyes connect with my daddy's.

"You do look nice, Genie," is all Daddy says, and he seems to only grudgingly release that much.

I still have no idea what Keenan said to him when they talked that day at the barbecue, or what Keenan has said to him since. Kee refuses to tell me.

Lus chuckles at Hadar. "Tell the boys they have good taste."

I shake my head and kiss him. "Don't say that. It's okay. Tell them I'm just your mom and you're the hottest one out here, babe."

My heart is about to burst for a lot of reasons.

"You're dating the man who pulled this together? That guy who was outside your job that day?" Victoria, my former client from Chicago, asks. I gave her my free concert ticket that I won at the dance contest on Memorial weekend. Her case is closed now, and she successfully had her kids returned to her, after she stopped messing around with their father.

To show her proof there really are Black people in the Hamptons, and that big things can happen for all of us, I gave her my ticket and made Keenan give me another.

"Keenan is one of the men. A ton of people all came together in this Hamptons community and made all this happen," I answer.

Victoria marvels while gazing at me. "You did that."

"Did what?" I ask.

"You actually did yourself what you told me to do—you stayed by yourself until a good man came who deserved you. Most people tell you one thing, while they go do something different. Hypocrites. But not you, Ms. Rouse. You practice what you preach. Respect."

"It's Ms. Jackson. And thank you." She has no idea that I wasn't waiting for a good man, and I had long given up on finding another one. Only once I'd accepted being alone, and was establishing my own peace, did Keenan show up.

"Baby girl." Nelson nudges me, and points behind the stage. "K-Dog wants you."

In his tux, a nervous, fidgety Keenan stands outside of Sasha Static's stage, hands on his hips, and waits for me to come back.

He took his meds right before he went up there, but to be sure, I grab the little case I now keep in my purse. Getting up and squirming past all the legs in this tight pantsuit, I go to where he is.

I barely arrive before he takes my hand and threads me through all the speakers, wires and sound equipment.

"Baby, you did a good job up there," I start gushing as I

reach for his cheeks, for his baby face. "It was powerful and I'm so proud of--"

Keenan's hands devour my body, he breathes me, and the manhood in his eyes finds me.

"Marry me."

The world freezes. "Huh?"

"You heard me, Genia." Fear and nervousness, intensity and urgency, love and hope, all etch his facial contours. Breathless, he speaks in a rush, trying to manage all his thoughts at once. "I was going to ask you tomorrow. I planned this whole thing at the cliff where we jumped, so I don't have the ring right now. But I don't want to wait another minute. I almost asked you after my speech, but I know you don't call attention to yourself willingly and I want this to stay about us, not everybody else. So I'm asking you now."

He lowers to his knee. I can almost hear it rattling. And he takes my hand that is definitely quaking.

And lifts my existence with his eyes that gaze up at me.

Over our heads a shuttle blares, reentering the atmosphere. The audience begins clapping and screaming. Somewhere out on the tarmac, Sasha Static is landing from space, and making history. Her backup dancers, costumers, makeup artists, and handlers all swarm around us, some of them stopping to swoon or pat Keenan on the back.

But he doesn't divert his focus from me.

"Eugenia Jackson, I can't breathe unless I'm breathing you, can't see unless I'm seeing you, can't explore anything else unless you're there exploring it with me, so will you marry this man who's crazy in life and crazy about you? Will you be my wife?"

I am no longer an empty vessel. And no longer do I question what happens if this young man leaves me for a younger woman. I'll live.

I am worth trying and hoping for, again. The riverbed of my soul, no longer cracked and dusty, now flows with water. "Yes."

EUGENIA

This morning, only two witnesses are here with us—Desmond and Princess.

Instead of me proposing like I originally planned, Pastor Arnold has come to perform our exchange of vows. Right here at the cliff, where she decided to take the leap with me, where I needed to know a few weeks ago if I was only nursing a hopeless crush or if she wanted me too.

I didn't invite our families even though they're in town for the concert festivities. I didn't invite my closest boys, Kevin and Lorenzo, and Genia didn't invite Illustrious or even her son, not this time.

This moment is not for them. What I have to say to Eugenia—*really* say to her— is not for public consumption.

We'll have a ceremony and reception in a couple of months once we roll through high-traffic season, and have time to plan a quiet, intimate affair that reflects her. I already know Roberta Middleton will be all over that, so no worries there. Mrs. Middleton's kind of taken Genia in like a daughter, and my baby certainly deserves that. And if I know my moms, Margaret McLain won't let shit stay quiet.

As far as me clearing my head, I haven't had time so far, with all the commotion leading up to the concert. But I also need to head home for a minute and process Showtime being gone.

Based on my conversation with Roach once we finally got

a chance to chop, Show came to New York to see me one last time. Not to cause problems. I had it wrong.

Apparently, my boy overextended himself with some cartel guys, and bit off more than he could chew. When I said no to letting Show use my business illegally, he knew his time was limited. But he wouldn't drag me into his problems or force my hand, the way I suspected he would.

Rather than letting his opps come for me, he prepared for the inevitable. And flew out to meet Eugenia—my future—himself, and to say goodbye, in his way. That was the weird vibe I picked up from him.

Roach never said a word.

I understand Shonathan's actions put him in that position, but when his back was against the wall, he could have played with my life, and instead, he laid down his.

Life is too short to be waiting and planning, so yeah, I asked Eugenia last night.

For today, in our relaxed summer 'fits, we take each other's hands and repeat the script Pastor Arnold gives us.

Genia's soft Afro, piled high on her head, is a crown, and falls down one side of her forehead. In a simple, long cotton maxi dress, my angel is au naturale perfection.

"Baby," I begin, "I didn't know what to expect when I jumped on a boat and rode it to your job. I knew you wouldn't just open up to me right away, but I was hoping I could open up the woman you hide under all those layers. I knew underneath your fake pretense of being super careful and disciplined, and saying no all the time, that deeper in you was somebody with fire and friskiness, who was nasty with a devilish side. I had a feeling your soul and your life was a mirror of mine, if only I could uncover the real you. And you battled me the whole way, but a nigga wasn't going down without a fight. Literally, you beat my ass to keep me from getting to you."

Princess and Desmond stifle their snorting.

"But here we are, and I'm glad you let me fight my way to your heart. Since I caught a couple of battle scars in there somewhere, you'd better believe I'm not letting you go anywhere."

Pastor Arnold's face is a bowl of vinegar as he manages a fake smile, and Genia and the others shake out their amusement.

"Keenan," Genia starts, her eyes misting, "you're right. I wanted nothing to do with you."

Princess and Desmond are definitely catching the comedy hour they didn't expect.

"But not because you are lacking in anyway, but I was trying to shield my heart from anybody who could abandon or disappoint me. What you saw was the big vault in which I'd locked myself so nobody could come in. So no pain could come in. So no excitement or hope could find me and set me up for failure. From inside my vault, I could protect myself."

Blinking, she wipes her teary eyes.

"But you didn't care about my vault." She huffs. "You showed up with your sticks of dynamite."

Seeing her vulnerable and truthful, I wipe some tears of my own.

"And you, my love," Genia continues, speaking from a well of love and peace that's nourishing me, "with your courage, hunger for life, curiosity, and strength—you charged right in and found the most valuable parts of me."

"*Every* part of you is priceless," I remind her.

"Keenan, you see with your spirit and not your eyes, and it inspires me. Your intellect cannot be contained in any book. Baby, your beautiful restlessness compels an adventure. You are the top of the mountain I climb, my eyes when I'm blind, the wind carrying me forward, the gold worth chasing all the way to the ends of the Earth... the roller-coaster in my world and between my thighs..."

"Aww, shucky," Desmond adds.

I pat the area over my damn heart to make sure it's still there.

Genia continues, "Thank you for your electricity that brought me back alive."

In one move, I'm all over her face and expressing my love with my whole body, because I don't need Pastor Arnold to say shit else.

EPILOGUE

KEENAN

"Keenan, I don't want you to be disappointed."

"Baby, don't do that right now." I'm already more nervous than a lotto winner about to get his check, my whole life flashing before my eyes.

Genia's finger presses the phone to activate the call, and she puts it on speaker.

After months of trying for a baby, we couldn't conceive on our own and had to go to doctors for in vitro fertilization. She takes this very personally, as a failure on her part, but I don't give that an ounce of oxygen. I refuse to let her wallow in it for a moment. While everybody's got fantasies of doing the deed and Heaven and Earth coming together before a magic baby springs up a month later, this is what it is. I have zero regrets. I'm grateful for modern technology.

If we can just get one, I'll be damn happy. And if it so happens we can't have any, I've got my forever who lights up my life anyway.

"Mr. and Mrs. McLain," the nurse says to us over the phone. "Congratulations! You're pregnant. And your HCG levels are high enough that you might be having twins!"

Oh, okay…

I sure as hell wasn't expecting that.

CAN Eugenia free her younger brother, Odell, from prison?

He has his own book. Lula is offering it at a discount on her web site for a limited time.

THANKS FROM LULA

Thank you for reading *See Through You*! If you enjoyed this story, please leave a review.

This is not the end of Sag Harbor. Not at all. The *Metamorphosis* series is coming in the summer of 2024, and it'll be a whole journey back into time. In *Circa 1979*, what secret betrayals and power grabs led to the hidden secret of Kevin Middleton? Be sure you stay in the loop. Or you'll miss this funky 70s and 80s saga.

Lula's Store: lulawhitebooks.myshopify.com

Web site: www.lulawhitebooks.com

Email: lula@lulawhitebooks.com

Join Lula's Luxe Suite Reading Group:

https://www.facebook.com/groups/lulawhite

Read the stories before they go on sale:

https://www.patreon.com/lulawhite

You can find me on my web site where I drop short stories once or twice a month. I will also be making books, videos and content available early as I write the books on my Patreon. Come hang out on my writing journey. Much love! 🤍

Books in the *Explore Men of the Hamptons* series

Explore You - Kevin & Cher

Taste You - Solomon & Chaitra

Drink You - Lion & Kamila

See Through You - Keenan & Eugenia

Find You - Roland & Neeraja

Books In The *Sag Harbor Black Romances*

Brown Sugar This Christmas - Maddy & Jerrell

Hot Chocolate This Winter - Chrissy & Sheldon Part 1

Flinging All Spring - Adella & Desmond

Overheated for Summer - Chrissy & Sheldon Part 2

Rouse Family Christmas - All Couples

Related to *Explore Men of the Hamptons*

A New Life for Christmas - Odell & Tazima

The Young and Luxurious Series

Love & Fire - Kori & Easton

www.lulawhitebooks.com

Email: lula@lulawhitebooks.com

www.blackluxuryromances.com